THE
DEMON
RACE

THE DEMON RACE

ALEXANDRIA WARWICK

Wolf Publishing

Published in the United States by Wolf Publishing

Copyright © 2018 Alexandria Warwick

Cover design © Alexandria Warwick
Map illustration © Alexandria Warwick

ISBN: 978-0-692-06803-8
First Edition

Printed in the United States of America

For my family

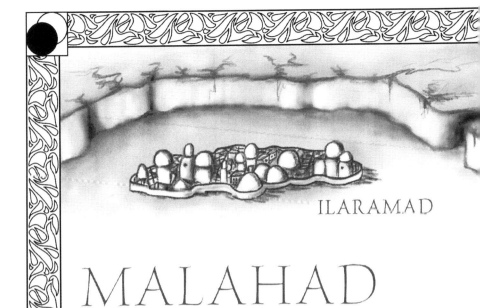

ILARAMAD

MALAHAD

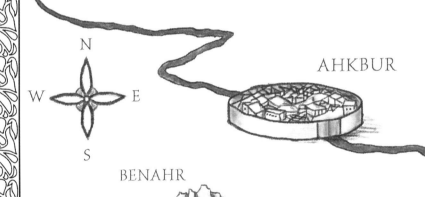

N

W   E

S

AHKBUR

BENAHR

THE SARAJ

YANASIR

PROLOGUE

IT WAS NIGHT. A cold wind howled through the narrow window chiseled into the western wall, salt and sand and hints of a sun long gone having blown in from the sparse, skeletal land. It was alive, and hungry, and it tore greedily at Namali's sleeping robe until she bolted upright, gasping for air. A swelling darkness pressed upon her eyes.

"Mama!"

From across the hall, the shift and sigh of cloth. Hurried footsteps on the cool, mud-packed floor. Namali clutched her skinny arms close to her chest, teeth chattering with a dread she feared might never leave. There were beasts here, lurking in the shadows. And they were in her mind, too.

A candle flared, then dimmed. Mama knelt beside her bedroll, eyes glowing like two dark wells. "What is it, my love?" Gently, she brushed a sweaty strand of hair away from her young daughter's cheek, her concern plain.

At the reassuring touch, Namali threw herself forward, burrowing into the softness and warmth. The nightmare had been a live thing inside her. Her mother, gone, and she and Baba all alone.

"I thought—" Her voice broke. "It was so dark. I couldn't find you."

"Shh." Soothing circles rubbed against her back—up, down, around; up, down, around. "It was only a dream. And look." She lifted the candle so the flame fluttered between them, warming the chilly air. Namali curled her hand into her mother's woolen robe, huddling close as the flame danced before her eyes, growing larger and larger until she knew nothing else, and her world was pure, flickering light.

"Mama?"

"Yes, my love?"

Her mother's heartbeat thrummed against her ear—slow, steady, strong. "Will you read me a story?"

The love in Mama's voice was plain when she replied, "You know you never have to ask."

Moving quietly, they padded down the hallway and sank into a pile of pillows heaped in one corner of the sitting room near the bookcase. The volumes unable to fit onto the cluttered shelves were stacked at their feet like great towers and bridges and walls, a castle of their own making. This was where they laughed, and cried, and breathed life into stories. It was home. It was theirs.

The crack of the book's spine cut through the quiet. "Where did we leave off?"

Namali pointed, then sank deeper into her mother's embrace. Her earlier nightmare was already beginning to fade.

"It wasn't long before the sun slipped below the horizon. Young Delir had traveled nearly three days across the Saraj without food or water, and he had begun to weaken. His daeva grew restless. He heard whispers in his mind."

"Who?"

"I don't know." The page crinkled in Mama's hand, but she did not yet turn it. "Should we find out?"

Namali nodded eagerly, the night growing longer, colder, as the candle burned low, wax pooling onto the floor.

"And then," Mama whispered, "a cold blackness grasped at Delir's mind. The daeva began snapping at his legs, running around in circles while he clung to its back. *Delir,* crooned the voice. *Come to me, Delir.* And the boy knew it belonged to the Demon King."

Namali's pulse surged, and she clutched her mother's arm with all the strength of a drowning girl in need of air.

Setting down the book, Mama cradled Namali close, lips pressed against her daughter's long dark hair. "There's nothing to be frightened of, my love. It's just a story. It's not real."

Her heart fluttered, little more than a bird with a broken wing. All she could think of was black eyes, black hearts. She squeezed her eyes shut. *It's not real. It's not real.*

This . . . this was real. Mama was real. These books, the paper worn smooth, were real. And then, the things she couldn't see. The love that filled her home. The slow exhale of breath, soft as a sigh.

This was real.

The story was not.

Mama asked quietly, "Do you want to continue reading another time?"

Resting her head in the crook of her mother's neck, Namali nodded, and she was lifted and carried back to bed, laid gently on her messy bedroll. Baba's snores drifted through the dark, quiet house.

As her mother turned to leave, Namali clutched her hand and squeezed. Felt smooth, unyielding bone. "Don't go." Her voice was small.

Mama pressed a kiss to her forehead, lingering. "Be brave, Namali." She tucked a thin sheet around her shoulders. "No one will be brave for you."

Namali tilted back her head, eyes wide with love and trust. Her pulse slowed as sleep pulled at her, leading her back to that warm pool of stillness, calm. She could be brave. She could.

Namali released her hand. Whispered, "I'll try, Mama."

The candle flickered, then guttered out.

CHAPTER 1
10 YEARS LATER

THE KNOCK REVERBERATED like the low tolling of a bell.

It was not the urgency that caught Namali's attention, but rather the lack of it. A slow, unhurried weight, ringing, ringing. A pot of water boiled in the hearth near the tubs of apricots and cherries, the sacks of rice and nuts located in the small kitchen in the rear of their home. Namali removed the pot from the fire, intending to answer the door, when Baba called from the other side of the house, "It's for me."

The door opened. Low voices. Laughter.

A man.

Treading softly, Namali peeked around the mud-brick wall of the sitting room, eyeing the stranger. Tall, lavishly dressed, a beard the color of charred wood. The man's smile eased some of the grooves around his eyes, though he could not have been older than thirty. And there was something between them, having been blown in with the breeze—awareness, perhaps. Her baba rarely had guests over anymore, and yet he gripped the man's hand in a firm handshake, the sort that cried *power,* before allowing him to remove his sandals and step inside their home.

"Namali," her father called.

Immediately, she stepped into the sitting room. Threadbare rugs warmed the dirt floor. Tapestries collected from the northern cities during a more prosperous time adorned the otherwise bare walls. "Yes, Baba?" Her neck prickled beneath the stranger's gaze.

"Go to the well and fetch some water, please."

Her fingers itched to curl into fists. Of course he wanted her to fetch water. Of course. If not the water, then feeding the herd, and if not the herd, then cooking or cleaning or some other menial chore. It was a polite way of saying he didn't want her overhearing, but not so polite that she forgot her place.

She said nothing, unsurprisingly, for they had guests. This man, who stared at her from the doorway. Stared and did not look away. Her father must not have noticed though, because he didn't say anything, and the man continued to stare until she averted her eyes again. "Yes, Baba."

Namali grabbed the wooden bucket with its rusted handle from beside the front door and heaved it down the staircase leading to the desiccated earth below. The wide, central road was moon-pale and smooth, a strip of goat's milk poured through the blood of stone thrusting upward, smoothed by wind, carved by men into dwellings that housed a town of four hundred strong. There had been water here, once, and greenery, and cool shade, before the sun had done its cruel work and baked the foliage into weeds, the wet soil into red hardened clay. Thousands of years had transformed the ground into a great immovable rock. Not even the wind could move it now.

Lifting a hand to shade her eyes, Namali headed to the well

located in the center of town, dust clouds bursting from beneath her sandals like small gasps of air. Even this late in the day, when the sun began its slow descent and drenched the land in fire, the heat was blistering, burning the tops of her feet to a deep, deep brown. Her mind was a restless storm. Whatever Baba and the man discussed must be important enough to dismiss her. She shook her head. It was best not to dwell. There was still much to do.

The western edge of town saw signs of reconstruction as sand spinners, identified by the white strips of cloth wrapped around their yirasafs, removed mounds of sand that had blown in from a passing sand hawk last week, its mammoth wings having swept the dunes into a frenzy. They worked in pairs, moving their hands with fluid grace to lift the sand and toss it back over the low stone wall surrounding Benahr. The few date palms present, more skeleton than tree, had been splintered from the force of winds. It was a miracle no livestock had been killed.

A line of people snaked away from the well, their expressions strangely muted as Namali took her place at the back of the line. She had not noticed earlier, too focused on what was beginning to unfold back home, but there was a stillness in the air, in the earth and dead trees. A lack of . . . something. Unconsciously, Namali straightened and slanted a gaze at the woman in front of her. Their eyes clashed; the woman's darted away. Mrs. Lamiri was her neighbor. They said hello every morning.

The line moved without haste. There was no laughter, no ease. It was strange. Her people did not hesitate to greet friends, ask after families. Perhaps it was due to the lack of rain in recent months? Men and women and children all but wilted in the heat. It was a burden, to want for water when there was none to share, and it was heavy. Most families survived on three buckets of water a week, but those with goat or camel herds were allowed up to seven. And yet the restriction did not stop the liars, the cheaters, the thieves. In the Saraj, water was life. And life made liars of them all.

Quiet conversation drifted down the line. Namali peeked around Mrs. Lamiri and spotted Farid and Hami, two brothers who wore dark robes over dark trousers like herself and white yirasafs, their heads bent close. Someone hissed for their silence.

She leaned forward. "Mrs. Lamiri."

The woman stiffened, but did not turn around.

Namali sighed and stepped back. Then she would not speak of it now. But when an older man ambling down the road caught her attention, his camel in tow, she set down her bucket and waved a hand in greeting.

He slowed at his approach and dipped his chin in wordless hello.

"What's going on, Mr. Kashmi?" The camel stretched its neck forward to lip the black veil shielding the lower half of her face.

He shook his head. Glanced around at those who would not meet his eye. "Best not to speak of it," he muttered.

Namali watched him for a moment, her heart pounding its uncertainty. A trickle of sweat slithered down the small of her back. "Did something happen?"

He did not reply, but she looked into his eyes and knew. *Not yet, but soon.*

Mr. Kashmi began to move past her. Without thinking, she reached out to grab his arm, but at the last second, she pulled back, calling herself every kind of fool.

Namali swallowed against the sudden dryness in her throat. "Sorry," she whispered.

At his retreat, the unease she'd felt earlier crawled out from the dark place it had retreated to. Namali scrubbed at her eyes. He would not speak of it. No one would.

The line shifted forward.

An unsettling energy sparked, coiling tightly, pulling each of them toward that inevitable dark ache of truth. From the corner of her eye, she watched men reach for their scimitars, the blades short and curved and forged of the thinnest, strongest steel, broadened at the tip. Dust churned around their shifting feet as ahead, voices rose in animosity. Namali craned her head in curiosity. Heard the word, hushed, "Demon."

The strike came from nowhere, and then Farid was on the ground.

The man who'd lashed out towered over him, breathing hard. "Shut it, boy." The skin around his lips tightened into whiteness.

Whispers punctured the air, too convoluted to pick apart or make sense of. A slow fear swelled against Namali's too-tight chest as people rushed back to their dwellings empty-handed, heads ducked against some unseen presence, like a sickness infecting the air.

Face red, Farid picked himself up off the ground and jerked Hami to the front of the line, where an official checked off their names from a piece of parchment and allowed them to lower their bucket into the well. It landed with a plunk and a splash. A few seconds later, the brothers hauled their bucket out of the well, untied the rope, and headed home, dragging what remained of their pride behind them.

Namali watched them grow smaller and smaller, and she could

not shake the urge of wanting to give chase, to sprint after them and learn more about this strange shift in the air, an uttered word that struck fear into the hearts of men. She yearned to lift the curtain of this small, unchanging town. Something told her this was greater than knowledge, greater than her insignificant life. An opportunity, if only she had the courage to act.

But she waited too long, in the end. Farid and Hami were nearly out of sight, too far away to call back. The opportunity was lost.

As the fired red sun sank behind the dunes and poured gold onto the land, Namali jogged home with the empty bucket banging against her leg. After setting it outside the door and removing her sandals, she stepped inside the cool, dark entryway and stopped, frozen. Baba and the stranger sat on two pillows across from one other, legs crossed. They did not speak.

Baba shifted to a more comfortable position. Said, "Namali, please bring food for our guest."

Her heart stumbled. Her feet no longer knew how to move.

"Namali," her father warned.

Somehow, she unglued her feet and hurried to the kitchen. Her hands trembled as she prepared the cardamom tea, one of the metal cups slipping from her damp fingers, the impact like a crack of thunder as it hit the ground. She thought of the things she had done this week, the things she had left undone. Had her father discovered her feeding Khorshan treats without his permission? Surely that was not grounds for punishment. And it did not explain the reason for this man's presence.

After pouring the tea, Namali transferred flatbread, pickled mangoes, and dates to a plate and arranged the food the way her father liked it: bread in the front, fruit in the back. She carried everything into the sitting room, face calm even as chaos raged in her heart. The stranger watched her. And watched her. And did not look away.

She placed the refreshments on the ground in front of him. *Breathe, Namali. You have to breathe.*

"Have a seat," said Baba.

She obeyed, tucking her bare feet underneath her. Baba's mouth drooped at the corners—his serious face. He sipped his tea, set it down, picked it up again. The stranger chewed on a date.

Namali picked at a hangnail, cheeks warm beneath her veil. The air hung in the room with the weight of a slaughtered goat bled dry. From outside the window, a child screamed, warning her of something yet to come. Often the Saraj knew things she did not.

Her father faced her. It seemed each time she looked at him more lines appeared, more signs of fatigue. "Namali."

Briefly, she closed her eyes. Maybe if she denied herself the evidence of her father, this man, herself, sitting together in this room, she could pretend this was not real, and that what was to come would not in some way irreversibly change things. "Yes, Baba?"

"I'd like you to meet Hazil Abdu." He gestured to the man, who, upon closer inspection, appeared to be in his mid-twenties, and rather handsome. A deep red yirasaf protected his head and the back of his neck from the sand and sun. "Mr. Abdu is a spice merchant. Perhaps the most successful in all of Malahad."

Namali bowed her head but didn't offer her hand. "Many welcomes."

"Mr. Abdu and I have been in contact these past few months. He's shown an interest in our family."

Unconsciously, she clenched fistfuls of fabric in her hands. The moment the man's gaze cut to her, she sucked in air as if the blow had been a physical thing.

"Namali." A pause, one that lifted the hair on the back of her neck. "Mr. Abdu is looking for a wife."

She was cold. She was so cold that her lips tingled, and she realized she had stopped breathing.

In that moment, there was nothing Namali did not feel. In truth, she did not know how to react. In Malahad, arranged marriages were fairly common—two families joining for financial stability, generally. Baba was a camel herder, but in recent years the available pasture near Benahr's oasis had been reduced. Too little food, too many animals. It was not sustainable, and she was certainly of marrying age. It was the next logical step.

And yet she could not think of anything but the unfairness of it all. What was there for her in Benahr, save her father? She yearned. My, did she yearn. Something different, something new, but she had caved, time and again, beneath the underlying fear that convinced her to stay. Because what if she was wrong? What if this was it? What if this was all there was in life?

What if there was more?

The knot in her stomach tightened, forcing her to hunch over to relieve the pain, and her father snapped, "Sit up. You're being disrespectful."

She obeyed, trying to stop her lips from trembling, and failing. She needed time, and there was none to hold. She must sit here and smile and be thankful that her marriage would bring an end to their financial woes.

"A union between you and Mr. Abdu is for the best. He would

be able to care for you and your family. You would never have to worry about going hungry or having a roof over your head."

A family? She wasn't even ready to get married, much less have children.

"Think of how proud your mother would have been."

At the mention of her mother, Namali inhaled sharply. If Mama were still alive, she would murmur comforting words the way mothers did, the ones that brought a racing heart down to a slow pulse. Her mother, who she missed every day.

"Mr. Abdu requests to speak with you privately."

Namali's mouth opened, then closed. It was a request from the merchant, but an order from her father. "Yes, Baba."

Setting down his tea, her father left the room. Namali peeked at the merchant, who approached and knelt in front of her. He smelled of man and sweat and cloves and the hot desert air. His face was browned from the sun. A handsome face, yes, but she could not help but think how those cheekbones might snag on his yirasaf if he wasn't careful.

"I know," said the merchant, "this isn't what you wanted."

"No," she murmured. "It's not."

The truth was a light she could not, would not, turn from. It was not what she wanted. It had never been what she wanted. But she was sitting across from this wealthy, worldly man who would bring stability to her father's failing livelihood, and that was also a truth.

The merchant pulled a metal object from his pocket. "I will do my best to give you a comfortable life. You will want for nothing. Anything you desire . . . it is yours."

A delicate gold bracelet rested in his palm, the square-cut ruby in its center catching the last of the dying light streaming through the western-facing windows. Namali's breath caught, for it was beautiful and pure.

"May I?" he asked, and before she could refuse, he caught her hand and slipped the bracelet onto her wrist.

She touched the thin metal with a fingertip. "It's lovely." There was no polite way to refuse the trinket, so she left it alone for now.

The merchant swallowed. "It suits you." He stared at the bracelet with dark eyes, made darker by a raw pain having quickly risen to the surface. She wondered what it stemmed from, and if he would eventually find peace. "I will see you soon then?"

She nodded, already feeling the walls closing in.

Satisfied, the merchant went to speak with her father before taking his leave. Namali wrapped her arms around herself, taking deep breaths. As soon as the front door shut behind him, she burst into tears.

Baba barged into the sitting room. "Namali, what has gotten into you?"

She covered her face with her hands, as if they could somehow erase this nightmare. The bracelet felt impossibly heavy. "I don't want to marry him, Baba." She lifted her tear-streaked face. "Please don't make me."

His bushy eyebrows snapped together. "You're being selfish, Namali. Think of our family. You know times are hard right now."

She knew. She *knew*. But was there not another option, another road that would lead to the same destination without requiring union with a stranger? She did not think she asked for much, but maybe she was wrong. Maybe desiring such a life was too high a cost for her father's happiness.

Baba knelt next to her and patted her back awkwardly, one of the few times he had shown her affection since her mother died. "Mr. Abdu is one of the wealthiest men in the Saraj," he said, voice gruffer than it had been a moment ago. "He could have any woman he wants. You should be grateful he wants you for a wife."

A sharp, metallic taste flooded her mouth, borne of all the things she could not change. She choked on the word—grateful. "If he can marry any woman he wants, then why doesn't he marry someone else?"

"Why does it matter?"

It mattered. It did. There was no why to it. But her father was of the water, and she of the sky, and could a fish ever understand what it meant to fly? How could she possibly explain what lay in her heart?

"I don't want to marry him. I . . . I refuse," she whispered, staring at the ground.

His voice sharpened. "You're my daughter. You'll do as I say."

"You can't make me."

"Namali." He waited until she glanced up. "I'm sorry you feel this way, but you don't have a choice. You will marry Mr. Abdu regardless of whether you want to or not. This is what's best for our family. Do you understand me?"

Choice. The word meant nothing and everything. Nothing, because she'd never had a choice, and everything for the same reason.

She nodded, not trusting herself to speak.

"Good." Straightening, he smoothed the wrinkles from his robe. "I'll be out in the corral if you need me."

Alone, Namali gathered the uneaten food and returned to the kitchen. Her thoughts were tumultuous as she scrubbed the dishes clean with sand and stacked them on the ground near the pot of water that had gone cold. Here she was, trying to speak to her father as an adult, and he still thought her a child.

Frowning, she wrapped the flatbread in a piece of cloth and set it next to a bowl of pomegranates. She wasn't a child anymore though. She was seventeen. A woman.

Namali gritted her teeth, swiped at the tears that welled and stung her eyes. With the acceptance of this bracelet, she had sealed her fate as a married woman. But still she asked herself, *How long?* How long did she have to live this life, *her* life, before it reached a bitter end? One month? Two?

It's not enough time.

With a sigh, Namali put the remainder of the food away and glanced around. The dishes were washed and organized. The sitting room was in order. All of her chores were completed for the day.

Then, because there was little else to do, she began preparing dinner. Baba didn't like to be kept waiting.

CHAPTER 2

NAMALI APPROACHED HER father's bedroom door a few days later, tea tray in hand. She had lain awake at night and thought of this moment, and as the sun had risen and chased away the darkness, she had thought of it, too. The words that would bring an end to this marriage. The motion that would set her free.

Her toes curled into the cool packed mud. "Baba?"

"Come in."

Pushing aside the blue cotton covering the entryway, she stepped into a sparsely decorated room, a bedroll heaped with pillows in one corner, and a shrine dedicated to Mahurzda, the Good Lord, in the other. Beside it rested a painting of her mother, who, even in the last days of her life, had been every form of lovely. Faded, frayed, but never forgotten.

"I brought you tea," Namali said, placing the tray on the ground. An elaborate, hand-woven rug brightened the otherwise sterile space.

Her father didn't look up from the book he was reading. He wore a pair of dull yellow trousers; a black, knee-length robe; and the usual indifferent expression. She couldn't remember the last time he had smiled or laughed. The last time they had done it together.

"Did you finish your chores?"

"Yes, Baba."

"You're sure the gate has been fixed properly?"

Namali bit back a sigh. Was it so hard for her father to believe she was capable of more than cooking a hot meal every night? "I'm sure. And Khorshan—"

Her father paused in the middle of turning a heavily scripted page. "What about Khorshan?"

She swallowed, searching for an explanation, but none of them held the ring of truth, and by the time she thought of an answer, the silence had stretched on for too long.

"You've been spending time with the kerespa again, haven't you?"

Her back went up, each vertebra locked into alignment. "His name is Khorshan, and he's my friend."

"Seven hells, Namali. How many times do I have to tell you? Khorshan is not a pet, so stop treating him like one. He is for work. The more you coddle him, the lazier he will become. I won't tell you this again."

Taking a step back, she murmured, "But he's lonely." She couldn't help that their hearts had been drawn to one another, that a non-human friend was better than no friend at all.

"He's an animal," said her father, and returned to his book.

Namali gripped her long, thick braid in both hands and gazed out the window, the baked stone buildings of Benahr an unfocused blur. A warm breeze fluttered the edge of her veil, coaxing her question out into the open. She had come to him for a reason, and it wasn't to discuss chores, and it wasn't to discuss Khorshan either. "Can I talk to you about something?"

No answer.

She turned around. "Baba."

"Hm?" He stroked his graying beard and flipped a page. "What is it?"

Releasing her braid, she clasped her fingers together. The time was now. "I wanted to talk to you about my . . . marriage."

"Mr. Abdu is arranging everything. Food, decorations, invitations. There's nothing for you to worry about."

A shiver rippled through her body despite the pressing heat. "It's not the decorations I'm worried about."

"Then what is it?"

Namali took a breath. *Be brave,* her mama used to say. But courage was one of those things, like gorgeous skin or the ability to stand on the back of a moving camel, that she had never developed. "I'm not ready to get married."

He sighed and lowered his book. "We talked about this the other day. I can understand why you're not ready to marry. It's scary having to go into it without knowing your spouse. Do you think your mother and I—" The book slipped from his grasp, thudding to the floor.

Namali knelt down to pick it up, unable to look him in the eye for fear of what she would find. It was a collection of Malahadi folktales Mama had read to her as a little girl, one that had sparked her love of the written word. When she thought of what had been, so different from what was, it brought too much pain for her to dwell on for long. *Do you remember,* she wished to say, *how I would laugh at Mama's silly impressions? The way you looked at her, as if you knew there would be no one else. Do you remember?*

She returned the book to his limp fingers.

Her father cleared his throat. "Do you think we had time to get to know one another before we were married? The first time I saw your mother was on our wedding day. She was the most beautiful woman I had ever seen."

Her chest squeezed. "Baba—"

His shoulders drooped, and the wall went up, too tall to climb, too thick to breach. "Enough. Mr. Abdu will make a dependable husband. He is a good man who has done much for us." With that comment, Namali wondered just how much the merchant had done, and what. "You should be thanking Mahurzda for this gift."

"I don't love him, Baba. I don't even know him."

He turned a page, then another, much too fast for someone to read. He had yet to touch his tea. "Love won't put food on the table or a roof over your head. Mr. Abdu has the means to give you that and more. You will have a comfortable life with him."

"I don't *want* a comfortable life. I want—"

His head snapped up. "Stop it, Namali. You sound ridiculous."

She flinched. These were her dreams, and her own father thought them ridiculous. In a smaller voice, she said, "He won't make me happy."

Something seemed to leave him. A strength, or a will to go on. "You don't know that. I didn't love your mother in the beginning, but I eventually grew to love her."

There was so much sadness in his voice, so much she wanted to say to comfort him, but in the end she said nothing, only stood there wishing he could understand the merchant was nothing like her mother. Mama was gone, and there would never be another like her. "It's not fair. You didn't even tell me I was going to marry him."

Leaning back against the wall, his eyelids fluttered closed. "You knew it would happen eventually."

"That's not the point."

"Your dowry has been paid. You're getting married at the end of the week, and that's final."

It felt as if her lungs had shriveled up and burst into a cloud of dust, for she could not take in air. She didn't know how long she stood there with her eyebrows lifted to her hairline, nauseous, out of breath. "I'm getting married at the end of the *week*?"

He exhaled through his nose, one long deflating sigh. "Yes."

"Wh—" Her stomach churned. "When were you going to tell me?" she managed. The end of the week was in five days. So little time.

"I was going to mention it at dinner tonight."

"You can't keep these things from me."

"I told you, didn't I?" He returned to flipping pages. "Now please, leave me be so I can read."

Namali wrapped her arms around herself, needing some sort of comfort she couldn't expect from her own father. In five days she'd be married, and all he cared about was his books. "Well. Don't let me distract you." She lingered in the doorway, hoping he would glance up and notice her distress, admit his misstep, hold her close, soothe her fears.

But of course he didn't.

She swept from the room, face utterly still. She'd been a fool to hope for as much.

•••

Needing something to distract herself, Namali grabbed the water bucket and descended the stairs to the corral located beneath the craggy outcrop her home had been built upon. The camels were gathered beneath it, their heads hung low, listless in the dry, sweltering heat, all save one.

The gate to the corral gaped, and she was not even surprised. With a sigh, Namali exchanged the bucket for the coil of rope slung over the fence and approached the lone camel munching on weeds beyond the fence's perimeter. Drowsy, half-lidded eyes regarded her in disinterest. She had taken to renaming this animal Problem. Quite fitting, as it escaped the pen no less than once a week and frequently chomped its food with what Namali believed to be a near-smirk as she went through the motions of fashioning the rope into a lasso, her hands moving from muscle memory.

It slipped over the animal's neck with ease, and she once again led it back to the corral, glaring all the while.

Once the camel merged with the rest of the herd, a creature that was most definitely *not* a camel pushed through the furry bodies and approached the fence.

Namali smiled. "There you are."

The kerespa was both power and grace. Burnished orange scales rippled over his equine body, long legs ending in claws instead of hooves, a barrel chest swelling with each inhale. She offered a hand for him to catch her scent, the forked tongue tickling her palm as it flicked past his lips. Behind, his serpentine tail trailed along the ground, a dark red ridge protruding upward, following the line of his spine.

He pawed at the earth, looked past her shoulder. Out there.

Namali couldn't help it. She followed his line of sight to where the horizon shimmered behind waves of heat. Eventually, it became too much, reaching but not being able to touch, and she turned her back. "Not right now," she said, understanding what it was he desired. Having already disobeyed her father once today, only the dark of night would offer adequate coverage from any unwanted attention. "I brought you something."

Khorshan's serpent eyes locked onto her hands as she removed a woven necklace of purple thread from her pocket and slipped it around his substantial neck. Weaving jewelry had been something she and her mother had shared, but now that Mama was gone, she wove to feel close to her. To remember.

Namali ran a hand down Khorshan's neck, his scales so hot it was a wonder flames did not flicker beneath his skin. "Do you like it?"

Instead of answering, he sniffed her pockets for possible treats. She nudged him. "Don't be greedy. I asked you a question."

Khorshan snorted as if to say, *Really?*

"I can take it back if you don't want it," she said, reaching for the necklace.

He stepped back, butting her arm in apology.

Her expression softened. There was something so pure about the love of an animal, and she never took it for granted. "Good." She pressed a kiss to his snout. "I'll be back later."

Picking up the bucket, she continued down the road. A few merchants had set up shop, but they never stayed for long, as

Benahr was not the most profitable of towns. Still, the main road was quite congested with herders, animals. Stray dogs picked at trash scattered in the street, dodging the creaking wheels of wagons piled high with the soft flesh of peaches and the round brightness of cherries. There were a few women browsing the wares, most notably the imported fabrics or jewels. But there were no women working the stalls, or selling their handmade goods, or directing a trade or sale. In Malahad, the law deemed women as property. They could own no title, no land. Once married, their bodies were not their own.

Namali moved into a scrap of shade, the thought churning her stomach. She knew what occurred when a woman lay with a man. Her mother had informed her of such things. She'd even said it could be pleasurable, but how pleasurable could something be when not given a choice? The status of a wife had expectations she didn't think she could meet. Especially in the bedroom.

From the corner of her eye, she spotted two familiar figures lumbering toward her, sacks of grain slung over their sweat-drenched backs. They passed her without notice, but she tracked them down the road as their figures diminished, bleeding into the sea of dull, dusty robes. Her mind was running. And then her feet were, too.

Namali raced after them, the bucket banging against her leg. "Farid! Hami!"

They turned at her voice, and after some hesitation, lowered their sacks to the ground.

She slowed when she reached them, the bucket coughing up

a cloud of dust as it thudded against the road. "Um. Hello." Now that she had their attention, she was not sure how to proceed.

They shared a glance, silently communicating in the way of brothers, then looked back at her. Farid, the older sibling, dipped his chin in acknowledgement. His eyes were shadowed, and his body had tensed slightly, just enough for her to notice. A smudge darkened his jaw from where the man had struck him.

She wiped her sweaty palms on her thighs. "Do you have a minute? I'd like to talk to you about something."

Farid slanted a glance over his shoulder to where a man drove his goat herd through the street, tapping the backs of the animals' flanks with a long wooden staff. Hami was younger by five years, and he was never without his older brother. They stood exactly the same—arms crossed, aware of the activity beyond this seemingly small and private space.

Farid murmured, "I know what you're going to ask me, and I can tell you it's best if you don't know."

Namali took care to keep her face and voice neutral. "That's a bit presumptuous of you."

"Namali." Farid's smile softened his rebuke. "I've known you since we were six."

"And *I've* known you since I was one," said Hami, not wanting to feel excluded.

"You saw me at the well yesterday?"

Farid nodded.

"But you won't tell me why that man hit you."

His fingertips alighted on his bruised skin and pressed in, gently. He only said, "It was deserved."

Namali knew Farid well enough to understand she would not find her answers here, but Hami . . .

The large smile she sent the younger brother was just startling enough to send him back a few steps. While her veil concealed her mouth, it did not hide the deep crinkling of her eyes. Namali took advantage of his momentary confusion by stepping between him and Farid. "Hami." She crouched down to his level.

"Don't listen to her, Hami."

She ignored Farid. "Do you remember last year, after the harvest, when Mr. Kashmi discovered someone had been stealing the apricots off his tree?"

Slowly, the boy peeked at his brother through his lashes, his panic so clear he may as well have shouted his confession. He was still young enough to have not yet mastered the subtle art of stoicism, and Namali struggled to contain her laughter under the weight of Farid's dark scowl.

"He never learned who did it," she said, so very grave. "But I did."

"Don't—don't tell him!" The younger sibling's face wrinkled in distress. "He's friends with our grandfather. I'll get in trouble."

"I won't say anything," she promised, then looked to Farid as she continued, "but don't you think it's a little unfair that I kept this secret all this time and asked for nothing in return, and you can't even tell me something so small as to what you and Farid were talking about yesterday?"

Hami whispered, "We're not allowed. It's bad luck to speak of it."

"I promise, your secret will be safe with me."

He looked to Farid for direction, fiddling with the frayed ends of his yirasaf. The char of sizzling meat carried on the hot breeze.

It appeared to pain Farid, for his pride to bend beneath the goodwill of fairness and trust. But when he nodded his permission, Hami leaned close and said, "We were talking about a race. It only takes place every one thousand years." He then folded his arms in an attempt to look as intimidating as his older brother.

Namali glanced between the siblings before heaving an internal sigh. It was too much to ask, she supposed—respect, truth. "Look, if you don't want to tell me, that's your choice, but you don't have to lie about it."

"We're not lying." Farid glanced around. No one paid them any attention, but he gestured for them to stand in the shade of a scraggly tree for additional privacy anyway.

After a brief hesitation, Namali followed. Technically, she was forbidden to be in the presence of men unless it was her husband or a blood relative, but no one would notice in the crowded street. No one would be looking for her. No one ever did.

Farid leaned against the tree trunk, hands deep in his trouser pockets in a casual slouch, though he continually scanned the surrounding area. "It's called the Demon Race, and it *does* only take place every one thousand years. People enter because the prize is worth the risk of crossing the Saraj."

That name . . . It was like an old friend she had not heard from in many years, and its knock on her door brought Namali back to a time when she had not known what it meant to be alone. Mama had settled seven-year-old Namali on her lap, cracked open the spine of a well-loved book, and wove her the tale of a boy crossing the Saraj, searching for an unimaginable treasure. The details had faded with time, but Namali remembered this: no one knew why the race existed, only that it did. Some claimed it to be the work of the Good Lord. Others thought it bore the dark mark of Mahurzda's foe, the Demon King.

Farid tilted up his chin, his smile small but pleased. "So you have heard of it."

Her mind was whirling, fast, fast, fast. A race across the Saraj. How liberating. How thrilling.

How deadly.

Namali licked her lips, tasting the forbiddenness of the conversation. There was a saying her people lived by. The man who seeks, knows. The man who knows, does. This race represented everything she wanted and feared, and nothing she could ever have. It was pointless to ask, as she'd never be able to watch it anyway. There were chores to be done, dinner to be cooked, a wedding to be had. But the mystery, the unknown . . . It made her want. "And the prize?" she asked, unable to mask the longing in her voice. "What do you get if you win?"

Farid's eyes crinkled from the small secret he harbored. "The deepest, most hidden desire of your heart." And, like spring, his smile bloomed. "A wish."

CHAPTER 3

THE UNEXPECTED MUSIC of that word pattered against her like soft rain, and it made Namali wonder if, like rain, she had imagined it because the very idea painted the world in such bright colors she was convinced it was real, it was now, it was truth. The brothers watched her with open, honest faces, no beguilement to lead her astray. Here, with them, was trust. And with such sweetness on her tongue did Namali dare to dream.

Her family was not rich by any means, but Namali thought that if she had all the jewels within the land cupped in her palms and piled at her feet, she would feel just as she felt now—poised on the brink of greatness. In one swift heartbeat, her world had transformed. It was no longer *if,* but *when.* With this key, all the wants, all the suppressed yearnings, spilled free.

Her father's love. Her mother's life.

A way out of this marriage.

Her cheeks burned, and she was grateful Farid and Hami could not see behind her veil. What was she thinking? She couldn't possibly enter the race. She was just a girl, and not a very brave one at that. If she attempted to cross the Saraj, she would probably die out there, alone and afraid, wishing she had stayed where things were familiar, where no growing ever occurred, where every day was praying to the Good Lord for something unexpected and new.

Namali looked to the sky. She had the unexplainable urge to laugh and she didn't know why. Did she want to stay because that was best for her, or did she want to stay because she was too afraid to leave? Fear was the chain she had toiled for years to break, and now she had been given a tool, an opportunity to do this very thing, and she still managed to dredge up flimsy excuses that would deny her what she wanted most. If she were to truly take this step, she needed to approach this realistically. Even if she entered, she wouldn't be the only one seeking to win.

After all, her people were of sun and sand. The desert was in their blood. Any race, no matter how small, drew competitors from hundreds, even thousands, of miles. And this race was the largest of them all, shrouded in mystery, its roots buried so deep no one knew its origins. The danger, the magic, the uncertainty, the thrill. It would attract people from all corners of the land, from every tribe and town.

Both brothers studied her with raised eyebrows, and she stepped closer, as if reaching for a flame despite knowing it would singe. The chatter and activity of Benahr slipped away. "What else can you tell me about the race? Where does it begin? When?" The words burned her traitor mouth.

The fervor in her voice caught Farid off guard. He straightened and slid his hands from his pockets. "Think of what you're asking."

"I know what I'm asking."

"No, you're letting your emotions cloud your judgment."

Their rising voices were beginning to draw unwanted attention. A butcher swatted slabs of bloody goat meat to keep away the swarming flies, observing them in interest. Lowering her response to a hiss, she returned, "All I want are answers. I think I deserve at least that." She shot Hami a look. "Right?"

The boy's mouth gaped. "Uh—"

Farid said, with worry, "It's dangerous."

Her bravado was beginning to fail. He intended to keep this information from her, hoard the words as if they were jewels. "It's not fair," she managed through an aching throat. "It's not fair that you, and all the other men out there, will have this chance to leave, while I stay here and rot. That could be me out there." She stabbed a finger in some aimless direction. "I could win. I *could* . . ." The last word died on her tongue. Her shoulders slumped. Perhaps, in another lifetime, she could be that person. But who was she now? Betrothed. Her father's daughter. She could not abandon the wedding, for it would shame her father, shame herself. Baba had done so much for her, and it felt like the deepest, most confusing of betrayals to want something different, something she felt was undeserved, for some unexplainable reason. But Namali had to ask herself, *At what cost?* What, after all was said and done, and she a married woman, would this cost her? Didn't she care about her own happiness?

The truth was hard and bright as the sun. And she could not look too closely for too long, lest it blind her.

"What are you thinking, Namali?" asked Farid, his face serious.

Her smile did not come easy, but she managed. "Nothing." And

if she was bitter about it, well, such was life. "I have to get back."
She picked up the bucket, heading for the well.

"Ahkbur," Farid murmured to her back.

She turned around. "What?"

His expression revealed his displeasure in letting slip this
detail. "The race begins at Ahkbur. In one day. At noon." He
blew out a sigh. "I'm probably going to regret this tomorrow."

Namali whispered, with all the gratitude she possessed, "Many
thanks."

After the brothers had gone, Namali remained in the shade,
pondering this newfound information, when she caught sight
of the merchant across the road, watching her. Slowly, she
straightened in uncertainty. He must have seen her converse with
Farid and Hami. And yet he had not made any move to interrupt.

Her stomach dropped as he crossed the busy street, his
features harsh beneath the glaring sun. She gripped the handle
tighter. It would anchor her against this tumultuous feeling—
dust on the wind.

"Hello, Namali." The clatter and cries of the market threatened
to drown out his voice, so quietly he had spoken. His manner of
dress was conservative, with only the occasional flash of jewel to
indicate his wealth.

She dropped her gaze. "H-hello."

Fingertips grazed her chin, tilted back her head. Namali
stiffened at the unwanted and unexpected contact, the boldness
of the gesture that allowed him to stare into her eyes and
murmur, "That's better."

His hand remained, his touch burning through the black
fabric of her veil. She wrenched her chin from his hold, her

back hitting the trunk of the tree Farid had leaned against earlier. Whether or not this was his right as her soon-to-be husband, it was unwelcome.

A sad smile softened the hardness gathered around his mouth. "It would be a shame," he said, "to hide such lovely eyes."

Lovely. She had never been called such a thing.

Her hand went to her cheek in a self-conscious gesture, and the motion drew his attention to the gold bracelet he had given her, which she had yet to remove.

A shift of emotion, a flash of something heartbreaking, intense. Namali convinced herself it was the shadows cast by the sun.

He said, "You don't remember me, do you?"

"Should I?"

It was an honest enough question, but the merchant did not seem pleased. "I suppose you wouldn't. It was over a year ago that we met, though the meeting was brief." Somewhere in the dusty streets, a child squealed, followed by a deeper voice booming its rage. A little girl raced past, a hot, freshly baked pastry clutched to her chest that Namali suspected had not been paid for. "I came to speak with your father, and you were sitting outside reading. The Book of Inala, you told me."

What was there to say? He was unrecognizable to her, but if he had approached her while she read, it was unlikely she would recall anything but the story. "I'm sorry. I wish I could remember."

He gave a resigned nod. "It's all right."

"Um." She still had the bucket. "I need to get this filled. It was . . . nice seeing you?" She edged around him and fled for the well, sending an apology to Mahurzda for her poor manners. In her haste, she rammed her hip into the edge of a cart loaded with pomegranates, and was scolded by a wrinkled old man with an unusually long beard.

She managed to reach the well intact. Once the official checked her off the list, she tied her bucket to the rope and lowered it down the dark, damp hole. Water poured inside. It had no choice, as that was its nature: filling what was empty. She heaved the bucket up to the well's edge, untied the rope, and began lugging it back home.

"Let me get that for you."

Namali jerked in surprise. She thought the merchant had gone. "I can carry it."

"I insist." He reached for the bucket.

She danced away, water droplets raining onto her burning feet. Even if it killed her, she would carry her own water. She had two hands, two legs, strong from her labor-intensive chores. She didn't need his help.

But his long dark fingers gripped the handle and tugged, disregarding her claim. Water sloshed onto the parched earth. She grimaced. Not wanting to spill more of the prized liquid, she released it and walked faster. If the merchant believed he was doing her a favor, then so be it. Her house wasn't far.

"Tell me how I can make this transition easier for you."

"You can't."

"There must be something I can do."

Her pace slowed, and she came to a standstill, looking straight ahead. "Do you really want to know?"

"I do."

He was so eager, so willing to please. She almost felt guilty facing him. "Marry someone else."

There was that look again, the one that was both separate and shared, as if he, too, wished for something else but had to make do with what was. "I can't do that."

"Why?" she wondered. "Why do you want to marry me?" For a man of such high status, there were far more beautiful women available. If he saw her bared face, he'd be displeased, having been led astray by the mystery of her eyes. The purple birthmark covering the lower right side of her cheek was not a thing of beauty, and once they were married, once he removed her veil, as was his right as husband, he would know she was tainted. "I don't understand." She was quiet, responsible Namali. Meek, obedient Namali. Shy, naive Namali. Namali who brought her baba tea. Namali who fetched water and folded laundry. Namali who did as everyone asked and never questioned what was best for herself.

Did she even like that person?

The merchant leaned in close. Close enough for her to see every pore in his long nose and the thinly veiled grief lingering behind those shining black pupils. "I understand how confusing this must be for you. I asked your father to give you warning before I arrived—I did." He stepped back, and Namali could breathe easier without the scent of cloves clouding her senses. "Your father is a good man. He told me about . . . about your mother. How strong you've been these past years. I admire that."

This man had no idea, *no idea,* what she had gone through. What she was still dealing with every day, for that matter.

"All I want," he said, "is to give you peace and comfort for the rest of your days. Whatever you desire in this life will be yours. Clothes, jewels—"

"Love?" she asked, and called herself every kind of fool.

He froze. "I'm sorry?"

She couldn't look at him. "Can you give me love?" Not that she could ever love this man, but she had to know. Since her mother's passing, it was as if all the love had been sucked from her home, leaving it as dry and cracked as an old carcass.

"Love." He turned partially away, a hand lifted to his forehead. "I . . . perhaps I can do that."

It was possibly the saddest thing she had ever heard, the confusion he must feel over so small yet so large a word. Maybe he didn't know what love was. She would likely never find it in the union between them.

"Like I said," the merchant continued, "this marriage can be pleasant for you. I'll provide for you and your family. You'll have new clothes, new shoes, new—"

She lashed out as her panic mounted. "I don't want new clothes. I like the ones I have."

"There's nothing you own that can't be replaced."

An emotion swelled in her throat, thick and stony. She tried to swallow it down. "So you're saying I can't bring anything with me? What about my books? Is there room for them?" And another thought, one so ridiculous she felt foolish for asking it. "What about Baba? Will I . . . will I be able to see him?"

The merchant's eyes were grave. "I would never prevent you from seeing your father." A pause. "I'm not a cruel man, Namali."

The air was locked in her chest. He was not cruel, but he was stifling. In many ways, that was worse.

"I need to get back," she said, yanking the bucket from his hand. Half of the water sloshed out, a waste.

"It will be all right, Namali."

"No. No, it won't." She rubbed at her eyes. The sun was too bright. "I'm sorry, but I don't want to marry you."

She was too cowardly to look at him, but she heard the merchant say, as he turned his back, "You don't have a choice."

Namali was not aware she had moved, but the bucket was no longer in her grip, and the front door slammed, and she was in the sitting room, kneeling in front of the bookshelves, yanking them from their cramped quarters, seeking a dark green, cloth-bound volume. Something dormant had awoken in her with the merchant's parting words. She was running out of time. Time to live. Time to leave.

If Mama were here, she would hold her hand, look into her eyes, and tell her not to be afraid. But for a girl who had spent her entire life hiding, unknown to everyone around her . . . she floundered.

Farid had given her information though, and had given it freely. Was she a fool, then, to allow that word—demon—to guide her? The book was in her hands. She flipped through the pages and returned to the journey of Delir, gleaning whatever details she thought might be of some use. Demon. Lost City. According to the legend, Delir had not been granted the wish, even though he had won the race. It did not explain why.

The race was one day away—tomorrow. Ahkbur was located five hundred miles northeast of Benahr. She had never ventured far beyond the wall. But she knew which landmarks would guide her through the monotonous sands. She knew how to read the constellations. And she knew if she didn't leave now, she never would.

Her hands tightened on the old worn book. Here was the path, and it was pure and cold and clear in her mind.

Be brave, Namali. No one will be brave for you.

She would enter the Demon Race. She would win. And she would wish this marriage away.

CHAPTER 4

THE WORLD SLEPT, but Namali was wide awake.

In the darkness of her bedroom, she slid from her bedroll, having already changed into a black wool robe and trousers, plaited her hair into a braid, and attached her veil. Her breath rushed in and out with such urgency it was a wonder Baba didn't hear her through the wall.

This is what it feels like to be brave.

A breeze stirred the tiny succulent withering on her windowsill. She must move quickly and quietly, no more than a shadow or wisp of smoke. Come morning, she'd be far from home, racing toward an unknown future.

Namali shouldered the pack filled with supplies she had gathered that afternoon while her father worked: food, a waterskin, a dagger she had no idea how to use, and rubies that could purchase more goods if needed. After slipping the dagger against the small of her back, she padded through the narrow hallway and pushed aside the cloth leading to her baba's room. He slept curled on his side beneath a blanket, face unlined in sleep.

A pang moved through her heart like an unhealed wound.

Her baba was the only family she had left in the world. No grandparents, no brothers or sisters or cousins.

No mother.

The idea of leaving him as he slept, unaware, did not sit well with her, and yet it was the only way. Namali removed a note from her pack and placed it next to his prone form. When Baba woke in a few hours, he would find the note. He would go to her room and discover it empty, unable to believe his shy, quiet, obedient daughter had stolen away into the night. She only hoped he could forgive her upon her return.

"I'm sorry, Baba," Namali whispered.

There was no response, but then again, she hadn't expected one.

•••

The sky was lit with stars, though none that she could see. A brisk wind ruffled Namali's hair as she pulled her robe tighter around herself and swiftly descended the stairs to the corral where Khorshan dozed. The cloud cover was so thick she could not identify the positioning of the two moons, nor the constellations. She would just have to make do with the landmarks, then.

From the back of the corral, the kerespa lifted his sleek, narrow head. Bright green eyes pierced the night, two islands in a black sea. The camels stood clumped together for added warmth in the middle of the pen, forcing Namali to travel the long way around to reach Khorshan. A forked tongue flicked past his lips upon her approach, which, admittedly, was more frenzied than usual. He pressed his snout against her chest, his way of saying he had missed her.

"Missed you, too," she whispered, returning the affection.

With her presence, a few camels began to stir, moaning their complaints at the disturbance.

"Quiet!" she hissed, shoving through their warm, sleepy bodies to reach the gate. Baba's snores no longer drifted through the window. Three minutes, and then she'd be gone.

A pebble rattled down the staircase, and Namali whipped around and pressed deeper into the crevice, until she became shadow and anyone walking by would see her as darkness.

No one came. Nothing stirred. After a few moments her heart lowered itself back into her chest.

She saddled Khorshan as hastily as possible with shaking hands, her blood throbbing through every inch of skin. The saddle was of pale hide, stitched together from animal sinew. It overlaid a thin blanket to prevent irritation. The bridle and reins were of the same soft leather, and as soon as she slipped the lead over his head, Namali mounted Khorshan and led him into that fathomless sea of rolling dunes. He jerked at the reins, nostrils flaring to inhale the dry, dusty air while Namali tucked her supply pack beneath her robe for protection and leaned forward in the saddle, thighs tightening around Khorshan's girth. The land was dark and open and waiting for her, Benahr's wall at her back. Khorshan shifted impatiently. His muscles coiled beneath her, ready to spring.

"Fly," she whispered.

The force of the explosion tossed her back in the saddle. Namali screamed and clutched the reins, the motion wrenching her shoulder joints as she pulled herself upright, a wave of sand blasting her face. The wind burned her eyes and darkness swirled around her. They were wind and water and light, untethered, unchained. Khorshan opened his gait, hitting his stride with the fastest sprint. The world blurred.

The desert unfurled before her like a glorious carpet, paving the way to Ahkbur. Her eyes drank in the night, so dark, so still. Khorshan's muscles stretched and contracted seamlessly, his scales imprinting into her skin like hard round coins, and she felt his elation with each pounding breath. The ride was like sweet wine, like laughter rolling out of her.

She didn't know living could be this way. She didn't know at all.

"Faster, Khorshan!"

They flew, so fast they could not be seen, and Khorshan's scales sparked from the breakneck speed, then burst into flames. Her heart thundered with such joy that she could not stop the tears. How she had longed for this, feared this. She had never needed to. The air was cold and pure in her chest, and she felt so small yet so large and it was everything, everything.

As the miles whipped by, the sky warmed to gold in the east. Namali blew past the various landmarks in a cloud of sand, the most recent a pile of bleached bones set atop a massive stone. She would not be fooled by the desert's beauty. Danger was all around. It was in the sun, the shifting winds. In the brightness of day, the land shone stark and cruel. Beautiful—and terrible.

The barest nudge sent Khorshan changing direction, so attuned was he to Namali's body language, almost as if they were one being. Lean forward, he sped up. Lean back, he slowed down. They surged through the timid dawn, breath for breath, and she knew he would run forever if she asked him to.

An hour before noon, a dark smudge appeared on the horizon. Namali slumped in dazed relief from the sheer unlikelihood of arriving safely. She slowed Khorshan to a walk upon reaching the outskirts of the city and dismounted, wincing at her sore thigh muscles. Khorshan's chest heaved like a bellows, his eyes still bright from the run, and Namali's heart swelled with love for her friend. In all the years they had ridden together, he had never failed her. Not once.

"Many thanks," she whispered, "for keeping me safe."

Ahkbur was a city of twenty thousand strong built around a sprawling desert oasis. The behemoth gates carved from the fortified, sandstone walls lay open to welcome those traveling the Old Road. It was said civilization had been birthed from Ahkbur's waters, beneath the shade of its many trees. With access to Shun in the east and Lomoria to the west, it served as the heart of Malahadi trade.

"Come on, boy." Namali led Khorshan through the heaping sand until it eventually transformed into hard, baked earth. She joined the congestion of travelers seeking entrance to the city, scrutinized by the watchful eyes of the guards atop the gates. She would need to ask someone where the race began. Maybe find a quiet place to gather her thoughts and strategize.

But as she stepped inside Ahkbur's walls, the thought disintegrated. The city was a riot of sound. Rumbling wagons, clanking chains, the snap and pop of sizzling meat, a high peel of laughter drowned out by merchants crowing to passersby of recently acquired goods, the best deals. The sheer force of volume assaulted her, and she nearly clapped her hands over her ears for reprieve. Gone was the hush, the muted undercurrent of voices, like wind-weathered stone. These sounds were sharp and bright.

Namali glanced around in confusion, her distress mounting. She followed the flow of traffic, as she had little choice lest she want to get trampled. The sheer crush of people was overwhelming, the presence of color an unusual distraction. Ahkbur pulsed with vibrancy and life. The robes, yirasafs, and veils were richly dyed, ornamented with small metal bells, thick tassels, intricate patterns embellishing the deep sleeves. Hand-woven Malahadi rugs hung on display like massive colorful flags. She did not understand the languages spoken, the choppy syllables of those with paler skin, straight black hair, and then those with lighter distinctions as well, eyes of blue or green, people from the north. The energy here was so strong Namali felt it seeping up through the cracks at her feet, and it wasn't long before her throat swelled with emotion. The brilliance of this city would overshadow Benahr even on its brightest days.

"Are you prepared?"

Namali whirled around and nearly plowed into a heavyset man wearing what must have been near one hundred wrought-iron pendants. Something in his wide, unblinking gaze made her pulse surge. "Excuse me?" She shifted back a step, out of the worst of the congestion.

"Are you prepared for what is to come?"

Namali inhaled shakily, the leather reins cutting into her callused palms. She could see it in his eyes. She could see what would come to pass. Who would live and who would die, and a land ravaged by night.

"Are you prepared for blood?"

She couldn't move.

"Or darkness?"

Blackness and shadow and smoke and night.

"Or death?"

No.

Slowly, he pulled one of the necklaces over his head, offering it to her. "Protection. From the daevas." He dropped it into her palm.

Namali jerked her hand away as if burned, the pendant clattering onto the ground. Their gazes clashed.

Daevas.

Fear sliced her clean through. It lived beneath the skin, breathing her breath and twisting her thoughts into sly, slithery things. Demons knew of darkness intimately. It was their hell and their salvation. Thousands of years trapped beneath sand and stone with no light to penetrate . . .

He leaned closer, his breath reeking of garlic. "The Demon King is ready. He has awaited this day—"

Khorshan lunged forward to snap at the man's shoulder, knocking him into a large clay pot that tipped and shattered. Namali used the distraction to slip away, weaving through the throng, dodging elbows and knees, but she could not escape the man's words, and neither could she escape the attention of the crowd.

People gaped openly at Khorshan. Children towing sacks of rice on giant beetles pulled their mounts to a halt, slack-jawed. A woman purchasing vegetables accidentally dropped her basket, sending onions rolling across the ground, while a father held his young son's hand and watched from the side. Namali averted her gaze. All this unwanted attention after a lifetime of invisibility. She wanted to be the dead lizard on the road, the fly on the refuse pile—overlooked.

Heavy traffic kicked up dust so it hung over Ahkbur in a dense cloud, filtering the light. Open, airy tent stalls were squished together on either side of the street with barely an inch of unclaimed space, allowing merchants and artisans to barter and sell. The goods were abundant and varied. Silk and black tea from Shun, a land of mountains and rivers and streams. Weapons from Lomoria to the west. Tubs filled with every imaginable spice—turmeric, coriander, cinnamon, cumin, saffron—sat in rows beneath various stalls, their gold, copper, and apricot colorings reminding her of miniature sand piles. And still there was more. Musical instruments, or bolts of wool and muslin, or colorful caged birds. But the most extraordinary were the jewels: fat, glittering rubies worn for youthful-looking skin; teardrop sapphires for removing blemishes; perfect spherical pearls for whiter teeth; and even those jewels unusual and strange, like the live iridescent beetles worn as earrings and necklaces.

The marketplace extended for nearly a mile, a mass of bodies growing denser and denser the farther Namali stumbled down the crooked street, and she couldn't move without touching or breathing or stepping on another person. The wave carried her deeper into Ahkbur, where the space narrowed, halting the flow of movement. The bodies were damp, smothering walls.

Someone rammed into her shoulder. Namali lost her balance and tumbled over a cart carrying baskets of figs and persimmons, the fruit exploding in all directions. People scrambled to scoop up the rolling fruits, flee, but there was little room to turn, and the frenzy of the crowd soon crushed her onto the ground, rocks biting into her palms as she twisted to catch herself. Her fingers caught beneath someone's shoe. A knee rammed into her cheek. "Get off me!"

No one spared her a glance.

The weight of hundreds of bodies bore down. Skin touching skin and groping hands and thick clogging air, and soon the sky, that perfect slice of blue, disappeared. Black dots erupted across her vision with the thinning air. She couldn't *breathe*.

The glassy fear that she would be trampled alive and left to die in this strange place sent a burst of adrenaline through her. In her desperation, she turned vicious. Her elbow rammed into someone's gut. Her knee went between the legs of a man who refused to let her stand. Namali shoved and kicked and carved a path through sheer will, her throat cinched tight, and then squeezed between two carts abandoned in the middle of the road as a slow panic swelled and burst over her. She practically climbed atop a young family to reach the perimeter of the street.

And then she was free. She was free from that prison of skin. Her legs wobbled. She pressed a trembling hand to her chest, gulping air. Nearby, men crowded around a single tent stall, shoving and swearing at one another, a tense hum. It smelled of sweat and something else she could only identify as *angry man*.

Namali pulled Khorshan to the side to watch the commotion play out.

The seller, a tiny, shriveled man with a network of wrinkles mapping his face, dangled a coil of rope over his head. "Last one!" he called over the demands of the crowd. "First one to pay walks away a victor."

One man, his physique more solid than a brick wall, shoved to the front, beefy hands clenched. "You're a thief," he growled. "A thousand rubies for a piece of rope is ridiculous."

The seller flashed a mouthful of yellowing teeth. "Not as ridiculous as competing in the Demon Race."

"No one has that kind of money," another man in blue garb argued.

"Think of what this rope represents," he countered, all smiles. "*Victory.*" He seemed pleased by his targeted manipulation. "You can't put a price on that."

Quick as a snake, the man in blue grabbed the vendor's robe and yanked him across the wooden barrier serving as a table. Less than an inch of space separated their noses. "Give me the rope, old man." The crowd crowed their thirst for blood.

The older man's hands fluttered, two brown birds uncertain of where to land. "L-let's not get carried away," he squeaked. "A man has to earn a living, you know." Steeling himself, he pried the fingers from his robe and darted to the back of his tent, where he attempted to smooth his rumpled appearance. "If you can't afford the rope, that's not my problem."

"If this wasn't the day of the race I could buy a piece of rope for only five rubies," the first man spat.

The old man appraised the wooden barrier, as if debating whether or not it offered adequate protection from his increasingly antagonistic audience. "Yes, but this *is* the day of the race, and times are hard." He dangled the rope before them, a decision Namali thought to be most unwise. "The price stands. A thousand rubies, or no deal."

The mob rumbled to life, swarming like locusts, feeding

upon the man's nervous energy. Their shifting feet stirred up dust and well-earned spite. "How are we supposed to enter the race?" someone cried.

"Find another vendor—"

"They're all sold out!"

"Sorry. Can't help you there." His attention darted to the clenched hands, the livid expressions. He reached for the ties securing the open tent flaps. "As of now, I'm closed. Please leave." A flick of his wrist, and the flaps descended, shielding him from view.

Namali watched in horror as the crowd surged forward with a heinous roar, yanking at the sealed flaps, but two officials arrived to neutralize the mob. The men disbanded, and Namali found herself following the man in blue who had yanked the vendor across the table. "Excuse me," she called, running after him.

He slowed, spat on the road with a glare in her direction. "What do you want?"

She shifted closer to Khorshan, who stepped in front of her body, partially shielding it. "Which way do I go to enter the race?"

His expression shifted, became distant. "If I were you," he murmured, avoiding her gaze, "I'd go back to wherever you came from."

"What do you mean? Can't anyone enter? I have a mount."

The man shook his head, the movement stiff. "That thing won't do you any good. In order to compete, you must ride a daeva."

A sudden chill burrowed beneath her skin. "A daeva?" It couldn't be. It was a lie. A cruel, cruel lie. "How . . . why do I have to ride one?" She tried to sound unconcerned, but the slight tremor in her voice gave her away.

"Look," said the man impatiently. "I understand why you want to enter, but do yourself a favor and go home. You won't survive the race."

The reins dug into Namali's palms as she watched him walk away. *You must ride a daeva.* The man had sounded serious, maybe even sorry for her. And that word: *must.* It was nonnegotiable.

Daevas. Shadow demons. Servants to the Demon King. When not in their shadow form, they wore various masks to prey upon those weak of mind, the most common ones being an old beggar in need or a young woman in distress. With one touch, the darkness swept in. Pulled them down to a state between waking and dying, a place of eternal night. And if she wanted any chance of winning, then she must race on one.

There was also the issue of Khorshan. What was she supposed to do with him while she competed in the race? She couldn't return him to Benahr because she'd never make it back in time for the start, but she couldn't abandon him, her father's most prized possession, while she attempted to cross the Saraj.

Namali glanced upward. One of the moons was round and whole and fully visible in the day. According to the story of Delir, the Demon Race began with the occurrence of a solar eclipse, and ended with a second eclipse on the thirtieth day. She did not have long.

"So are you going to enter?" asked a low voice from behind.

Namali turned, shielding her eyes against the sun. A young man of a similar age stood in the space between two merchants' tents, having managed to escape the pull of traffic like herself. A blue yirasaf, vibrant as a jewel, concealed his hair, but a few strands peeked out, as dark as her own. She frowned. "Are you going to tell me I'm wasting my time, too?"

He tilted his head, his expression quietly serious. "Why would you think that?"

She shrugged, suddenly self-conscious of her bold question. "I don't know. You wouldn't be the first to say as much."

"As far as I'm concerned, you have as much of a right to enter as anyone else."

She probably looked like a fool with her mouth slightly agape. No one besides her mother had ever told her she had the right to something, and this coming from a man, no less. "Oh." And that was the extent of her brilliant response.

"The man was right about one thing though. If you don't have any rope, you won't be able to catch a daeva, and if you can't catch a daeva, you can't compete."

"Why can't I ride Khorshan?"

The young man turned to admire the kerespa appreciatively and without a hint of greed. "Only the daevas know the way to the Lost City," he said. "That's the finish line, and where the wish is being held."

Of course. Delir had sought the Lost City with nothing but the clothes on his back. Some claimed it a myth. But so were all things too impossible to prove.

"You said I needed rope," she said. "Is there another vendor I can buy from besides that one?" She jerked her thumb at his tent.

It was too bright to make out his reaction in the sunlight, but Namali felt as if he smiled at her. "As far as I know, he's the last one left."

"That's what I was afraid of," she muttered.

"Can you afford it?"

A thousand rubies? She would never see that much money in one lifetime. Not even two lifetimes. "I don't have enough." The laugh snagged in her throat. It was an impossible price.

"Hm." He glanced at the kerespa again, his focus drifting to where her hand lay flat against the creature's neck, and her fingers twitched as if that look were a touch.

"What is it?" she asked when he remained quiet.

"I was thinking. The vendor might be interested in a trade if you're willing to part with him."

Namali inhaled sharply at the stabbing sensation in her chest. "I don't know if I can do that."

"It doesn't look like you have many options."

She looked to the cracked, dusty ground, the truth pressing upon her chest. He was right. She hadn't many options. Either move forward in this journey alone, or return to Benahr with a friend, but powerless.

Namali looked up to find him watching her. She swallowed and lowered her gaze once more.

"Good luck in the race," he said, before hobbling in the direction of the front gates. She couldn't see very clearly, but his right leg appeared to be twisted inward.

It didn't seem fair, somehow, that to get what she wanted, she would have to give up what she had. A choice—it was not how she imagined it to be. When she looked deeper, she saw how it had dressed itself in lavish silks and pleasant scents to better conceal its true nature: sacrifice.

Closing her eyes, Namali huddled closer to Khorshan, her throat tight with remembering. The first time Baba had brought him home. The first time she had ridden on his back, arms spread wide, knowing he would not let her fall. And when her world had shattered all those years ago, Khorshan had allowed her to cling to him, heartbroken, for as long as she had the strength to stand.

Every memory, every quiet and joyous moment, had led them here.

But this was where their journey came to an end.

CHAPTER 5

THE WIND PICKED up, twining around her legs as she squeezed through the marketplace, as if to say, *Hurry, hurry.* The sky had darkened subtly, the moon's silhouette crossing the edge of the sun's stark face, casting a sliver of shadow upon the land.

She reached the tent, Khorshan in tow. The neighboring tent had already packed up for the day, though it was early yet. "Excuse me, sir?"

"I'm closed," the gruff voice answered through the flaps. "Come back tomorrow."

She retreated before her mind registered the action. Obedience was as much a part of her as the blood running through her veins, but there was no Baba telling her to fetch water, to feed the camels, to leave him be. She could speak up for what she wanted, just this once. "I'm interested in buying your rope."

"It will cost you a thousand rubies, and you likely can't afford it."

Namali pressed her forehead against Khorshan's warm, muscular neck. He shifted, sensing her unease, and her heart sank so low she was surprised she did not find it dragging on the ground. She had no words to explain what Khorshan meant to her. It was less of knowing and more of being. A kind of quiet joy in her chest from the language they shared, that there was never a need for anything more than the two of them, together.

"I'm sorry," she whispered, unable to look him in the eye, "but this is the only way."

She said, loudly and clearly, "I can offer you a trade."

"Not interested."

The words slapped against her. She ducked her head, just . . . wishing. Her eyes filled, the world a blur as she said, "I will trade you my kerespa for one piece of rope."

The silence in the tent was complete. A crash sounded, and the old man poked his grisly head out. When his gaze landed on Khorshan, he sucked in a breath. She didn't know if he was breathing or not. "Seven hells. Come in. Quickly now." He practically hauled Namali inside.

Oil lamps flickering in each corner of the tent drenched the hide in a golden glow. A jumble of wares occupied the back: massive clay pots, bowls of spices and herbs, black and red teas, silk robes, thick furs in softest white—treasures of a world she had never seen. The tent was spacious enough that Khorshan could stand without his head brushing the ceiling.

The man's attention slicked over the creature's powerful frame, the long slender legs and shredding claws. She may as well have been invisible. "You say you're interested in selling this kerespa?" he said, expression skeptical.

She gripped the reins tighter. Had it been only yesterday that she had slipped the woven necklace around Khorshan's neck, bantering as old friends did? "Yes."

"One kerespa for one piece of rope?"

Namali clenched her teeth. This was a lousy, laughable deal, and under any other circumstances she would have walked far, far away.

But she wasn't laughing now.

"Shall I go somewhere else then?"

The man grinned. It was almost as if he could smell her desperation. "It's a deal—"

The oil lamps flared with a harsh, unearthly scream that seemed to echo inside Namali's head, her gasps ringing as the flames guttered, plunging them into a slick and seedy darkness, a place where light came to die. Her heart was beating in her ears, in the soles of her feet, for the air thickened and charged as if alive, though with nothing she could see. She began to notice not what was, but what was not. The shouts, the tread of feet, had vanished, and from the man's expression, he noticed the change, too.

She lowered her voice to match the hush. "Did you hear that?"

Gone was the earlier ease of luring in a deal. The man barely stirred. "There's nothing to hear."

So he had not heard the scream.

"We should close the deal," he said, reaching for the reins. "The race will begin soon."

"Hold on." Namali stepped aside, out of reach. Her eyes gradually adjusted to the dim. "This creature is worth twice the price of the rope. It doesn't seem like a fair trade to me."

A brief flash of annoyance crossed his face, though it soon melted into the charismatic façade, the one that made her think of falsities or equally ugly things. "Of course. I have many other wares for sale." He scoured through his mountain of clutter, sending items toppling over in order to reach something buried. "Here's an absolutely stunning robe." He showed her a green dress-robe with emeralds woven into its belled sleeves. "Made of silk. Brought all the way from Shun."

She shifted back onto her heels, wishing he would relight the oil lamps. It was a struggle to focus with the shadows crowding everything. "How will that give me an advantage?"

"What about this necklace? Every woman needs something pretty to drape around her neck."

Namali gritted her teeth. "I'm not interested in clothes or jewels. I need something to help me survive the race."

"I have food. A waterskin."

"I already have those things."

"Um . . ." Then his face lit with realization. "As a matter of fact, I *do* have something that may interest you."

Muttering to himself, the old man began searching through the mess. He soon realized, however, the difficulty in completing a task with little light, so he relit a few of the lamps, much to Namali's relief. "One minute. I know it's here somewhere." He tossed aside a robe, some baubles, gold and silver coins, a pair of camel hide sandals, a pair of silk slippers, a thin mat woven of dried grass, a bowl full of what looked like teeth that thumped across the carpet.

Khorshan flicked out his tongue, smelling something in the air. Namali rubbed a soothing hand down his neck.

The man whirled around, grinning hugely. As if he had already won.

"What is that?" Namali asked, studying the small cloth bag he held.

"Depending on how you look at it, your greatest weapon or your greatest defense."

She glared. "That doesn't tell me anything." As if she would expect anything else.

"This will come in handy for you, I guarantee it. On my honor as a merchant, this is worth the price of your kerespa."

"Merchants have no honor," she countered, yet unable to tear her attention away from the bag. A second later, thunder growled, shuddering through the rock. Her gaze snapped to the closed tent flaps, something about the noise lifting the hair on the back of her neck, that buzzing sensation in the air having returned. She didn't remember seeing storm clouds earlier. The sky had never been a brighter blue.

Namali returned her attention to the bag, unable to relax. There was a wrongness to it all. Everything. Even this man. "May I touch it?"

Sensing victory, he shoved it into her waiting hands. "You must not open it until you absolutely need it. What lies inside this bag can only be used once."

She accepted the flat, flimsy piece of cloth, a piece of twine tied around its end. It felt weightless. "Are you sure there's something in here?" she asked with a frown.

"I promise you, a great power lies within this bag."

It was clear he would not be revealing that power anytime soon, if ever. "That's nice, but since I have no idea what's inside, I don't think this, plus the rope, plus the supplies, are worth—"

The oil lamps dimmed, then sparked, causing her to throw up her hands against the brightness. She stumbled back into Khorshan's chest. "What's happening?"

He said, voice oddly without inflection, "The daevas are trying to break through the barrier to the mortal world. They'll be here soon."

Sweat broke out on her hairline. What would that mean for Malahad, for humanity? Her time for questions had come and gone. She needed to reach the starting point, now. "What you offer me is nice," she said hurriedly, blinking away the bright spots, "but it's not enough."

His face fell.

"However, I have a proposition for you."

His gaze latched onto Khorshan, then darted back to her, trying not to express how much he yearned for this rare and beautiful creature. The greed of men, however, was not easily masked.

Namali met his stare with a confidence she neither felt nor believed. "You give me all the things you offered: the rope, the supplies, and the bag. In return—" She swallowed. It was for the best. That's what she told herself and would keep telling herself, after all was said and done. To go forward, she must leave something behind.

"In return," she continued shakily, "I will give you Khorshan."

The kerespa's ears perked at the sound of his name.

The man grinned. "Splendid—"

"However," she cut in, "if I return from the race alive, you return Khorshan to me, and I'll return you your rope. I get to keep the supplies and the bag, because their price is worth the difference." She fiddled with a piece of unraveling thread along the edge of her sleeve. "Does that sound fair?"

The man bent his head in consideration, scratched his patchy gray beard. Weighing the chance she would return as she had claimed against the likelihood she would die. "It is not as I had hoped . . ."

A high, keening wail crested in the distance. A child's cry, so foreign in the quiet. "Final offer. Take it or leave it." She was bluffing. If he refused, she'd most likely give him Khorshan outright, because she needed this rope more than he wanted her kerespa. She sensed Khorshan's uncertainty in the taut lines of his body. A part of her wanted to shield him from the man's greed, her betrayal, but she did not. To comfort him would be to lie.

The child was screaming now, crying for its baba. Namali's knees trembled with the will to remain standing, to not collapse and clap her hands over her ears to block out the wretched sound that pierced something fragile within her, a memory she did not dare revisit. *He's not coming back,* she thought, and broke a little at knowing the child would grow up fatherless. *You'll never see him again.*

The man stepped forward, hand extended. "I accept your offer."

The deal was done.

The seller gave her the bundle of supplies, as promised. She placed everything but the rope and empty-looking bag in her pack. Those she stuffed between the folds of her robe next to her dagger. If the bag was indeed the best weapon or best defense, she wanted it close at hand.

Now all that remained was goodbye.

It felt as if her heart had hardened into lead and been pounded into something unrecognizable as Namali wrapped her arms around Khorshan's warm, sleek neck, clinging to the familiar, her last memory of Benahr. Baba had been wrong. He was far more than a kerespa. He was her mother and father, her modest bed, the front door that creaked when opened. He was home, and she had traded it all for a piece of rope.

"I'll be back for you," she whispered, tilting back her head to look into his crystalline green eyes. "Don't . . . don't forget me, all right?" She passed the reins to the seller, could do nothing but say, "Take good care of him," and hope that he would.

The ground shuddered again, rattling the clay pots. The man stroked Khorshan's neck so, so slowly. "It won't be long now."

Namali did not give him the satisfaction of revealing her mounting anxiety. "I'll be back," she said.

The man chuckled. "I think this was perhaps the best deal I ever made." He flashed those broken teeth again, his sunken cheeks giving him a skeletal appearance. "I won't be holding my breath."

When the tent flaps fell shut behind her, Namali stepped foot into a darker, starved version of the market she had left. There was neither human nor animal along the strip of paved gravel—merely footprints left in the dust. Without the people to clog Ahkbur's streets, Namali could not help but notice the prominence of its walls, how small she felt among the abandoned stations, the food and wares left untouched. "Hello?"

Not even the wind stirred.

Her hand trembled as she pushed aside the strands of sweaty hair clinging to her forehead. Everything was black and fearful and unexplained, the land cast in spindly shadows that writhed on the ground, shifting and slithering and spilling down the cracks. Not a soul, not a sound. She was alone in a world made dark by the moon.

The earth rumbled a third time, and her knees buckled. "Hello?" she called again, voice cracking. "Can anyone hear me?" It was nearly noon, and she did not have long before the moon cloaked the sun completely, but there was no evidence of where the race began, how she should get there. She should have asked the boy from earlier for directions.

As the land darkened further into night, Namali climbed to her feet and sprinted toward the front gates, her sack banging against her side. She recalled seeing a small group of people congregating outside the city, but had she wasted too much time? Was she too late? Even the guards atop the wall had abandoned their posts as she flew through the deserted entrance and spotted a shifting entity between two shallow cliffs, the crowd appearing more sinister from this distance, feeding upon the fear of others. Once she hit the dunes, she stumbled. Namali thought of the life waiting for her, *out there*, and the people wanting to hold her back. She pushed her legs faster.

Above, the moon snuffed out the final ray of light. She raced through a black wasteland, a place of eternal night, where shapes melted into shadow and the packed bodies she pushed through blocked the dinge-colored sands. Darkness wrapped her in its suffocating embrace. *Welcome me,* it whispered. *Stay.*

The earth groaned, an icy, hair-raising shriek erupting as chunks of rock ripped free and tumbled from the cliffs to shatter on the ground below, shooting up clouds of thick, scorching dust. Her breath sounded harsh and wild in her ears. *Demon, demon, demon.* Whatever she had imagined this to be . . . it was so much worse. It was the blackest nightmare made flesh, and it had yet to truly begin. And she was here. She was here and she was a fool, and Namali choked on each inhale in her struggle to breathe in such a tight space. Thought, control—gone. All gone.

Another crash, an echoing boom. It sent the cowards fleeing, sent the pious to their knees, sent the ruthless forward, the beginnings of a stampede stirring, the men like animals, like beasts. Through the darkness, a gaping chasm appeared where two halves of the earth wrenched apart. The swell of people pushed toward the earth's black maw, crashing down on those too slow, too reluctant to move and trampling them with little thought or remorse. The violence, the mindless greed. The horror of it all.

"They're here!" someone screamed.

The roar of noise shook the earth. She jumped, trying to spot the daevas beyond the crowd, these beasts made of shadow and smokeless fire, but she saw nothing, only a great fathomless mass flying toward them, and darkness all around. The crowd surged forward, alive with frenzy and a base, animalistic need erupting like the hottest of flame, and Namali burned among them, caught within that dark current. It was all hands and teeth and nails. Then came the daggers. Then the first drop of blood that soaked the sand.

CHAPTER 6

NAMALI RACED AFTER the crowd, her heart feeling as if it might seize from the overbearing roar that built and built until it reached a high keening and the pressure bloodied her ears. The rumbling had stopped, but now a different, more terrifying sound emerged, freezing the blood in her veins: the sound of the dying.

The dust cleared, and there they were, their eyes like pits, their snarling mouths crowded with glistening black fangs. They were neither water nor air. Not insubstantial, but the way their forms passed through space, so unearthly, reminded Namali they did not belong to this world, that their spindly legs and bowed, twisted spines represented the ominous place from which they had come. And now they were here. Ravenous. Unleashed. Ripping each other to shadowy shreds. Men tossed their ropes eagerly, attempting to capture one of the beasts, and Namali slowed and clutched her side while war raged around her and the land continued to buck and roll, the avalanche of crashing stone drowning out the worst of the screams. Clapping her hands over her ears, she dropped to her knees. Insanity—this was insanity.

She could not fathom how quickly order had dissolved. These

men were like slavering dogs, mindless with the possibility of reward. In gruesome fascination, she watched one of the few competitors who had succeeded in roping a daeva yank the snarling, bucking animal closer, the muscles in his neck bulging with the effort of controlling the beast, this monster from another world. He threw himself onto its back, where the brush of shadow against his skin ripped from him an agonized scream that could only come from the deepest, blackest depths of hell. It was the sound of a man torn apart, a sound of wretched, unimaginable pain.

She couldn't look away.

The man's eyes rolled up in the back of his skull. His spine bowed forward to the point of snapping. Then he kicked the daeva into a run, straight toward the cliff.

Time seemed to slow. Her heartbeat was a low tick, tick in her ears. She stumbled to her feet as if to stop this tragedy, this one among many, as the man barreled toward the slab of solid rock, sand flinging around the demon's legs.

"Watch out!" she cried.

The man crumpled from the impact, his face caving inward like a chick pea crushed between her fingers. The daeva flung off the corpse, unhurt, and kept running. Away. Away from it all.

The sight of slaughter encased Namali's legs in ice. Around her, the sands bled black with blood. Men lay dead and dying, impaled by swords, dismembered, weeping from the agony. Those who did not escape back to the safety of town watched, sickened, as the remaining competitors mounted the daevas and turned on themselves, became their own worst enemies. A boy wrapped his hands around his throat and squeezed tight, tighter, and blue flooded his lips even as his mouth worked to inhale, to keep on living. He couldn't have been older than twelve—too young to know of death. Another man sobbed as he gouged his eyes out, blood raining down his cheeks and staining the top of his robe. When he removed his hands, his eye sockets were empty, red, inflamed. Blind.

The screams drummed against her back like a furious downpour, and the world was a writhing, grinding mass that swelled and filled every empty pocket, every abandoned corner, every hollow space with bleeding darkness, and the people were swimming in its ichor, slashing, dodging, fleeing death or running forward to meet it with hearts already touched by violence. The black tide bulled her over as Namali clenched her hands into fists, took a steadying breath, tried to block out the worst of the screams. She searched for peace amidst the chaos, turning inward, to the deep well in her mind, the place of calm. *I am not afraid.* But it was a lie. She had spun herself a web of fear seventeen years deep and had somehow convinced herself it was the only way to live. The thought of leaving behind everything familiar squeezed her lungs in a tight fist, and now *this*: complete and utter destruction.

Had she made a mistake?

The initial stampede of daevas had dwindled. Soon the moon would part from the sun, and light would flood the land once more. Of the few thousand people initially present, less than fifty remained, most having fled. The men who succumbed to madness vastly outnumbered those who did not. Those men, the ones who failed, looked like liars and cheaters and thieves, their hearts already tainted with greed. And yet there were others, few, like this man fighting for dominance, who managed to regain control, his goodwill having somehow given him an advantage. As he raced into the distance, Namali imagined him a father, a brother or son, on a journey to seek a better life for his family. The smaller he became though, the lower her heart sank. One less demon to choose from.

Rough hands abruptly clamped down on her shoulders, jerked her back. Someone pawed at her supply bag. "What—" She tried twisting around. "Stop!"

The strap snapped, and her pack fell into the man's waiting hands, the tip of a scimitar blade rushing upward to kiss her throat. Namali stilled. Around her, the action slowed and slipped into a dull murkiness. The line separating nightmare and reality blurred.

"Unless you want your throat sliced open," he hissed, expression stony, "don't come any closer."

Raising her hands, she stepped back, giving him space and the chance to escape. A black, toxic emotion curdled in her stomach as she watched him clamber onto a daeva's back, the echo of his screams lingering long after he had disappeared.

The shock at having been taken advantage of with so little remorse brought the swift rise of tears. Namali swiped at her damp, sandy cheeks with shaky hands. It was all so overwhelming. So many variables to this day and so little she could control. But if she were being honest with herself . . . she was less affected by the theft and more by her own inaction. Why hadn't she fought back? Why had she stood there and allowed that man to take from her?

Without food or water, she would not last long. The sun would eat away her flesh, her bones would disintegrate to dust, and she would become a memory. If she could not protect what was hers, what chance did she have at winning? She should turn back. This was not her world. She would marry the merchant. She would do her best to fulfill her duties as a wife. That . . . that was her world.

But she had come all this way, and for what? Why was it so hard to make this choice?

Namali looked at the now-bright sky, where the last sliver of moon shadowed the sun. Already, she had gone farther than she ever thought possible. She must remind herself of who she was and where she had come from to keep hold of her tenuous grip on the situation. Despite the turmoil, all was not lost. She had her rope, a dagger, and the bag from the vendor. A few daevas lingered. There was still time.

Compared to the beginning of the eclipse, the daevas emerging from underground were smaller, their features less mutated. She spotted the smallest one, about half the size of a camel. No one tried to capture it. They wanted the largest, the strongest, the swiftest, but she hadn't the strength of the other competitors. This was her best option: the most overlooked.

Hurriedly, Namali uncoiled the rope and fashioned it into a lasso. Her pulse beat in time with the cries of the wounded, as inhuman as those of the demons. She only hoped death came quickly for them.

Digging her feet into the hot sand for traction, she swung the rope around and around, the motion creating a sharp *whomp whomp whomp* as it cut by her ear. The daeva lowered its head, its black eyes burning with the heat of a banked fire.

She released. As the rope slipped around the beast's thick neck, its chest swelled, and a deep, guttural growl ripped from its throat. The first thrash nearly yanked Namali off her feet, but she held on, teeth gritted, beads of sweat clinging to her eyelashes.

She heaved the rope close, closer. Blood leaked from her abraded palms, dripping onto the sand to mix with that of hundreds dead. The beast was sleek and vicious and out for revenge, but she would not let go. She would not give in.

When it was close enough, Namali launched herself forward, scrabbling at its neck for a hold while it snapped at her legs and flung itself from side to side. She gripped the creature's fur, all flowing black shadow and smoke.

And a scream tore from her throat.

Agony in her eyes, in her chest, in her back, legs, and head. It was white hot, flooding her veins, seeping into every pore. Deeper and deeper, the pain slipped into her body until she could not separate herself. It was her heart, her world. She writhed from the excruciating sensation of someone peeling back her skin strip by strip to reveal the bones, muscles, and tendons beneath.

Darkness trickled into her vision, its tentacles probing the edges of her mind. She flinched. The foreign entity was as cold as it was oily, and with its presence the light inside her withered, crushed beneath its immense weight. The desert disappeared into a void, someplace fathomless, empty. A place of anguish, too dark for her imagination. An end to something.

Namali tried lifting her hand, shifting her leg. In desperation, she ordered her limbs to *move*.

She no longer had any control over her body.

Horrifyingly, Namali felt her arm jerk in the direction of her robe, manipulated by a cold, unseen force. She felt her fingers splay, felt her hand clasp around the heavy dagger and slide it from its sheath with a high whine. The wind shrieked across the sandy plains, demanding blood. She tried to push away the arm holding the dagger, to scream *no,* but the darkness uncoiled beneath her skin, overpowering. She thrashed inside the walls of her cage to no effect. If she'd had the ability to weep, she would have, but even that small mercy had been taken from her. Stolen from the one whose voice hissed a soft *yes* in her ear and slowly drove the blade against the tender skin of her belly.

Inside, Namali began to shake. *I will die by my own hand.* She could barely process this realization, so surreal it was, so implausible. The darkness imprisoned her mind. This black nothing-land was punishment for abandoning her father, and she felt the pieces of herself separating in a process that would eventually unmake who she was at the core. A large part of her recognized this was it. She would become like the man who had clawed out his eyes, the boy who had strangled himself: weak, easily controlled. But a smaller, more timid part of her hoped this was not the end. She could shed that skin if she wanted. She could begin to learn of her own strength.

Amidst the consuming darkness, a light flared, like an oil lamp ignited in those forgotten corners no one could see. The black cowered against the flickering red and gold. The fog clouding her vision lifted.

All around, people were begging, writhing on the ground like beetles, gnawing their fingers to bloody stumps. And as the moans punctured the air, the moon slipped past the sun at last, and the fissure in the earth snapped shut, closing the portal for another thousand years.

With the end of the eclipse, the air lost its unusual current, and the beast calmed and looked around, as if momentarily forgetting its purpose. Namali fashioned the rope into a pair of reins as quickly as possible with shaking hands, eyeing the daeva warily. Adrenaline was a fever in her blood. She had survived the first test, but only just. Thirty days to reach the Lost City. Survive, or perish.

She finished securing the reins when the demon came to attention, ears perked. Before she could cry out, they were bounding north at full speed.

The sun chased them across the land, the sky so vast she feared the blue might swallow her. She, a mere girl slipping through light and sound. Only now did she realize how small Benahr was, hardly more than a speck among all this sand. Curved over the back of the daeva, Namali sank into the feeling of wind and blistering heat. Ice beneath her legs, fire along her neck.

Running.

And running.

Forever.

She did not know how much time passed before her neck prickled in sudden awareness. Tightening her thighs around the demon, she glanced over her shoulder as steel flashed in the corner of her vision. Namali gasped and jerked to the side, but the man's sword descended, slicing into her upper arm. She screamed. Her demon veered close, snapped at his legs, and Namali could do nothing but cling to her mount and grit her teeth from the agony of fire licking down her arm, her robe in tatters from where the blade had sliced through. She didn't dare remove her hands from the reins. The demon, as much as she loathed its power, was her lifeline in this race.

The man raised his sword again, and for a single heartbeat, she glimpsed his face, the need carved into every line of skin, his pupils so large they swallowed the whites of his eyes in what she only assumed was the daeva's influence. Namali's demon swerved, the blade screaming past her ear. Digging in her heels, she urged the demon forward, fast, fast, fast. They were speed and wind and rushing water, racing through the desert as two dark blurs. Her heart fluttered, quick and furious. She fumbled for her dagger.

When he gripped her arm, Namali didn't hesitate. She plunged the blade into his shoulder.

The slap of the man's body against the packed sand chased her through the desert, the reins slick with blood. *Don't look back. Don't look back.* If the man wasn't dead, he was gravely injured. She'd never hurt anyone before, even out of self-defense, even during those rare times she wished she had the courage to do so.

It did not take long before the blood loss began to take effect. Sweat slithered down her face, coating her burning lips in salt. Her skin practically throbbed with heat, and her mouth was a dry cave with not a drop of moisture for relief. Hunched over her mount, Namali tried focusing on the dunes ahead, unsure of what direction she headed, her disorientation quickly descending into unconsciousness. The thought of turning around and seeking a healer slipped from her grasp. She could not hold it. Once it drained through the cracks, she forgot she had ever considered the idea.

Her body remembered though. Her heart and lungs recognized it had begun to fail, and so her left hand clutched the rope fiercely, her useless right arm dangling like a slab of meat. Whispers pulsed in her ears, a thousand buzzing flies crawling into the canals and burrowing into her brain. Namali gasped as paralyzing cold speared through her limbs. A wounded girl one hair away from slipping into oblivion? It was almost too easy.

The dagger sat heavily at her waist. Her teeth were chattering and her hands were shaking. The whispers grew more insistent. *Take it,* they said, crowding her mind with bloody thoughts: screams and dead, gaping eyes; mouths full of broken teeth; dismembered limbs; the shudder of her weak, fearful heart. She thought *yes* and *no* and *please,* but were these her thoughts? Or were they someone else's? Why did she suddenly think such horrific things?

By the time the sun began to sink in the west, chills wracked her feverish body. She squinted in the distance, where the sunset bled onto the land. The desert played tricks on the eyes, luring people into its burning center to feed its insatiable hunger. At one point Namali thought she heard a voice behind her, male and far away, but soon a warm haziness cocooned her, and she couldn't be sure she had imagined it. To lie down, if only for a minute. To close her tired eyes and forget. This, too, was a danger. She must heed her baba's warnings—*Never stop unless you are under cover.* She must not stop.

But then darkness wrapped her in its comforting arms, pulling her under, and she had no strength left to resist.

CHAPTER 7

NAMALI'S SENSES AWAKENED first.

The sand, mildly warm beneath her. The air, cool and dry. The hiss and spit of a fire a few feet away. Familiar sensations, but not as she knew them, for the air smelled of danger, and the fire indicated someone else was nearby, someone she did not know.

Wincing, she rolled onto her side and pressed her cheek against the soft sand. Her shoulders ached and her back throbbed, and a headache drilled into the back of her skull, but here was the dark that soothed her tired eyes, as she was no longer subject to the bright, fevered boil of the sun. A small mercy. The memory of yesterday had been reduced to fragments splattered in the bones and sinew of slaughter. Namali loosed a shaky breath. It was past, it was done, but it was not gone. The residue of such an ordeal was one she might never be completely rid of. Experiences like the day of black sun did not just *happen*. They changed you.

"Glad to see you're awake."

Namali stiffened. The voice was deep, friendly. *And male.* Her hand flew to her veil. Thank Mahurzda it still covered her face, but what should she do? Should she run? Whoever awaited her knew she was no longer asleep.

Cautiously, she sat up and faced the boy sitting cross-legged on the opposite side of the fire. And by boy she meant young man. The same young man who had spoken to her before the race.

Her hand strayed to the dagger hidden in her robe.

"I'm not going to hurt you," he said, and shifted his focus from her hand to her face, "although I don't blame you for being wary."

Her fingers twitched against the hilt. It did not seem as if this was a trap. Indeed, his expression was sincere, his body relaxed, no weapons visible, though that did not mean much. But if he were a foe, would he not have left her to die?

After a moment, she abandoned the dagger, instead bringing her knees to her chest and wrapping her arms around them. Fire danced in the young man's eyes, the flames warming them to the color of steeped tea leaves.

"How is your arm?" he asked in concern.

Only now did Namali notice her wound to be dressed in a strip of faded black cloth. His threadbare robe revealed a piece torn off from the bottom hem.

"I stitched it up to the best of my ability. I'm sorry I couldn't do more."

She felt strangely light. No one had ever helped her in such a way before, and from a stranger no less. "Better." Then she added, "Many thanks." It seemed like the right thing to say to someone who had saved her life and probably risked his own to do so.

The answer pleased him, as he dipped his chin in a friendly manner. "Are you hungry?"

Namali nodded stiffly, and the boy passed her two apricots,

her favorite of all the fruits. Maneuvering the fruit beneath the hanging fabric of her veil, she bit into the bruised flesh, the sweetness causing her teeth to ache.

The boy took a bite of his own apricot, his grip loose. "Do you remember what happened?" The question was gentle.

When she recalled the chaos of that day, it was swallowed up by a man's black, black eyes. "A competitor attacked me," she rasped. Her throat burned.

"You collapsed from blood loss. You also suffered from heat exhaustion. Here." He offered her a waterskin made of soft oiled hide, similar to the one that had been stolen from her. "You should drink."

So used to following orders, Namali obeyed. But then the water brought her back to life, and she closed her eyes and gulped the liquid down until her belly ached from fullness.

When she opened them, the boy was watching her, still smiling. She didn't understand how he could so easily find something good in this situation. Nothing about it was ideal. It was every possible death wish tossed into a poisonous concoction she had voluntarily ingested. She had already welcomed death in and was miraculously still alive, but what other obstacles would she meet on this journey, and would they see to her demise, or would she outlast them all?

Her gaze fell to his feet, which were donned in ratty camel hide sandals. His right foot was pointed inward, the ankle bone warped and jutting under his skin. She recalled the start of the race, the men strong and quick on their feet, tireless. The odds of him winning with his disability were slim.

At the thought, Namali ducked her head in shame. She was in

no position to judge. She was a girl among men. Fool's hope had brought her here.

He tucked his foot behind the other, then tossed a few twigs into the fire. He didn't meet her eye. "Drink more. You're dehydrated."

Namali took another generous gulp, then two more, before looking around. A jagged outcrop protected their backs from the wind that grew cold with the rising of the moons. Stunted trees gasped for life between the cliffs, their limbs gnarled and bare. Supposedly, the land had once been lush and green. Or so she'd heard.

"I'm Sameen," said the boy.

She peeked at him from beneath her eyelashes. He wasn't handsome by any means. His nose was too large for his face, and his eyes too close together, but when he smiled it didn't matter. His mouth was made for smiling.

Clearing her throat at the direction her thoughts had taken, she returned the container. "Namali." It emerged as a whisper, as if the merchant might somehow overhear her speaking even though he was over five hundred miles away.

"Namali," he repeated, rolling the name around on his tongue. He said it softly, without the curtness used by her father. "It's a nice name."

Namali froze as a low growl reached her ears, the sound taking her back to a shadowy land and black rivers of blood. In the corner of her eye, something moved. She began to shake, not knowing how it was possible to burn from cold. The nightmare was real.

"It can't hurt you," Sameen said. "It's tied up."

She wasn't so sure. The daeva jerked against the rope binding it to a nearby tree, its tail flicking in agitation. In comparison to the demon's bulk, the rope appeared to be nothing more than a piece of thread. And there was only one daeva she could see.

"What happened to my demon?"

He studied her for a moment before casting off his yirasaf and running his fingers through his shaggy hair. "I don't know." Firelight threw the planes of his face into sharp relief. "I found you lying on the ground. I didn't see your demon anywhere."

Namali released a soundless breath. How was she to race without a demon? How was she to find the Lost City? She didn't even have a map. "Do you know where we are?"

"Let's see." He glanced around. "We seem to be sitting in the middle of the desert." His teeth flashed, a line of shocking white in the dark. When Namali did not smile in return, it disappeared. "But in all seriousness, no, I don't. Daevas are instinctively drawn to the Lost City, so I was going to keep traveling in the direction it wanted to go and pick up more supplies when I came across a town."

His lack of concern, well, concerned her. She had already lost half a day. She could not afford to lose more time. She needed to cover a lot of ground, and with much haste.

Namali stood and brushed sand from her robe while Sameen tilted his head in question. "Many thanks for the water and . . . everything else." As first impressions went, she wasn't particularly proud of her behavior, but there were more important matters to address. Like how to locate a single demon in a million square miles of sand. Forcing her feet to move, she walked away from the safety of the fire and into the darkened landscape.

"Namali!"

She walked faster, shoulders hunched. She would melt into the dark and disappear. She would become the night.

Sand shifted and sighed as Sameen limped up beside her. "Where are you going?" His right foot sunk sideways in the soft earth, but he was half a foot taller than her and matched her pace easily.

"To find my daeva." And food. And water. The presence of rocks and foliage indicated habitat for wildlife, the possibility of a watering hole.

Minutes passed. They walked in silence. Down one dune, up another, again and again. Either Sameen didn't notice he was leaving his daeva behind, or he didn't care. She tried not to stare at his foot. He walked with a strength that defied his limp, a strength painfully absent in herself. It wasn't that she didn't wish otherwise, didn't want to be strong, too. She just didn't know where to start. How did one go about such a change?

"Why don't I help you?" he asked, stumbling on a deep sandy patch.

That would be the second time he offered his help since the start of the race. It was two times too many, two times she felt like a burden. "I can find it myself."

"Another pair of eyes couldn't hurt."

Namali whirled to face him. "Why are you doing this? I don't even know you." Showing he cared, a stranger, made it that much more apparent how little her father cared. She wondered how he had reacted this morning upon reading her note.

His brows lifted at her harsh tone, but he didn't step away. "Of course you know me. I'm Sameen, and you're Namali. We met ten minutes ago."

The absence of his smile almost made her regret lashing out. Almost. She wrapped her arms around her middle. "I'm competition. Helping me means hurting your chances of winning."

"Isn't helping others the right thing to do?"

He was right, but . . . *why was he helping* her? There must be some other reason aside from the satisfaction of performing a good deed.

When she didn't respond, Sameen smiled, bashful and childlike. "Two people traveling together will be safer than one. I can help you search for food and water, teach you how to build a shelter."

If they hadn't already stopped walking, she would have at that moment. Instead, she brushed past him, quickening her pace. It wasn't Sameen's fault he had found her wounded and half-dead, so he probably assumed she knew little of surviving in the Saraj. An honest mistake. Still, that he assumed so little of her stung.

"Did I say something to offend you?" he asked in confusion once he caught up to her.

Yes, she wanted to say. Couldn't say.

"Namali—"

"Yes, if you must know." Her voice was quiet and clear. She didn't look at him. "I'm perfectly capable of taking care of myself." In case he misunderstood, she added, "Finding my own food and water, building my own shelter, mending my clothes, tending my wounds, counting to five . . ."

Namali felt rather than saw the moment Sameen realized his mistake. "I wasn't trying to criticize you. I just thought we could travel together for a time, and when you find your demon we'll part ways."

Her steps grew slower and slower, and she eventually stopped walking entirely. It wasn't right to accompany this man alone. He wasn't family, and he wasn't her betrothed. But he knew the Saraj, knew the dangers it held.

No one was around to see her with this man. This Sameen.

Namali swallowed and lifted her chin. "All right, but only until we find my daeva. And I'll walk."

"Sameen," he said gently. "My name is Sameen."

The knot of tension in her chest loosened, just slightly. "All right . . . Sameen."

●●●

They traveled north, Sameen riding his demon beside her. The Great Northern Constellation—flecks of stars outlining the shape of two wolves, leaders of the Great Pack—guided them through a night so thick Namali felt it pool in the well of her cupped palms. There had been a time, thousands of years before, when Mahurzda would have called the pack down from the heavens to banish the daevas and their evil, but with their disappearance, nothing could stop the chaos that reigned for these thirty days. There were those, however, who prayed and held hope in their hearts. Who still believed in a brighter existence.

The air was sharp with cold, the wind full of whispers. Every few minutes, Namali found her attention drawn to the daeva's shadowy form. It moved with unnatural grace, slinking through the sand, ears constantly twitching in various directions. She did not envy Sameen's position atop its back, for it reminded her of what she would rather forget: that glimpse into the blackness of her heart. She did not know if touching the demon injected darkness into her, or if it simply peeled back a curtain she had formerly been blind to. Her hands shook with the memory of attempting to impale herself on her own weapon.

It was a strange thing to be wandering the desert in such unusual company. She and Sameen did not speak, but the silence was neither uncomfortable nor awkward. It was easy to share space without the pressure or expectation of conversation. She wouldn't know what to say, really.

"I was born this way," he said, breaking the silence.

She stiffened, drawing her attention away from where she had been scanning their surroundings for movement, a flash of metal, a tortured cry. "What?"

He continued looking ahead. "My foot. You keep staring at it, so I assumed you were curious. I was born like this. The healers were not able to fix it because my family couldn't afford payment."

"Sorry." Her voice softened. "For staring, I mean."

"It's fine. I'm used to it by now." But the bitterness chipping at his words indicated otherwise.

Namali understood, to an extent. They were traveling down the same river but in different vessels. She had the luxury of a veil to cover the birthmark on her face. Only family ever saw it removed.

"Still, it was rude. I'm sorry."

"You said that already."

Her mouth opened, then snapped shut.

She stayed quiet.

"Did you ever end up making the trade?" he wondered after some time had passed.

Trade . . . ?

Khorshan.

"Yes," she said. "And I feel awful for betraying my friend."

"Friend?"

His tone reminded her so much of Baba that she shut down. "Never mind."

The demon hopped to the side in agitation, forcing Sameen to tighten his hold. The beast settled but continued walking, ears perked. Sameen then said, "Was he truly your friend?"

Namali rubbed her hands along her upper arms for warmth, taking care to avoid the bandage. "He was—is." For she would see to his return. "I don't have many friends where I'm from, sadly."

His attention returned to her profile. "No," he said slowly, as if having finally processed her earlier reaction. "I suppose I don't either."

"Is that by choice?"

"Circumstantial." The word sagged with exhaustion. "I've been busy the last six months. Too busy to keep in touch with friends."

"Busy with what?"

He shook his head. "Nothing of interest."

Namali placed her feet carefully as they topped the dune's round shoulder and slid down its broad back into the deep valley between. What Sameen meant was, it was none of her business and not her secret to keep.

"I have to ask." His glance was too fleeting to catch. "After you first caught your daeva, did you . . ." He chuckled self-consciously and sat up straighter. "Um . . . *feel* any different?"

Namali couldn't look at him. Otherwise he'd see her reliving the memory of darkness crawling over her, inside of her, and he'd know she was weak. "I d-did—" She shuddered and tried again, aware of how close the demon walked beside her. "I felt . . . not like myself."

His throat bobbed. "How? In what way?"

Should she tell him of the turmoil? The voice of rot and decay, how its stink clung to her heels?

Neck prickling, Namali glanced back as they topped the dune, the set of footprints, two abreast, marking their trail. It would be easy for a competitor to track them, to slip up behind, silent and unseen, and bury a dagger in her back. Dead before she had a chance to scream.

They began a slow descent. "I would rather not say." Her voice grated from the dryness of her mouth.

"Did you imagine yourself killing those you loved?"

She stopped, and the silence inside her widened until it swallowed the sound of her beating heart. "What do you mean?"

His shoulders lifted with breath. She suddenly wished she had never asked this of him.

Voice low and raw, he began, "When I first touched the daeva, I saw my home. My family was sleeping. My three brothers, my mother. I . . . I was standing in the doorway watching them sleep, and I was h-holding—" He cleared his throat. "A knife. I was holding a knife."

Namali stared at Sameen, speechless. "Did you . . . ?"

"No." He hesitated. The love for his family was plain, and the pain at the thought of losing them. "I managed to break free of the vision, but I knew—" Another deep breath. "I knew I would have gone for my youngest brother first: Mirza."

The atrocity bubbled in her gut. How awful. Would she soon suffer from similar thoughts, to wish those she loved dead?

"Mirza warned me about the daevas and the Lost City." His lips pressed together. "He's interested in old myths. He's only eight, but he's smart."

"Did he mention a way to stop the thoughts from intruding?"

"No." His next words chilled her to the core. "I only hope I'm the same person going out of the race as I am coming in."

"Me, too," Namali murmured, but secretly she hoped she would emerge as someone more.

They reverted to silence again, gradually making their way up and down the heaving back of the Saraj. The air was dead. The land was empty. It meant nothing. The sense of being watched followed them, but Namali was too shy to mention it for fear of experiencing this paranoia alone.

Which was why, when Sameen pulled his mount to a halt after perhaps the thousandth dune they had traversed and suggested they stop for a break, Namali kept quiet, watching with large eyes as he dismounted. A slight wind stirred, like a huff of breath against the back of her neck.

He dropped his pack on the ground. "I'm going to . . ." He pointed vaguely behind him.

Namali jerked a nod, avoiding his gaze. How awkward!

He started to leave, then pivoted back around and lifted the demon's reins. "You wouldn't by any chance want to watch it while I'm gone, would you?"

If she never had to touch one again, it would be too soon. "No."

His mouth twitched. "Just thought I'd ask." And he soon melted into the night.

Plopping down on the still-warm sand, Namali sipped from the waterskin. Above, stars cloaked the sky, hard and cold and bright. The clouds from earlier had mostly dissipated, both moons, each displaying one half of a separate whole, offering silvery light. Knowing Sameen was nearby steadied her, another breathing, beating heart. She was glad she had agreed to his offer to travel together, because he was right. Two pairs of eyes *were* better than one.

She began to take another drink before lowering the skin. They would need to conserve as much water as possible in the coming days, for the towns were lost among all this sand. There was a smaller city located directly west of Ahkbur, but they were heading north and most likely nowhere near the vicinity. Without the ruthless sun stinging her back, there was time to think and plan. Come sunrise, time would become as all things were, strangled in the bands of fire: an illusion.

She didn't know what changed. Possibly the night-sounds. Possibly the air. It came down to a feeling, a heightened awareness of another's presence. A subtle shift in the world.

Slowly, so slowly she didn't think she moved at all, Namali twisted her head around, gazing into the moons' pearly shine. A shift against the backdrop drew her eye. There, a dark figure stirred.

What to do, what to do? She sat, paralyzed and lightheaded with fear. Sameen had not returned. From this distance, she could not distinguish the figure's shape, but on the small chance it had not spotted her, aglow in the patch of moonlight, she did not want to draw attention to herself. Animal, demon, man? She didn't know. She just didn't know.

The figure shuffled closer, hunched, curled into itself, either old or wounded or something else entirely. Adrenaline flared in her limbs. She fumbled for her dagger with trembling hands, praying she wouldn't drop it. The thing moved with purpose now. If she must defend herself, then she would as she had done before, sinking her blade into the man's shoulder. She had not meant to kill him.

She sucked in a breath to scream.

The figure emerged into a strip of moonlight spearing through the clouds, and Namali tensed. Not an animal, but it may as well have been one. The hunched old man was certainly hairy enough. A scraggly gray beard covered half of his face and fell to his scrawny, wrinkled chest, a strip of white cloth wrapped haphazardly around his head. Simple brown trousers flowed around his legs. He wore no shoes.

His grin revealed diseased gums, teeth worn to nubs. "People!" His voice was ancient. It was wind-weathered rock and roots buried deep.

She gripped the dagger tighter. An old man in the middle of the Saraj with no camel, no daeva?

"Don't come any closer," Namali warned as he took a step toward her. She gripped the hilt in both hands, the blade pointed outward like a spear. Sameen had been gone too long.

The man observed her awkward grip, the obvious inexperience of holding a weapon. "There's no need for that, now."

"I mean it." She willed her heart to slow and stood her ground. It felt as if she were wearing someone else's clothes, and they did not quite fit right, but they were not completely uncomfortable either. This was her hand wielding a weapon, her voice, shaky as it was, demanding, "What did you do to Sameen?"

His gaze sharpened.

"I said, what did you do to Sameen?" Harsher.

The man considered her question, one hand wrapped around his beard. "I did nothing to your friend. It was he who decided to wander off alone, not I."

These words were more than their surface. She was convinced of this. Except Namali was not sure of their deeper meaning.

She called out, "Sameen!"

"This encounter does not have to be one of fear," said the man. "We are two travelers passing through. You must trust in yourself. The Demon Race is a time of confusion and uncertainty, but a stranger is not the same as a foe."

She didn't know who to trust—this old man, who carried neither water nor provisions traversing these brutal plains, who spoke nonsense and riddles, or herself. She should trust herself. She could rely on no one else. But the truth was unfamiliar in this ancient, ravenous land. She could not fully grasp it.

"Namali!"

Relief poured through her, loosening the tension in a sudden flood. So he had been telling the truth, strange as he was. "I'm here!" she called, voice surprisingly steady. She spotted him topping the rise, unharmed, and looked back at the old man, saying, "I apologize—"

She stopped. Her head whipped left and right.
The man was gone.

CHAPTER 8

AT HIS APPROACH, Sameen slowed, the demon trailing him. His focus narrowed on her hands, body braced in sudden caution. "What's that for?"

Namali followed his gaze. She still clutched the knife. Her joints creaked as she unpeeled her fingers from the metal and slid it back into its sheath. "There was a man here. Five seconds ago." The words felt flimsy in her mouth.

He glanced around the bare, moonlit landscape. "Where?"

Namali took in his bewildered expression, the fact that she pointed to a patch of empty sand, and deflated. "I swear on Mahurzda there was a man here," she said, looking to him for support, a shred of belief.

"Was he a traveler?"

"No. At least, I don't think so. He didn't carry supplies. He was . . . he was . . ." Her eyebrows snapped together.

Sameen watched her expectantly. "He was . . . ?"

But the thought eluded her. The memory eluded her. There was nothing to grab hold of save the knowledge that he had been a man, nothing less and nothing more, and old. She could not even recall what he had been wearing. Why had the man stirred in her such unease? And why could she no longer remember?

Namali placed two fingers to her temple and shook her head. This place had already begun to creep beneath her skin. "Let's keep moving."

Thankfully, Sameen didn't press for more information. He grabbed his pack, swung it over his shoulder, and mounted the daeva with an effortlessness that should not have come to someone making contact with such a corrupt creature. He may as well have mounted a camel or a horse, for there was no sign of struggle. Namali decided not to mention it. She was no expert on the matter.

They traveled beneath the carpet of stars extending from sky to sky, slowly, surely, as humans had each night since the dawning of the world. The constellations were like glowing oil lamps floating by the billions: Three Brothers—a trio of stars forming a triangle; Khalid, the great warrior; his steed, the Great Horse. Under the cloak of night, it was easy to forget they traversed a desolate wasteland. Easy to believe themselves safe.

"Do you know the story of Khalid?" Sameen asked a few hours before dawn.

She did, but Sameen's voice, smooth and deep and calm, was its own music. She wanted it to last. "Remind me."

So he wove her the tale of Khalid, a man standing sixty feet tall, who fought the Demon King's dragon of darkness and chained it beneath a mountain for all eternity. And afterward, Namali told him the tale of the tortoise who had no name, the goat and his boy, the girl who stole the sun, and as each story sent Sameen's laughter rolling across the hills, his head thrown back, teeth flashing white in the dark, the door inside her creaked slowly open.

As the sun began to rise, transforming the landscape into a rich golden field, Sameen offered her the waterskin.

Namali washed the dust from her mouth and returned it to him, scanning the horizon. They would soon need to seek shelter. She'd spotted a cluster of boulders about half a mile back that would provide adequate protection, and began to inform him of her suggestion when a shadow shifted in the corner of her vision. Her attention snapped to the front.

There were no ghosts in the Saraj, only the fear of them.

Namali continued the long trudge forward even though the urge to turn and look was unbearable. She held herself stiffly. "Sameen, I think—"

"Wait." Calmly, he dismounted the daeva and moved to her side, pulling the beast behind him. "Don't turn around. Keep walking straight ahead."

So he knew. She did as he said, one foot in front of the other, aware, always aware. Everything was fine. She could do this. She could pretend.

"When I say so," Sameen murmured, "I want you to drop onto the ground."

"Where is he?"

"It doesn't matter. Just do as I say."

Her ears strained. The sand shushed around their feet like a mother comforting a crying babe, but the Saraj was no mother she wanted. There was another sound, two. Labored footsteps, labored gasps. "I can hear him," she whispered.

"Me, too." His chest rose and fell in one deep breath, and the demon, as if sensing the growing tension, tugged at its bindings. "He's coming up on your left. No, don't look."

All right, she wouldn't look. But she needed at least the illusion of safety. And so, without thinking, her hand strayed to her dagger.

"Namali!"

She fell to the ground. No, a hand *pushed* her. Light flared, a ray of sun catching the shining metal of a sword blade. The thin, blue steel had been forged in the mines of Lomoria, though the man was certainly Malahadi beneath the monstrous bruise coloring his face, his skin dotted with scratches and half-healed scabs, his wheezing pants whistling through purple swollen lips.

The man hacked at Sameen's side, putting his entire weight behind the blow. Sameen stumbled back but recovered quicker than she expected, grasping a chipped knife he must have been hiding on his person as his arms lifted for the block. The *shing* of metal on metal sent a wave of raised bumps rippling across her flesh. She scrambled to her feet out of range of the danger to watch in awe while Sameen slipped under and around the blade like water, like wind. He darted in and out, his movements smooth and practiced in a way only hours of repetition could achieve. The man grunted, stabbing the weapon like a spear, but Sameen knocked the sword aside, a shower of sparks raining down.

They circled one another, dancing in and out of reach, testing the other's strength and stamina and control. They sprang apart for one heaving breath before Sameen threw himself back into the fight. He struck left, right, his face immobile, agleam with sweat from the sun that had now pulled free from the earth. A dusky flower bloomed on the man's chest, and then another. The sand sucked at the drops of red.

Namali jolted in surprise as the daeva began to thrash from the commotion, clamping onto the rope with its shadowy maw and shaking it furiously. A growl rumbled, coming from that deep place where thunder churned. Its roar burst free, building in the stillness until the silence cracked beneath its weight. Sameen cried out as the demon jerked him to the side, almost into the sword's path.

He shot her a frantic look and thrust the rope in her direction. "Take it!" The man's weapon skimmed his side, missing by inches.

She stared at the demon, paralyzed by the pull she felt, to reach out and stroke a palm along its rounded spine. Its teeth were glistening black knives.

"I can't," she said, shaking her head. "I can't." The last time she'd touched one, she had become blind. Her mind had turned against her. She never wanted to experience that nightmare again.

Sameen muttered a curse. He lurched away from another blow and attempted to right himself before the sword impaled him. "Yes, you can, you can do it, just take it." The words were wrenched from a place of utter desperation.

The fight grew downright vicious. Though evenly matched in height, the older man had more muscle, his shoulders thick and solid as a bull's. He used that strength to his advantage, bearing down his Lomorian steel against the pitiful knife. The daeva worked itself into a frenzy, gnashing its teeth and compromising Sameen's tenuous balance. His arm, trembling from the strain, looked like it might snap.

Sameen bared his teeth and held on. "Namali, please!"

She watched the exchange with wide eyes. The older man pushed down harder, forcing Sameen to bend backward. Pain tightened his features as his bent foot twisted at a deeper angle. Slipping.

Namali's mind was a tangle of uncertainty, words unearthed from her past whose only purpose was to solidify her powerlessness, and yet the truth was a tangible thing, unfolding before her eyes. If she did nothing, if Sameen fell, he would die.

And then the man would come for her.

She grabbed the reins, freeing Sameen's hand. He dropped and rolled and rose again, slashing and stabbing until the man's knees buckled and he fell, blood pooling beneath him. Dead.

Sameen's back heaved, arms dangling limply at his sides. Namali dug her feet into the sand to prevent the daeva from yanking her off balance, a slight tingle gathering in her fingertips. After a moment, the daeva quieted and curled up on the ground, and Namali used the opportunity to stake its rope into the earth, trying to think of possible apologies for Sameen. They were inadequate. Useless. Looking back on all the times she had remained passive, she cringed. Yet another reminder of the cage she had unintentionally built for herself.

Finally, he turned. He didn't look at her as he used his robe to wipe the blood from his blade and sheathed it. He knelt in the sand, opened his pack, and began building a shelter with sticks, which he shoved into the ground in a square shape. Once he arranged a sheet over them, he stood and approached.

"Do you have your dagger?" he asked.

She swallowed. "Yes."

"Can I have it?"

Namali stepped back, throat noose-tight. He wouldn't do what she thought he might . . . but why not? She had hesitated, had risked both their lives out of fear. So why not take her dagger and punish her, end her?

He sighed and rubbed his palms over his face. "I'm not going to hurt you. I only wanted to show you how to use it, since I'm assuming you don't know how." He looked at her more gently, and the warmth in his gaze melted the ice running through her veins. They were like small suns, his eyes. "Am I right?"

The silence tugged, stretching and fraying into nothingness. She released a shaky, shallow breath.

Namali passed him the weapon, feeling lighter to be rid of its weight.

He said, "Think of the blade as an extension of your arm," and wrapped his fingers around the hilt, thumb covering the index finger. "Your blade should always be pointed out, away from your body. Notice how I hold it in a way that makes it easy to see where it is at all times?" He handed her the dagger. "Now you try."

She gripped the hilt where he had moments before, the metal warm from his fingers. He shifted her hand's position, his skin rough and dry, like a pebble not quite smoothed. Worker's hands, like her own. No one had ever touched her so gently. No one had ever taken the time to teach her something as useful as defending herself, as if she would even be allowed that right. Her throat tightened further, though no longer in fear.

"Keep your wrist locked forward," he said. "Be careful about having your arm too far away from your body, as it makes you vulnerable. You can also place your thumb on the side of the blade if that's more comfortable for you, like this." He shifted her thumb so it lay flat against the metal. "How does that feel?"

Awkward, but necessary. At least the next time a situation arose, she would know enough not to accidentally stab herself. Maybe. "Better. Many thanks."

His attention slid to the dead man. "We should rest before it gets too hot." Then, despite the corpse lying ten feet away, he crawled into the shelter.

Namali fingered her veil, gnawing on her lip with enough force to draw blood. The shelter was hardly large enough to fit one person, much less two, and she knew nothing about Sameen except that he had a crooked foot and a beautiful mouth, or maybe even a crooked mouth and a beautiful foot.

But she couldn't stand around forever. In the Saraj, you either found shade, or you let the sun destroy you.

She wanted to live.

Namali crawled beneath the sheet, where it was at least ten degrees cooler than the surrounding air, and scooted as far away from Sameen as possible—all six inches of it. A bead of sweat slithered down her nose, clinging to the tip. "How are we going to find my daeva?" she asked, a breathy whisper.

His eyes met hers. Even when she shied away, he continued to watch her. "Hopefully we'll come across it on our way north, since it should be attracted to the Lost City, too."

That told her nothing she hadn't already known. With every passing hour, competitors closed the distance between the Lost City, save her. Twenty-nine days remained of the race. Considering the Saraj encompassed a million square miles, it was no time at all.

"Did your brother ever tell you the reason why daevas are attracted to the Lost City? If we knew that information, it might help us find mine." In the story of Delir, she could not recall the detail ever being mentioned. What purpose would these creatures have, to seek a city most claimed to be a myth?

"He didn't, unfortunately."

Namali shifted to cross her legs. "They say there's a great library east, deep in the mountains of Shun, that holds the great histories of the world." She paused. "It's a shame there's nothing like that in Malahad."

"It is a shame."

She was still mulling over the thought when her stomach growled.

"Hungry?" Sameen asked, digging through his fraying pack. He offered her a piece of latki: deep-fried sweet dough drizzled with honey.

She blinked, mouth softly parted. After nearly a day without food, it was a feast, and yet she said to the ground, "Many thanks, but no."

He rolled his eyes good-naturedly. "Take it." Before she could protest, he shoved the food into her hands.

Namali curled her fingers around the dough. The last thing she wanted was to burden him further. He was helping her find her daeva. He had fought that man to protect them. And now . . . now she was taking his food. She didn't deserve his kindness.

Sameen must have noticed her indecisiveness, because he said, "Please eat it. You need to keep up your strength."

In the end, her hunger won out. Lifting the bottom of her veil, she shoved the entire pastry into her mouth. Sweet, golden honey. Flakey, buttery crust. Delicious. "It's really good." Memories lingered in this taste, ones of laughter and standing beside her mother in the kitchen, flour coating their hands. "It tastes a bit different than what I'm used to."

His expression dimmed. "Well, when you can't afford all the ingredients, you have to make do with what you have."

Namali bowed her head. "I apologize. I didn't mean to insult you."

"It's not that." He rubbed the back of his neck and gestured to the latki. "My mother made this three days ago, but she didn't know I planned to enter the race. She wouldn't have wanted me to go. Would have said I needed to stay to care for our family, but what she doesn't understand is that this choice I made, this is me caring for our family." He formed a small pile of sand near his legs. "Do you know of Yanasir?"

Namali shook her head, fiddling with the bracelet around her wrist, the ruby throbbing dully. A reminder of the life awaiting her, should she fail.

His mouth slanted into his cheek. "I wouldn't think so. It's a poor town near Malahad's southern border. It's home, but this kind of opportunity . . . it doesn't exist in Yanasir."

The half-smile he sent her eased some of the tension from her body. She had already guessed from his clothes, patched and threadbare, that Sameen did not come from wealth, but she tried to overlook such things, because money defined no one.

Regardless of class though, the latki Sameen gave her was delicious. Even with missing ingredients, it tasted better than her mother's, because this latki had something to prove, whereas her mother's had not.

Lowly, Namali said, "What I meant to say earlier was . . . this is my favorite food in the world."

She glanced up to his surprise, the way the smooth expanse of his forehead folded into wrinkles. The slight tilt of his head. "Why?" he asked.

She shook her head. "It's silly."

"No, it's not. It's important to you."

And now she was the one caught unaware, for how could this boy, whom she had known for less than twenty-four hours, know something as deeply personal as this, something she kept safely hidden in her heart? It was this entirely helpless feeling, her words unfurling as if they were petals, and he the sun.

Namali said, "Because whenever I taste latki, it reminds me of what's good in the world. The care that goes into making such a meal"—her voice softened—"and the people you share it with."

Sameen looked at her as if he had never seen her before. He held out his share of the dessert. "Here."

Namali drew back, staring at his outstretched palm. The unexpected sweetness of the gesture dissolved like sugar upon her tongue. "But—" She looked up. "That's yours."

He held her gaze for two uncomfortably long seconds.

"You deserve it," he said, "for seeing beauty in the ordinary."

She fisted her hands in her lap. "I shouldn't."

"Consider it a gift." He placed it on her knee.

The small act of kindness caused a shift inside her. She felt . . . like an equal. She grabbed hold of the feeling for as long as she dared.

"Why did you help me," she asked, "back in Ahkbur?" It was still so strange he had stopped.

He thought for a moment before responding, as if searching

for an answer other than the truth. "A girl entering the Demon Race? I'll admit I was intrigued."

"And now?" she challenged, bolder than she had intended. A small thrill went through her. "Are you still intrigued?"

His smile unfolded slowly, and Namali caught her breath at the intimacy. "Most definitely."

She flushed and quickly changed the subject. "This is a decent shelter," she began, "but I have some suggestions to keep ourselves cooler."

His eyebrows shot upward. More surprise than disbelief. "You do?"

There was the slightest hesitation before she nodded.

"Then by all means, show me."

Namali began to break down their meager shelter while Sameen stood off to the side, observing. "When I was a little girl, my baba taught me the basics of survival in case I ever found myself alone." Twice a year they had ridden out to camp, search for food and water, and practice basic first-aid. "He made me build this shelter so many times I can do it with my eyes closed." She arranged the sticks by memory. "The structure you had before was adequate, but it didn't completely block out the sun, and if you use a square shape, it makes it harder to trap in the heat, which, as you know, is dangerous when night falls. A triangular shape is more effective."

Sameen crossed his arms. "Are you implying my shelter wasn't good enough?" he said in mock indignation.

She smiled, tucking the sheet down into the sand. Then she stepped back to admire her handiwork. "Yours was good." A touch devilish. "Mine is better."

Sameen made the most ridiculous, over-the-top scoff, which had

Namali giggling into her hands. She glanced over his shoulder, her laughter fading.

A sand cloud bloomed in the distance.

Namali lowered her hands to her sides. "Are those more competitors, do you think?"

Sameen came to stand beside her. "It's possible."

She looked at the dead man's splayed form. She had no desire to meet his fate. "What should we do?"

"Let's wait. They might not have seen us."

Namali had never been more aware of another person until this moment, with the heat from their bodies flaring out, mingling in the space between while the thick, dark curtain hurtled toward them. The hot air moved in waves, distorting the image of three riders on horses, but when a gust of wind shifted the sand, her attention snapped to the flash of color, a red stain against the gray-brown backdrop of whirling debris.

Her world narrowed to a pinpoint, until she knew only this: damp, sticky palms; dark spots scattering her vision; the breath that was never enough.

How did he find me?

"It's not competitors," she quavered. The memory of the merchant slipping the bracelet onto her wrist slithered through her. *Mine.*

"Who is it then?"

She avoided Sameen's eyes, which only had to look at her to know. "Someone who's looking for me." In her haste to prepare for the race, she had forgotten all about the merchant. Had thought him still in Benahr with Baba.

"Who?"

No time to explain. Maybe not even time to get away. "We have to leave."

His eyebrows snapped together. "Where would we go?"

"I don't know. Away. Come on." Tugging his sleeve, she pulled him from the shelter and toward his demon. Something was tightening in her chest, pushing out all her air, a bending branch ready to snap. Her hands shook with coiled energy. She could barely think beyond the knife of possibility. What would occur if he caught her, brought her home.

"Namali—"

"Please, Sameen."

He caught her gaze, the fear uncoiling behind her eyes. And understood.

"Break down the shelter," he said, eyeing the daeva.

Namali yanked the sticks from the sand and stuffed them, along with the sheet, into his pack. A glance over her shoulder showed the merchant shouting to the heavy-set man on his right.

Sameen swung himself onto the daeva's back and offered his hand when he suddenly went rigid, a muscle fluttering in his jaw. "Get—" He choked, tremors vibrating through his stiff form. "Get on."

She froze. That slithering, hungry voice was not of this world.

His hands clenched and unclenched, moving to his face, then down again, as if trying to decide whether or not to claw out his eyes. She remembered when he had told her of his murderous thoughts, and wondered if he thought of them now. Did looking like a monster make one a monster? Did one's thoughts?

Something compelled Namali to approach. "Sameen, it's me. Namali. Can you hear me?"

He looked at her, and his expression flickered in recognition. For a brief moment, she saw Sameen return to himself.

Then his hand latched onto her throat, fingers crushing her windpipe as the whites of his eyes succumbed to the blackest of inks, two wide pools absorbing all light. He lifted her up with impossible strength, dangling her three feet above the ground with one hand. Behind his gaze lay a void, and behind that void lay a future dark and bleak.

"Sameen," she rasped, clawing at his hand. She clawed and clawed and shredded open his skin, but it wouldn't budge and she couldn't breathe, couldn't *breathe*. His grip was iron. "This isn't you." The words burned with the force of squeezing through her windpipe. "It's the demon." White flooded her head, a burst of starlight in the ever-growing darkness. "Fight . . . back . . ."

His mouth stretched, and a growl rumbled in his chest, and his eyes transformed, light to dark to light again. The horror of Sameen fighting for control of his own body was almost worse than the carnage witnessed during the eclipse, because here was someone good, and the demon was trying its hardest to destroy it.

But then he released her and she was falling, breathing, *alive, alive, alive*. Namali hit the ground, gasping for air, clutching fistfuls of sand, legs twitching like an insect that would die here, shriveled in the heat.

Sameen's breath rattled out, brittle with the gravity of his actions. His face had cleared, but the guilt pooled in his eyes, taking root, lingering with quiet intensity. "Namali. Seven hells." His voice trembled.

She couldn't stop shaking. She was still on the ground, safe.

It's all right, she wanted to say. *It's not your fault,* she couldn't seem to say. His hands at her throat. His fierce, snarling expression. Gently, she touched the tender, bruised skin of her neck.

Sameen could have killed me.

She studied him warily, sprawled on the ground and looking up, the angle making him appear larger, broader. Her thoughts tumbled one over the other, running, running. He didn't appear to be under the daeva's control anymore, as his gaze no longer held that frightening emptiness. The sand plume, the merchant, hurtled ever closer. She reminded herself that Sameen was not the daeva. It was the demon's influence she could not trust. They were each fighting their own darkness.

She pushed to her feet. "I'm fine." Her legs wobbled, but that couldn't be helped. Grabbing the supplies, she passed them to Sameen. "Help me up."

"I don't know if I can trust myself. Your neck—" He swallowed and fell silent.

"I'm fine. Really." The bruises would heal. "We have to go."

Reluctantly, he nodded. His callused hand grasped her softer one, gently, and he pulled her up behind him so his broad back pressed against her furiously beating heart. Namali was so focused on escape she did not notice the stirring in her limbs until she was fully seated, the cold coming alive and roaring through her weak human body. A body she no longer controlled as she thrashed and clawed at her chest. A voice hissed in her ear, riddled with death, and her only response was to scream from the pain ripping apart her skin, the brokenness of her life, this crazed thirst for blood.

Feeling returned to her limbs, and Namali blinked away the disorientation. Sameen was shaking her shoulders, their faces inches apart. "Put your arms around me," he said.

Her hands fluttered near his waist. The merchant would see her touching another man.

"Namali, hold on to me." He wheeled the demon around.

It's just a waist. It doesn't mean anything. But the waist was one of those body parts, like the hand or mouth, that represented something incredibly . . . intimate.

Steeling herself, she wrapped her arms around him and pressed her forehead to his back. "Go!" she shouted.

The daeva lunged forward in a burst of speed, and they were flying, speeding, racing away in a cloud of dust, the demon's tail streaming behind like a swath of black fabric. The wind roared in Namali's ears. They cut through the air like an arrow as the demon's legs ate up miles and miles of sand. They were smoke and mist and other insubstantial things.

"How close are they?"

Namali squinted through the tears distorting her vision. Three men gave chase, but the merchant shone brighter than them all. The distance between them diminished. She could now see the whites of his eyes. "Too close. Try to lose them."

They ran harder, faster. The daeva soared over dune after dune after dune, a shadow among a sea of sand. The beast propelled them forward, all strength and power and control, and its muscles stretched and contracted, but it never faltered, never slowed.

"Do you still see them?" he cried.

Pressing closer to his back for stability, Namali glanced behind. She scanned the area once, then again to make sure. Heat waves shimmered in the distance, but the Saraj was otherwise empty. "I think we lost them."

"Are you sure?"

"I believe so—" But something slithered on the ground to her right. Without warning, a sandy tentacle ripped her from the demon before she had the chance to scream.

CHAPTER 9

NAMALI CLAWED AT the slippery ground as the tentacle dragged her through the burning sand. "Sameen!" she screamed.

Sameen vaulted from the daeva and ran toward her, his face pale. "Namali!"

Two sandy arms exploded from the dune and wrapped around his stomach, flung him up, hurled him across the sand, where his body flailed in the air like a bird with a broken wing. He slammed into the ground and was still.

Namali slumped in shock. *No, no, no, no.* Was he dead? He lay crumpled in the distance like a piece of trash, his yirasaf a pool of water that would soon evaporate. She screamed at him to get up, to rise even as she choked on a mouthful of grit and the tentacle dragged her farther away, but this was no mirage, no illusion. The world was cruel and unforgiving. One more person taken by the Saraj. One more light snuffed out.

A flurry of sand blasted her face. She scrabbled for purchase, tearing her fingernails to shreds, but couldn't gain any traction in the slippery earth, which doomed her to an ugly fate—wife—when all she really wanted to be was Namali.

The air cleared to reveal the merchant and his two men. The skinny one, whose face resembled that of a hawk with his long, beakish nose, moved his hands in an elaborate pattern before him. *Sand spinner.* The man manipulated the sand so it dragged her in front of them before disintegrating, halting her movement forward.

The merchant watched her with bright, fevered eyes. "You're hurt."

Teeth chattering, she followed his attention to the bandage covering her arm, now hanging in tatters, and forced her jaw still. Yes, she was hurt, but more importantly, she had survived. Against all odds, she had survived.

Namali pushed to her feet, locking her knees to remain upright. "What do you want? How did you find me?" Her voice was weak, and her heart afraid, and she hated it.

His mouth sagged at the corners in genuine confusion. "I was concerned. Your father's worried sick. He claimed you ran away, but I can't believe that. Did that boy steal you away? Force you into this situation?"

So Baba had noticed her absence, the emptiness in the house. It was a small comfort, and one she didn't entirely believe. "No. I left of my own freewill."

The merchant looked incredibly young as he asked, "Why?"

"I told you," she said, exhaustion roughening her tone, "back in Benahr." *I don't want to marry you.* "You didn't listen."

He did not look at his men, their curiosity plain. "Perhaps I was too hasty in the preparations. I can give you more time." His attention never leaving her, the merchant dismounted from his horse, stepped forward, and held out a hand. Offering something she had no desire to claim. "Your father wants you to come home." After a bit of awkward throat clearing, he added, "I want you to come home, too."

She had done it, had abandoned the known for the unknown, had proved everyone wrong, even herself, and now they wanted her to return to a life of mindlessness. As if her only purpose was to serve others.

The merchant reached for her arm, but she slipped from his grasp. "Don't touch me." Her blood hummed. All the times she'd repressed the *no's* even when she wanted to scream them to the world bubbled up, ready to burst free, and she . . . she was ready to welcome them.

So this was what it felt like to have a voice.

He blew out a sigh, the first sign of his mounting frustration. "I don't want to tell you again."

She didn't move.

"You'll listen to Hazil if you know what's good for you," the hawk-man snarled. He lunged for her.

"Stop!" the merchant cried as Namali unsheathed the dagger, having moved to intercept the strike. "Don't hurt her." He shoved the man back, a warning.

The hawk-man caught his balance before he fell, scowling. "Does she even know how to use one of those?"

Sweat trickled down her neck, dampening her palms until the hilt began to slip in her clumsy grip. She took another step back and gripped the weapon tighter. Her thumb moved to cover her index finger as she'd been taught, the blade pointed away from her body. She wouldn't be able to outrun them, especially the sand spinner.

The merchant dragged a hand over his face, across the lines that spoke of loss and grief. "Enough of this, Bijala." His voice cracked. "I've been patient enough with your silly games. Now come. Everyone is expecting our betrothal in a few days. You can return with me, and we'll pretend this never happened. It will be a fresh start."

The woman's name rang in the air. The merchant's eyes widened. What he had said and not said, and the quiet that spoke louder than them all. This time, it was *he* who dropped his gaze first, turned away as if he could not bear the bedraggled sight of her.

Who was Bijala?

"I—" He shifted back onto his heels. "Namali. I meant Namali. We mustn't waste any more time. Your father expects you home within the week."

"No." A shock of a word, foreign to her ears, delicious on her tongue.

The merchant pulled back in shock. Something dangerous lurked in his expression.

Namali didn't see him lunge, but suddenly his hand wrapped around her arm, bruising, and she screamed and slashed at his chest as a night-dark voice unlocked a slumbering, violent rage within her. The weight of his bracelet. The cloying scent of cloves. He cursed, stumbling back, and Namali gaped at the oozing wound on his chest, the red tears weeping down, drop by drop. She had intentionally harmed a Malahadi man.

The fat man caught her wrist and bent it backward until she cried out and released the dagger. She twisted around, tried yanking free. He was too heavy, too strong, his hand engulfing, the friction alighting against her skin. She managed to connect a well-aimed kick at the man's groin. Color drained from his face faster than she could blink, and he collapsed onto the dune, covering himself, cursing her family name in a wheezing voice.

The merchant clamped a hand on the hawk-man's shoulder to prevent his attack. "Don't." His eyes snapped like thunderclouds, unleashing years of suppressed agony, the kind that left you gutted with no hope for repair. The depth of that pain frightened her, for she had been there once, in a dark place, too.

Namali's chest tightened, near bursting. She was alone among a pack of wolves. They surrounded her, these men, the hostility in the air so thick she grew faint.

Admittedly, Namali was woefully unprepared for this lifestyle, this race. When she had first reflected on the traits needed to succeed, she thought of strength, agility, power, speed. It was true—pure physicality gave many men the advantage. She could not fight the merchant and win.

But as she stood there, patting her robe with increasing urgency for another weapon, and touched a piece of twine, a smooth patch of fabric, nearly forgotten, Namali decided she had been wrong. Her desire to shatter these bonds burned with such intensity she would blaze a trail brighter and more beautiful than those qualities she had believed to lack. Not power of force, but power of spirit. Not strength in arms, but strength in heart. And she would see this through.

Your greatest weapon or your greatest defense.

Namali pulled the seemingly empty bag from her waist. She didn't want to consider what would happen if there was nothing inside it. "Don't come any closer," she said. Her heart was brittle ice, but her voice was stone.

The merchant stilled. Blood flowed sluggishly from his wound. "This won't solve anything. You'll only make both our lives more difficult by putting off the inevitable."

What was inevitable? Her cage? Her unhappiness?

"You don't know what you're doing, Namali. Whatever is in that bag, put it away."

She very nearly laughed. People never missed an opportunity to underestimate her. That was the price of invisibility, and she didn't want to pay it anymore. "I know what I'm doing."

Removing the cord, she opened the pouch.

Typhoon-force winds erupted from the bag. Slammed into the three men and their horses with the force of a mud-brick wall. They soared into the air: fifty feet, one hundred feet, far away, miles away, until they were specks in the distant sky, and then until they were nothing at all.

Her watery knees buckled, sinking into sand that could be soft when not used as a weapon. Namali tried to slow her breathing, muscles still hot with adrenaline. Somehow, whether from Mahurzda's hand or dumb luck or both, she had escaped the merchant. With a bag she had believed to be empty, she might add.

Luck, most likely.

Wiping sweat from her brow, Namali lifted her head. And there he was, hobbling toward her, leading his daeva by the rope. The force of relief overwhelmed her, so much more intense than expected.

He was *here*.

Sameen slowed upon reaching her, his expression mirroring her own, a mixture of wonder and shy affection. "I saw what happened. Are you hurt?" Sand clung to his robe, and sweat plastered his dark hair to his neck beneath the yirasaf, but otherwise he appeared miraculously unharmed. He offered her a hand.

After a brief hesitation, she allowed him to pull her to her feet. "I'm fine. Are you?"

"My ribs are bruised, I think, but I'm not dead, so that's good." At her raised eyebrows, his lips twitched.

As if it was the most natural thing in the world, her mouth curved in response. No, he was very much alive. "That *is* good."

He began brushing sand off her arms, oblivious to her heated cheeks, the sudden stillness of her body. "Were those Trade Winds? I didn't get a good look. Everything happened so fast with that sand spinner. Are you sure you're not hurt?"

"I—" She swallowed when he moved to her shoulders, his hands firm and sure. The touch burned. "I said I'm fine, see?" She stepped aside to finish the job herself.

Sameen dropped his hands, his face as red as her own. "Sorry," he mumbled.

She pretended she hadn't heard him. "I didn't know they were Trade Winds. The vendor who traded them wouldn't tell me." It was an unexpected miracle, really, that she'd carried an object so valuable. The Malahadi had used Trade Winds since the beginning of civilization, scaling the rock formations along the northern border where they blew the strongest to capture their force. Their people exported the bags to the Shunese, who used them to power their navy and cargo ships to the east.

Sameen looked in the direction the three men had disappeared to, deep in thought. Another minute passed before he said, "I know it's none of my business, but . . . who were those men?"

Bending down, Namali picked up her dagger and slid it back

into its sheath, buying herself time to think. The merchant was wealthy, handsome, successful, and yet the thought of revealing their betrothal twisted her stomach into a snarl of knots. She did not want Sameen's perception of her to change. She no longer had a desire to live in someone else's shadow.

When she spoke, her voice was quiet. She wondered, then, why it seemed so loud. "His name is Hazil Abdu."

Sameen's eyes narrowed.

"Do you know him?" she asked.

"I've heard of him."

"Anything good?"

"Just that he's extremely wealthy. He's done business in Yanasir once or twice, if I recall."

"Yes, well—" She exhaled. "I'm betrothed to him."

Sameen frowned, but his mouth could not hold the shape, and soon it softened back into one of his half-smiles. "Which one was he, the fat one, the one with a bird's beak for a nose, or the normal-looking one?"

Her lips twitched. Even in times of high stress, he could put her at such ease. "The normal-looking one, unfortunately."

"You're to marry this man and you tried to stab him?"

"I never said I wanted to marry him," Namali snapped. A second later, her gaze dropped, and she was back in Benahr, waiting for her father's clipped, unfeeling voice. Too much sun, too much mind-numbing terror.

Sameen tilted his head. She thought she detected pity in his expression, but it could have been her imagination. "Why is he looking for you?"

Because she wasn't a person to him. She was an object to be

ordered about. And by openly defying the merchant, she mocked him. Rich men valued their pride nearly as much as their gold. "I ran away," she said. How angry Baba must be, how humiliated.

"I see." A breeze beat the dry desert heat against them, and their robes whipped around their legs. "Is that why you entered the race, because of him?"

"Yes." Then she cleared her throat and said, louder and with more force, "Yes." She would have to work on her decisiveness. "I wanted a chance to live my life for me, not based on someone else's decisions. If I win this race, I'm going to wish myself free of the marriage."

His smile wilted. She wouldn't have noticed unless she was watching him closely, which she was. "Oh." The word plummeted between them. "That makes sense."

She could see it quite clearly now. To be allies in this race was impossible. They were competing for the same prize. A piece of her ached to think of crushing something so honest and pure, but she could not risk winning for the sake of this tentative friendship. Before the race ended, she intended to reach the Lost City first, to claim what she had worked so hard to achieve. To win.

After all, there could be only one.

CHAPTER 10

DAYS PASSED. THE sky was a vast ocean above the red-gold sand. The air shimmered beneath the oppressive heat, swirling and dancing in front of their eyes. And as the sun rose and set each day, the Saraj lured them farther and farther into its fiery heart, where the chance of returning grew ever distant.

Namali and Sameen settled into a routine. They traveled between sunset and a few hours past sunrise, catching small reptiles for food and using Namali's knowledge of the terrain to locate fresh water sources. When the heat drained their energy, they sought shelter, rested, and talked until the stars emerged. Sameen taught her more of knife-fighting, the various stances and grips. Namali told him stories from the books she had read and wove a bracelet of black thread from her fraying robe. It went back and forth, this giving and taking, listening and learning. They never discussed anything more than surface topics, never spoke of family, never asked personal questions. Namali didn't ask Sameen why he had entered the race, or what he would use the wish for, or why, when he thought she wasn't looking, he watched her with a smile softening his night-dark eyes.

But that didn't stop her from wondering.

They scanned the horizon constantly. Sometimes they spotted a competitor in the distance, a black silhouette moving quickly north. Other times they wouldn't see life for days, and during those waking hours Namali was convinced they were the last people alive in the great sea of sand, doomed to wander until their hearts gave out. They passed wounded men and piles of bones. Pools of black blood and vultures circling overhead. They passed all these things, and each gruesome death reinforced the danger, the knowledge that they could be next, another body butchered and forgotten.

CHAPTER 11

IT WAS HIGH noon. Gritty heat billowed against them in waves, drying out their eyes, their lips, their skin. Beneath the blistering sun, Namali curled forward, pressed against Sameen's damp back as the daeva plodded onward, sweat dripping steadily from her nose. The inferno roared around them, and it was not kind. She dreamed of home, the structure that managed to remain cooler on the inside, protected from a heat so consuming it gnawed at flesh, rock, bone.

Her eyelids fluttered shut, then snapped open. These days, she craved the darkness. Night was blind and blissfully cool. In this dry, deadened heat, she had forgotten that anything existed beyond sun and sweat and sand and stone. She had forgotten many things. Time was an illusion here.

Sameen suddenly straightened in front of her. Everything was blindingly, searingly white. "Is that . . ."

Namali unwrapped her arms from around his waist, wincing at the heaviness in her chest. Her neck prickled, but when she glanced over her shoulder, nothing was there.

Warily, she turned back around. When she scanned the horizon, she always searched for red cloth, a group of three: the merchant and his men. Blown far away, but not far enough. Never far enough.

Following Sameen's finger to where he pointed, Namali soaked up the sight before them. Death was all around, but here was green amidst desolation. Not just one plant, but an entire forest, a family of plants. Growing, persisting, living.

They stopped. There was no question that they wouldn't. It had been days since they encountered a source of water or a town, and while Namali long ago stopped caring about the grit sinking into the creases of her skin, the light dust clinging to her eyebrows, a chance to wash would be a welcome relief.

Sameen pulled the daeva to a halt, allowing Namali to slide free of the demon's icy touch, move away so she had room to breathe. The cold in her chest lingered—a hard, frigid diamond. It would be some time, she knew, before the sensation faded. Before that shredded bit of black prowling her mind quieted, calmed.

Once they tied up the daeva, they set up shelter in comforting silence near the edge of the ring of palms and scrub encircling the oasis, Sameen burying the stakes in the sand and Namali draping the cloth over them. After spreading a blanket on the ground, Sameen asked, "Do you want to wash first?" He was nearly as dusty as she.

Her hand pressed to her breastbone, fingers slightly curled. It was hard to focus. The light flickered and dimmed in the corner of her eyes. "You go ahead." Perhaps silence and solitude would help rid her of this . . . this *thing* inside her.

"Are you sure? I can stay—"

"I'm fine," she snapped, then winced. In a softer tone, she said, "Don't worry about me."

But he would. He *did*. It was in his eyes, and the turbulent emotion darkening those irises, the rims like burning coal. He didn't argue, though. With a worried look, he disappeared through the foliage.

Blowing out a breath, Namali laid back on the blanket, cool sweat dotting her brow. The black sheet cloaked her eyes. Soothed. In another life, Mama would lie on one side, Baba on the other, their hearts beating in sync. There had not been much to fear with her parents looking out for her.

Tears stung her eyes. She squeezed them shut. There was sadness, and then there was grief. It was never truly gone, the loss. At odd times it resurfaced, crushed her heart, crushed her lungs, and she ached. How could she live when she could not breathe?

"I miss you, Mama," Namali whispered, a tear trailing down her cheek. "I'll always miss you. And Baba . . . Baba does, too." She shuddered with sudden cold. "I hope he's not angry with me."

From outside, the daeva paced back and forth with a warning growl. Namali sat up, needing to do something with her hands, so she pulled the black bracelet from her pocket, intending to work on its weaving, when her fingers began to cramp. Not a dull twinge, but excruciating pain that radiated along her tendons and gathered at the joints. She whimpered. Clutched them to her chest. And watched as gnarled black veins flared beneath her skin.

Namali did not move. Did not blink. The faint tendrils shifted of their own accord.

Then everything jolted into motion, and she hissed, "No . . . *no*," and scrubbed at her skin to wipe away the evidence, half-mad with denial of this imminent change. She did not choose the darkness. It would not be her fate.

The ink bled away, her skin red with irritation but unblemished. Namali stared at her wrists and palms in case the tendrils returned, but they did not. She would not mention this to Sameen. It was not his business, and she did not want to give him reason to abandon her. As far as she was concerned, this had been an illusion, too.

Hands shaking, Namali shoved the bracelet back into her pocket. She didn't want to be alone. Didn't want to dwell on dark thoughts.

The edge of the foliage etched a hard ring of shade against the sand. Namali followed Sameen's footprints to where the forest extended its palms and cool shade embraced her. It smelled like water and pungent earth and something else entirely.

Peace. It smells like peace.

Light seeped through the canopy, its warm fingers brushing the ferns cloaking the floor, and soon the world opened up again. Namali stood at the edge of a shallow cliff with greenery wrapped around the hollowed-out center. Stairs chiseled into the rock led to a glassy body of water below, where a few birds waded near the shore and jeweled lizards sunned themselves on smooth boulders. But her attention wasn't drawn to them. It was drawn to a dark young man below. A gloriously half-naked Sameen.

Oh. My.

Wearing nothing but a pair of loose-fitting trousers, Sameen waded into the water up to his waist, causing shallow waves to lap against the rock. He slipped beneath the surface and emerged, dark hair slicked back against his scalp. In all her life, she had never seen so much beautiful skin. And that broad, muscular chest—

Steeling herself, Namali darted behind a rock and peeked around it. Sameen moved to the sloped bank, his back to her. A magnificent back, truly. Brown and broad and strong. A bead of water slid down his spine and disappeared below his waistband as he reached his arms above his head, stretching.

Then he stripped off his pants.

Namali's cheeks burned so hot she thought they might burst into flame. Eyes wide, she fanned herself with her hand. What was she *doing*? There was the definite possibility she might actually evaporate in a whiff of steam. This was so wrong. And so right. Appalling. Exhilarating. She had absolutely no shame.

After completing his wash, Sameen emerged from the oasis, water beading on his skin, and began to dress. Namali used the opportunity to flee back to camp, picking up the hem of her robe so she wouldn't trip. Ten minutes later, Sameen spoke beyond the shelter walls. "Namali?"

Swallowing hard, she said, "I'm here." As he entered, her cheeks flushed from the small secret she harbored. "Um . . . hello."

His eyes crinkled in puzzled amusement. "Hello," he replied, and settled beside her. His hair was still damp. "When I was washing up, I realized something."

Namali blew out a long, silent breath. Willed the heat in her cheeks to drain away. "What?" He hadn't spotted her amongst the rocks and trees. She hoped.

"It's Asraba."

Her hand flew to her mouth, and her earlier embarrassment faded. "I forgot."

"Do you think we should pray?"

They wouldn't be able to celebrate in the typical fashion, with dancing and costumes and elaborate feasts, but they could make do with what they had. In the end, it was the intention that mattered. "I think that's a good idea. Is there anything to eat?"

Sameen rummaged through his pack beside her, their shoulders lightly touching, and set out their food. "Flatbread and pomegranate seeds." A slight pause. "But no figs."

Long ago, when Mahurzda first hatched the world from an egg, he planted a fig tree to suck the evil deep from the cracks in the earth. By consuming the fruits the fig tree bore, the Great Pack did their part to expel the darkness. Eating figs during Asraba acknowledged the banishment of evil, but without them, they would unfortunately have to skip that part of the ceremony.

Namali said, "I'm sure Mahurzda will understand."

Sameen arranged the food for their small, last-minute ceremony in a circle, which represented the connectivity of the universe. That done, they knelt in front of the ramshackle display. It was appallingly sparse—pitiful, even—but it would have to do.

Head bowed, Sameen began, "Mahurzda, Good Lord of Malahad," and Namali joined him, their voices—one a soft murmur, the other rich and deep—melding into a complex harmony. "We kneel before you in sorrow for the loss of the Great Pack, known for its goodness in the world. For thousands of years they drove away the darkness the Demon King had unleashed, but that is no more."

Namali lifted her hands to her forehead, palm to palm. The rustle of cloth indicated Sameen did the same, and the closeness felt like a touch, as if there was no space between them and she could feel his heartbeat in his chest, soft and persistent, an underlying steadiness as constant as the sky.

They continued after a moment of silence. "Yet there are those who still believe a day will dawn when the Great Pack returns, restored by a heart without greed. In this, we believe."

Namali started to turn toward Sameen, but the knowledge of what followed held her in place. Normally, Asraba was celebrated in the presence of family. Never among strangers, and certainly not between an unmarried girl and an unmarried boy of no relation.

Sameen cleared his throat. "We can stop here if you want." He caught her eye and looked away.

Namali found her metal bracelet to be extremely interesting at this moment. Honestly, she needed as much help from Mahurzda as he was willing to give her. Skipping another portion of the ceremony did not seem particularly wise.

"I'm willing—"

"Do you—"

They both stopped, watching the other. It was hot and airless beneath the sheet.

"You go ahead," he said.

She tugged on her veil. "I was saying that I'm willing to finish the ceremony if you are."

"I'd like to finish it. With you, I mean." Sweat clumped his dark lashes together. They were so much longer than her own, but there was nothing feminine about them. Nothing feminine about any of him. "That is, if you want to." He grimaced, his cheeks reddening. "I'm going to stop talking now."

Her mouth twitched, but she held the smile inside herself. Wordlessly, Namali gripped his right hand in her left one, not knowing whose sweat was whose, and met his gaze despite wanting to look elsewhere. Then she took a breath, picked up a pomegranate seed, and moved it toward Sameen's mouth.

His lips parted. His breath blew against her fingertips, warm. The seed dropped inside.

Namali snatched her hand back as if burned, turning away so she couldn't see his expression. In a way, she didn't need to. His body hummed with tension.

They recited the next section of the prayer together. "And when one with a selfless heart restores the Great Pack, the Demon King will weaken. Darkness will give way to light, and Mahurzda will once more rise to power for all the remainder of his days. In this, we believe."

This time, Sameen tore off a piece of flatbread. Unlike her, he didn't meet her eyes, instead studying a point beyond her shoulder as Namali lifted the fabric to reveal her mouth, careful to keep her birthmark covered. Sameen placed the flatbread on her tongue before facing the front. They finished the prayer with a final, "In this, we believe."

It was done.

Outside their shelter, the daeva curled up on the sand and laid its head on its paws. A hot gust whipped over it, sending the shadows swirling like flames.

Namali took a sip of water to give her hands something to do. "My father always enjoyed this ceremony. His relatives would visit, and it would be an all-day affair."

Sameen rested a palm on his ankle. "My father is dead."

Slowly, she lowered the container from her mouth, a pang moving through her chest. "I'm sorry." How swiftly she understood. And felt for him. And ached. Too much to consider mentioning her own loss. It was too personal a topic for someone she had met less than two weeks ago.

His expression grew distant, settling on a memory she could neither see nor experience, but that she wanted to understand regardless. "When someone you love leaves you, they're never coming back. People are funny in that respect. Always looking ahead or behind or all around, seeing things others have, things we want, and we're too blinded by our own greed to recognize what's in front of our eyes. Maybe I didn't always get along with my father, but I can't ever forget I had one, and that he was a part of my life. I can't forget that he loved me."

Namali traced a swirly pattern on the blanket. Did Baba care she was gone? Sometimes it felt as if she'd lost both of her parents. They were father and daughter of blood but not of heart. A handful of words over dinner did not build a relationship, and a handful of words, unless they were *I love you,* did not repair the brokenness between them.

She had not heard those words in over three years.

Namali plucked at a loose thread dangling from her robe, figuring there was no harm in voicing a concern that had prowled her mind for days. "I've been thinking about darkness and . . . and daevas." Her head was full of it, full of them both. "Do you think Mahurzda is angry with us for participating in the race?"

"Why would you think that?"

"Because Mahurzda is inherently light, and the Demon King is inherently dark. We're playing into the Demon King's hand."

Sameen shredded a piece of flatbread thoughtfully. "I've thought about this, too." His eyes were far away. "While I'm not sure Mahurzda completely approves of what we're doing, I think he understands human morals are sometimes blurred. There is conflict in all of us. You and I, we made this choice. Morally, life is more convoluted than the deities wish us to believe. Light, darkness . . . one cannot exist without the other, for the very definition of light is the absence of dark. They are both necessary for the balance of the world."

"I guess I'm worried about our actions being justified. Doing something wrong, or what we think is wrong, for the right reasons. Does Mahurzda understand the wants and needs of mortals, or does it only look like greed to him?" She scrunched up her face at his surprised expression. "I don't mean to be so philosophical. It's just something I've been thinking about."

"No," he said. "I like these types of questions. They make me think."

And then Sameen bent his head, pondering the thought, pondering her words, with all the seriousness they deserved.

"I believe he can recognize greed for the sake of greed. But I also think he can see the reason behind one's intentions, whether they're fueled by violence or wrath or love, whether that's love of self or love of someone else. We all place importance on different things. I believe Mahurzda has a plan for all of us, whether we realize it or not."

"But what about my plan?"

"I'm sorry?"

"You said Mahurzda has a plan for all of us, but what about the plan I have for myself? Are they the same plan?" She swallowed. It was not too much to ask, she realized. "Shouldn't I have the ability to shape my future?"

Sameen frowned, as if he hadn't before considered the possibility. "Honestly . . . I don't know."

"What do you mean you don't know?" Her tone had an edge.

"I'm not a fountain of knowledge, Namali. I believe Mahurzda puts us on a path, but whether you choose to remain on that path is up to you." The crease between his eyebrows deepened. "I can't answer your question because I'm not you. Do *you* think you should have the ability to shape your own future?"

Not that she thought Mahurzda would strike lightning down from the sky in punishment, but she spoke quietly when she answered, "Yes."

His eyes warmed. "Then you have your answer."

"Do you think he knows about the race?"

"Mahurzda? I'm sure he does. He might even have a stake in it."

She started to reply, but the scream had Namali on her feet before she understood what was happening.

It ripped into her, pushed her forward so she was moving, running across the sand. The cry held such anguish it sent a wave of bumps over her body. Was it a woman? A child?

Sameen caught her arm, yanking her to a halt. "Don't," he said, jaw clenched.

At the second scream, she jerked free of him. It sounded close. Right over the next dune. "Someone's hurt. We have to help them." Hadn't Sameen told her the same when she'd woken to a crackling fire, a kind stranger?

"It's not what you—Namali!"

She raced in the opposite direction, struggling up the incline, her feet sinking into loose, deep sand while Sameen's voice chased her, telling her to stop, to come back. The sun burned a line of fire down her back. Cruel, unforgiving. She topped the dune and looked below.

Three men in dark robes surrounded a fourth, who lay on the ground in a pool of blood. She swayed. The sand was black with it. The men laughed as they took turns slicing into their victim, who flailed and screamed and wept from the agony of a knife peeling back his flesh. And Namali watched. Watched, and wondered why he didn't fight back, didn't do anything but shout his pain to the empty blue sky.

Then she noticed two objects lying on the ground next to him.

They had cut off his hands.

She clapped a hand over her mouth, her stomach heaving. They were torturing him. Looking upon his mutilated form with their black demon eyes and playing a cruel, sadistic game.

And for a single breathless moment, she wanted to play, too.

Sameen reached her side, turned her away. He shook her shoulders, saying, "It's not real, it's not real, it's an illusion."

Her chest hollowed out from the violence of the sight. How could this be an illusion? It was as real as the sand beneath their feet. There was the man's blood on the ground, and his severed hands, and his pale face drenched in sweat, twisted in pain. Sameen was wrong.

"We have to help him," Namali choked out. She was going to be sick.

"Listen to me." He pushed his face close. The inner rings of his irises glowed like molten bronze. "What you see is not real. It's an illusion. Do you understand?"

Sunlight seared her eyes. She couldn't see, but she didn't need to. She heard the screams.

"Those aren't men. They're daevas, and they're tricking you. They're tapping into your fear to try and take control."

Was it true? She'd experienced loss of control and could remember how it felt: sudden, a vice. It had not felt like this. "But . . . but it *looks* real." She shook her head to clear the confusion. "They're torturing him!"

"I promise you, it's not. The daevas have been following us for a number of days now."

His hands imprisoned her. She looked into his eyes, those dark, calm pools, and a thought occurred to her. How did she know *this* wasn't an illusion?

Namali studied him more closely. Large, slightly crooked nose. A mole coloring his chin, like a tiny round nut, currently covered by dark stubble. He certainly looked like the boy she'd met a few weeks ago, but she could be wrong. She'd been wrong before. Maybe this fake Sameen was trying to trick her, too.

Namali wrenched away, palms up. Something was different about this young man. She felt it in her bones. "Stay away from me."

The fake Sameen sent her a helpless look. His hands were still open from where she'd jerked free of his grasp. "I'm real, Namali. Trust me."

"Prove it."

"You entered the Demon Race to wish yourself free of your arranged marriage. You like reading and weaving bracelets in your free time. You showed me how to build a proper shelter. You owned a kerespa when we first met. Khorshan." His voice hardened. "You hate how restrictive your life has become, but even more than that, you hate how you're too afraid to change it."

She recoiled as if slapped. "I never told you that." How had he known? Could he read her mind?

The twisting of his expression said so many things. "You didn't have to."

Namali gasped and bolted down the dune toward the bloody, tortured man. She had to get away from this fake Sameen, this liar. As she neared the men, all four of them morphed into shadowy daevas, smoky tendrils licking around their grotesque forms. But she didn't see this. Her mind had been covered with a thick, dark curtain. It told her to trust these creatures. It told her not to trust the boy, who chased after her, shouting.

It told her to climb onto the closest demon, to grab the reins dangling from its neck, to dig her heels into its sides and not look back.

So she did.

CHAPTER 12

THE DAEVA STREAKED across a desert she could no longer see.

A pounding in her blood. A chill in her bones.

They flew like the wind.

She and the daeva. The daeva and she. Her hands sank deep into billowing fur, tendrils crawling up her arms and legs, though there was no prickling sensation, no pain. Her heart punched a hole in her chest. Shuddered against her ribcage. The air tasted of ice and blood.

The demon leaned right, and she leaned with it, bodies merging. They inhaled the same darkness, breath for breath, and it was easier than it had ever been, and welcome. The demon's fear became her fear. Its rage her rage. She suddenly understood what it was like to attract hatred when she had never asked for it. That was the demon's burden.

Namali strained her ears. Two men gave chase close behind. The harshness of their breath. The scrape of swords sliding free of their sheaths. They were hungry, and they were almost here.

A blade whooshed by her ear. Namali jerked away, snarling, but she didn't anticipate the daeva lunging in the opposite direction. She slammed into the ground.

The world flashed white and dissolved into grays. She sucked in a labored wheeze, blinking at the sky until her vision cleared and the darkness leached away, thick as paint. Shards of memory returned, bits of humanity nearly destroyed. She remembered now. She remembered the danger.

The men dismounted from their daevas and swaggered over, blades up, grins stretched wide, a touch sinister. One was thick with muscle, the other lean as a snake. Their eyes were black fathoms.

She climbed to her feet and gripped her dagger the way Sameen had taught her. Struggled to recall his fluid movements, the placement of his feet as she backed away slowly, but her mind had become a blank slate, wiped clean from the will to survive. These men had no reason to spare her. They would make her beg for mercy as they celebrated her blood flowing thick and red. What would they do once she was incapacitated and screaming from pain? Remove her hands so she couldn't defend herself? Cut off her feet to prevent her escape?

She bolted as fast as her leaden legs could carry her, pushing through the burn creeping up her thighs and down her knotted calves. The men gave chase, not ten feet behind. Her chest heaved. Her robe weighed a thousand pounds. She hurtled down a slope, arms wheeling to keep her balance, trying to remember which direction she'd come from, how far she'd ridden. It couldn't have been very far. If she somehow found her way back to Sameen, he could help her, fight for her.

One man caught hold of her braid, and her head snapped

back. Namali screamed and twisted around, clawing at any patch
of skin, and she spat and thrashed even as her scalp split apart and
tears seared her eyes. They could pull her hair out. She didn't care.
She only needed to get away.

One hard shove and she was on the ground. The skinny man
covered her screaming mouth with a hand, mashing his sweaty,
grimy palm against her lips. Then a heavy weight crushed her
chest, and the screams cut off. The man straddled her, grinning,
grinning. Like it was a game.

Namali tried to buck him off. She lunged forward, wanting to
rip into his skin with her teeth, make him cower, make him bleed.
He yanked her head back by her hair to bare her throat, a knife
in his hand, another scream building, beating against her ribs to
break free in one last act of defiance. It couldn't end this way. Not
in this forsaken place. Not like this.

Then she saw her chance.

The man shifted, and her fingers shot out to stab him in the eye.
The strike sent him tumbling onto the sand, one hand covering
his face, and Namali kicked him aside and ran and ran and ran,
not looking back, not daring to stop until she left the competitors
far behind and her knees collapsed, body shaking from adrenaline
and shock. The sand engulfed her small form. The wind howled
a shriek of rage, her life having been spared. Now she was truly
alone.

Slowly, her hands crept into her hair, gripped tight at the roots
as she curled over her knees. A haze clouded her mind. Familiar,
unsettling. She couldn't remember why she had left Sameen,
what had compelled her to run. That part of her memory was
barren. Deep grooves formed on her forehead from her efforts

of concentration. It had only occurred mere hours ago, right? The last thing she remembered was performing the ceremony for Asraba, and then . . . and then . . .

She didn't know how long she lay there with the sun beating its fiery fists upon her back, but eventually her daeva returned, its eyes shining a strange, muted blue. Namali was mindless. She hadn't the energy to think, only *do*. So she climbed onto its back, slumped against its neck, and let it lead her where it may.

•••

When Namali opened her eyes, the land was still. The sun had begun its slow descent. Her mouth and throat burned with the need for water, that cool kiss of moisture her body craved. *Water, water* . . .

"Hello, there."

Namali bolted upright, poised for flight. Her knuckles whitened atop the reins. "It's you."

A familiar old man sat cross-legged on the ground in a pair of loose wool trousers, regarding her steadily. Impossibly, his beard was twice as long as it had been eleven days ago, pooling into his lap and covering his legs like a second pair of pants. "Yes. It is."

Warily, she dismounted. This man was real. The camel resting beside him was real. And he had brought her here to meet him. There was no doubt in her mind, for such a coincidence would otherwise be impossible. The question was why.

"Who are you?"

He smiled, as if the answer were obvious. "I think the better question is: who are *you*?"

"I know who I am."

"Do you?"

He didn't believe her, and Namali realized he shouldn't. Back in Benahr, she would have answered him without hesitation, but now . . . things were different now. *She* was different. A flower gently blooming, no longer squeezed tight into a bud. Perhaps she didn't know who exactly Namali was yet.

"I imagine you're quite hungry," he said. "Would you care to join me for dinner?"

There was no food anywhere she could see. No supplies except for the blanket he sat on. Again, she wondered why he had brought her here, and for what purpose. Aside from the camel, they were alone.

Namali stepped toward the demon, away from the odd man and even odder situation, a tingling sensation spreading through her limbs. "Unfortunately, I don't have time."

"A pity," he said, watching her.

The dagger burned through the cloth at her waist. The world leaked darkness at its edges. She'd been here before, that smoky voice hissing in her ear, coaxing her to take the dagger and drive it into flesh, but the old man's heart was so much more tempting than her own. That sad, weak heart.

Her right hand reached for the weapon while her left tangled in the demon's fur. Her breath came harsh and fast. This was wrong. These thoughts were not her own. They were tainted, smelling of death. A part of her reveled in the power she held in these moments, for it was as addictive as she always thought it would be. The wrongness came not in the power itself. It was in trying to convince herself she was somehow innocent of these crimes.

She wrenched away from the daeva, breathless, stumbling, lost. The man's gaze flitted between her and the demon, all too keen. Could he see? Could he see into her mind and the violence that prowled? Lately, it had become difficult to separate herself from the pull she felt even in sleep. It was clear now. The path was set. Continue along its pitted road, and she would reach a very dark place indeed.

"Please, have a seat." The darkness of his eyes gleamed a pure, liquid black. "I insist."

Her feet moved of their own accord, as did her knees, bending forward before him, reminiscent of a bow. She may as well have been a plank of wood for how stiffly she shifted to sit on her bottom and cross her legs. *Demon, demon, demon,* whispered her heart. This man, who might not be a man at all, but rather someone wearing a human skin. She was afraid. How could she not be? But there was anger there, too, at her lack of control. She'd come far, but there was still much distance to cover, and she did not want to travel its length without the promise of change from within, the collapse and rebuilding of certain qualities she loathed in order to experience an independent life. She didn't care who this man was, or if he was even a man. He did not hold the right to command her body. It was not his decision to make.

"What do you want?" she demanded, lips stiff. Her daeva sat on its haunches, as if under the man's influence as well.

"A moment of your time."

"I do not recall you asking."

"Would you have agreed to it if I had?"

The intensity of his gaze turned her eyes downward, before they snapped up. She would no longer reinforce this absurd notion of inferiority. "Release me."

Reaching out, he scratched the camel's bristly head. The sudden weightlessness of her limbs indicated his power had been lifted.

She began to rise when he said, "You are free to leave. However, the demon answers to me."

Namali wished she had never left Sameen. She didn't even bother grabbing her dagger again. If this man was who she believed him to be, a mortal weapon would be useless.

"You are frightened."

"It should not come as a surprise. Are you not the Demon King, master of darkness and chaos? Is this creature—" She stabbed a finger at the demon. "—not your servant?"

A minute passed as the man stroked the camel's furry back leisurely. "This is perhaps the worst kept secret in the world," he said. "Everyone has both light and darkness inside them. Even you. I'm simply calling the darkness inside me to better connect to the daeva, since that is what it understands."

"You didn't answer my questions."

A small smile formed, his eyes no longer black, but brown. A trick of the light, then. "And I don't plan to."

He would not answer her, and she would not leave without a mount. It made sense, what he said. The demon used the darkness inside her as leverage to corrupt and bend her mind to its will. How many times had she wanted to rage at her father for keeping his affection locked away? How many times had she lashed out, given others her pain, in order to lighten her load?

Darkness inhabited her, hidden deep, but the demon brought it to life.

Wordlessly, Namali settled between the man and the camel. If she was going to die, she may as well do so with a full belly. Wrinkles carved deep trenches in his face, along his mouth, and his deeply tanned skin sagged around his neck. His eyes held a terrible ancientness, as if he had walked the earth for a hundred thousand lifetimes.

Her stomach rumbled. Loudly.

His smile widened a touch. "What would you like to eat?" It sounded almost . . . kind.

Again, she looked around. The sky, an unusual yellow-violet, announced the day's end. The sand had flushed a deep, burning red. "I don't see anything."

He flicked a shriveled, bony hand. "Irrelevant. Do you like oranges?"

Saliva flooded her mouth. Who knew a piece of fruit could have such power over her. "That sounds wonderful."

"Anything else?"

"I think the orange will be enough."

"You *think* or you *know?*" He shot her a pointed look. In many ways, he reminded her of Baba, though perhaps a bit more weathered. "Tell me what you want."

What do you want, Namali? Perhaps they were speaking of oranges, but then again, perhaps not. And if they weren't, how did this man know her reluctance to speak, but more than that, her desire to be heard?

"Well," she said, drawing out the word, "I wouldn't be opposed to eggplant with rice."

He bobbed his head up and down. "And?"

And something other than water. "Cardamom tea."

His laughter tinkled in the air like a high, sweet bell. "Splendid!" Then he reached into his bushy beard and pulled out a perfectly ripe orange.

Namali gaped.

Again, the man reached into his beard, rummaged around a little, before removing a plate of rice and eggplant, two cups of steaming tea, and, even though she hadn't requested it, a waterskin filled to the brim.

She blinked and rubbed her tired eyes. The food was still there. "How did you do that?"

"The universe works in mysterious ways, does it not?" He gestured at her untouched meal. "Please, eat."

Namali dug into the food without hesitation. The steamy rice warmed her chest against the rapidly cooling air, and the orange was bright and sweet.

"I am surprised to see only one of you."

Taking a sip of water, Namali discovered the liquid to be as chilled as if it had been sitting in an ice house. "Only one?"

He stared at her. "Weren't you traveling with a young man before?"

She lowered the skin. "I was." Until she'd left him in the dust. Now here she sat, stuffing her face, gorging on this rich, filling feast. The rice turned in her stomach. At the end of these thirty days, they would meet one another as enemies across a red field, and Namali would choose herself. That was the plan. It had always been the plan. So why this sudden guilt? Any advantage given to Sameen was a disadvantage for herself, this she knew. There was no honor in war. One winner, one wish. "We decided to part ways."

The man nodded as he removed a teapot from his beard and

poured himself another cup. The sky had bruised to deep indigo, and the sun was a ghostly sliver where the earth kissed the sky. Wrapped in the folds of color, the Saraj was quite beautiful. "A wise decision."

If she kept telling herself that, maybe she would eventually believe it. "Sameen is a good man."

"Maybe he is. But there will come a point in this race when he no longer thinks in terms of light and dark, right and wrong, but dark and darker. The daevas are designed to crush those who are weakest. Do you think prolonging a friendship doomed to die within the desert sands will lead you to victory? It is better to be alone. Grow close to those you care for, and you will open yourself up to a world of pain."

More than anything, Namali knew this. And still she said, "You're wrong."

He laughed darkly. "Am I?" The white of his yirasaf glowed against the night backdrop, as fiercely as the moons.

She wondered what tragedy had befallen this man to cut himself off from beauty and compassion and grace. Namali understood pain. It hurt *because* they loved you, *because* you loved them. Love was pain, but love was also kindness and salvation. And when you found yourself broken upon the road, love would do its part to heal.

Namali allowed everything she was feeling to resonate in her voice. "You're right. By cutting yourself off from others, they would not have the power to hurt you." She then added in a whisper, "But they would not have the chance to love you."

Setting down his tea, the man looked at her for a long moment. The night shrouded him in even more mystery.

"Maybe I'm wrong then. Maybe there is hope for you, for your friend." He shrugged. "It would be nice, to hope." He looked to the daeva as he said, quietly, "It would be very nice, indeed."

For the remainder of their meal, they did not speak. Though no longer hungry, Namali cleared her plate, for it would be days, possibly, before she ate again. The stomach craved fuel. The mouth craved flesh. The man's description of what would befall Sameen chilled her, a lodge of ice in the pit of her stomach as the knowledge took root. The man, in all his knowing, had been mistaken, had been wrong.

It was not Sameen who had to worry.

CHAPTER 13

NAMALI LEFT THE old man behind on her journey north. She traveled until sunrise before seeking shelter beneath a bluff, and when the shadows finally merged with the night, she continued onward. She passed no towns, no competitors. No indication anyone else existed. The Saraj surrounded her, cruel and toxic and desolate, day after day after day. She would find no comfort in its barrenness, no guidance in the vague, umbrous valleys and hills. Sitting stiffly atop the demon, Namali pulled her robe tighter to ward off the nightly chill. The press of a thousand eyes only agitated her disquiet. She must remain aware, always, of what lay ahead and behind. She was not safe in a land where men turned to beasts.

Sand.

Stone.

Namali . . .

Blood.

Bone.

Sometimes she swore she recognized three dark figures on horses, chasing her and chasing her, and Namali could barely catch her scream before she realized no, it was her imagination, it was false, it was a nightmare made flesh. The shadows slipping from her line of vision, the whispers emerging from nowhere . . . was anything real?

Focusing her energy on gathering food soothed her nerves, at least for a short while. Years had come and gone since she and Baba camped together, but Namali still retained much of what she had learned. She kept watch for rock formations, as those would offer shelter for small mammals and reptiles, and on the second day to the east, she stumbled across a pile of wind-battered boulders half-buried in sand. A directional landmark, most likely. She searched between the cracks and crevices. Peered beneath a shallow overhang of gray stone. The chameleon was quick, but she was faster.

Namali skinned the lizard by the light of the moons, exposing the tender flesh beneath. It was a few mouthfuls at best, but hunger gnawed a hole in her gut, saliva pooling in her mouth from the sight of muscle, tendon.

Sand and stone and blood and bone.

She choked the chameleon down raw.

The daeva grew more restless with each passing day. Snarling and whining and random bursts of speed and head cocked as if listening for something important, something that made its muscles coil in anticipation or dread or both. During these times, Namali felt as if her skin might split down her spine, and she didn't know if the heat caused the tight, itching sensation across her back or if she was truly going insane. A film clouded her vision, cloaking the burning sun from her eyes. Her hands curled into fists, elongated fingernails digging into her palms hard enough to puncture and draw blood. And when that bold red ink stained her skin, when her fingers were sticky with it, she brought them to her nose and inhaled. Deeply. Hungrily.

Time spun out. Dawn brought more whispers, more agony. Sparks ignited down her body, setting her skin aflame, and a dreadful buzzing filled her ears. She forgot her intentions. She forgot her name. She considered using the wish for something else, something the Demon King desired most of all.

With the rising of the moons, Namali's paranoia teetered on a knife point. Drenched in cold sweat, she gazed up, up, waiting for the mouth of the world to swallow her whole. Her thoughts turned nightmarish, gorging on those fleeting images of claws protruding, limbs extended, face transformed to that of a beast. The unbalanced realm, that liquid conscience between waking and dreaming, trapped her with cruel intentions, where the horror of locusts crawling over her body would wrench her from sleep, and Namali would scream and claw at her skin until she wore a coat of blood. Afterward, when her head cleared, she would stare at her hands, unable to remember what had caused the red scores running parallel to those bubbling black veins. And, curling around herself, would cry until sleep took her again.

Her thoughts turned to Sameen. In his absence, she noticed how dark the night could be. They did not even have to speak. Being in his presence, sharing his space—it was enough. But . . . it was better this way, to complete the journey alone. As the transformation took effect, she could not be his friend without at some point endangering his life, acting out of selfishness, succumbing to the restless greed. He would look at her, a stranger, and see a wild, disgraced animal. She did not want to see in his eyes what she knew to be true. She was her own worst enemy. She could not be trusted.

On the sixth night of her solo journey, a low moan broke through the buzzing in her ears. Namali pried her burning eyes open to the moonlit landscape, wincing at her cramped muscles. The moan sounded again. She knew the sound well. Once every few years, Baba culled the herd when the animals grew sick. The splatter of fluid as he cut into their throats would follow her for the rest of her days. In suffering, it was best to put the animal out of its misery.

The demon's paws sank deep into the sand as they halted atop a dune. Below, in the depression between two sandy hills, a man lay sprawled on the ground, one hand clutching the handle of the knife buried in his chest, his legs crushed and useless. Blood soaked the ghostly sand beneath him, dyeing the earth red.

The man turned his head and squinted through the low light. "Please." The rasp scraped against her ears. "Water . . ."

Namali gripped the reins, hands trembling. Another competitor left for dead. The vultures hadn't descended yet, but they would. When the sun beat down on his fetid corpse, cooking it from the inside out, they would swarm and feast and pick his bones clean. And he would be forgotten. That was the real tragedy. For many of these men, they had no families to honor them by. For others, they were leaving their loved ones behind.

The thought twisted her gut. She wanted to go. She wanted to stay. She wanted to share her water, share life. She wanted to hoard it for herself. She wanted so many things, but most of all, most of all . . .

She saw the man. Saw him lying in the sand with the protruding dagger, and the need to shove the blade in deeper shredded her tenuous control. She wanted to watch his blood flow, hear him scream, witness the life flee from his eyes, for he was weak, and sad, and pitiful, and looking at him sent ice branching through her limbs. The trembling grew worse. She was not herself. Somewhere along this journey she'd become lost and could not find her way back.

I'm not a killer. I'm not.

But the demon was trying its hardest to convince her otherwise.

She dismounted jerkily, stumbling forward, fighting the force pushing her to the man, wanting so badly to close her eyes, hide herself from his suffering, and she feared it was already too late. A part of her, tangled and unclear, wanted this. The Saraj called for blood, and she was giving it its due. Who would have known the race would lead her here? In all honestly, Namali had anticipated an early death, much like this, subject to the power of another, and maybe a part of her wanted to prove she was strong, and cunning, and ruthless, more than her veil suggested, more than one would expect of a shy girl from a small town. The daeva knew her heart. And so it would not deny her this kill.

Her knees hit cool, soft sand. The black presence loomed near as she stared into the man's ashen face. A husband's face, a father's face. Flies circled him lazily, already anticipating the end.

A grin stretched across her mouth as her fingers darkened with shadow. Her tongue touched the tips of her pointed teeth, anticipation a thrilling hum in her blood. Blood, death—both were old friends. It had been too long since she'd seen them. Far, far too long.

But something else stirred to life: light, the part of Namali still present and known, not yet lost to violence. Somewhere within the murk of morality, the light wavered, trembled in the shadows diving and circling the glow, doing their best to douse it. It was fragile, that light, and so much smaller than it had been weeks ago. But still it stood, a pillar risen against war and adversity. Her smile slipped, teeth beginning to retract. She could walk away clean, let this man die in peace, die with honor. All she had to do was rise. All she had to do was choose.

Stand up.

But it was like the day of the eclipse, the first time she had encountered the darkness. The wave, the pressure, the *force*—she must swim with the tide or drown. Returning to a place she hoped to never again visit only succeeded in breaking further what was broken. No matter how she raged or begged, her limbs wouldn't listen, wouldn't move. They served another master now.

Stand up, Namali.

Her ragged sobs slapped the air. The whispers grew to a thunderous roar. She could do this. She could do this one small thing. Namali fought to fortify the barrier protecting her mind from outside influence, but a feeling like rock shards scraping over her scalp threw her back into the helpless, shadowy pit, down, down. There was no bottom. Her hand wrapped around the hilt as she plummeted, and the man wept, a soft, feeble sound. The sound of a man knowing he was going to die.

This isn't you, Namali. This is the darkness. Don't listen to it. Don't—

Shadow snuffed out the light, victorious, and her hand pushed the knife deeper into the man's chest. He screamed, a sound so riddled with pain it tore into her insides, tore a hole into the world.

Murderer.

Unwrapping her fingers from the hilt, Namali fell back with deep, soulful gasps, shaking so hard her teeth rattled as blood bubbled up his throat and mouth. She had done this to him, an innocent man. It was her hand that held the dagger. Pushed it in, twisting, twisting. Hers, and no one else's. She was cruel, she was sick, she was done.

But the evil wasn't through with her yet.

Shapes swirled before her tear-choked eyes. Pictures, moving images—a vision.

Her breath hissed through her teeth. She tried to shove the vision away, to clear her mind and heart, but the darkness was strong, so strong. It bore down.

It conquered.

•••

When Namali came to, she stood in a city of palest stone beneath a still-bright sky. Stark shadows crisscrossed the roads, the pathways wide and curved like bands of water and inlaid with fat, glittering jewels. Rubies and sapphires and emeralds and opals dazzled her eyes, and only when she was able to tear her attention away from the wealth heaped beneath her feet did Namali realize the structures were not actually stone at all, but bone. Smooth, carved bone bleached beneath a beating sun, faint cracks streaming through.

The sight robbed her of breath. If Benahr was roughened rock, then this was a diamond, a jewel. The sprawl of buildings enveloped her, cradling Namali in its lush, opulent hands. Glazed tiles crowned the vast, domed rooftops, shimmering like a turquoise sea. Massive columns soared to dizzying heights, framing the arches and curves so that one felt small. Carved within the walls were high arched windows with long, flowing curtains, the fabric sheer and green, fluttering from a phantom wind that drifted through the city, fragrant with the smell of cinnamon.

Her chest swelled with something close to awe. She couldn't speak. The words were lost to her. How could she describe something she didn't understand? It was a feeling like light after years trapped in the dark.

Drawn by an unnamed force, Namali stepped through one of the wide, scalloped doorways. A long hallway unfolded, archway after archway, corridor after corridor, and the walls were as breathtakingly beautiful as the domes, painted a crushing blue overlaid with threads of gold. Her sandals scuffed along the paved gray stones. North, in the capital of Ilaramad, temples much like this one graced the arid grounds. A sacred space for her people to worship in solitude. They had been built a thousand years past, and would stand for a thousand more. It was a comfort, Namali thought, as she turned into a vaulted chamber and tilted back her head.

Mirrors. Thousands upon thousands of tiny, octagonal mirrors layered the domed ceiling, reflecting the sunlight pouring through the open doorways. In all the years of her life, never had she witnessed such splendor. The walls were intricately carved: birds and leaves and feathers and swirling rivers. Life this city once held. She skimmed her hand along the carvings and entered what appeared to be a courtyard, the ceiling having been replaced by azure sky. A long, rectangular pool stretched the length of the open expanse, framed by smaller, thinner columns spaced evenly apart. The walkways transitioned to polished marble inlaid with sandstone cuttings. Nearby, a sweet, gurgling fountain bisected the shallow pool.

Namali continued to wander until she eventually returned to the streets. The area was deserted, but it didn't feel empty. There was laundry drying on the line. And there, sandals and slippers placed neatly outside the temple walls. People lived here. They walked these roads and breathed this air, and yet she was alone. Where had the people gone? And why?

At the next turn, she spotted motion. A few yards from where she stood, near a small fountain, two Malahadi men appeared to be arguing. One wore a black robe and yirasaf. The other wore white. Although their mouths moved, no words emerged. The silence was complete, as if she were standing in a tomb.

Namali looked around. The buildings were carved from bone, and nothing grew. Maybe this *was* a tomb.

Shaking his head, the man in white stepped back. He mouthed *trees* and *all gone,* his hand slicing through the air in a sharp, restrained gesture. His dark counterpart mouthed *loved her,* followed by *rain.*

Namali's attention slid between the two men. They stood chest to chest, of equal height, as the animosity transformed into a thick, palpable cloud, and she didn't know why, but the sight kicked her heart into a gallop. This was not a chance meeting of strangers. These men loved one another. And despised one another.

Whirling around, the man in white stalked away, cutting

through the massive columns to stop beneath an archway and look into the distance, shoulders hunched, head bowed. Protecting himself from whatever pain he experienced.

Behind him, the man in black drew his blade.

Namali lurched forward, her only thought to stop him, but the man in black was quicker, far quicker than she would have possibly believed. His sword descended, a blur of molten metal, and she braced herself for the inevitable spill of blood, another untimely death, but the man in white sidestepped smoothly, and the blade whooshed past, harmless. The man in white was already turning, already raising his own scimitar to block the next blow, and the next, as if he had known this moment would come. They thrust and parried, dodged and blocked, the man in black cutting at his opponent in vicious strokes, driving him back through one of the gleaming courtyards, moving parallel to the glassy pool. A misguided swing sent fountain water spraying over the marble slabs.

Namali tracked them down the road, shadow and light, moving as one, both equally skilled. High strikes and low strikes and high blocks and low blocks. A dance that was not a dance. A game that was not a game.

They circled the pool for what seemed like hours before the man in white caught his ankle on the raised corner and faltered. His opponent's blade was already cutting into his stomach, his thigh as he fell, and the man in black raised his blade for the killing blow when his white counterpart twisted onto his feet, lunging forward, moving through the pain. Mouth open in a silent scream, he drove his sword into his foe's heart.

The man jerked from the force, his expression childlike with surprise. It was only when the light fled his eyes that Namali realized there had been any to begin with.

The man in white sank to the ground. His tears shone like the jewels hammered into the earth. Namali stepped forward, thinking to comfort him, to let him know he was not alone, but stopped. With cold horror, she watched as he lifted a hand, as he gripped the sword buried in the dead man's chest—

And cut out his heart.

With the bloody organ cradled in one palm, he stroked the heart tenderly. He had lost someone today. A brother, a friend, she didn't know. The wind sighed, stirring the sand around them. If there had been trees, the leaves would have shaken in grief. If there had been a lake or stream, the water would have rippled with quiet sobs. But there were none of these things. Only the stillness that comes with death.

The man in white leaned forward and placed a kiss upon the dead man's forehead. Seconds later, light flashed. When it cleared, the man in white had vanished.

Namali hardly dared to breathe. The man was a puddle of smoke splayed over the earth: silent, still. But then a cold force dragged at her, sent her kneeling beside him. She was lifting her hand. She was pressing her palm over the hole in his chest, firm.

As if awakening from a dream, the dead man stirred. His fingers twitched, followed by his arms. His legs. And when his black eyes fluttered open, the man took one look at Namali's pale, stricken face.

And grinned.

●●●

Namali gasped and bolted upright, sand clinging to her sweat-slickened skin. It was night. The city of bones had vanished, the jeweled roads and gauzy curtains replaced with sandy hills stamped by moonlight. Not five feet from where she sat lay the dead man. Killed by her own hand.

Bile surged up her throat, too forceful to stop. Rolling onto her hands and knees, Namali heaved, vomit splattering the sand, the stench causing her body to clench painfully. Her skin was like ice, and she no longer knew what it felt like to be warm. Was this how it felt to lose oneself? To annihilate the feelings of good, hope, and happiness and replace them with pain, death, and greed?

Shaking, she sat back and wiped her mouth on her sleeve, waiting for her heartbeat to slow. She stared at her outstretched hands, seeking some recognition. Blood stained her fingers, but when she tried to wipe it away, she only succeeded in pressing it more deeply into her skin. The change was too apparent to ignore. Paranoia frayed the edges of her nerves, her energy near depleted. She felt . . . empty. Helpless. How was it possible to weigh so heavily, fight for breath as if a ball of steel pressed upon her lungs, when there was nothing inside of her?

The vision had faded, but its importance was only beginning to grow. She didn't know the reason for the vision. She didn't know who the men were or why they had fought or who betrayed who. She didn't know anything anymore.

As for this man . . . she could not take back what she had done. He probably had a family. A wife who loved him. Children whose eyes brightened as they saw him walk through the front door. None of that mattered now.

I am a monster.

Namali dragged herself away from her sickness to the other side of the dead man. Curling up next to him, she held his still-warm hand in hers, pretending this was another time, another place, and her past was not her own. When she closed her eyes, she saw blood on her hands, blood on her robe, blood pouring from her eyes. And she wept with the knowledge of innocence lost, and evil lurking in her black, black heart.

CHAPTER 14

THE SKY WAS a pearly, timid gray.

Namali knelt beside the dead man, head bowed in the morning's quiet, hands fisted atop her thighs. The cool breeze hushed her churning thoughts, whispering things she did not want to believe, that this man's death had been necessary, that she had proved herself in the valley, in the dark, beneath a shadowed sky. She squeezed her eyes shut. She had gained nothing, but she had lost much. Her heart was an empty cavern.

It was another cruelty to beg for his forgiveness when it was undeserved, so she did not. Still, she asked Mahurzda to guide him on his journey to the afterlife, to keep him safe where she had failed. She had prayed for the dead before, but never like this. This was . . . so much worse than she could have ever imagined.

Heavily, Namali stood and faced the demon. Its tail hung low, grazing the ground. The thought of riding it, of touching its strange insubstantial skin, riddled her with revulsion. What purpose did this beast serve except to spread its lies and destruction and fear? It was a monster. Like her.

And yet . . .

And yet it knew nothing else. If a creature was born into darkness, did that make it inherently evil? She used to think so. She used to think of a lot of things. But even the deepest blacks contained shades of gray.

Against her better judgment, Namali stepped forward to brush the daeva's neck, and it leaned into her touch. Those eyes, which had always been without color, glinted a pleading blue, but when she blinked the color disappeared, leaving behind two gaping pits.

Namali shook her head. She desperately needed sleep.

After fortifying the mental wall surrounding her mind, she set out, wearing caution like inner armor. Urging the daeva faster, Namali let the wind sting her eyes, the sand scour her skin. Punishment for her awful deeds. Regardless of how fast or how far she traveled though, she could not outrun her past. Memories of the man's screams clung, trapped her in a perpetual cycle of self-loathing, where every slice of remembrance cut deeper than the last.

The desert flickered past in patches of sand and rock alike. Shadows lengthened, and sharpened, and stretched west as the sun claimed its massive blue throne. Namali clenched her legs around the demon, her body moving in rhythm with its loping gait. Above, the sun poured its liquid heat upon her, making her skin stretch and crack and bleed, while below, the demon's shadow combined with hers to form a single black entity rippling over the desolate land. The Saraj was not a place for living or growing. It was a place for dying.

Before long, Namali came across fresh tracks in the sand, and it was then the daeva changed. Subtly—so subtly she couldn't be sure she had imagined it. It was the deepening of twilight into night. It was a sigh's soft, almost hesitant, release.

The demon surged forward, a hunter pursuing its prey. She gave the beast its head, allowed it to charge in the direction it desired, through wind and sand and light. Soon, a dark smudge materialized, larger than a man, larger even than Benahr, sharpening in clarity as the distance closed. White, needle-like spires stabbed the perfect cerulean sky. A gold wall soared upward to encompass the sprawl of buildings, near blinding in its brilliance.

Namali startled at the sudden pull she felt, the otherworldly touch. The Lost City. She had made it. She was *here*.

"Faster!" she screamed.

From the corner of her eye, men swarmed atop the dunes from every direction, bruised and bloody, their faces savage and haunted and wanting. It was too many, and their numbers continued to rise. A group of five broke off from the larger stampede to surround a trio of men, cutting off their escape. They slaughtered two in a spray of blood. The third they yanked from his demon, and even yards away, even amidst the cruel ring of weapons and ferocious screams, she heard the sickening crack as he slammed into the ground, bounced, and lay still. The fall had snapped his neck.

Namali watched as they abandoned the body to the vultures, as they cut down seven more competitors in their path, as they razed a bloody path toward the entrance gates, any shred of humanity long ago buried, and then, as their attention locked onto a man hunched over his mount far ahead, his yirasaf the bright, burning hue of sapphire.

Sameen.

Namali dug her heels harder into the beast's sides, and the

shadows flowed out, away, before curling around her legs. *Go, go, go.* She cried his name, but he was too focused, too far, and the men steadily closed the distance between her friend. He didn't know, couldn't know, of the danger snapping at his heels. His attention was ahead, leaving him blind to what lay behind. *Look,* she thought desperately. *Look over your shoulder and* see.

The leader maneuvered his demon closer, lifting his blade. The remaining four fanned out behind him, acting as a buffer.

"Sameen!"

The wind snatched at her words, stole her voice.

Then the rope around her neck stole her air.

It cinched tight, snapping her head back. Namali didn't have time to prepare before the ground rushed up to meet her, legs crushed from the fall. Whoever held the rope dragged her through the sand like a sack of grain, and her hands shot to the abrasive collar, clawing, tugging as pressure built behind her stinging eyes and her face flushed hot with blood.

The dagger. She must get the dagger.

Namali fumbled at her waist, a tingling sensation spreading through her face, arms, and legs. Black dots burst behind her pupils. She shoved aside the folds of cloth, scrabbling for the weapon as fire scorched a pathway up her throat, as her heart fluttered against her ribs like a dying bird. Her movements jerked with desperation, and she tore at her clothes with everything she had. It was all soft, dark wool, mounds of it. Had she dropped the dagger unaware?

But then her fingers bumped the hilt, wrapped around its heavy reassurance. She slashed at the noose, again and again. The rope fell. She wheezed for air, choking on her hands and knees.

Bodies dotted the landscape. The daevas swarmed around the Lost City's entrance, ripping themselves to shadowy shreds, the men half-mad with bloodlust, driven by a terrible need. She should be there too, running for the city, lunging and snarling, howling and biting, doing what needed to be done to ensure victory, this chance to change her fate.

But she didn't run to the city. She ran toward Sameen, who fought off two men with a competitor's sword, whose twisted foot was the blade on which he danced. He cut and parried, darting forward and backward and side to side, unaware that Namali trudged through the sand with mindless intention, barreling through the wall of wind. The last time a competitor attacked, she had quailed in fear, but not this time, not again. Her blood was laced with fire.

There was no thought in gripping the dagger. No thought in the careful, detached way she stabbed it into the man's shoulder, through flesh and sinew. She wanted to be that blade, deadly and precise. She wanted to conquer, and claim, and teach him the language of death.

Sameen's eyes widened in recognition before the man roared and whipped around. Namali ducked. His blade screamed past her head, and her heart thrilled with the savagery of it. *Yes,* said the voice. *More.* She managed another strike before his fist plowed into her cheek.

Pain exploded through her face. She was falling, and crashing down, and he was on top of her, and then, as he raised his sword for the killing blow—

Became stone.

Her blade was buried, hilt-deep, in the man's chest. Behind him, the other competitor lay dead.

Sameen shoved the dead man off her so she could stand. He swayed on his feet, gulping air, skin glistening with sweat. The scimitar slipped from his fingers. His skin was darker since she had last seen him, his beard having grown in. She had never felt such joy at seeing his face, bruising and chaffing aside. Here was Sameen, a friend. She smiled so hard her lips cracked.

"Namali."

One word—one single word.

He said her name like a prayer.

Their eyes locked. The emotion in his gaze made her heart beat faster, and not because she had been running.

Namali looked around. The chaos had calmed. The daevas wandered aimlessly, as did the men. No sight of the gilded gates, the spires and domes.

The Lost City was gone.

Namali blinked to make sure she wasn't imagining things, yet the landscape remained deserted. "Where did it go?"

Sameen's throat worked. Flecks of blood spattered his face, evidence of all the men he had killed with a swift and fearless blade. She glanced down at her clothes, stained with the same dark red. In some places the cloth was black with it.

He said, roughly, "I don't know."

Legs trembling, she sank to the ground. It felt like the sand had turned into water, the world shifting and widening and coming apart beneath her feet. She did not know the Lost City could appear and vanish at will. How was she to find it again? What if she had squandered her only opportunity to save Sameen?

Sameen knelt beside her, jaw tight. After so many days alone, she found herself leaning into him, his strength. "What's wrong?" Tentatively, he curled his arm around her back.

She covered her face with her hands, for her veil was not enough. How could she possibly tell him what she had done?

"I hate the violence, too," he said, misinterpreting her silence, "but you do what you have to do to survive, to see the sun rise and set for another day."

In the Saraj, the fight for survival trumped everything else, but how did one move forward, knowing the past could potentially repeat itself? Knowing she could, and would, kill again?

"Do you want some water?" he asked.

Water. The man had asked for water.

When she didn't respond, Sameen slipped his hand into hers. It was all so very natural. "Come on. Let's get you out of the heat." He helped her stand and led her back to her daeva, which meandered in circles, around and around and around. Namali hadn't the energy to defend herself from the darkness, but luckily the beast seemed too distracted to attempt anything. After helping her onto its back, Sameen mounted his own demon. "I passed an oasis a few miles east, close to Farhan. We'll rest there."

Soon they reached a body of water surrounded by lush greenery, sunlight reflecting off its surface like a wide, flat mirror. Sameen tied their demons to a tree, where they curled up together, like brothers. He then sat Namali on the cool muddy bank, soaked a piece of cloth in the water, and placed it on her brow, two creases grooved on either side of his mouth. Her swollen cheek throbbed. She stared into the distance, dazed.

"Namali."

The mists faded from her eyes. There were trees. And birds.

Sameen's presence warmed her side, their shoulders nearly touching.

"A lot has happened this week," she murmured. "I'm not sure my body knows how to cope."

Sameen dipped his fingertips into the warm, murky pool, and ripples disturbed the quiet waters. His voice came low. "I was worried about you. I didn't know where you had gone."

"I'm fine, Sameen." It didn't sound like her, not at all. "I arrived here on my own, the same as you. You don't need to coddle me. I'm not a child."

A flush rose to his face. "I didn't mean . . . I wasn't—"

Seven hells. What was *wrong* with her? It wasn't his fault he cared. Under different circumstances she would have welcomed it, but after that ugly, wretched night, any concern scraped along her skin.

She focused on a point over his shoulder where the trough of two hills merged. "You were right before, back at the campsite. I am afraid."

"You don't have to—"

She raised a hand for his silence. Her voice was important, too. It had always been important. She just hadn't seen it. "It's all right."

His chin sank toward his chest in obvious remorse. "I shouldn't have said that. It was unfair to you."

"I'll admit it did . . . does . . . hurt." If she concentrated hard enough, she could still feel a tenderness in her heart where the blow had made contact. "I believe it's important to be honest with others, honest with yourself." She straightened, her demeanor hardening by slow degree. She hoped to never again reach that point, where the honesty hurt not because it had been spoken, but because she had avoided its face for so long. "But you were also wrong."

She didn't know where to start. They did not have time to discuss the seventeen years of her life. "When we met, I was already taking the steps necessary to overcoming that fear. It wasn't as if I had done nothing. Entering this race was a big step for me. I was trying my best. I really was."

"I know. I know you were."

"No, Sameen. You *don't* know." Her frustration began to shift in agitation. "You have no idea how hard it was to leave my father. I grew up thinking I could do nothing without him, that if I left Benahr, I would fail. For a long time, I believed that. But now I know it's not true."

"It sounds like you think I don't understand."

"I'm not asking you to understand." In truth, he never would, not in the way *she* did. "I'm just asking you to listen."

He jerked a nod in her direction. Not that she expected an apology, but it would have been nice. Namali sighed. She did not want to argue with Sameen. There were larger issues to address. "I met a man when we were separated. Elderly, and rather strange."

He lowered his shoulders from his ears. "Did he happen to pull things out of his beard?"

Namali barked a startling laugh. So she was not alone in her insanity. "I thought I was hallucinating."

Sameen's eyes crinkled at the corners like a leaf held to flame. "If you were hallucinating, then I was, too."

Namali snorted, a sound most unlady-like, and Sameen chuckled in response. Soon they were both laughing at the absurdity of the situation. "What did the man talk to you about?" she asked once her laughter was under control.

"The race. My . . . my home life." He didn't look at her as he said this.

"Is life at home difficult?"

He shrugged. "In some ways, yes."

"Because of your foot?"

Sameen grew still and sent her a slanting gaze, eyes unusually chilly. "No." He drew out the word. "It's unsurprising you would think that though." He snapped a twig off a nearby branch and dug it into the wet sand. "I guess, like you assumed about me before, this is something you will never understand."

Clearly, she had misspoken. They were both low on energy, strung tight from recent events. She learned in that moment she could be proud too, choosing to ignore her blunder rather than apologizing for the hurt she had caused, the impact. Slipping off her sandals, Namali dipped her feet into the earthy, tepid water. The oasis reflected back a girl with dark eyes and a wild recklessness shifting in their depths. A girl she no longer knew. "I saw a vision I think might be related to the race."

His back curled with a long, unspooling sigh, as if making an effort to let go of his anger. "What was it?"

Heart-wrenching in a way she couldn't explain. "There were two men in a white city. A city of bone. It was . . . lovely." And lonely. "One man wore a white robe, the other wore black."

He stared at her hard. "A black robe and a white robe?"

"Yes."

"You're sure?"

"I know what I saw."

"It might be the Lost City. It would make sense. Supposedly, that's where Mahurzda and the Demon King were born."

Was it true? Had she really seen the Good Lord and his foe? Darkness and light, shadow and sun. Doomed to fight for all eternity. It explained so much and yet so little, for while she knew of the myths and legends surrounding Malahadi culture, her knowledge was not comprehensive by any means.

Sameen shifted to face her more fully. "What else do you remember about the vision?"

"They were arguing." Her brow furrowed. Words that, had she been able to hear, would have battered the air with their spite. "Mahurzda said something about how the trees were all gone, and the Demon King mentioned a girl he loved."

"The story of Barandi."

"Who?"

He shook his head, indicating for her to continue. "I'll tell it to you sometime."

Namali eyed the waterskin. He handed it to her wordlessly. After drinking her fill, she went on. "The Demon King attacked Mahurzda, but Mahurzda killed him and cut out his heart." And wept as he did so. "Afterward, the Demon King came back to life."

"He came back to *life?*" He was staring at her. When a god struck down another god, their reign of immortality reached its end. "How?"

"I'm not sure, exactly." She shuddered from the memory of his empty eyes. Shuddered again because of what she was about to say, and how she still didn't understand it. Any of it. "One moment I was looking at him, and the next moment my palm was covering the hole in his chest. He woke up after that."

Again, that stare, though warier now.

Namali asked, "What do you think it means?"

He scratched his bearded cheek in thought. "It seems Mahurzda killed the Demon King specifically for his heart." The heart was where the soul resided, locked up tight within flesh and blood. "Taking the soul from the Demon King's body, having power over it . . ."

Namali remembered one of their very first conversations. The daevas, Sameen had said, were drawn to the Lost City. She hadn't paid much attention because she hadn't understood why, had assumed it was inherent. But what if it wasn't inherent? What if it was more?

The wheels of her mind were already turning, offering a glimpse into what was perhaps the dawn of the race's creation. "Mahurzda would want to prevent the Demon King's rise to power by any means necessary. But we also know a god's soul survives death, even when the body does not. Even after cutting out the heart, Mahurzda would not be able to destroy it. The only solution would be to make sure it's hidden in a place the Demon King couldn't reach."

"Yes," Sameen murmured behind the fingers pressed to his mouth. "And with the daevas drawn to the Lost City . . ."

They looked at one another simultaneously, and it clicked. The Demon King desired power. Without his heart, he was nothing. But there were these demons, these creatures whose existence lived and breathed darkness, and she imagined, in their servitude, a single, mindless purpose: to reach the Lost City in these thirty days. To find their master's soul.

"What happens when the daevas find the Demon King's

heart?" Sameen asked with gravity. "What happens when his soul is restored?"

She shook her head, not wanting to give life to the answer by speaking it aloud. Terrible, terrible things. The strangest variable, however, was the wish. If this was, in fact, the Demon King's purpose for the race, why offer such a prize to mortals when the daevas could reach the Lost City on their own? Unless there was a different role humans played she couldn't see?

"You still seem upset," Sameen said.

It went far, far deeper than that. "After I left the old man behind," she began, "I traveled by myself for a while." She didn't mention how terrible those days had been, how her despair almost made it impossible to go on. Even now, she didn't know if she had the strength. "I came across a man lying in the sand."

She stopped. It hurt to breathe. "There—there was a dagger s-stuck in his chest, but he was still alive."

A shadow fell across Sameen's face. His dear, sweet face.

He knew.

"What happened, Namali?" His whisper was the loudest thing she had ever heard.

The danger of words lay in knowing they could not be unsaid or unheard. Once she revealed her actions, he would know of her heart's slow and ugly decay.

"The darkness overcame me, and I . . . I sh-shoved the dagger into his chest harder." She covered her mouth with her hands on a broken sob, wanting nothing more than to curl up and rot. She was a hideous, disgusting thing. "I killed him. I wanted to watch him die."

The shock in his expression was unmistakable, and the horror.

Then she noticed his focus lock onto her hands, onto the cracked fingernails, which were sharp and elongated like claws, the darkening at her fingertips, palms, and wrists, as if they had been dipped in ink. "It . . . it wasn't you," he said, trying to convince her, convince them both. "It was the darkness. You're not that person."

But I am, Sameen. I am.

Sameen rubbed the back of his neck, darting a worried look in her direction. "It's been a long week. Why don't we head into town and find something to eat. We'll rest for tonight, then set out in the morning." His gaze met hers, searching. "Does that sound reasonable?"

No, it was not reasonable, but sometimes pretending was all she could do to keep going, to keep on living.

So she stood, feeling every bit of violence she'd experienced these past weeks seep into her bones as she followed Sameen over the bare, rocky ground. She was ancient, a piece of rock eroded by time and wind.

Her heart had never felt so heavy, and the land so still.

CHAPTER 15

FARHAN WAS A city of many names.

The Red City.

The Sacrificial City.

City of Blood.

It was a city chiseled from hard black stone, a city few dared to venture. Black mineral did not exist in Malahad, or anywhere she had heard of. The opaque structures gleamed as if having been pounded into a glaze. There were no windows. The doors were crude holes in the walls. It was clear this city had not been built, but made.

As she and Sameen led their daevas under a gleaming archway, people emerged from their dome-shaped dwellings to line the bare, narrow street. Chunks of rock protruded from the earth, and sunlight bounced off the reflective surfaces, forcing Namali to squint against the glare. It did not take long before the hair along her arms stood on end, a tinny voice shrieking in the back of her mind to run, quickly, quickly now. When she glanced down, her stomach dropped. The brick was stained an unsettling deep red.

She grabbed Sameen's arm to stop his progress forward. "I

think we should turn back." The sharp scent of rust tinged the air.

He pulled his attention from a tall, skinny post scarred with hundreds of notches. "I'll admit this is less of a welcome than I was expecting, but we *are* intruding on their home. They probably don't see many travelers."

Yes, because who in their right mind would ever want to come *here?* "I would feel safer if we went elsewhere."

"I'm not going to let anything happen to you." He tipped his chin down the road. "It shouldn't take long."

With reluctance, she resumed walking at Sameen's side, though more cautiously than before. The townspeople tracked their progress, eyes hard behind their painted masks. Unmoving in the doorways of their homes, aggression colored every line of their stances: rigid spines, knotted shoulders, feet planted flat and firm. Even the children watched them like something to be stepped on. Their bald, sweaty heads shone like brown orbs beneath the midday sun.

Namali stared straight ahead, cheeks burning. No one wore a single article of clothing save the masks, not even yirasafs or veils. "Why are the people here so . . . different?" she whispered. So much flesh exposed, and so little caring. What was this madness?

"I don't know," Sameen replied, trying not to gawk.

The sinking sensation in Namali's stomach surprised her. Of course Sameen would notice. With so many stunning young women present, she couldn't hope to compare. Their skin was smooth and unblemished, and so deep a brown it appeared almost black.

Namali shoved the emotion aside and walked faster, forcing him to jog to keep up. "Let's keep moving."

The city revealed a meager existence: no color, no laughter, no form of expression aside from the masks. The air crackled with aggression she didn't often encounter. In the sweltering heat, most people took refuge in what little shade the buildings provided. Children crowded around clusters of rocks, stacking them into various shapes. Old hags crouched on their front stoops, whittling branches into stakes while the men sparred beneath the burning sun, their sweat-drenched bodies moving in a bizarre, violent dance.

"Sameen, I *really* think we should turn back," she murmured. The copper stench was stronger now, scratching at her eyes.

"Where else would we go?" His hand hovered over the small of her back, yet didn't quite touch. "We need to resupply, and I'd feel safer sleeping in a town rather than out in the open."

Did he not *feel* that? The press of a hundred burning eyes; the suspicion billowing through the streets, trailing them; that fully saturated silence. She shuddered. If he did not feel the danger, then she must make him see it.

A splintering of wood. Namali turned, a strangled wheeze catching in her throat.

"What? What is it?" Sameen rushed in front of her, scanning for danger. Someone beat an oiled canvas steadily. The echo slipped through the dwellings. A weak, pulsing heart.

THUMP *thump.*

THUMP *thump.*

Namali fumbled for his sleeve. "There." She lifted a shaking hand.

Sameen swore.

They were three young children, knobby elbows and knees, and they were kneeling in a pool of blood. A dead animal had been tossed before them. Possibly a goat, but from this distance it was difficult to tell. Internal organs spilled from its severed abdomen, stinking in the heat, and the children—two girls and a boy—were ripping out its innards, lifting them to their mouths, gnawing on the raw flesh with dull, glazed eyes as blood smeared their chins.

Namali clapped a hand over her mouth, gagging. She had to turn away. She would. Except now one of the girls was digging her finger into the animal's eye socket, cooing something beneath her breath. The eye popped free and rolled on the ground, squishy and tender and—

Sameen stepped in front of her, cutting off her line of sight. "That's enough," he said.

She licked her cracked, salty lips. Touched her tongue to the tips of her pointed teeth.

Yes, perhaps it was.

A man, naked as the day he was born, stepped from a hidden doorway to block their path. His mask dripped red, with charcoal lines darkening the eye sockets. "You offend Mahurzda on this day." The mask muffled his words, but not the sharpness of them.

Namali shifted closer to Sameen, who said, "We don't want any trouble. Only food and shelter for the night. We have rubies to pay."

The man's eyes glittered like shiny black beetles. "You dare bring the Demon King's servants, his evil, into our home? Leave now if you value your traitorous lives."

"We only ask for your hospitality so we may rest safe," Sameen said. Either he wasn't afraid, or he hid his fear better than her. The people watched them through their masks, unblinking, still as stone. Living, breathing statues. "We'll be on our way tomorrow morning."

"We will not house you."

Before Namali considered otherwise, she stepped forward. "Why not?"

As if in some unspoken language, the crowd pressed in with their sweaty, naked bodies. She flinched, remembering the marketplace at Ahkbur, the groping hands and walls of musky skin. Their whispers crept along the ground, stinking of carrion.

She forced her attention back onto the man, but remained aware of the people outside her line of vision. "You would refuse us food and shelter? Is this what Mahurzda teaches us?"

The man sneered. "You think to speak of Mahurzda's teachings to me? You, who associate with the Demon King, tempted by his dark ways?" He stepped closer. Only six inches separated his unclothed body from hers. "Mahurzda grows angry."

Namali retreated a step, her confidence shriveling beneath the uncertainty of leaving this place unharmed. "If you send us away without food and water, we will die."

"Mahurzda does not protect the weak. Only the strong can do his bidding." He dipped his chin.

Instantly, a wall of masks surrounded them. Frozen faces and sneering mouths, red and black and black and red, blood and death and death and blood, the promise of both painted in slashing lines and heavy splatters. Namali stumbled back as the groping hands descended. Tugging, scratching, crawling over her skin like millions of insects. The demons growled, yanking on their bonds, and someone pulled on Namali's braid. She cried out and jerked free, into yet more awaiting hands.

Sameen's wide eyes cut to hers. "All right!" he shouted, curling one arm around her shoulder protectively and pulling her to his chest. "We'll leave."

The crowd parted. A low, thrilling chant trickled along the ground, building, building as the drum boomed, chasing Namali and Sameen through the streets. The voices descended into animalistic shrieks. They were mad. They were all mad here. Namali's robe caught around her ankles in her haste to flee, and she half-stumbled the last few feet to that initial black arch when a voice hissed to their right, "Girl."

In the shadowed niche between two buildings, a young woman shifted into the light. She wore no mask. Her head wasn't shaved. She also wore clothes—a dark blue robe and a yellow veil.

Namali lifted her eyebrows in question, and the woman gestured them over.

After checking to make sure they hadn't been followed, they trailed the woman down an alley. Once out of sight, the woman said, "I heard you were looking for food and shelter."

Namali and Sameen shared a look. "We were," Sameen answered slowly. He maneuvered his body slightly in front of Namali so she had to peek around his shoulder to see. "Who are you?"

The woman licked her lips. "You may call me Janu. I have food if you are hungry, and a place for you to rest." She jerked in response to a man shouting in the street, shrinking back into the gloom. "Follow me, quickly."

"Wait." Namali scrutinized her. She did not recall seeing this woman in the crowd. "How do we know we can trust you?"

The woman looked between them. "The people here are set in their ways. When I offer food and shelter to strangers, they scorn me, for they believe Mahurzda rejects those who seek help, rather than Mahurzda favors those who offer it. They look at me with my clothes and say I am hiding myself from the Good Lord, just as they see me without a mask and assume I am much too free in my identity." She stopped. "I will not force it upon you, but you will be safe in my home."

Namali looked to Sameen, and when he gave the smallest of nods, she turned back to the woman. "We accept."

"Good." She disappeared around the corner.

They gave chase, their daevas close behind, darting across the open street to another alley smelling of decomposed flesh. Left, right, left again around the buildings. Pieces of rock protruded from the austere homes, threatening to impale them at every turn. As they moved deeper into the city, all noise disappeared except for their feet slapping, hard and loud, against stone.

"Namali, listen to me." Sameen heaved the words, his limp more pronounced, but they kept running, not wanting to lose sight of the woman. "We can't know for sure if this woman is trustworthy or not, so stay close to me."

Namali steadied him when he tripped on a deep crack in the road. This was her friend, a drop of water amidst all this dust. She would be a fool to deny him. "I will."

They wound through a courtyard with the same shiny black

rock spearing from the ground. What appeared to be scorch marks blackened the brick streets, bold strokes etched of ash and soot. The woman glanced over her shoulder to make sure they still followed before darting down another street choked with decrepit homes and heaps of filth. Crumbling stone walls, roofs caving in. A thick stench of dung hung in the air.

Janu stopped in front of a squat building with a red cloth serving as a door. "Wait here." She disappeared inside while Namali and Sameen caught their breath. A few minutes later, she emerged. "You can tie the daevas to that post. No one will touch them."

They tied their demons to a lonely stone spear before removing their shoes at the woman's front door. Namali began to step inside when Sameen clasped her arm. "I'll go first."

She didn't know what to say, how to identify this feeling. It was fragile as a baby bird. It was lovely and brand new.

She had never noticed how *warm* his skin was before.

The low ceiling forced them to stoop. Janu fussed with a cloth hanging in the corner, probably to better conceal her sleeping area. The rest of her home contained a small fire, a few pillows, and a stack of dishes and bowls. It was small, yet cozy, and it made Namali yearn for home.

The woman cleared her throat and said, "Please, have a seat."

Exchanging glances, they settled on the plain mud floor. Sameen pressed his wide palms flat on the ground, as if welcoming its coolness. She wondered if this made him yearn for home, too.

Namali asked, "Will you get in trouble if someone finds out we're here?"

Janu didn't respond for several moments. Crouching near the hearth, she removed a clay bowl already warmed by the flames. "The people here do not like me because I refuse to follow their customs. They believe the daevas are evil, and maybe that is true, but they cannot change their demon nature any more than we can change our human nature. People here do not understand that." She glanced around the room for seemingly no particular reason. "But yes, I would get in trouble."

"How much trouble?"

She swallowed and tucked a strand of hair behind her ear with a trembling hand. Pushing up the long sleeves of her robe, Janu revealed the bloom of bruises on her deep brown skin, shocks of sickly green, acidic yellow.

Namali stifled a gasp. Sameen's face darkened.

"They stoned me two weeks ago." Her voice was strong, her chin lifted. They had not broken her. "I also have whipping scars on my back, burns on my chest."

"Why stay here if you are suffering?" Sameen demanded.

Janu spooned jelly into a shallow clay bowl and placed rice-stuffed grape leaves on top. Cut pieces of flatbread and poured water from a basin into two chipped cups, pushed the food and drinks toward them. She settled on the ground, legs crossed, hands resting on her knees. She did not speak.

Namali bit into the soft, slightly acidic grape leaf. She understood the woman's silence. Time to consider the question carefully, to piece your thoughts together, to think on your answer. Baba always said to wait and think. To be impeccable with your word.

Janu lifted her head. "It is not easy to leave what is familiar. Farhan is all I know. Do you think I have not considered leaving?"

"No amount of pride is worth this pain," Sameen said.

Shock flashed across Janu's face before a raw, broken laugh tore free. Namali, too, felt laughter swell in her chest, needing some way to release her blatant disbelief. Janu's situation was not about pride. No, pride had nothing to do with it.

Janu said as much. "Tell me, why does my fear of leaving have anything to do with pride? Are these"—she gestured to her bruises—"also a matter of pride?"

"I mean . . ." His throat worked, and Namali sensed his confusion. She hoped, for his sake, he was remembering their last conversation and tying the two threads together. "Couldn't you ask someone to help you?"

She met his look squarely. "You are a man. It is easy for you. But for me and your friend, things do not come as easily. We fight twice as hard to get half of what we deserve. If I asked for help, it would not come." Her entire body vibrated with turbulent emotion. "Pride is a luxury I cannot afford."

His attention slid between the two women. He opened his mouth, closed it.

Today, now, was a beginning. Privilege wore many masks, but Sameen could never again deny that being born a man lent a wider, freer worldview than a mother or daughter or sister or wife. She hoped this new and tentative self-awareness challenged him, broke down the world he knew and rebuilt it into something better, for that was how one came to grow.

"It appears," Sameen said, "there is still much for me to learn." His eyebrows drew inward. "I apologize for my rudeness."

For the first time, Janu's polite expression wavered. "You are forgiven." She gestured to the food before them. "Please, eat. You must be hungry."

"It's very good," Namali told him, dipping another grape leaf into the warm jelly. She chewed happily, relaxed and at ease with food warming her deprived belly.

His lips twitched. "It is, is it?"

Her gaze jumped to his, light from the hearth captured in the glow of his eyes, and Namali thought she had never seen a color so warm or so pure, the dilation of his pupils cradled in the inner ring of bronze. Her palms grew sweaty. Any possible response vanished in a puff of smoke. This close, she smelled the desert on him: hot, dusty, *alive*.

Namali bobbed her head, gulped her water. Except she momentarily forgot how to swallow and ended up choking and spewing it everywhere, coughing as Sameen thumped her on the back with an amused, "Someone's thirsty."

Her cheeks—no, her entire face—was aflame. Oh, how nice it would be to melt into the floor. If only Sameen did not have such a nice smile. "Just a little."

"Only a little?"

Her lips curved quite helplessly. The space between them was electric, and her heart pounded out a wild, thrilling beat. "Stop distracting me."

"Distracting you?" His eyes danced at the confession. She tried not to look at them, their warmth, but it was impossible. They positively glowed. "Whatever do you mean?"

Namali choked out a half-laugh. This slow, maddening dance was one she had never experienced before, and yet she wondered where it had been all her life. "You know what I mean."

"I'm quite sure I don't. Rather, it's *you* who distracts *me*."

Though her pulse surged at the unexpected delight, she tried to remain casual as she said, "I do not."

With their upper arms pressed close, the vibrations from Sameen's laughter traveled through her body. In the background, Janu puttered around her home, tidying up. "So if I were to tell you that when I look at you, I forget myself, forget that we are supposed to be enemies in this race, would you deny my claim?"

His expression softened a touch. "You," he murmured with absurd fondness, "are absolutely a distraction."

Ohhh no. This was a bad idea. A very bad idea. Because the way he looked at her . . .

Was the way she looked at him.

It was all one heaping, stinking mess, and she didn't know what to do about it. "Eat your food," she demanded.

"Yes, Grandmother," he replied in a mock serious tone.

Namali released a slow, silent breath. *Get a hold of yourself.* To give her hands something to do, she reached for her cup of water, only to realize it was empty. Sameen noticed and pushed his cup toward her.

"But you didn't have any," she protested.

That warm, slow smile sent her stomach fluttering. "Take it. I'll be fine."

Closing her eyes against a wave of dizziness, she sipped his water. Dehydration, exhaustion. The inevitable end bore down. The days were shorter and the nights were longer, and time was beginning to move more swiftly. Only sixteen days of the race remained. Sixteen, before the darkness came. Their plan remained: travel north, or wherever the daevas may lead them. But they must make haste.

With a sigh, Namali reached for another grape leaf.

Her fingers closed on air.

Sameen leaned in close. "Is everything all right?"

Her friend's question sounded far, far away. A bare wisp of sound. She held up her hands, frowning. *Strange.* A gray curtain shielded them from view.

"Namali?" Concern sharpened his voice.

She forced her lips to move, her tongue to shape the sluggish words. The world tilted dangerously, and she would have fallen into the fire were it not for the strong hands that caught her. "I . . . can't." There, that ought to fix things.

"Can't what? Can't eat? Can't speak?"

Namali faced him. By now he'd become a vague blur. "I can't . . . s-see." The words stumbled.

"What—" Then Sameen cursed. "It's happening to me, too."

She heard him struggle to his feet. "What did you do?" he demanded to the woman.

Namali's dulled senses softened Janu's sobs, rounding out their harsh tones to something close to an elegy. "I'm sorry. I'm so s-sorry. I wasn't—I couldn't—"

Sweat trickled coldly down her back, but it could not pull her from this strange and maddening floating sensation. "Sameen?"

No response, only the woman's sobs. Had she spoken the words aloud or merely thought them? The more her thoughts raced, the darker the room became, and now the light was gone, vanquished, and she suddenly remembered how she had gotten here, in this room, with ragged gasps splitting the air.

The woman had betrayed them. Had smiled while sliding a knife into their backs. Namali should have known better. She had allowed the woman's suffering to cloud her judgment. She had believed there could still be goodness and honesty in humanity.

Sameen pressed his large palm against hers, grounding her in a world slowly slipping away. She felt cocooned. "I'm here."

Sameen's voice, steady and sure. He was here. She was not alone.

Then she remembered no more.

CHAPTER 16

A PRICKLY RUG scratched Namali's back, tiny claws digging into her skin until her eyes flew open and darkness flooded in. For a moment, all was shade and gloom. The world rebuilt itself with painstaking slowness, made slower by the disorientation. Shadows unfurled at the edges of her vision like long, grasping fingers, and her breath expelled in one long hiss.

It was as if the night had swallowed her.

Her hands moved on either side of her, eventually touching cool, dry sand. Here was the familiar, the steady and calm. Her heartbeat slowed as her eyes gradually adjusted to the dim. It was mostly grays, but every passing minute brought more clarity. Whatever she thought dwelled in the corner curled up and went to sleep.

Namali sat up in the cramped, shadowy tent. The blankets were tangled around her legs, damp, perfumed with an aroma that caused her stomach to clench. Sweet. Overwhelming. She knew this scent. Of this she was certain. But she could not remember from where.

The bustle of the city was gone, replaced by the desert's quiet.

Namali touched a trembling hand to her head, trying to recall what had happened, but the acute throbbing behind her eyes made it difficult. She and Sameen had been eating in the woman's dwelling in the city of black stone. The woman had eased their worries with warm food and hospitality, a glimpse into her suffering. It had been genuine. It had reached across the divide and touched them both in a rare show of humanity. But then came the fog, and Sameen's voice, reassuring her she was not alone.

Except she was alone.

From outside the tent, laughter peaked and died. She froze, the tang of metal flooding her mouth. Her first instinct, still, was to do nothing. But it was no longer an option. In order to escape alive, she must push forward with ferocity and unwavering belief. She had done it before. She could do it again.

Unfolding herself from the ground, Namali crept to the edge of the tent and lifted the flap a few inches. Ten feet away, three men sat around a small campfire. The fat one, with his flattened nose and piggish eyes, the sand spinning hawk-man, and beside him, slightly more separate from the others, the merchant. He stared into the fire, a cup curled in one hand. The last time she'd seen him he was clean and impeccably groomed, but now food stained his robe, his beard a tangle of weeds, his hair long like a vagrant's.

The fat man glanced at the tent, and she ducked out of sight, nausea sliding into her belly. The Trade Winds should have blown the merchant hundreds of miles south. How in Mahurzda's name had he managed to catch up? The woman from Farhan must have cut a deal with the merchant. Janu, with her bruises and scars and lies. Namali assumed, while she and Sameen ate the woman's drugged food, that the merchant lay concealed behind the fabric blocking off her sleeping area, waiting. It explained why the woman had sought them out.

The wind moaned like a hoard of dying men, rustling the tent flaps. Namali shivered, trying not to think about her skin tightening over bones, the tent blocking all light except for whatever managed to slither through the cracks, the all-encompassing feeling of isolation. She needed a plan, fast, but these walls trapped her here, and she knew nothing except that the merchant sat ten feet away, perhaps waiting until he was sufficiently drunk before barging into the tent and claiming what he deemed rightfully his. The heat of his hands pawing at her, the press of his mouth. The thought turned her stomach, and she shifted, trying to find a more comfortable position, when a hard object dug into her hip. She brushed aside the cloth, brought the slim metal strip into the sliver of moonlight, where it gleamed with such promise she very nearly laughed.

Her dagger.

Gripping the hilt eased the tension coiling inside of her. The men had forgotten to check her for weapons. Their mistake, her gain. She would not squander this opportunity. Nothing mattered but staying alive.

She peeked outside once more. As the two men conversed, the merchant remained apart. He swallowed his drink, going through the motions, not appearing to taste it. Behind him, three horses and a pack camel dozed, huddled close for warmth. She would have to wait for them to fall asleep before stealing a mount, but until then, the conversation might give her a clue to their location.

So she settled back to watch. And wait.

The hawk-man stared into the flames. Firelight glinted in his cold eyes, unable to warm them. "I'll be happy when this blasted race is over so I can return home to my wife."

His companion snorted and took a swig from his cup. "When your wife finds out you've been sleeping with the neighbor, you—"

A sandy rope shot out to constrict the fat man's neck, lifting him into the air. "And who's going to tell her?" the sand spinner hissed. "Not you, surely?"

His hands scrabbled at the tightening noose, eyes bulging. "I swear . . . on Mahurzda's . . . life." His face flushed hot with blood, deep as a bruise. "Please."

Sneering, the hawk-man released his hold, but only after a warning shake. "Pathetic."

The fat man heaved on the ground, the only sound besides the crackling fire. The merchant leaned back in the sand and moved his bare feet closer to the flames as he gazed into the distance, eyes unfocused.

"What of the girl?" the hawk-man asked. "It's been over an hour."

"She's fine," said the merchant. "There's nowhere for her to go."

The fat man scratched his large, lumpy head. He did not seem very bright. "Seems to me like the girl is more trouble than she's worth. You could have any woman you want. Why this one? She might not even be attractive beneath her veil."

Namali fingered the fabric concealing the lower half of her face, and her grip tightened on the dagger. Whatever lay behind her veil wouldn't make one difference whatsoever in escaping.

"I have my reasons for marrying her, and none of them is your business," the merchant spat, chucking his cup at the fat man. He then stood. "I'm going to check on Namali."

A bead of sweat slid down her spine, the droplet rolling over her skin maddeningly slow. She darted to the rear of the tent, searching for a way out, already knowing there was none. Her hands skimmed over the thick canvas. Not a hole or crack in sight. Maybe if she crawled under the walls—

The tent flaps burst open, light from the fire briefly outlining his silhouette. The merchant halted in surprise. "You're awake."

The wall brushed her back, preventing her escape. In this corner, she felt small, but the merchant seemed smaller too, less of a god and more of a man, battered and bruised like the rest of them. She was glad of it. Not that she believed the merchant to be a bad person, but he needed to learn that sometimes, a *no* really meant just that: *no.*

"Namali . . ." He sighed, at a loss for words. "I don't want to do this anymore. I'm tired. You're tired. All I want is for us to return to Benahr so we can be married."

Though she trembled, the word rang with unwavering conviction. "No." It grew easier every time.

The merchant cleared his throat. "I don't think I'm explaining myself very well," he said, "so let me make this clearer for you. We are returning to Benahr, where we will be married. You have nowhere to run to. Your game has reached its end."

Hidden behind her back, Namali's knuckles whitened around the knife. The man had hardened since their previous meeting, repressed emotion—anger, grief—having risen free of the murk. In his eyes, she had dragged him, for weeks, across hell: desolation and long days in the saddle with no reward. But she had not made this decision for him. He had chosen this path, and Namali would not be guilted for actions *he* had made. She was not a dog to whip into submission, not a jewel to be bought or sold. "Where's Sameen?" *Please let him be unhurt.*

His lips thinned, though his response was pleasant enough. "Your little friend? Probably passed out on that woman's floor."

Those eyes, savage yet polite, belonged here, in the dark. And maybe a part of her did too, hidden in the corners, the crevices, the areas where light refused to penetrate. Maybe the dark revealed people's true selves, for here in the dark lay uncertainty, but also power. And it was power Namali wielded when she next spoke. "I want you to tell me something, and I want the truth."

Her boldness caught him by surprise. "I'm listening."

To not ask was to not know, and that was worse than learning the truth. "Why do you want to marry me?"

Everything about him tightened, as if readying himself for a blow. "Do you even care about what I have to say, or are you just trying to buy time so you can think of a way to escape?"

"Does it make a difference?"

A muscle fluttered in his jaw. Tense, relaxed, still. "Caring makes all the difference in the world."

To the merchant, of course caring made all the difference. Those with something to prove to others always cared. Namali had nothing to prove to others—only to herself. "Then yes. I care."

He was transformed. His face cleared, his shoulders straightened, his mouth thawed into something resembling a smile. Suffering had aged him ten years. So much like her father. "Not that it's any of your concern, but I was married once."

Married? She wiped her face of emotion. "Why aren't you married anymore?"

At once, his grief clouded the air. A complex web twisted with misery and resentment, a tangled mass of regret. It was no less real than her own grief. "She died," he said. "A long time ago."

Unbelievably, a pang shot through her heart. She didn't want this, didn't want a reason to empathize when he had chased her and chased her, when she did not want to be caught. "I'm sorry to hear that."

Crossing his arms, he studied her. It wasn't difficult to imagine him as the man he once was: happy.

"You remind me of her."

She didn't know how to respond to that. "Oh."

"You . . . you have the same eyes."

Namali tried to step back, but could not. "I'm sure you loved your wife very much, but sharing similar features does not mean we're the same person."

He didn't hear her. He was somewhere far off, caught in memory's tightly woven threads. "You remind me so much of Bijala."

Enough, Bijala!

And now . . . now she understood. "But I'm not. I'm not like her." How to make him understand? She was her own person. "And I'm sorry, but I don't want to marry you." Another step toward the exit. "So if you could please let me go—"

"Wait." He reached for her.

Her hand shot out, the blade slicing into the merchant's upper arm, and he howled, his face twisted with every sort of pain.

Namali bolted from the tent.

"Namali!" he roared.

His accomplices sprang to their feet, drinks sloshing over their cups as the merchant burst outside. "Stop her!"

Namali tripped on the hem of her robe in the uneven sand, falling on her hands and knees. The dagger flew out of her grip. A second later she lurched to her feet, abandoning the weapon, and charged through the night, one foot in front of the other, her attention locked straight ahead, the merchant's shouts driving her forward, away. Her lungs seared. The disorienting effects of the drug lingered.

Almost there.

She managed to grab the reins of a chestnut mare when someone yanked her back. Screaming, Namali twisted around to scratch and bite. She clawed at the hawk-man's nose, breaking skin, and then at his neck, his chest, anywhere she could reach. If she was going down, he was too. Blood called for blood.

The hawk-man squawked, fumbling for a hold. He finally managed to pin her arms to her sides.

"Bring her here," the merchant gritted as the fat man bandaged his wound. The fire's glow sharpened his haggard appearance.

The hawk-man half-dragged Namali to the fire. He shoved her to her knees and held her down, his fingers digging into her skin hard enough to bruise. Flames licked at the hem of her robe, the scent of burning hair strong. The world tilted dangerously, its edges dipped in red.

The merchant held up her dagger, firelight reflecting off the dull metal. His hand trembled as he asked, "Do you know what becomes of thieves?"

An eye for an eye. Something of hers for something of his. Swallowing, she replied, "I didn't steal anything from you." Smoke scratched the back of her throat, stung her eyes. If he was referring to the bracelet, that had been a gift, given freely.

He looked like he was trying very hard not to cry. "You did, Namali, whether you realize it or not." He glanced at the larger man, who placed a flat, solid block of wood in front of her knees.

Her heart raced faster than it had ever raced before, each beat tumbling into the next. It looked like a cutting board. "What's that?"

"Your punishment," the merchant whispered. "A thief deserves his—or her—punishment."

A large, heavy stone sank into her stomach, settling at the bottom. Maybe he *was* referring to the bracelet. But if that were the case, why not take it back? She made no effort to hide it. "I'm not a thief."

"Yes, Namali." His voice was so, so soft. "You are."

The hawk-man wrapped his bony fingers around her wrist and forced her palm flat on the smooth wooden block, fingers splayed. Tremors shuddered through her body. She tried wrenching free, but the man pressed down with his weight until her bones ground together and her nerves shrieked in pain. She stopped struggling.

"What did I steal?" she quavered. Hairline cracks crept inside of her. They fractured, and creaked, and eased apart. She would stop this somehow, stop this insanity, but without a weapon, she was helpless.

"Perhaps the most valuable thing I own." He traced the cold

metal tip of the blade around her fingers. Up, then down, then up again. The blade scraped along her skin. Once he reached her thumb, he traced the opposite way. "Can you guess?"

She tracked the weapon. "N-no."

When he'd spoken of his dead wife, she thought there had been warmth in his gaze, maybe even kindness. But something else replaced it now—a mad, terrifying light.

"My reputation," he said. "You stomped all over it for the world to see. I am Hazil Abdu, the richest man in Malahad. What right do you have to refuse my offer of marriage? What right do you have to run away and humiliate me?" His voice cracked on the last word.

The hawk-man shook her. "Answer him!"

Something snapped in Namali, as clean and pure as shattering glass. She strained against her captor, a cold blackness swelling in her chest. They could take her hands and they could take her dagger, but never again would she be silenced. "Right?" she snarled with ferocity. "I have every right. My purpose in life is not to please you." Her struggles intensified, vision blurred by furious tears. "You can't force someone to love you. Why are you doing this? Why do you treat people this way?"

His eyes widened at her obvious fangs, the shadows blotting beneath her cheeks, a frenzy. The merchant stared at her with borderline revulsion, and she thought, perhaps, it was for the first time. "Because," he said softly, "it's the only way I know how."

Namali slumped over with a small sob, spent. The merchant wore a most convincing mask, but inside, he was as confused and trapped as she. She wanted to hate him. He deserved her hatred. But she couldn't. Grief had broken him in the cruelest way.

The night grew darker. The wind sighed, blowing every which way, whispering the desert's secrets in her ear. It sounded like weeping.

The merchant shifted closer. "Will you come back to Benahr with me?"

She kept her eyes on the dying embers, for it was the only light in this cold, desolate place. "Never."

He studied her hand on the wooden block with a childlike expression. "I don't want to hurt you, Namali. You can change your mind. There's still time. We can be married. We can be happy together. Isn't that what you want?"

Numbness blanketed her. *Happy*. It sounded like a lie. Nothing felt real. Not the sand beneath her, not the prickling of her skin, not even her own body. She was a shattered cup hastily glued back together, waiting for the next gust of wind to break her again.

His breathing grew ragged. "You're making me do this," he said, tears trickling into his beard. It was painful to watch. "I don't know how else to keep you here, to prove we belong together. You understand, don't you?"

"You don't have to do this," she whispered, lifting her head. "I know it feels like nothing will ever get better, but it will. I promise you."

He was long past the point of listening. "You're a thief, Namali. You know the price of stealing." The merchant nodded to his men. "Hold her down."

She came awake then, screaming, thrashing, begging for mercy she would not find from this empty, broken man.

The merchant raised his arm, the weapon gripped tightly. The blade descended.

It felt like minutes passed, but it was truly only a second, time enough for a quick blink, a sharp intake of breath. The blade hit the wooden block, severing flesh, and Namali's screams tore into the night.

CHAPTER 17

SHE WAS SINKING. Sinking into warm, deep waters. They tugged her down to a murky, gray existence, where shadows twined around her leaden limbs, absorbing into her skin until they disappeared below the surface. A faint light pierced through the haze but could not penetrate the water's deep.

Memories drifted, hollowed-out, senseless. A bird fluttering its wings behind the bars of a gilded cage. A girl peering into a body of water, her reflection depicting black, soulless eyes and a mouthful of broken teeth. And yet another of a smiling young man, telling her to hold on, hold on.

Wanting to wake coaxed her nearer to the surface, but darkness held her under. *Not yet,* it whispered. The agony grew steadily worse. Flames licked through her fingers, a shredding heat that ripped open her skin and ate away flesh. It consumed her. Burrowed into her bones until she knew nothing but fire and blindness and the deep ache of loss. If she'd had the ability to scream, she would have, but she could barely move, could barely breathe, and after struggling for so long against the pain, Namali let it carry her away. If this was death, she didn't care anymore.

•••

An uneven rocking motion coaxed Namali awake, her drowsiness lifting as if it were dew burned away with the dawn. Peeling her crusted eyelids apart, she met a night so thick and dark it was like velvet drapes tumbling down from the heavens. It was true what people said: the world appeared most beautiful on the eve of death. She had always wondered how someone knew their time was at its end, but it must feel similar to how she felt now, as if some core spark or energy had depleted itself. Cool air brushed her feverish skin, and a musky odor wafted from the springy fur tickling her cheek, her neck bent at an awkward angle. She was tied to the back of a camel.

They had left the sand behind in exchange for hard-baked earth and pillars of rock. Weeds and stunted trees pushed between the cracks, clinging to the rock faces with their spindly roots. A few desert blooms unfurled their petals in the splash of moonlight, but otherwise it was a bland, colorless landscape: flat, gray, ruthlessly battered by the wind. The Great Southern Constellation—a line of ancient Malahadi kings—guided them south.

As Namali shifted to relieve the pressure of the rope cutting into her stomach, she accidentally bumped her right hand against the camel's back.

The world flared red.

Her breath exploded in the quiet. Her muscles spasmed from trying to remain as still as possible, the hot flush of blood pulsing in her ears, beneath her clammy skin. She remembered, years and years ago, a sudden fall, the snap of broken bone, but this pain incinerated that memory into ash. A howl unrolled along her tongue and struck the back of her clenched teeth, over and over. White fire seared the edges of her consciousness, making it impossible to forget what the merchant had done. How, in his selfish cruelty, her pleadings had fallen on deaf ears. Bringing her hand close, she studied the thick, blackened bandage. A sickly-sweet odor oozed from the goopy cloth.

Namali turned away from the gruesome sight. If he did not intend to seek out a healer, then what? Time was bleeding out. She clung to these frayed threads of awareness and would do so until her last breath, wishing things had ended differently, in laughter instead of screams, in togetherness instead of isolation. If she could not win this race, then the victory belonged to Sameen. He would fight. He would fight to the end. What a shame she would most likely not be there to witness it.

Slumping onto the camel's hump, Namali closed her eyes and willed the blaze in her hand away. There was nothing left to do except wait for the dawn.

The hawk-man jerked the camel forward. "Move it," he barked, and the animal picked up the pace with a disgruntled groan, small stones clattering beneath its splayed hooves. The shift and sigh of rustling cloth came from Namali's left side. She thought it might be the fat man, but the faint tinkle of bells indicated it was the merchant.

"I'd like to tell you men something."

"If you're going to complain about how we didn't clean your wound well enough—"

"It's not that."

A surprised silence descended. The men's uncertainty feathered the air around them, causing Namali to tense and the horses to shy away. It was not the harshness of the merchant's voice that ensnared her, but rather the lack of it. All those prickled edges, suddenly worn smooth.

"I want to thank you both for aiding me. I didn't think the journey would take this long or be this arduous, but your help has been invaluable. You will be handsomely rewarded when we return home."

Namali shivered from the sweat pooling between her breasts. What she wouldn't give for a glass of chilled water, fresh from an ice house. The heat was slowly, quietly smothering her.

A half-laugh. "There must be something wrong with me. What kind of person severs his betrothed's finger?" Namali felt, rather than saw, the shake of his head. "She deserved it though. I mean, after everything I did for her, for her father, and she spits in my face."

"I'm sure the girl—"

"Her name is Bijala," he snapped.

Namali swore her heart pounded loud enough for them to hear. The merchant couldn't remember the difference between her and his deceased wife, and maybe . . . maybe he didn't want to.

The horses' hooves scraped along the ground. "Hazil, Bijala died two years ago."

For one agonizing moment, the merchant did not speak. "That's right. Namali. I meant Namali."

A lizard scurried across their path as they squeezed through a tumble of boulders, sinking into shadow before emerging once more into moonlight. Namali caught sight of a small stone house built into the rubble, an empty doorway leading to shelter, warmth. There could be water hidden behind its walls, fresh grain left from a generous traveler, or medicine to slow the infection poisoning her body. The men, however, were too preoccupied to notice its presence.

"Do you think she's right?"

"Who?"

"Namali. Do you think she's right about how I treat people?"

The fat man said, "You're being too hard on yourself. What happened with Bijala was unfortunate, but give it time. The girl may come around."

Did they think her so foolish, so desperate for a sense of belonging, that she would settle for less than she deserved? *Never.* Her life belonged to no one but herself. Did they not see? His love was soaked in blood.

"I can't give it time," the merchant said, and now the words poured from his mouth, full of ache. "I waited too long to tell Bijala how I felt, and it was too late. The raiders . . . they took her from me." He was breathing deep, ragged breaths. "I didn't even get to say goodbye."

"Hazil—"

"I remember our wedding day. She had flowers in her hair, blue ones and red ones, and her eyes sparked with fire. She was the loveliest thing I had ever seen.

"When she looked at me in the months after we were married, I knew she loved me. But I never said the words to her. I was too afraid." His voice softened, and Namali strained to hear the last of his confession. "She was too beautiful, too kind, for the likes of me."

"Hazil." The hawk-man's voice. "I know you loved Bijala, but she's gone. You are chasing a ghost. She's never coming back."

The horse reared as if the merchant jerked hard on the reins. His voice whipped out, low and cutting. "You dare?"

"I only meant—"

"This discussion is over."

"Hazil—"

"I said," he spat, "this discussion is over." He took a deep breath, released it. They had reached a clearing nestled against the base of a plateau. "We'll stop here for tonight."

Namali squeezed her eyes shut while the men dismounted and set up camp. Pebbles shifted around their feet, and sticks clacked together as they raised the tents. During this time, Namali remained motionless, keeping her breathing slow and even. Asleep—she was asleep.

The sharp scent of cloves enveloped her a moment before someone loosened the rope around her waist. As soon as strong arms lifted her from the camel, starlight burst behind her closed eyes, tears leaking down her cheeks. Crushed between their bodies, her wounded hand throbbed. But it reminded her she was alive.

The tent flap whooshed open, and the merchant laid her on a mat, surprisingly gentle. After covering her with a heavy blanket, he brushed a strand of hair away from her temple, hand lingering. "Forgive me," he said. And as his footsteps died away, sleep pulled her under once more.

CHAPTER 18

A HAND CLAPPED over Namali's mouth, tearing her from a restless sleep. A dark shape loomed, filling the small space, stealing her air. She tensed, unable to breathe or fight or flee, because it was the merchant, he was here, intent on claiming her at last. A scream built in her throat.

And a pair of warm brown eyes stopped it.

Namali sagged against the bedroll, blinking back the sting of tears. The shock and relief was so profound she could only stare, slack-jawed, at this miracle, this prayer she had believed would never be answered, a man whose smile warmed her like a fire in the hearth. Her heart felt full. "Sameen." Even when he removed his hand, the warmth on her lips remained.

Tenderly, he brushed her cheek through her grimy veil. His face was haggard with fatigue. "Are you hurt?"

At once, sweat broke out on her hairline as she realized what he had done. He was here, with her, in the merchant's tent. The merchant, who sat right outside. The merchant, who made her scream and thought it love. "You have to get out of here," she said, not daring to raise her voice above a murmur. The sound expanded in the closeness, stretching and softening until darkness ate away at it. "If the merchant finds you—"

"He's sleeping now, him and his men." He still touched her cheek. It was the only part of her that felt warm. "I drugged them. They won't wake for a few hours at least."

"You *drugged* them? How?"

"I added some sleeping powder to their wine while they were busy setting up camp."

Namali pushed herself into a sitting position, hissing out a breath as pain knived through her hand. It took a few moments for the world to stop swaying.

His attention snapped to her bandage, the smoke-like tendrils curling around her wrappings. He moved as if to reach for her injury, yet pulled back. "What happened to you? Did they do this? Did those men hurt you?" He clenched his jaw, eyes fierce.

Namali cradled her mutilated hand against her chest. Not that she blamed him for what happened, as it was not *he* who had harmed her, but she wondered if events would have unfolded differently had they left Farhan immediately upon her request to leave. Would she still be a whole person? Would he? The seed of resentment made it difficult to move past. "How did you find me?"

If Sameen noticed her avoidance of the question, he did not pressure her to respond. A gray tinge washed out his coloring, the blue smudges sinking in atop his cheekbones more vibrant in contrast. "When I woke up, you were gone. The woman said she didn't know where the merchant had taken you, so I left the city and made for Khalmad. I figured he'd stop there for supplies. That's where I bought the sleeping powder." His hands curled, very slowly, into fists. "It wasn't until the third day when I saw them traveling outside the city. They . . . they had slung you over the back of a camel. Like a sack of grain." Choked, furious. "I honestly thought you were dead, but I followed them anyway." His gaze locked onto hers, quiet and full of secrets. "And then I found you."

Her mouth quivered in a watery smile. He had come back.

For her.

In some ways, it felt like being born. In others, it felt like dying. She could experience this wonder, but only as long as she allowed herself to dream. Whatever existed between them would die on the thirtieth day, and with this wound, she might not even survive that long. In truth, she wanted nothing more than to sleep.

Sameen peeked through the tent flaps, saying, "We need to get you somewhere safe." He grabbed her unwounded hand and tugged, yet stopped when she made no move to follow. "What are you doing?"

His hand was warm, strong, comforting. And not hers to hold.

Namali extracted her grip. "I can't let you risk your life for me. If the merchant finds out you helped me escape, there's a very real chance he might kill you." And she did *not* want the responsibility of another death. Would it be a quick demise, a sudden stab to the heart? Or would he remove Sameen piece by piece?

He stared at her in disbelief. "What are you saying?"

"I'm saying . . ." She pushed out the words through a half-closed throat. "I'm saying you should go on without me."

"What? No, I won't—"

"If I leave him again, he'll do something worse to me, and you. I don't want to see him hurt you. At least this way one of us has a chance at winning."

"Namali, listen to yourself." His words were low and fierce. "This is what the merchant wants. He wants power over you. He wants you to give up, to believe leaving him isn't worth the effort." He touched her shoulders, her arms, checking for injury while simultaneously trying to comfort. "You're not thinking straight."

"I *am* thinking straight."

Blowing out a breath, he dropped his hands, then changed his mind and rubbed them over his face. "The drugging set us back a few days, but if we leave now, we can make up the time. The race is already more than half gone. Come with me. *Please.*"

She bit her lip, worrying it as she had worried this thought, until it bore the scrapes and dents of too much use. This door had remained shut between them, out of uncertainty, out of fear, but no longer. "What's going to happen when we reach the Lost City? What if, somehow, we arrive there first? Who will get the wish?"

Sameen's expression was pained. "This isn't the time—"

"You can't tell me you haven't thought of it." She had, far too much. The worst part was she had seen this storm brewing far in the distance, had done nothing to avoid being drawn into its whirling, burning center. She was starved for affection, starved for friendship. Who could blame her? Sameen was kind, and loyal, and caring, and strong. She had learned much about herself in his company, as he inspired her to test the boundaries she had set for herself. But she could not have both. She could not have Sameen's friendship and also win.

Bowing his head, he replied, "No, I . . . I have. This hasn't been easy for me either." His shoulders slumped. "I don't know what the future holds. I don't even know if we'll survive to the end of the race. But I do know I care about you, and I won't leave you here to make a choice you will regret. When the time comes for us to address the wish, then we will. I promise you, we will figure something out. Not now though. Now, we need to put as much distance as we can between ourselves and these men."

Her weighted eyelids fluttered, then slid shut. She was sinking into a vast pit, one so deep she could not see the light. They were so close to reaching the end. It ached, this wanting. "No matter where I go," she slurred, "the merchant will never stop looking for me."

"What do *you* want? That's the important question. If you want to marry him, then fine." His voice broke with heightened emotion. "But I don't think you do. I think he has you running scared, and when someone has you running scared, you need to stop and fight, for your future, for your *dreams*. I have seen so much growth in you in this short period of time. Don't throw it away. Where's that courage I first saw, when you woke up to a stranger and went for your knife?"

Namali's chin wobbled at all she was feeling, which her heart could not possibly contain. "That wasn't courage," she admitted through a watery chuckle. "That was fear."

He smiled into her eyes just as she smiled into his. "You cannot have courage without fear."

This was true. Look at all she had done. Namali could hardly believe it. It must be some other girl with a death wish who had come this far, but no, it was her strength, her determination, her resilience that propelled her legs forward even when they threatened to buckle. The merchant's actions, however, had shaken her. She said, with unashamed honesty, "I don't know if I can do this alone."

Sameen slipped his hand into her uninjured one, as if it belonged there. "Then what about with a friend?"

Namali looked around the small, cramped tent. The air was close and stale. She couldn't see what lay beyond the shadow and the dark, for its walls kept her from the light. This would be her life: alone, wishing for a door leading elsewhere, somewhere free.

She squeezed his fingers. "Let's go."

The men were passed out around the flickering embers. Namali struggled to keep up with Sameen as they fled from camp, veering toward higher ground. She stumbled on weak, watery legs, unable to catch her breath no matter how much she heaved. Their daevas stood silent in the night, shadow upon shadow, tied to the merchant's camel with a thick, sturdy rope. The camel regarded the demons in disinterest and huffed a breath as if bored.

"Can you ride?" He began securing the supply packs to the camel's back.

The world was tilting and swirling before her eyes, never still. "I don't think so." A chill leached into her legs, seizing the muscles and tendons and bones.

"We'll ride together then." Grabbing a handful of his daeva's fur, he pulled himself onto its back before offering her a hand.

Namali stared at his outstretched palm for longer than was necessary. She should take it. It was an almost instinctive compulsion, to press their hands together, skin to skin. Except she couldn't comprehend why he wanted to help, what hidden motive guided him. Tentacles were probing her mind, tearing down the barriers she'd built, and the longer she studied his face, the more he looked like an enemy.

A helpless sound slipped out. "It's happening again. You have to help me." And then her back hunched, molded by hands cold and unseen, and her eyes melted into wide flat pools.

Namali.

The boy's lips formed her name, but there was thunder in her ears and static sparking like veins of the hottest, whitest lightning. She stood in a strange, desiccated land that reminded her, vividly, of a place having once held the color green. And this land would lead her to a city carved of bone, a prize that would restore her master to power, return him to his divine right to rule.

Darkness embraced her like an old friend. Canines crowded her mouth with their bulk, and her body shook and shook until her knees buckled, and when she heard that faint, fluttering pulse beneath the boy's delicate skin, she fought the need to tear into his throat, to peel the skin from his body and drape it across her shoulders, a warm and well-earned coat.

Look at me.

She looked, but saw nothing but a black void.

It was the hardest thing she had ever done, pulling herself back from that void, from whatever coiled in its depths. She glimpsed its churning heart, the leak of ichor and slime. There was no need to hesitate. She was not fully dark, but she was nearly there, and to be free of this mad, mad world, she must reveal her true self. But her master wanted her to wait. It was not yet time.

The boy's hand dropped from her cheek to curl around her shoulder. Fingers elongated into claws, puncturing skin.

She screamed and wrenched free of the darkness, shuddering, gasping, aching. The boy snarled at her, baring black fangs.

"Sameen!" She screamed again as the claws sank deeper into flesh, lashing out to club him on the chin. At once, the claws disappeared, and the fangs, and the cold, fathomless eyes. Slowly, Sameen returned to himself. Horrified, sickened, but gloriously human.

"Namali." He covered his face with his hands, every inch of him trembling. "I'm so sorry. I couldn't . . . I wasn't strong enough."

Shakily, she smoothed the wrinkles from her robe. Sameen could have killed her. He could have, but he didn't. It was she who killed a man with darkness in her heart. She whose mind was twisting, darkening. "It's not your fault."

His nod was not entirely convincing. "You're right. It's . . . it's the daeva's fault."

"No, it's not."

Sameen studied her, brows creeping inward, and Namali shut her mouth as the implication sank in. Where had those words come from? Of course it was the daeva's fault. It was evil. It served the Demon King.

But she remembered its eyes after ending that man's life. Its blue gaze had held such turmoil she couldn't help but step into its pull and comfort it. Confusion, desperation—those weren't the emotions of a monster.

"Should we go?" His words were distant.

Her right side burned with fire, and her fangs poked into her bottom lip, and her skin slithered and pulsed with chilled breath, but it could be worse. It could always be worse. "Please."

Sameen looked like he wanted to say more, but instead he nodded. They couldn't waste any more time.

With the adrenaline wearing off, her fatigue returned at full force. Sameen lifted her onto the daeva and settled behind her, where she slumped in his arms gratefully. He scanned the sky for the Great Northern Constellation, and, wheeling the daeva around, they headed north with the other two creatures in tow.

•••

Namali must have fallen asleep because Sameen was suddenly shaking her awake, dragging her from a numb and mindless existence. She didn't want to leave, but he was insistent. As soon as she pried her bleary eyes open, she wished she hadn't. A brutal headache stabbed at her temple. "What?" she snapped.

He led the daeva at a trot through heaping piles of rust-colored sand. The sky had lightened with near-dawn. No shadows yet, but they would come with the rising sun. To the west grew spare, spindly trees and bushes starved for water in what appeared to be a former watering hole, the image distorted by heat waves wavering in the distance. "We're stopping soon."

Her burdens wrapped around her. That dreamless world awaited. "Let me sleep," she rasped, slumping more heavily against him.

"Namali!" He pulled the demon to a halt, and she whimpered from the agony radiating through her shoulder at the movement. He froze. "I forgot about your injuries." She felt him shift behind her, as if he were scanning the area for danger. "I'm going to help you down."

Taking care not to jostle her injuries, Sameen lowered Namali to the sand. He pressed a palm to her forehead. Searingly hot, blessedly cold. "You're burning up. Give me your hand."

His words evaporated into mist. She couldn't be sure they were real, so faint was his voice, but she did as he asked, tipping her face toward the sky so the light burned red behind her closed eyelids. *Red.* She had not chosen this color. Rather, it had chosen her.

Namali was long past the point of resistance, long past denial. She thought she had pulled herself back from the edge of that abyss, but it was her own mistake. She was falling, and the only question remaining was when she would hit the bottom of the deepest depths of this personal hell.

As he unwrapped the bandage, a strong, sickly odor wafted in the air. He inhaled sharply.

She looked at him, wanting to know the truth. "It's bad, isn't it?"

Clenching his jaw, he replied, "The infection has spread to your bloodstream."

She heard what he did not say. Unless they found a healer, she would be dead in a matter of hours.

Everything about Sameen tightened, ready to explode at the slightest trigger. "The merchant did this to you, didn't he?" When she didn't answer, he demanded, "Why?"

Namali studied her wounded hand, a gruesome mass of dark, sticky blood, oozing yellow puss, and flaps of mutilated skin. A bloody stump took the place where her pinky had been. "He was angry," she said thickly. Even talking required energy she didn't have. "He was angry because I ran away when I learned I was to marry him. He said I ruined his reputation." She looked east.

Dawn's pale fingers began to creep across the Saraj, bringing with it strange dark clouds. "So he punished me."

Sameen curled his lip in obvious disgust. "I would never treat a woman that way."

A hard smile cut into her mouth. As a man, Sameen could never understand her position. Did the sun know anything other than light? The moon of darkness? "In some ways, you do."

The unexpected barb jabbed, just as she expected it to. "Forgive me if I somehow forgot the time I laid a hand on a woman . . . oh yes, that's because I never did." He glared, a bit of hurt seeping through. "You must know I would never raise a hand to you, or to any innocent person, be it man, woman, or child. I know I *did* hurt you." He gestured to the congealed blood covering her shoulder from where his claws had punctured. "But that was the demon's influence, not mine."

So what did that say about her, when for Namali, they were one and the same?

"I'm not speaking from a physical standpoint," she said, pitching her voice to carry as the wind picked up. Life, after all, was often subtle. "Remember the woman from Farhan?"

"You mean the one who drugged us? How could I forget."

"Do you remember what she said? That women fight twice as hard to get half of what we deserve? Well, it's true. When I lived in Benahr, I believed myself powerless. It's why I entered the race. I thought the wish was the only way I could free myself of the marriage."

"I mean, was it really that bad for you?"

"Sameen." Her expression closed with the gravity of his implications. "Oppression is very real. And it's not always obvious.

Even something as small as invalidating my feelings—" She shot him a pointed look. "—which, really, isn't that small, forces me into a cycle that's extremely difficult to break. In many ways, I'm grateful for the Demon Race, because if it did not exist, if I hadn't decided to leave, I would not have fully recognized the unfairness of my situation." Because in all the days and all the years of her life, Namali had never asked herself, *Why not?* But now she knew. The answer lay in the glint of metal, a warm wash of firelight, a blade cleaving through air and flesh. *Her* flesh.

The beginning of Sameen's self-awareness evolved slowly: doubt, confusion, respect, distress, shame. He fought to tuck in a length of fabric the wind had pulled free from his yirasaf. "I don't mean—"

"I know." She touched his sleeve. "We are the products of our environment. It will never be perfect, but I believe it can be better, with time and effort on everyone's part."

He finished adjusting his yirasaf, lifting his head. "I'll do better. I *want* to do better." A softness touched his eyes. "You're a good person, Namali. The type of person the world needs more of. And you . . . you deserve so much better than a man who can't recognize how lucky he is to be marrying you."

Her heart swelled, so much that it became difficult to draw breath. Truly, that's all she had ever wanted—to feel like she *mattered* to someone.

"Many thanks," Namali murmured. She gazed east again. The clouds loomed closer now, and the air smelled different. More alive. "Can I have some water?"

Sameen was up before she finished the question. He crouched

at her side and offered his waterskin. "Can you eat anything?" he wondered, a deep crease worrying his brow.

She lifted the container to her mouth with a shaky hand, dribbling water down her chin in the process. "I don't think my stomach can handle it."

Sameen nodded in understanding. "When I was in Khalmad, I spoke with some artisan jewelers who claimed they saw the Lost City near Zeminir. Supposedly, a *lot* of people saw it. They say it's been there for close to a week now."

"Do you think . . . ?"

"No one has reached it, as far as I know."

There was still time. "Then we need to head straight for Zeminir. No more stops. We have enough supplies to last us until the end of the race . . ." Her attention kept returning to the clouds. Even as the sun rose, the world dimmed with an eerie gray light.

He followed her gaze. And froze.

The sudden shift in his demeanor sent her on high alert. "What's wrong? Did they find us?" So soon?

It was almost as if a part of Sameen had shut down, giving itself over to a mechanical quality, one that did not require thought, only action as he stood in one liquid movement and said, in a strange inflectionless tone, "We need to get to a town." Without warning, he scooped her up, practically threw her onto the daeva. Namali swayed. A hot gust slapped against her, plastering her robe to her body and tearing at her hair. The binding still lay on the ground. "My bandage—"

The wind tossed it away before Sameen could reach for it, and the sight of her bandage blowing out of range sent cold dread sloshing in her stomach. She looked at the horizon with different eyes. The massive clouds stretched from the red-gold floor to the lavender ceiling. They cloaked the weakened sun.

Sameen wheeled the demons and the camel west, in the opposite direction of the clouds. Then they were riding the wind itself, hurtling for a town they could not see. The beast plowed through the sand, trying to pick up speed, every lunge jerking through her sickly body with abrupt force, and in the presence of this mammoth phenomenon, she felt her own mortality, the fragility of her human body, weak, so *weak*. The camel brayed in distress. It could barely keep up.

"Is that—?"

"Sand hawk!" he shouted in her ear.

Her head whipped around. Yes, she saw it now. Not clouds at all, but huge mounds of sand racing toward them with sickening velocity, a churning storm rimmed in hard crimson, a dark devouring wall ripping apart the land and leaving it in ruin. The hawk beat its immense wings far above, hidden by the force of its own destructive nature. Whole towns and cities had been lost to these storms. "Can we get back to where we were a few hours before? With the boulders?" The rock faces would provide safety, shelter.

"Not unless we want to go through the storm."

Again, she looked behind them. A wall of red haze swamped the land, the curtain billowing, reaching out to touch. "Go faster!"

"The camel's too slow." Both daevas strained in an effort to haul the camel's weight while the storm crashed and moaned its rage behind them, grasping at their legs as they rode the crest of the descending wave.

Ducking her head from the wind, Namali prayed for shelter, prayed for time, something to protect them from the winds strong enough to bury them, the sand deadly enough to flay the skin from their bones. And maybe Mahurzda did hear her. Maybe he wanted to see her succeed, for when Namali glanced up, a black dot appeared on the horizon.

Refuge.

"I think that's a town!" Sand twisted and churned, a thick, impenetrable cloud of chaffing particles that clogged her eyes, her nose, her mouth. She couldn't hear, couldn't see, only felt Sameen's arms around her waist, grounding her. They had to keep going. If they didn't reach the town in time—

Ahead, the dark speck wavered, then vanished completely.

The sandstorm had swallowed them up.

CHAPTER 19

A POWERFUL GUST ripped Namali from the daeva. Screaming, she hit the ground, her wounded hand crushed under her body, pain obliterating her shredded nerves. She vomited on the ever-moving dunes. The wave had overtaken them, sucked them into its ferocious center, but when Namali lifted her head dizzily, half-delirious with exhaustion, she realized there was no *them*. There was her, and the sand and the storm, and little light to see.

Namali wiped her mouth and struggled to her feet, using one arm to block her face from the worst of the storm's might. Another burst of wind sent her lurching sideways. "Sameen!" she cried, and choked on dry, dusty air.

The wind howled in answer. No, not the wind, the *world*. Not a howl, but a thunder in the earth, a roar that blasted outward in waves of sound and set the air to trembling, the vibrations sinking into her pelvis, into her teeth, the force of the eruption building in pressure and power and tossing her back as it reached its peak. Namali screamed as the earth screamed. The earth, which could not shield itself from this upheaval, a story doomed to end in decimation. She could barely see beyond the dark, tumultuous curtain, the swirling mass of debris.

She was alone.

Namali began to shake. The wind was tearing at her hair and tearing at her robe and tearing at her face and veil with its claws and she couldn't think beyond the conflicting battle between her head and her heart, to search for Sameen or stay. There was no direction. There was no clarity, no time. She had no food, no water, no shelter. Sameen had the supplies. Sameen had the daevas. He had . . . everything.

The next gust plowed into her back, launching her forward. She went down. The sand was already burying her, encasing her legs and moving toward her waist, but the sick rush of fear pushed her upright, where she stumbled blindly onward in search of her friend. Through slitted eyes, Namali scanned her surroundings, seeking a shadowy form. She did not know how much time had passed since her initial fall. Her worst fear was not death, but a missed opportunity to say goodbye. The distress sent her running in a random direction, shouting his name. She could not say goodbye if he was lost to her, and she was not ready to say goodbye. They had barely said hello.

But then she turned. His head was tucked low, his back to her, silhouette wavering from the shifting air—a tree sprouting from the earth. Namali lurched forward and grabbed his arm, and Sameen whipped around, pressing her face against his wide chest, one large hand cupping the back of her head. His heartbeat echoed like a drum in her ear. "We need to find shelter!" His other hand clutched the demon's reins.

Namali squeezed her eyes shut against the horror. No shelter existed except for Sameen's arms. The wind wailed at the top of its lungs, filling her head with a high keening, while the storm sucked the oxygen from the air and left her gasping. The sun was gone, swallowed up along with everything else. It was possible they'd never see it again.

As one, they sank onto their knees. Sameen's grip on her tightened. "Namali . . . I don't know what to do. The storm . . ." His voice died as a pitch cleaved the air. The purest, highest, longest note, poised on a brink, ringing. A beam of white light tunneling into her soul.

The camel brayed in distress from the hawk's cry, and it triggered a memory from long ago: Baba returning from his travels, face grave from the death of a friend. They had left with one camel each, and he had returned alone, empty-handed. *You do what you can to survive.*

Namali touched her mouth to Sameen's ear and screamed, "We can use the camel's hide for shelter!"

Nodding, he towed her toward the animal, using his body as a shield. The wind pummeled them, shoving them back two steps for every one step forward. The blast of sand scraped her skin raw. She gripped Sameen's fingers tightly enough to feel the creak of his bones.

The camel came into focus, curled up against the storm with its head tucked into its chest, and the world pulsed around Namali in one large wave, sharpening her awareness. A wash of cold swept through her. It looked so small lying on the ground, fighting to stay alive. Small and helpless and weak. The daevas watched, almost expectant, as Sameen drew a dagger from his belt.

"Wait." Something called to her. Something that had waited until this moment, this perfect moment, before making itself known. "Give me the dagger."

Sameen squinted through the agitation. She couldn't see his expression very well, but it *felt* like hesitation, unease. "I don't think—"

"The dagger," she growled. "Now."

The moment the hilt touched her palm, Namali sank the blade deep into the animal's heaving neck and yanked it across in one fatal incision. Blood spattered, filling her pocketed hollows. She hated herself for wanting this, *needing* this. *She* was small, and helpless. *She* was weak. The creature's death breathed life into her shriveling soul.

She sliced through the tough hide into the soft underbelly. Sawed away its insides, flinging the organs aside as she went. The carcass gaped: a warm, wet cavern.

"Get in!"

Namali crawled into the body cavity one-handed, Sameen right behind her. Cramming into the hollow together, they pulled down the flap of skin so it blocked out the worst of the wind and sand. Her legs were crushed against her chest with Sameen twisted in the same position, one hand holding the rope attached to the daevas outside. Namali gagged from the stench and switched to breathing through her mouth. Their harsh panting crashed in the dark, enclosed space.

"Are you all right?" Sameen asked, shifting so his arm pressed against hers.

Blood dripped from the ridged walls of the carcass onto her shoulders. She hardly felt it, hardly felt anything. The cold had receded, leaving behind a spreading numbness. She recalled the dagger in her hand, its heavy weight, and how, when it came to ending a life, there had been no weight at all. "I don't know."

Going into the race, she had taken care to guard herself against things wanting to harm her, but she had never considered the idea of becoming a danger to herself. She had never believed herself to be the enemy.

Am I all right?

Was *broken* a synonym for *all right?* Or how about *possessed?* She was a lost and shattered girl, and she was certainly not all right.

"It's a part of me," she whispered. "I don't know how to make it stop."

"We'll . . . we'll fix this," he reassured. But she heard the quaver in his voice, the shallow ripple of fear.

Then she started to cry.

It seemed as if nothing would ever be right again. The merchant could not be stopped, or the darkness, or her feelings for Sameen. And it made her feel so much worse. She never wanted to give Sameen a reason to fear her, but this was not the first time she had seen its seedy underbelly. And she wasn't supposed to care. The more she cared, the harder it would be when they reached the Lost City, if they reached it at all. One winner, one wish.

"I know—"

"Don't say it," she hissed, whipping her head around. Sameen watched her as he would a wounded animal, a savage, a monster. He knew the truth of her, for she was all of those things. "Don't tell me everything is going to be fine. Don't tell me it's not my fault that—that this evil lies inside of me. Just . . . don't." She did not want to hear more lies. She did not want to hear him at all. His gaze flared in mounting anger. "I wasn't going to say that." She wished he would stop watching her. Those eyes saw too much, even in the near-dark. "Yes, you were."

"No," he said, "I wasn't."

"I see the way you look at me sometimes." As if he couldn't quite believe a girl like her would know intimately of death. "It's only a matter of time before you leave. I'm not the person I was. I'm not that naïve girl anymore." A part of her sensed the unfairness of the accusation. She was too far gone, too deep into the transition, however, to pull back. "But it's better this way. This is how I'm going to win." She could hate what she had become while also recognizing she would not have made it this far without the change. "I know you look at me and see something monstrous, something—"

"Seven hells, will you *stop*? Yes, the change scares me, confuses me, but I'm not going to abandon you, and I wasn't going to say everything was fine before, because it's not. It's not fine. But I can listen if you need to talk. I can try to understand."

"How could you possibly understand how hard this has been for me? I don't see the darkness overtaking you. I don't see you changing because of it." She pointed to her teeth, hand trembling. "They're getting pointier. And look." She drew up her sleeves. Burning black veins dominated her forearms like overgrown weeds, tangling around her wrists to end in shadowy fingers, nails curved and elongated into claws. "You don't know what it's like," she whispered.

"What don't I know? Struggle?" He spat the words as if they

were poison. "Maybe the darkness doesn't affect me as much as you, but you forget I know hardship more than anyone." He stabbed a finger at his foot. "You think I don't know what it's like to fight against the world? To work twice as hard as everyone else just to prove I can do things half as well? I do. I really do. So don't think you're the only one out there struggling. Everyone is fighting their own battles—"

"I only meant—"

"Let me speak!"

His fury was so startling her mouth snapped shut. He had never shouted at her before. A crimson tear dropped from the cavity's ceiling onto her robe, where it was absorbed.

Her eyes had adjusted to the gloom enough to make out Sameen scrubbing his hands over his face. "I'm sorry for snapping at you. I know this journey hasn't been easy for you, but you have to understand this hasn't been easy for me either. Believe it or not, it's not always about you."

She did not look at him. She looked at the carcass walls, the shadowed indentations between the camel's ribs. Mouth tight, she ran a finger over the slippery white bones. There had been a heart here at one point, caged within the hollow structure, but now there was nothing.

"I never asked you to come back for me," she said coldly. "Leave, if you think I'm so much of a burden."

His sigh slipped into a humorless laugh, the carcass clogging with the heat of their breath. "I never said you were. You're twisting my words around."

"What am I supposed to think? I told you to leave me with the merchant, but you wouldn't listen." Outside their shelter, the storm raged and raged. She let its anger feed her own, let it feed the bottomless pit that had become her. "It would have made your life easier."

Sameen turned his head, his face a vague smudge. Lowering his voice, he asked, "Do you honestly think I would have let you stay with that man? Is that the type of person you think I am?"

Her cheeks burned, and tears clouded her vision. When would she stop pushing him away? "I know nothing about you," she said, but it was a lie. She had never known someone so well besides her mother.

Jaw clenched, he turned away. "Fair enough."

But she wasn't done. "Why do you stay with me when I keep holding you back?"

"You're not holding me back."

"Yes, I am. You lost three days going after me, and you're still here."

He lashed out. "Is it so wrong for me to care for you? To want to protect you?"

"I'm not your responsibility."

He flinched hard, withdrawing into himself. "No," he said softly. "I guess you're not."

Turning away, Namali shifted to lay on her side. Her heart hurt. She tried to curl into a tighter ball, tucking her legs close to her body so they wouldn't touch Sameen, but it was impossible. Their bodies filled every inch of space.

Sameen shook her shoulder. "Don't fall asleep."

She brushed him off. "Leave me alone. I'm tired."

"I know, but you have to stay awake until we reach a healer."

The town was miles away, and the storm could last hours, days.

He couldn't expect her to remain awake for that long, but she said, "Fine." If only to stop him from worrying.

For a long time, they didn't speak. The air clouded with their breath. The things she had said, the things he had said, the spite behind the words, the pain. There were truths and there were lies, and they all twisted together until she couldn't tell one from the other.

The silence was so unbearably heavy.

Was Sameen right? In her efforts to fight the Demon King's influence, had she grown selfish, blind to others' feelings? *You don't understand.* She assumed that of him more often than she was comfortable admitting. And it was unfair. It was unfair because in doing so, she invalidated his opinion simply because they, as people, were different. How hypocritical. Petty. Narrow-minded. Arrogant—

She stopped, tucking her chin to her chest. Dragging herself down would not lift Sameen up. He was right. This journey was not solely hers, and in her determination to reclaim her life, she had stripped Sameen's experience of value, believing it did not, could not, belong to him as well. The error was hers. But she vowed to do better.

Softly, Namali said, "Can I ask you something?" But what she really meant was, *I'm sorry.*

His palm came to rest on her back, and the tension deflated somewhat. "Anything." But it sounded like, *I forgive you.*

Turning back around, she asked, "Could you tell me a story?" She needed to hear one now, with the sandstorm raging beyond the thin carcass walls and their future so uncertain. When her mother had been alive, she'd read Namali tales of far-off places, of adventure and heroics and deceit. They'd been small gifts of hope, feeding her desire for more.

A smile touched his mouth, and her heart warmed in response at having put it there. His mouth was made for smiling. "I think I can do that."

He shifted position, trying to stretch his legs out in the cramped, putrid space, then sighed and gave up. Blood trickled down the slickened walls of their shelter. It pooled around their legs, mingling with the shadows.

In a soft voice, she suggested, "It might be more comfortable if I leaned back against you. It would allow you to stretch out more, since you're taller than me."

Their eyes met for a span of one heartbeat, then two. His warm and forgiving, hers shy and wary.

Avoiding each other's gaze, they shifted to a more comfortable position inside the camel. Namali settled her back against Sameen's chest, his long legs stretched out on either side of her. She struggled to relax. His body was warm and firm and coated in sand. Strong.

Sameen cleared his throat when the silence had stretched on for too long. "So. A story."

If she turned her head, she could hear his heartbeat. It was thrumming as fast as her own.

"Do you have a preference?"

So many possibilities. The king who hid the moons. The girl with the serpent's eyes. All of them, however, reminded her of Mama, and she thought it was time, perhaps, to hear something new, something focusing on the future rather than the past.

"Surprise me," Namali said, settling in the curve of his arms.

So Sameen's voice filled the cramped space, taking her

someplace safe, someplace only for them as he said, "This is the story of a boy who loved a girl. This is the story of how the Saraj came to be."

CHAPTER 20

LONG AGO, BEFORE desert covered the land, there was forest all around. Great massive trees skimming the sky; flowers bright and plentiful; flat bands of water carving through a landscape lush and green—things no longer present in Malahad.

Among the clouds lay the celestial kingdom of Alamir. It was a peaceful kingdom, a gentle kingdom. The inhabitants were of sun and sky and rain. They rode great colorful birds, traveling far and wide in search of delicious fruits. Their ruler, Mahurzda, awoke the sun at dawn with his powerful staff and laid it to rest at dusk. His daughter, Barandi, brought rain to the lands. It was this way for a long time.

But far below the earth's surface dwelled another kingdom: Iyazka. Whereas Alamir burned with light and happiness, Iyazka teemed with sadness, misery, and hate. The people lived in fear of their dictator, Mahurzda's exiled brother, who was known to all as the Demon King. Envy for his beloved brother had transformed the Demon King into someone unsettled and confused. He yearned for acceptance, understanding, yet these things eluded him, happiness most of all.

Every year, on the eve of the longest night, the gateway between the kingdoms would open, and the people of Alamir and Iyazka joined together on earth for a merry time of dancing, drinking, and celebration. Usually, the Demon King remained in his kingdom on this day, wanting to avoid the hatred and hostility, yet one particular year, after a few glasses of wine, he gathered his courage and climbed above ground to join the festivities. But it was as he had feared. When the beautiful people of Alamir noticed his presence, they shunned him, believing his heart to be too evil, too dark for the likes of them.

Fleeing the celebration, the Demon King hid deep in the forest in a quiet grove, where no one would come looking for him. For hours, he cried. He cried so hard and for so long his eyes were swollen, and he nearly missed the snap of a breaking branch nearby.

He turned. He saw . . . an apparition, or what he thought to be one, for he had never seen such beauty. She was tall, slender as a reed. Long blue hair framed a pair of kind, curious eyes, as dark as her skin. She seemed familiar.

"There is so much happiness at the festival," said the girl, "yet there is such sadness in you. Why?"

The Demon King bowed his head against the song of her voice. There was no music in Iyazka, but if there had been, he thought her voice would be even more beautiful than that. "You would not understand."

"How could you know if I would understand or not if we have never met?"

"I should not have come here," he growled, cheeks hot from the humiliation of being caught in a vulnerable position. "People look at me and see darkness, despair. They see where I come from, not who I am. I am not loved. I am hated and feared—" He stopped. "That's why I stay below ground, so no one will have to suffer my presence."

The girl tilted her lovely head. Her eyes crinkled as if amused. "I do not see darkness when I look at you."

He paused, his self-loathing giving way to confusion. "Then what do you see?"

"Someone misunderstood."

The Demon King averted his gaze, swiping the dampness from his face. "I don't want your pity."

The girl watched him for a moment before saying, somewhat hopeful, "You could always return to the festival with me."

"I would not be welcome there."

Her sigh soothed him like the gentlest of winds. "I believe you're wrong, but it is your choice. I will not force you."

The Demon King lifted his head as she retreated through the dappled woods. "Wait." She turned. "What is your name?"

She smiled. A true smile, radiant as the sun. "Barandi."

The Demon King was struck by sudden loss. His exile had ostracized him from a young age, a decision he had been forced into simply by being born an illegitimate son. This girl was his niece—his half-brother's daughter, whom he had never met. Technically, he was forbidden to interact with his family. But the strange lightness in his chest would not leave, even after the girl had returned to the festival alone. In the few minutes he'd spoken with her, he had felt . . . happy.

So that night he devised a plan. Under the cover of darkness, he returned to the celebration, drugged her wine, and stole her away to Iyazka so she could bring him happiness for all eternity. The next morning, Barandi awoke, frightened and lying in a strange, dim room. When she asked where she was and what had happened, the Demon King approached her side. "You are home now, my queen"

The girl began to cry. "I beg of you, return me to my family. Without the sun, I will die. Without my rain, all the plants and animals in Malahad will perish."

The Demon King did not listen. Here was someone who brought him joy, who made his world a little less bleak. Why should he give up this small gift of peace after being denied it for so long? "I am sorry, Barandi, but you belong with me now."

Weeks passed, then months, yet Barandi did not leave her room. The food brought by the servants remained untouched outside her door. Generally, the Demon King left her alone, thinking she would come to her senses and join him in celebration of their union. But after nearly six months of her absence, his patience had reached its end.

Late one morning, the Demon King barged down the hall and pounded on her bedroom door. When no one answered, he pushed it open and stepped inside. The sight of his queen stole his breath. Barandi was rail thin. The blacks of her eyes had dulled to muddy brown, and her hair, once a vibrant blue, had leached into a sallow, watery gray. She lay curled on her bed, barely breathing.

He rushed to her side. Ran a finger down her cheek. "Barandi." Her skin was like ice.

She turned her head with great effort. "I need sunlight . . . or

I will die. Do not force me here. You cannot make me love you by doing this."

Something tightened in his chest, an emotion utterly new to him. He fought the urge to crush it. "There has to be another way. I can't . . . I can't lose you."

"You will . . . if you do not free me." Her face tightened with a spasm of pain. "Please."

The Demon King pressed the heels of his palms to his eyes, unable to witness Barandi's suffering. In his heart, he knew what he must do. She was not his to keep. And though she was the only person to ever show him true kindness, to keep her here in the dark, hidden among the shadows, she would surely die.

So he decided to let her go.

With firm but gentle hands, he carried her above ground. The sun blazed, and the sky was a blue quilt with white clouds stitched in. But there were no trees, or flowers, or streams. Barandi had been absent for so long that every living organism had died from lack of rain. Malahad had transformed into desert. Mahurzda's creation was destroyed.

Laying the girl on the sand, the Demon King stepped back to wait. It didn't take long.

Sunlight absorbed into her skin. Color bloomed high on her cheeks. Her hair darkened to deep, deep blue, and the clouds dissipated from her eyes, leaving behind shining black pupils. She had been born and remade with the sun, and stood strong and healthy once more.

His shoulders drooped.

"Why such sadness?" she asked.

"Once you leave, I will be alone again." He looked into the distance. "My brother will come after me for what I did."

She laid her cool palm against his cheek. "I will speak with my father about this misunderstanding. But know that you are no longer alone, Demon King, for I am with you. In here." Touching the area above his heart, she leaned forward to kiss his cheek. Then she turned to leave.

"Wait." He stepped forward, hand outstretched. Tears slid down his cheeks. "Will I ever see you again?"

Barandi wore a sad smile. "I have much rain to give the earth, for I have been gone a long time, but I will try and visit you when I can." She peered around the desert, a place that no longer held life, and her eyes welled with tears. "There will never again be rivers running through Malahad. This is what comes of stealing things that do not belong to you." With those parting words, she floated upward, swift and graceful as a feather, soon disappearing into the clouds.

Heartbroken, the Demon King returned to Iyazka. He spent his days weeping, his nights staring into empty space, hope slowly dwindling as he awaited her. And he dwindled too, alone under the crush of earth, unable to eat or sleep or dream. Only months later did something startle him from his trance-like state: a soft pitter patter on the earth.

Quickly, he climbed above ground to meet the rumble of angry gray skies. Lightning flashed. The sky cracked open. And as the rains fell over the Saraj, the Demon King felt peace in his heart, for he knew Barandi had returned to him.

•••

Silence filled the space where Sameen's voice had moments ago, heavy with the weight of thoughts unspoken. Namali, curled into a ball against his chest, murmured, "I've never heard that story before."

He brushed a strand of hair from her sweaty face. "I suppose that's because most people find the idea of the Demon King falling in love a bit uncomfortable, considering who he is."

And who was he, exactly? Namali had never pondered this question, for she, like many of the Malahadi, grew up loathing Mahurzda's foe, yet without any reason as to why. In the stories, the Demon King unleashed chaos among the realms. Yet Mahurzda was not wholly pure either. The Good Lord, who sent famine, war, and suffering onto the world. The Good Lord, who watched his half-brother pace in his cage beneath the earth, and did nothing. So was the Demon King truly a symbol of hate?

Or a symbol of truth?

"I wonder . . . If the Demon King had not been driven from the celebration, if the people of Alamir had smiled and welcomed him into their space . . . I wonder how different life would be." Would there be no daevas, no race? Would he and Mahurzda have greeted one another as brothers in the Lost City, rather than having fought as enemies?

"I didn't mean to upset you."

"I'm not upset." But wetness coated her cheeks, sticky with salt. She didn't even remember crying. "At least, not about the story."

It was about more than the story. It was about her, and Sameen, and his arms embracing, holding her close, and the steady beat of his heart, and how these things filled her in a way she'd never been filled before. It was about the solar eclipse looming closer each day, the knowledge that her time with Sameen would end. It was about life, and death. Love, and loss. It was about returning to an empty life.

Taking a breath, Namali said, "Listening to you tell that story reminded me of my mother."

Outside, the wind died. "Is she . . . gone?"

A lump caught in her throat. Gone was too kind a word to describe the emptiness of someone who used to be, and now was not. "Yes."

His chest rose and fell, touching her back and retreating. "How long?"

In many ways, too long. In others, not long enough. Namali felt herself opening to him. It was not like this in the beginning, when their bond was merely one of convenience. But as with all things, change had made its mark. This was real. She *wanted* to let him in. It was a deep and vast relief.

"She died three years ago," Namali said. "I was fourteen. My father never truly got over it." And how could he, when every time he looked at his daughter it was into the face of his dead wife?

"What do you remember about her?"

The question caught her off guard. More surprisingly, it warmed a part of her that had grown cold. Remembrance did not always have to be steeped in pain. It could be a comfort, too. "I remember she was kind. And she could make my father laugh like no other." Often, she would fall asleep to the sound of her parents giggling in the sitting room. "She was born in Ilaramad, but she wasn't happy there, so she left. Traveled alone, then met my father in Ahkbur. She was brave in that way. Choosing a path that would best bring her happiness."

Sameen tightened his hold, his chin propped on top of her head. "She sounds lovely."

"She was."

"I don't know what else to say except I'm sorry."

There was nothing else *to* say. It was enough. "I'm proud to be her daughter. My mother saw the potential in me when no one else did. I will always be grateful for that." Frowning, she examined the claws protruding from her fingertips in the faint light slipping into their shelter, the way her skin expanded and contracted with shadow as if breathing. She grimaced and dropped her hands with a dark laugh. "If only she could see me now."

"When my father passed, I took over the role of both father and brother when I still needed guidance of my own. And I'll be honest. I hated it," he bit out, his hand curving around her unwounded shoulder. Despite the hard words, his grip was gentle. Like his heart. "I never had time to grieve, and I started to resent my brothers, my mother, for putting all this pressure on me to provide."

He was trembling. Namali wondered if he noticed. "You were just a child."

"I know, but I was old enough to be considered a man, too. And then something . . . happened. There was nothing I could do." Frustration gnawed at his confession. "After my brother—" He swallowed.

She vaguely recalled he had three of them. Or maybe she'd made that up. Her eyelids drooped, half-closed. She couldn't remember the last time she had a decent meal, a decent rest. "Which brother?"

"Mirza."

The youngest one. The eight-year-old. "What happened to him?"

Her hair stirred with his exhale, and he said, "Honestly, I'd rather not talk about it."

Namali wanted to know him, wanted to know everything about him, but in the end, she didn't ask Sameen to elaborate. She would take whatever he chose to give, even if it wasn't enough. "I hope he's . . . all right," she mumbled. Her chin drooped, touching her chest. Suddenly speaking became a chore.

He shook her shoulder. "Namali."

She stirred. His voice sounded distant. "Hm?"

"Don't fall asleep."

"I was just resting."

"You have to stay awake until we find a healer."

The darkness pooled around her, cool and blissful, but she knew he was right. If she fell asleep, she would likely not wake up. With a groan, Namali opened her eyes.

That's when she realized they were already open.

Trembling, she reached out a hand. Blood slicked across her fingers, made her flinch as the darkness grew darker, vaster, deeper. The damp air gathered close. The swelling black seemed to swallow that, too. "I can't see."

"That's because your eyes are closed."

"No, I can't *see*, Sameen." Her voice cracked, crumbling into tiny pieces and raining down. "It's black. Everything is black." The light had vanished, leaving the intense rush of decay in her nostrils and the dead, eerie silence outside. There was no beginning and no end, only a crushing sense of hopelessness. Her breath shuddered in and out. Her heart squeezed in a tight fist. Scrabbling at the rough fabric, Namali tried to loosen her robe, but her fingers couldn't seem to work. "My chest," she choked out. Was this what dying felt like? Panicked and alone?

Tension rolled off Sameen in waves. She counted his heartbeats—one, two. She thought she might faint in the space between his exhalations, thought she might die in the belly of the camel she had slaughtered. Then he yanked her from the carcass to where the sunlight warmed her fevered skin. She didn't need eyes to know the storm had passed. The world was completely still.

"Hold on," he said, and swept her into his arms. He lifted her onto the demon, threw himself behind her, and kicked the beast into a sprint. They ran. Over sand, beneath sun and sky. The wind dried out her sightless eyes while Sameen's arm, banded around her waist, kept her seated as the daeva's gait jerked her forward and backward, the other not far behind. Her hands, which were beginning to turn numb, shook too hard to grip anything.

"Stay with me, Namali," he said in her ear. "Stay with me."

Namali slumped against Sameen's chest, her strength leaking out like sand slipping through a sieve. She wanted to stay, she did, but something else called her name, whispering promises of a life without suffering. Eventually, she felt nothing but the rapid flutter of her dying heart.

"I can see it!" he cried. "I can see the town!"

Namali leaned her aching body forward. Praying to Mahurzda, she *willed* her eyes to see.

But that was the difference between dream and reality. From one did miracles grow, while the other crushed hope beneath the heel of bitter disappointment.

CHAPTER 21

THE WOMAN WHO entered the healing tent wore a black robe with gold thread embellishing the sleeves and sandals made of rope and hide. In one arm she held a bucket of water, and in the other a bowl of figs. "Good, you're awake," she said matter-of-factly, shoving the bowl beneath Namali's nose. "Eat."

Namali ogled the bowl, her mind cluttered with fragmented images and remnants of half-forgotten memories. The rush of tears when she'd opened her eyes and seen color, light, as if it had all been a nightmare. She would never stop being thankful for another day on this earth when tomorrow was not guaranteed.

But the nightmare wasn't over. For hovering at the perimeter of her vision, a mask of fog drifted in. It didn't matter if she shook her head and it didn't matter if she blinked and it didn't matter if she rubbed her eyes. This was not a side-effect of dehydration or blood poisoning. These shadows were inside herself.

"I'm not going to stand here all day."

Startled, Namali reached out to accept the bowl. A thick wrapping encased her sore, throbbing fingers. A second bandage padded her shoulder.

The woman pulled back with a narrowed gaze. "What?"

Namali realized she was staring at the woman. At her bare, unveiled face. She could see her full mouth, her straight nose and stubborn chin—thrust forward, proud. She could see everything. "Why aren't you wearing a veil?"

Her suspicion eased into understanding, and she passed over the fruit. "It's not uncommon to see an unveiled woman this far north."

Namali fingered her own veil, filthy though it was. There was, after all, no one way to live. She sat on a pile of pillows in a spacious healing tent, the crisp scent of mint permeating the air. On the far side, three patients slept on folded rugs. A small fire crackled in the center of the tent, an opening in the top allowing the smoke to escape. "Excuse me, Grandmother?"

The woman snorted, batting aside the comment as she would a locust. "Please. Call me Farah."

Upon closer inspection, the healer was probably only ten years older than herself. Faint lines fanned from her eyes, displaying a history of laughter and hardships alike. "Farah then." She dipped her head in respect. "Where am I?"

"Kashgan." Farah set the bucket near a small work area cluttered with herbs, teas, and medicines. "Do you know that man out there, the one with the blue yirasaf? He keeps pestering me about whether or not you'll live."

Heat flushed all the way up to her ears. Of course Sameen was here. He was always here, even when she didn't want him to be. "He's . . . a friend." Though was it normal to think of him as more? As someone who'd never had many friends, it was hard to say. "Can he see me?"

"A friend, is that all?" Her mouth quirked. "Well, if he's not your husband, it's not proper for me to leave you two alone."

Her stomach jittered. *Husband.* She heard the word, the power and solidity in a sound so compact, but in her mind she twisted the inflection, the shape of the vowels on her tongue, until it became a different word entirely: enemy. "Have you seen a man recently? About six feet tall, most likely angry, with a bushy beard?"

Farah huffed out a laugh. "That doesn't exactly narrow anyone down around here."

"His name is Hazil Abdu."

At this, the woman fell silent. She scooped water from the bucket into a pot for a fresh batch of tea. Only when the pot was full did she reply. "Someone with that name stopped by a few days ago. He was searching for a girl your age."

She felt ill. Was he here, in Kashgan, roaming the streets, no home or place of business left unsearched? "What did you say to him?"

Farah placed the teapot on the fire. Next, she turned to the iron cage hanging from the ceiling and slipped fruit slices through the slats, appearing not to have heard her. A palm-sized bird, scarlet red, twittered on its perch. Healers often kept lotarbirds as pets, as their ability to replicate song was said to aid the sick. Admittedly, its song did ease a bit of the tension from her muscles.

With a sigh, the healer faced her. "I told him I hadn't come across anyone recently. He acted a bit . . . off. I certainly wasn't going to turn you over to a potentially unstable man, especially in the condition you were in."

Namali pressed her unwounded hand against the ground for support amidst the swaying room. "Many thanks." She didn't elaborate, but from the way Farah watched her, she suspected the older woman understood.

She started to lie back down, then stopped in sudden clarity. "Wait, you said he came by a few days ago. How long have I been here?"

"Four days."

Her jaw dropped. Four days? The sun, rising and setting four times. And she unconscious. "Have any other competitors come through?"

Pursing her mouth, Farah ticked off her fingers. "Six yesterday. Four a few days ago. I've seen about thirty since the race began."

Namali counted the number of days remaining in the race. When the sandstorm hit, it had been day twenty-two. Today was day twenty-six. If Sameen had learned of the Lost City materializing outside of Zeminir, it was likely others had as well. And if someone *did* claim the wish first, would she know? Would the world shift in some irreversible way? Or would life continue seamlessly, beguiling her into thinking there was still time?

She set aside the figs without having eaten any, a restless energy buzzing beneath her too-tight skin. Said, "I have to leave."

To which Farah laughed. But one look at the younger girl, and the smile vanished. "You're serious?"

Why wouldn't she be serious? "There's less than a week left of the race."

"I'm sorry, but I can't let you leave. You'll need to remain here for at least three more days to recover."

Namali practically choked on the word. *"Three?"*

The gravity in the older woman's expression seemed to press upon the room. In the back, one of the patients shifted in sleep.

Namali found she could not look away from Farah's eyes. They held some sort of frightening truth, like water cupped in the well of her palms, and if she looked away, if she denied it, the water would trickle through, leaving her hands empty.

"Do you realize how close you came to dying?" Farah asked. "If you leave now, you will die. And I will not have that on my hands."

It seemed Namali was a little closer to death with each passing day. In her heart, the shadows grew and grew. Even now she considered punishing this woman to prove she would not be manipulated. A life she could not control, a world drained of color. Was that, too, not death in its own way?

Beyond the tent walls, two voices rose in argument. She recognized Sameen's immediately. The other sounded like an ornery old man.

Farah poked her head outside. "Shame on you! People are trying to sleep." She snapped the flaps shut against the offending conversation and puttered around the tent, brewing tea, checking on patients, brewing more tea, checking on patients again.

Namali tried to catch the healer's eye. "Please," she said. "If you won't allow me to leave, at least let Sameen see that I'm well." He had stayed with her and fought for her and looked at her with soft, understanding eyes, and he deserved this one small thing: to know she was alive and thinking of him.

Farah straightened to her full height and crossed her arms, every bit the intimidating woman. "Like I said, it's not proper for me to allow that." But a smile hovered around her mouth. "However, suppose I left for about, oh, twenty minutes and he just *happened* to visit while I was gone, well, then I guess that wouldn't technically be breaking the rules now, would it?" With a wink, she whisked outside, and a moment later Sameen entered the tent and knelt beside her, face stricken. Namali forced herself to breathe. In and out, slow, the air between them tightening with an unbearable pull.

Sameen touched the claws poking from her blackened fingertips, and her stomach fluttered. This was not appropriate. This was foolish. This was . . . what she wanted.

She glanced over her shoulder at the other patients. Warm bundles of cloth. Drowsy limbs. Asleep.

"What was going on out there?" Namali asked.

"A man started yelling at me for loitering. Said it was bad for his business." He shook his head in obvious irritation. "It's not like I had anywhere to go. I told the healer we were friends, but she wouldn't let me see you."

Of course she wouldn't, because that wasn't the way of things in Malahad. Men and women were not friends in the way coyotes and camels were not friends. It simply wasn't done.

He went on, unable to sit still. "I couldn't wake you up. You weren't breathing very well, and she had to sacrifice an animal so you could live. She said your spirit was almost gone. I thought—" He bowed his head, at a loss. Sometimes words were not enough.

So Namali squeezed his hand with her good one, even when a voice screamed at her to avoid it. Because while she didn't have the words to ease his fears, she had a hand, a thing often overlooked until it rested on someone's shoulder or rubbed someone's back, saying, *You are not alone, I am with you, I understand.*

Reaching up, he removed the yirasaf from his thick dark hair and ran his fingers through it. "I felt so helpless."

Helpless. It was the thread binding the fabric of their lives together. Imagine carrying the limp body of someone you cared for. Imagine if you did not know whether they were dead or alive. "Sameen, you can't blame yourself for things that aren't in your control. You did the right thing by bringing me here. You *saved* me." Again and again he had saved her, and again and again she wondered why.

He dropped his hands, dropped his eyes. The sight sent a lick of fear through her, for she had never, not once since meeting Sameen, seen him this despondent.

"Whatever it is," she said, "you can tell me."

He stared hard at the ground. "Seeing you so sick reminded me of Mirza."

Namali hesitated. There was pain here, fresh like a gaping wound. "You mentioned him before. Is he . . . ill?"

"Very." He pulled away. "He's dying."

An ache stole through her chest, one she wasn't prepared for. "Do you know what's wrong with him?"

In the most desolate voice she had ever heard, he said, "He has the wasting sickness."

Namali looked away, nausea rolling through her as she fought tears. What a tragic way to die. Skin and bones—it's all that remained of the lives taken. "I'm so sorry." Her words were inadequate, but she didn't know what else to say, how else to comfort him. With this glimpse into his very personal home life, she began to piece together details surrounding his brother, the questions she had been unwilling to ask these past weeks.

A fierce light smoldered in his overly bright gaze. "Mirza is only eight years old. And the wasting sickness . . . there's no cure." He fisted his hands on his knees, the knuckles turning white from the skin pulling over bone. "That's why I entered the race, so I could wish my brother well."

Breathlessness took her quite suddenly, as if a fist rammed into her sternum. How could she wish herself free of a marriage when it came at the cost of knowing Sameen's brother, a boy who hadn't a chance to live, would die? An unwanted marriage seemed so small a problem compared to the loss of a loved one. Who was she to decide whose life took precedent, whose time on earth should end and whose should endure? She wasn't a god. She was a girl, painfully mortal.

Namali winced as the voice in her head screamed, *Me, me, me!* For seventeen years she had allowed others to mold her into obedience, timidity, passivity. They had carved out a life she no longer wanted, in an unchanging town, on a road leading nowhere. And she hadn't a choice. Perhaps the question was not *if* she would put herself first, but *when*. *If* was uncertain; *when* was confidence, assuredness.

When was also seventeen years past due.

But she couldn't make that decision. She could not choose her life over his brother's. Despite her dark heart, a trace of light still flickered somewhere deep inside the yawning cavern behind her ribs. So where did that leave them? In the end, one of them must choose. And if she did not choose herself, then why was she here? Or was it possible she didn't need the wish? Would her refusal to marry hold enough weight against Baba and the merchant?

Looking at Sameen's distraught expression, she remained quiet. It was not about her now. It was about Sameen, and his brother, and offering comfort during a time when he expected none. "I believe you can do it," she said, because it was the right thing to say to someone in his position.

His smile was genuine but all too fleeting. Before this moment, she had never noticed how much joy it brought her. How it effortlessly lit up the room. "Many thanks," he murmured. "I think I needed to hear that."

A quick peek at the door showed it still empty. Farah must be taking an especially long walk. Not that she was complaining. "You're from Yanasir, right?" she said, hoping to lift Sameen's mood with a more pleasant topic. "What's it like?"

"Small. Poor." He shrugged. "My mother likes to hang objects she's traded for her wool from the roof of our home—shells, beads, bones. It makes her happy."

"If you're not well off, how did you get to Ahkbur for the start of the race?" She assumed he did not have a pack animal at his disposal.

"Um . . ."

It was endearing how he casually scratched his chin as if deep in thought, when he quite obviously knew the answer.

"I sort of . . . stole a camel." He blinked at her innocently.

She fought the smile tugging at her mouth. The idea of Sameen stealing anything, least of all a slow, lumbering animal, was absurd. "I see."

"In my defense, this was the worst camel I've ever had the displeasure of caring for. It peed on me. *Twice*."

"You mean you don't know? That's how camels show they like you," she teased.

"That was terrible."

"I thought it was funny."

"You know what's funny?"

"What?"

"My uncle looks like a camel."

They held each other's gaze for a painfully long moment, then burst out laughing. Sameen howled, leaning on one arm to prevent himself from toppling over and clutching his stomach with the other. "It's true," he gasped, "especially when he chews his food." He demonstrated, and they laughed even harder, gasping for air like they were dying. Namali laughed until tears streamed down her face, until it hurt to breathe and every laugh was sweet pain in her side and a song in her heart.

She was so, so alive.

After they calmed down, they watched each other carefully—the dark young man with the quick-smiling mouth, and the shy young woman who was learning the terrifying, exhilarating feeling of falling.

As if detecting some emotion in her unguarded expression, Sameen grew serious. "Namali." His voice, whisper-soft, wrapped around her with invisible threads. "Can I ask you something?" His eyes were night-dark.

Her heart quickened. They weren't talking about camels anymore, she didn't think. "All right."

He swallowed once, twice. He looked behind him and clasped his hands together. She thought he wasn't going to speak at all, but then he asked, "Will you take off your veil for me?"

Namali never thought she'd hear the words capable of stopping her heart, but those were it. Appalling because he would ask such a thing. Embarrassing because she was glad he did. Take off her veil? For someone she wasn't married to? It was unthinkable.

And yet . . .

Would it be so terrible to remove the mask of fabric, to show her true self to the one person who accepted her for who she was? "Sameen," she whispered, head bowed. He knew what he asked of her, the gravity of it. Any respectable woman only removed her veil in the presence of her husband and family.

No matter how deeply she cared for him, no matter how she yearned for their friendship to blossom into something more, it could never be. The truth was a piece of jagged glass, snagging on her if she held it too close. Was it right to sacrifice her own desires for a possible future with Sameen? Out here, buried deep within the sand, she had discovered something precious, something that had eluded her for years: free will. And it was so, so bright. If she stayed with Sameen, she would care for him, and yes, she would love him, but soon that love would wilt. Soon it would become a withered black growth, choked with weeds. Knowing she had put his needs before her own during a time when Namali desperately needed to love herself first would kill any possibility of long-term happiness. The resentment would smother her. And then she would truly be lost.

Namali bit her lip to keep from crying. It hurt because in different circumstances, she could see that future. She knew he did, too. "I can't, Sameen."

His mouth curved, but it held no warmth. "I understand," he said, and began to shift away.

"No." Grabbing his hand, she said, "You don't understand. It's not you. I just . . . don't know if Malahad is the place for me anymore." Because somewhere along this journey, she realized she had outgrown it.

"You don't have to make excuses." Gently, he extracted his hand from hers. "Even if there was a chance to be together, I don't know how I'd be able to provide. I'll never be rich. I'll never have enough money not to worry." His words hardened into small stones. They dropped into the pool between them, disturbing the water. "You deserve someone better than that. Better than me."

That wasn't the reason. That wasn't the reason at all. How could he not see the truth? It was in the energy humming between them, in the way she looked at him and he looked at her, like the flare of a candle in the dark.

"If the timing were different . . ." Her shoulders slumped. Why did life have to be so difficult, so unfair? Why couldn't the stars align just this once? "You could come with me if I leave," she said, hopeful.

"I can't. I have to care for my family, especially Mirza. I'm the only one with steady work at the moment." His voice wavered, causing her heart to pinch. "I always knew this was temporary."

"I've never liked anyone as much as I like you," she said. "You're smart and genuine and kind and—" Her face crumpled on a sob. She covered it with her hands, trying to hide even though it was futile. She couldn't hide from someone who truly *saw* her.

"Namali . . . Namali, I shouldn't have said anything." His lips trembled. "I really like you, and I thought—" Shaking his head, he sighed. "I'm an idiot. I don't know what I thought."

Namali cried harder, curling into herself. She should have

never entered this race, because then she wouldn't have met Sameen. *You can't have something that was never yours to begin with.*

Sameen brushed the curve of her neck, a delicate, fleeting touch. Thinking he'd remove her veil without permission, her pulse spiked.

But no, he only pulled her closer so she leaned into his chest, his palm rubbing her back in long, languid strokes. Her tears dampened his robe, releasing every bit of frustration warring within her over this strange, confusing predicament as he rocked her, steadfast, until she drifted into sleep.

CHAPTER 22

A GLEAM OF metal bathed in firelight jolted Namali awake, pulling her into the twilight realm between waking and dreaming. She gasped for breath, body drenched in sweat, unable to calm her racing heart. Her hand throbbed with a phantom pain. The merchant was here, staring her down with those cutting eyes. He would hurt her again. Physical hurt, but the psychological hurt, too. The slow, lethal injection of terror. The planting of doubt. The complete annihilation of confidence.

Without thinking, her hand sought Sameen's in the dark, its strength and familiarity. The threadbare rug blanketing the ground grazed her fingertips. Empty.

Namali sat up in alarm. Firelight drenched the tent walls, bleeding into the shadows. Farah's bedroll was vacant, though a strong earthy scent lingered in the air, as if she had recently steeped a pot of tea. While Sameen was not allowed to sleep inside the healing tent, he had situated himself on the opposite side of the canvas in order to slip his hand inside so she would know he was there. But he wasn't there now.

"Sameen?" she whispered so as to not disturb the sleeping patients.

No answer.

Rising to her feet, Namali poked her head outside. The brick roads zigzagging through the clusters of tents were deserted. It wasn't that Sameen had disappeared. It was that he hadn't told her, and she didn't know where he had gone. Or if he was coming back.

Guilt nagged her at the thought. Sameen was too decent a person to leave without warning, but after their last conversation, she would not be surprised if he wished to continue his journey alone.

She stepped fully out into the night. Rock dwellings of hard red stone glowed in the moonlight, and the fortified towers flanking the corners of the mighty sandstone wall protecting the city jutted into the thick night-dark. Upon first exploring Kashgan's old-world elegance, she had discovered a city as quiet as it was clean. Temples lay nestled among the taller, multi-storied edifices, and it was not uncommon to hear music drifting from the open doors in passing. During the day, the air swelled with song and chant, the roads thick with the flurry of movement. But here, in the absence of sun and color and sound, everything seemed to be . . . less.

Namali started down the road. For the past two days, competitors had come and gone, men from every tribe and town, dust and sand coating their robes as they led their snarling daevas through the towering city walls. They didn't notice her, quiet Namali with the bandaged hand. She was invisible behind her veil. A rival hidden in plain sight.

The streets were mostly deserted. Namali lengthened her stride, picking up her feet so she wouldn't draw attention by scuffing her sandals against the ground. Her spine tingled. She was awake and aware. Moments later, a figure emerged into her peripheral line of vision. The bulked body of a demon wandered the area, limping as if injured.

She shrank back into the shadows, having realized her mistake. Not a demon, but a man already half-gone. His teeth were long and sharp and broken, clumped in his mouth like a handful of knives. And his eyes . . .

She tried not to look at his eyes.

Eventually, the demon-man loped down an alleyway and disappeared. Namali hurried to turn another corner when a low whistle pierced the night.

She slowed, but didn't stop walking. Ahead, in the niche between two ice houses of the same red stone, a tall, handsome man stepped into her path. He smiled. "Hello, lovely."

Namali stopped. He blocked her way forward.

His laughter skittered across her skin as she watched him warily. "Don't be afraid," he cooed, sidling closer.

Her eyes flared, and she jerked up her chin. The stench of his sweat flooded her nostrils. "I'm not afraid of you," she said, and her voice was deeper now, resembling a soft growl. Shadow prickled at the base of her spine, slithered up her arms. To not have to hide from this need. To not pretend this wasn't what she truly wanted.

She loved it.

And loathed it.

Mouth twisting into a leer, the man stepped forward when a black blur shot between them, Namali's daeva planting itself before her, lips peeled back. A tattered rope dangled around its neck from where it had broken free.

The man reared back, watching with newfound wariness as she rested a hand atop the demon's head. Sweat dripped down her neck and pooled greasily beneath her arms. She looked at this man, his black, fathomless eyes. Her skin itched and burned, stretched taut over aching muscles. She was shaking and growling and thinking *no no no* and *yes yes yes* and finally, finally the *no* won out and her vision cleared, and he was just a man, a hollowed-out man scraping by in life, equally lost, equally confused.

Before she caved to the need, Namali fled to the outer wall, the daeva on her heels. Upon reaching the entrance, she slowed. A silhouette cut into the backdrop some yards ahead: Sameen, sitting in the sand, knees drawn to his chest. The moons shone like the white of a luminescent pearl, casting their unearthly glow along his profile. His jaw spoke of strength, his eyes of kindness. Had he given more thought to what would happen once they reached the Lost City? Even now, paranoia stirred from its restless sleep. Another competitor might have already reached the end. Might he receiving the wish this very moment, palm outstretched, crushing her hope for an independent life. All her hard work, destroyed.

Suppose that wasn't the case though. Suppose *they* reached the end first. Then . . . then she would have to ask herself the question she dreaded most.

Who deserved the wish more?

Sameen, who risked his life to save his dying brother, or Namali, who risked her life for freedom?

Could she live with herself knowing she had sentenced Sameen's brother to certain death? She could not, in good conscience, end a child's life, but when faced with the decision, she did not know how the darkness would manifest. Sameen, too, had begun to darken, though the change was not nearly as severe. Did he anticipate the race's end? Did he weigh his brother's life against her own? She had never asked, afraid of what his answer might be. Afraid he would not choose her.

You are a fool, Namali. A thousand times a fool.

"Are you all right?" she wondered.

He did not immediately turn around, as if he had known of her presence. "I was just thinking."

Namali hugged her arms close. *About the wish?* She wanted to bring the issue, her worries, to attention, but for some reason, Sameen seemed very far away.

"Is something troubling you?" he asked.

She dropped her arms. "How did you know?"

"You are very easy to read."

"I could say the same about you."

"Oh?" The night shrouded his expression. "Then what am I thinking right now?"

Namali's smile faded as her thoughts clouded with teeming entities. This ominous storm bearing down, chasing them forever, it seemed. She looked at Sameen's softly curved mouth, and the sight of it was too much, too bright, for her weary eyes.

"You're wondering," Namali whispered, looking straight ahead, "what will happen when we reach the end. Who will win and who will lose, and what it will cost you." She licked her peeling lips, the words falling from her mouth like ripened fruit, devoured by the night. "You're wondering," she said, her voice barely audible, "if you have ever seen a night so dark before."

There was an almost unbearable silence, broken only by the sound of their breathing, the soft hiss of sand as he shifted to study her more fully. How loud silence could be in the dark, the places untouched by light. When Sameen finally spoke, the words were low, strained, rising from a place of deep uncertainty. Thirty days' worth of exhaustion and fear.

"Darkness always yields to light," he said. "It is the natural order of the world."

Of whose world? Mahurzda's? "Are you sure about that?"

He huffed out an incredulous laugh, as if he couldn't believe the breadth and depth of her negativity. Honestly, she couldn't believe it either. She dug the hole deeper and deeper without even realizing it.

"You don't know what the day will bring when it comes," Sameen said.

"Neither do you."

He didn't respond, but she didn't expect him to. The truth was, upon reaching the Lost City, one of them *could* win, in all possibility. One of them could step through the entrance gates and emerge with the wish, brightly burning, in hand. But she didn't know who that person would be.

"Namali—"

She wasn't listening. She was thinking, still, about the wish. The shape of it.

The weight of it.

She wanted to win, wanted to harness that power, wanted the ability to change time, change the world. But not for herself. For her master.

For the Demon King deserved the wish most of all, which meant *she* had to be the one to reach the Lost City first, not Sameen. Sameen, who would use the wish for himself. Sameen, who would prevent the Demon King from returning to power for another thousand years.

Namali curled her hands into fists, claws pricking the tender flesh of her palms. "I was a fool not to see it before," she growled.

"Excuse me?"

The air between them snapped with aggression, sparking against her skin and drawing the hair along her body straight on end. The shadows uncurled and pooled in her hands, drawing further up her arms.

"You lured me out here, in the dark, where no one can see."

He watched her as a rat did a viper: unblinking. "I'm aware that we're competitors," he said, "but trust me when I say I would never intentionally hurt you."

Trust. Such a fragile word—one that had no place here. "You're lying." The menace prowling her mind trickled down. "You're trying to kill me so you can have the wish all to yourself!" The words tore from her throat in a beastly scream.

She couldn't let the boy win, couldn't let him kill her for the wish.

So she would have to kill him first.

Her legs and torso bled into shadow. Then she was off, sprinting through the sand on all fours to rip Sameen from his seated position, her mouth stretched wide over ebony fangs. The end would be swift. She did not want him to suffer.

But the boy fought back. He pushed his legs between them.

Kicked her off. Crouching on all fours, he snarled in answer, flashing teeth as jagged as her own.

Namali didn't hesitate. She charged him, a black shadow under a black sky, and pulled him into a dark abyss.

•••

Around them, the landscape blurred. Swirling grays and blues and greens, the purple haze of twilight, the soft blush of dawn. After a moment, her vision cleared. Enough to notice she no longer viewed the world through black eyes and stood in the middle of the Lost City on her own two feet.

But the city was not as it once was. Duller, dimmer, less. Like a crown having fallen from dizzying heights, the walls had cracked and crumbled and caved. Piles of rubble and toppled pillars cluttered the jeweled roads, the stones winking dimly beneath inches of thick dust. Namali emitted a small, distressed sound. Only eight days ago had she walked the glittering ribbon of hammered jewels, marveling at their brilliance, and yet it felt as though much time had passed. Centuries. Many of the glazed tiles covering the domes were missing, the empty spaces like gaps in a mouthful of otherwise perfect teeth.

The vision had dropped her in the center of a marble courtyard. Algae choked the shallow pools and fountains, clinging to the edges in a slimy gelatinous mass, and the artful embellishments chiseled along the curve of the scalloped archways were no more. The wind had beaten the carvings into submission.

Something inside Namali broke, a fragile hope she'd held close.

This place had been beauty, splendor, grace, and now . . . now it was dying.

The clothes were gone. The sandals were gone. The people were gone. The mirrors, too, were gone. Shattered.

The emptiness gaped like a wound.

Namali glanced down at her hands and choked back a scream. Knobby knuckles protruded under a layer of deep, deep black, her fingers stubby and grotesque and animalistic. Tendrils whispered around her legs. The soft hiss of wind roared in her ears, the sound overly bright. They, too, had changed. Pointed. Silken with a layer of fine hair. Her fingers trembled as she traced the ears' triangular edge. If she could, she would rip out the claws, the ears, the fangs. Tear them from her hideous body.

But as she turned to Sameen, those thoughts faded. His robe hung in tatters around his lean frame, shreds of cloth soaked red. Deep scores marred his chest, his arms and shoulders, his neck and face. Namali curled her hands into fists, as if hiding them would erase the evidence of her betrayal. She had caused it, his pain. It was right in front of her, weeping blood.

What have I done?

Dazed, Sameen wiped a palm over the oozing cut on his cheek, having mostly returned to a normal human appearance. He did not look at her. He did not look at her, and that was the same as saying he did not know her.

Namali swallowed. All around, a hollowness encompassed them, the sound of absence. She was frozen with fear of this friendship breaking without hope of repair. Somehow, she had to fix this. Show him she wouldn't hurt him again, her friend.

Hesitantly, she stepped toward him. A puff of dust lifted

where her sandal hit the earth, and Sameen's head snapped up, his gaze shuttered. His shoulders tensed when she tore off a strip of her robe and gently wiped the blood from his face and neck. Her hands hovered above his chest, unsure of whether to clean those wounds too, but in the end she dropped them and moved aside. During all of this, he looked straight through her, as if she were a pane of glass.

Namali turned away, ignoring the pang in her chest, and looked around. Before her, beneath one of the dilapidated archways, Mahurzda and the Demon King were locked in battle. The clash was a beautiful dark dance, each swing of the blade telling the story of how they had failed one another. The Demon King bore little resemblance to his former self. His face was an indistinguishable dark smear. He loomed at least twelve feet tall, a towering figure of the blackest evil, his brother puny in comparison. She could not believe this was the same person who had once loved.

The Demon King opened his mouth as if to roar, a black mass rocketing from his throat, speeding toward his brother in deep silence with unleashed ferocity. The shadows shifted and multiplied, a swarm. Volatile. It hurt to watch. To even consider the idea of sympathizing with the Demon King was absurd, but . . . she did. Mahurzda had lost much during his daughter's abduction, but what about his brother, abandoned, shaped by the very darkness he had been unfairly sentenced to?

The Good Lord flung up a hand. Light burst forth, a thousand suns harbored in a single beam. The Demon King flew back and struck the ground, skidding across the cracked marble before coming to a halt near a murky pool, his body still.

Mahurzda strode forward with a thunderous expression. He

stopped. Looked down his long nose at a man he no longer knew. Then he began to speak.

For your treachery of stealing my daughter, I cut out your heart. For destroying the land I so carefully crafted, your privilege of accessing the world above is now revoked. This is your punishment: until the end of time, you will know only pain and suffering. You will know only darkness.

Mahurzda clapped his hands together. The ground rumbled, vibrations shooting through the soles of Namali's feet, and soon a wall erupted from a chasm in the earth, solid gold and impenetrable, dividing the two siblings. The wall was still rising when the Demon King stirred awake and lunged, a silent shriek erupting from his mouth. The wall towered above, agleam. It would not allow him to pass through, throwing him back each time he approached.

The Demon King stopped, panting like a madman. His eyes burned a sickening red.

Then he threw back his head and laughed. And laughed. And as he laughed, a flash caught Namali's eye: a wolf, brilliant gold, with eyes like sapphires. Struggling against an invisible chain pulling it from the heavens, it was soon wrapped in the Demon King's embrace, shadow eating at the creature until only a vague shape remained—a daeva, servant to the Demon King.

Namali stumbled back in mounting horror.

It can't be.

Fifty, one hundred, five hundred wolves. All torn from the sky, all transformed, all their light snuffed out.

Stillness entered Namali's heart. This was greater than anything she had ever known, greater than the world around her, and yet she was helpless against witnessing this tragedy. This sickening, monstrous tragedy.

The Good Lord fell to his knees, his composure cracking beneath the weight of his disbelief. He could do nothing. The wolves had turned, beyond his influence, beyond his control. Weakly, he brought his hands together again. Another flash of light, a fierce, animalistic rumble, and the earth split apart. With all his remaining strength, Mahurzda drove his brother and the newly created daevas into the abyss, trapping them inside.

In an instant, Mahurzda disintegrated into dust, and the bone buildings collapsed, and the gold wall crumbled, and the clouds disappeared, and all that remained were miles and miles of sand, touching one end of the world to the other. Namali blinked at the spot the Good Lord had stood, hardly daring to breathe. When she looked to the sky, there was no light. The moon had turned the sun black.

CHAPTER 23

NAMALI'S EYES FLEW open to the wide, gaping night. No sign of the Lost City among the half-darkened sandy waves. Beside her, Sameen stirred. He sat up with a pained groan, cupping his head. At the sight of her and the demon curled against her back, he froze.

Namali brushed sand from her arms, moving slowly so as not to startle him. It spattered on the dunes like rain. "Hello," she whispered, afraid if she spoke too loudly he would flee and never return. Gashes marred his shoulders and chest, but she didn't make any move to clean the wounds. His body language made it clear her touch was no longer welcome.

Namali buried her hideous claws in the sand. "I'm sorry." It was not enough. It was painfully less than it needed to be, yet she could give nothing more.

Sameen turned away, but not before she saw the disgust in his expression.

She pressed a hand to her bruised heart. Yes, it was deserved. And yes, in the moment before the attack, she could have pulled back, had she chosen to. In the end, she had trusted the silk and croon of a far-off voice more than she had trusted her friend's word. How she wanted to wrap her arms around him so they could pretend to still be on the same side. She knew better though. That was a time of the past, blown away by the wind. Gone forever, perhaps.

She looked into the moon's pale glow. Its brother had not yet breached the horizon. "Did you . . . see Mahurzda's Great Pack?"

"Yes."

At least he was speaking to her, however reluctant the response. All this time. They had been with members of the Great Pack all this time. The wolves' disappearance was no accident. It was an act of revenge. A strategized blow meant to cripple the Good Lord's power.

She began to piece together the missing links from the story of Barandi. Mahurzda punished his brother because of what he had done: stolen his daughter; destroyed the world he had created, a land of lush green with sparkling blue waters. After cutting out the Demon King's heart, he hid it in the Lost City, which the Demon King could not pass through. But she would bet her life the daevas could.

When she said as much to Sameen, he shrugged, avoiding her gaze. Avoiding the monster's gaze. "I suppose." A minute passed in silence. "I still don't know how the wish fits into all of this though."

I, not we.

It hurt more than she could say. Linking her fingers together, Namali tucked them under her chin and did her best to focus on the topic at hand. The myth. The race. Somehow they were linked. Somehow the wish brought everything together.

Before, she had not understood the role humans played, having assumed the daevas could restore their master's soul without aid. But maybe that was wrong. Maybe humans must be the ones to do so. It made sense. Offer them a chance to claim their heart's desire, and they would win by any means necessary.

Which made her wonder . . . In order to restore the Demon King's soul, did a mortal have to wish for it? Was that the true reason for the prize? If competitors succumbed to darkness by the time they reached the Lost City, they would be too far gone to use the wish for anything other than malicious intent. In life, nothing came free. There was always a price. And this was perhaps the darkest price of all.

But how would the Demon King be granted access to such a prize in his containment? Or was she again missing some vital clue that would paint her a larger picture?

Namali peaked at Sameen from the corner of her eye. His body was one line of tension. She had shredded his robe with her claws, and then, as if that were not enough, she had taken his trust and shredded it, too. The one person who had never failed her, who had remained steadfast and loyal and true. The one seemingly good thing in her life. And she had burned it all to ash.

Namali could barely speak the words. "Before the vision—"

"I'd rather not talk about it."

"Oh." It was difficult to swallow. "All right then."

Namali lay back on the sand, willing her heartbeat to slow. Her transformation rose like a wall between them, and neither one desired to climb it. Not tonight. For now, they would set it aside for a calmer time, when the vision and revelations weren't vying for attention. When she didn't feel so torn.

The earth trembled beneath her, but from what she couldn't say. Above, streams of clouds blotted out the moons. "Do you have bad dreams sometimes?" Her voice, whisper-soft, carried in every direction. They would have to leave eventually, but she wanted to hold onto the quiet for as long as possible before the coming day shattered it.

From the corner of her eye, she watched his chest rise and fall. Steady. Always steady. "Sometimes."

"What—" She cleared her throat. "What are they about?"

"What do you think they're about?"

The ice in his voice stabbed her battered heart. She didn't know how he had become such an important part of her life. It had happened when she wasn't looking, him creeping in like the dawn. "I think they're about your brother. I think they're about me." Her voice softened further. "I think they're about whatever you're afraid of."

Sameen stiffened and looked into the distance, his eyebrows drawn inward. He didn't speak for a long time.

Maybe she had gone too far. "Sameen—"

"I don't want to discuss this anymore."

Namali bit her lip, determined not to cry. The distance between them ached. "Will you look at me?"

He didn't. He stood and brushed the sand from his robe.

"Sameen, *please*." She was losing him. He was moving away, moving on, and she was not welcome to follow. "I'm sorry. I'm so sorry for what I did. I couldn't control it." It wasn't an excuse though. Had she been stronger, or wiser, or more determined, maybe she could have. "Please. Can't we talk about this?"

He approached the outer wall, and she ran after him, catching his arm. A spark of heat erupted where their skin touched. "Tell me what I can do to fix this," she said, voice thick. "I don't want to fight. Not with you. I can't . . . I can't do this."

Because now it was not Sameen's disappointment she saw, but Baba's. Baba pulling away. Baba turning his back on her, on his only daughter. Day after day of wondering what she had done wrong just by *being*, and not knowing why she deserved it.

"Sameen!"

He continued walking as if he hadn't heard her.

And Namali . . . Namali was done.

She gritted her teeth, snarling fiercely through a sheen of tears. Anger and hurt she could understand. Disrespect she could not. "So that's it then? After everything we've been through, you're just going to walk away? You act like you're this good person, like you're too strong to let what everyone else thinks hurt you, but deep down, you're exactly like me, exactly like everyone else. The demon affects you just the same."

When he finally turned to face her, she wished he hadn't. Never had he looked so cold. "Not nearly as much as it affects you. And you know why? Because I know myself. I know I'm better than being treated like a lowly servant to the Demon King." He laughed harshly, smooth round stone fracturing into shards. It was so unlike his normal laugh Namali thought she was looking at someone else.

"Maybe I don't always know who I am," she spat, "but I never believed I knew the answers to everything. I thought I knew who you were though." Kind, loving Sameen. Had it all been a lie? "I guess I was blind."

The storm clouds dissipated from his expression. In a softer voice, he said, "This is who I am, Namali. It's all there is to me." Running a palm over his head, he added, "This journey hasn't been easy for me."

"You think this has been easy for *me?*" How wrong he was. How horribly mistaken. "I run away from my father, the only family I have left, to ride across the desert on a demon that tries to infect my soul, and I have to pray every day I'll survive." Her voice rose to a shout, the sound filling even the infinite sky. After seventeen years, to finally be heard. She'd wanted this for a long, long time. "Meanwhile, the merchant captures me, cuts off my finger, and makes me think I'm worthless. That is the life of a Malahadi woman, Sameen!" She screamed it until her throat bled, until she thought her chest would cave in from the crushing pressure, a lifetime of harbored resentment unleashed. "*That is my life.* So I'm sorry I tried to change my future because I thought I deserved better. I'm sorry you got stuck with poor, naïve Namali. If you think I keep holding you back, then *go,*" she said, voice cracking. "I told you to go on without me. I told you, but you wouldn't listen. So go to the Lost City and get your wish. Clearly you deserve it more than I do for wanting to make a better life for myself."

"I never said I deserved the wish more than you. When I say it hasn't been easy for me, I mean it hasn't been easy traveling with you. The more I get to know you, the more I—the harder it is for me to decide who will get the wish if we reach the end first."

And there it was. Though they had not spoken of it since before the storm, he had thought of it. Why hadn't he come forward to discuss it with her? She would have listened, would have worked with him to find a fair solution. Her stomach churned. In her anger, she said the exact opposite of what she wanted. "Then I'll make the decision easy for you. Go on without me and get the wish. I was never going to reach the end anyway."

"You know that's not true."

Perhaps. But it was hard to distinguish truth from lie when there was no light to illuminate it. She had been trapped in the dark for so very, very long.

Sameen turned his back and drew his shoulders up to his ears. "Maybe . . . maybe it's best if we take some time to think about what we truly want."

The words slapped her across the face, a sudden, stinging pain. Namali bowed her head, speechless. This was it then—the beginning of the end. Or rather, the end of the end. She did not think it would arrive this soon, if at all. They'd had time.

She never knew how fragile the heart could be.

"I'll be at the tent."

Face damp with furious tears, Namali watched Sameen disappear inside Kashgan's high stone walls, and even long after he had gone, she stood there for some time, the wind whipping around her weak knees.

CHAPTER 24

THREE HOURS PASSED before Namali dredged up the courage to return to the tent. She had her apology ready. A few heartfelt words mashed together into coherency. As she trudged back with the daeva flanking her, she practiced what she would say.

"Sameen, it's all my fault . . ."

"I know I hurt you . . ."

"You have every right to be angry with me . . ."

"How can I make it up to you?"

Namali groaned in frustration. Her hands were stiff with cold, and she looked forward to warming them by the fire.

But when she reached the healing tent, the fire had burned to ash. Next to her bedroll where Sameen's supplies had been lay a single desert bloom, the white petals just beginning to unfurl.

Sameen was gone.

CHAPTER 25

"YOU'RE LEAVING THEN."

Farah stood at the tent's entrance, the flaps pulled back to let in the breeze. The night was full of deep, sleeping breaths, and the frigid air bit at Namali's cheeks as she adjusted her veil and pulled her small pack over her shoulder. Day twenty-nine. She couldn't afford to wait any longer, not even to heal. It was time.

Straightening, she looked the older woman in the eye, feeling worn-down and on edge, a volatile combination. Farah, who had tended her wounds. Who reminded her that goodness persisted in these darkening hours. "I know it's not what you wanted—"

"I understand." With a bittersweet smile, she came nearer, even with Namali's recent morphological changes between them. Shadow now encircled her neck like a ruff of fur. "Are you afraid?"

Namali almost didn't answer her. Who admitted terror, fear? But the truth was sharp and bright. Yes, she was afraid, had always *been* afraid. Had even taken comfort in that fear from time to time. But now Namali realized something else, something that would set her on a different path.

That fear no longer shamed her.

"I would be a fool not to be afraid." The Saraj was a woman of many faces, and Namali had yet to see them all. The mother, the savage, the deceiver, the thief. One you should never turn your back on. Which one would she have the privilege of witnessing today?

Farah's smile deepened, her dark eyes enfolded behind soft creases of skin. "Do you have a plan?"

"Ah—" Her laugh was strangled. "No."

Moving further into the room, Farah stared into the fire. Namali clenched and unclenched her hands, then clasped them together to stop their trembling. Her feet wanted nothing more than to carry her away from Kashgan, toward the bright, distant star that was her future, but this was the woman who had saved her life, and she deserved her respect.

When Farah spoke, it was hardly more than a murmur. "There's a place my people speak of known as the Gods' Table. It serves as a shortcut to Zeminir. I assume you've heard of the Lost City sightings."

The firelight flared, then dimmed.

Namali's pulse galloped forward. The lack of light was not unlike the old vendor's tent in Ahkbur. "That doesn't sound very safe." Unconsciously, she had lowered her voice as well.

"It's not. Safe, I mean. But if you're looking to reach Zeminir— and the Lost City—quickly, it will cut your travel time in half. I sent your friend in that direction as well."

Sameen.

Night swelled against the tent walls. Her attention snagged on the tent flaps, the darkness beyond. Nothing. A ravaging black hole. But if she looked closely enough—there. A dusting of stars. "Why would anyone choose to take that path?"

"Oh, no one *chooses* anything," Farah said on a half-laugh. "They take it because there are no other options." The healer tended the fire, and a spark popped, startling. The flames devoured the pile of twigs as if starved.

Namali said, with rising panic, "There's always another option. You said it yourself it's not safe. Why would I risk it if there's no guarantee I'll reach Zeminir?"

"Is that what you want? A guarantee?" She clucked her tongue. "You should know by now the Saraj never gives guarantees."

What was there to say? She was right. Namali wanted comfort, security, to *know,* but the threads slipped between her fingers no matter how she grasped for them. Not because she didn't deserve them. Not because they were for someone else, but because they didn't exist. Not out here. Maybe not anywhere.

Setting down the branch, Farah looked her straight in the eye, so very grave. "Tomorrow is day thirty, Namali. There's nothing left after this."

There's nothing left after this.

Hadn't she known this for some time? It had been driving her forward for weeks now, the knowledge of what awaited her back in Benahr: a lackluster life in a stifling, stagnant town. When would she open her eyes? There was no such thing as a safe place in the Saraj. Either you died from a sand hawk or you died from dehydration or you died from a knife in your back. If she died, at least it would be with the assurance of having fought to the bloody end.

The path was set. "Which way do I go to reach the Gods' Table?"

"North. And Namali?"

She paused at the tent's entrance, turned.

"Good luck."

•••

Namali left to the light of a full, single moon. Her pace was quick. Desperate, even. With her attention focused on the horizon, she clutched the reins and leaned forward as if anticipating the moment when the daeva scented the Lost City and plunged ahead, through wind and liquid night. Cold breath hissed through her lips like steam. There was a hunger in her veins, ravaging her sick, twisted body with its need, pushing her and pushing her toward that dark, inevitable end.

Alone, she understood it had to end this way. She could depend on no one but herself. But she was strong now, stronger than she had ever been. Namali needed only the courage in her heart, to remain steadfast in the midst of adversity. Tomorrow the day would dawn, hard and bright, and she would meet it with eyes wide open.

The Great Northern Constellation guided her. Deep into rocky valleys. Winding through cliffs. Up and down the endless rolling dunes. A hush pressed upon the desert, wrapping the smaller silences inside itself. It lay before her like a wide clear pool, so that every sound was a ripple in its waters. The hush grew and became a presence. It chased her through the night.

Long ago, before her family had fractured, before she knew of death's dark heart, there had been a time when running beneath a river of black silk released her heart from its stifling cage. Baba would fly with her atop Khorshan as Mama watched from a distance, his laughter rumbling against her back as she squealed in childish delight. The way their voices soared, that feeling of light, of air, in knowing this . . . this was everything. Father, daughter, mother—family. And she knew what it meant to be free.

But she had forgotten now. She had forgotten the simple pleasure of laughter, song. She had forgotten what it felt like to belong. Out here, she had no one. No family, no friends, nothing save her lonely beating heart. The slow, tortuous realization burrowed deeper into her mind until it became her.

Her body shuddered with need, cracks erupting along her spine, almost as if it were . . . realigning itself.

Faster, she snarled, and the daeva obeyed.

Namali managed to top a dune when something shifted in the corner of her eye. Her head whipped around, muscles tensed for an attack.

Nothing was there.

Slowly, she dismounted the daeva. Her gaze cut left and right. Something gloomy and mist-like hovered near, fading in and out of the darkness, and it wasn't the fog clouding her vision, she didn't think. The substance contained a distinct ethereal quality, similar to the daeva's pelt. When she reached out, her hand passed through, chilled. Her ears strained for sound, nose lifting for a scent. The dry air filled her chest.

"Hello?" she called, curling one hand into the demon's fur. She didn't want to hope, but the shape had been human.

"Sameen?"

Another shift of darkness, and she whirled, dagger out, a sliver of cold, cold silver. Perspiration dotted her forehead. The shifting mist migrated around her body, the air thrumming with a weak pulse. Namali's awareness of the area expanded, but . . . there was nothing. Absolutely nothing.

She could no longer trust her eyes.

The wind wailed, and small dust clouds lifted from the ground to swirl around her. Namali willed her heart into silence and, vigilantly, sheathed the dagger with a shaking hand. No, she wasn't imagining things. She had definitely seen a human, although it could have been an animal, or maybe a shadow cast by one of the clouds overhead. But she *had* seen something. She had.

Her gaze swept the desert. The dunes were bare, the horizon clear.

She was alone.

"I'm not imagining things," she told herself, the heels of her palms pushed against her stinging eyes. "I'm not."

But the press of a thousand eyes lingered.

Moving in cautious silence, she remounted and continued north at a trot. Every so often the demon whined and turned to look at her, but Namali ignored it, sinking further and further into herself. The land was shadow-dark. Night wrapped her in a silence so thick there was no sound but her beating heart. It was the pure stillness before dawn. It pushed her forward, saying, *Hurry, hurry.*

A trot kicked into a mad dash, and she was running, running, even knowing she might not reach the end, might die out here, abandoned, sucked dry from the heat. Doubts began to manifest. She tried to ignore them. It would do no good to dwell, after all. What was it Sameen had told her back in the merchant's camp? You could not have courage without fear. Maybe that's what Mama had meant. Be brave *despite* the fear. Be afraid, but be brave, too.

Namali scanned the horizon, ever watchful. The sun would bow before the moon today, but which one would reign?

A few hours later, the sun cast the land in fire. The landscape transformed into sheer cliffs, massive mountains of sand and stone. Boulders lay broken at the base of a great divide, two sheer walls rising at least two hundred feet on either side of a whip-thin path, the lands to the west cloaked in leaden shadows that had yet to sharpen.

The Gods' Table.

Structures such as these had not been built by human hands and only served to remind her how the earth was a crushing force which could not be mastered. A thousand years had shaped this pass. What was her life but a blink?

Namali reined in her demon, staring at the murky entrance. The wind had hewn the rock in two by sheer force, leaving the edges smooth, polished. Some ancient magic pulsed in the cracks of this indomitable rock fortress, beckoning. Her nostrils flared, and she instinctively leaned away from the scent. This place held the taint of death.

She fought against the upwelling of fear by settling into the pool of calm inside herself. There was only this moment, the demon shifting beneath her, the wisp of a voice growing louder and louder in her mind. Sameen had made his choice: to not falter in the face of fear. To go on, even when it seemed impossible. Now she must make hers.

Be brave, Namali.

Gripping the reins tighter, Namali nudged her daeva in the sides with her heels. The beast loped forward, head low, ears flat against its blocky skull. Apparently it had reason for caution, too.

The long, winding trail slithered between the two cliff faces. The rust-red stone emanated coolness, but in a few hours it would sizzle beneath the midday sun. Namali kept to the very center of the path, moving as quickly as possible without ramming into the cliffs. The trail widened in some areas, allowing the sun's pale fingers to creep down the smooth stone, while other times the narrowness forced her to dismount and lead her daeva on foot, where the rock scuffed her shoulders and scraped along her arms as if wanting to keep her here. What an agonizing way to die. Slow suffocation within these barren walls.

The wind whistled and howled between the rocks like the moaning of the dead. The sound was nothing she had ever experienced. Every few minutes the ground trembled, the onslaught of pebbles forcing Namali to duck her head from shards of tumbling rock. An oily sensation slicked over her, a warning, a promise, a curse. And hovering in the air, an unsettling intensity.

Deeper and deeper she went.

Sand.

Stone.

Hello, Namali . . .

Blood.

Bone.

The vibrations intensified the further she moved in the pass. The foul taint strengthened in potency. Despite her growing disquiet, Namali slowed their pace, wanting to avoid disturbing whatever slumbered between the rock. It took hours to travel a handful of miles, so twisty was the path. Hot stickiness clung to cloth and skin.

Namali jerked to a halt. Adrenaline sharpened her awareness, saturating the world's colors until tears flooded her vision. The cliffs had opened up, the sky a true, crushing blue. She could not remember why she had stopped. A need for something, now lost. Her memories were pale shrouds.

Every instinct was screaming at her to flee. Live, or die. Namali hooked her claws into the rock, feeling a trembling deep below the surface.

And then the wind died.

Her hair rose on end, pebbling the skin of her arms. It was so quiet she was certain her heartbeat echoed within the narrow passage. "Hello?"

Hello . . . hello . . .

The words: small, smaller, gone.

The air was thick as blood.

She glanced back the way she had come, then to where the path curved up ahead. Both were deserted. "Who's there?"

Who's there . . .

Her skin was like ice.

This place. It played tricks on the mind. These rust-red cliffs, the uneven pitted earth, an image dragged from the depths of hell. She was a young, frail girl, a jumble of bones. The towering walls pressed close, a maze without end. They could crush her with little effort.

Leaving her daeva behind, Namali forged ahead, her mind blanking in brief increments before memories rushed in at full force. She was determined to find out who, or what, sought her attention. The voice slipped past her defenses so easily. *Namali,* it whispered. *Namali, Namali, Namali.* Urgent. Restless. It did not sound like her master, yet it called to her all the same.

Sand and stone.

"Tell me who you are," she growled.

Blood and bone.

Namali clenched her jaw so hard her teeth creaked. The shadows came alive, twitching like fat worms burrowing into the soil as they clung to the rock faces. Panic surged through her at their slithering undulations, and Namali suddenly saw a future cut into ribbons by screams beneath a black sun, and she turned back around when her mind blanked again. The shadows stilled.

Time to leave. It was far past time to leave.

Namali began to mount up again when a faint voice drifted from around the bend.

Namali . . .

"Hello?"

Hello . . . hello . . .

. . . Namali . . .

She knew that voice.

Hurriedly, she pulled the demon along as she jogged ahead, ducking beneath an archway carved of the same smooth stone. Her hands were sweating, and her legs ached, but she didn't falter, didn't slow. The promise of what lay ahead drove her forward. The Lost City, the wish, a boy whom she had wronged.

She rounded a corner, and there he was, bent over his knees, wrapping a strip of fabric around his right foot. Her heart gave one hard throb.

"Sameen."

His head snapped up, and he stood, eyes wide. "Namali, what are you—"

The faintest of tremors buzzed along the ground, rattling the chips and pebbles scattered at their feet and migrating from her toes to her ankles, knees, and hips, settling in the joints. A harsh scrape drew her attention to the tumble of rocks as the ground shuddered and rumbled and groaned. It was alive. It was gnashing its ancient maw. A second heave sent Namali lurching into Sameen, and his arms wrapped tight, steadying her.

She feared she had stopped breathing.

It began again, and it was the rawest, most brutal form of song, the screech of a splintering waterfall. The ground bucked and rolled like brutal ocean waves, forming fissures in the earth, and she clutched Sameen for balance as her pulse grew to a dull roar in her ears and a furious animalistic shriek pierced the air, shattering in its purity. A sound like thunder followed, and the earth exploded in front of them.

CHAPTER 26

"RUN!" SAMEEN SHOUTED, vaulting onto his daeva. She whipped around, searching for her demon, the smudge of darkness. Great clouds of dust filtered the light from where the boulders exploded on impact, and the rocks rained down, down. Her feet were moving, seeking, then still.

Nothing was there.

The beast was off, a chaotic shadow streaming north. Namali cried out. Why would the daeva leave without her? Its form blurred into the red-gold rock, rippling along its smooth, weathered edges, too quick for a human to catch. It rounded a corner and vanished.

She did not anticipate the demon's abandonment to strike her with such force. It was nothing short of ridiculous, really. Did she expect the beast to care for her? *I see you,* she wanted to reassure it. *I know who you are.* But she had built a fantasy around what the daeva could be instead of what it was. It was simple. She had trusted something that did not exist.

Another tremor sent her knees slamming into the cracked, rutted earth. Sand rained as the rocks did. She squinted through the choking dust to where movement caught her eye. Sameen's daeva bucked and lunged, wanting to follow its kin, and Sameen's expression burned with indecision as he fought for dominance, to stay or abandon her, this demon girl.

She went cold.

But then he looked at her. He looked at her and his eyes changed and he said, "Namali," and it was like coming up for air.

She bolted toward him, kicking up dust. Placing a foot atop his, she pushed off and settled behind him, arms wrapped around his hard middle. "Go!"

They tore through the wall of sand, hurtling across the land like wind over water, the creature's cry lashing against their backs. The cliffs streaked past. Widening and narrowing, twisting every which way, the turns so sharp they almost crashed into the walls, and Namali ducked her head against the slicing air, clutching Sameen with all her strength as the beast chased them through the rocky maze, tunneling through the passage with single-minded intent. She wasn't sure which thundered louder: her heart or the earth.

The daeva jerked to avoid the onslaught of careening rocks, and Namali squeezed Sameen tighter, trying to make herself as small as possible. If Sameen had left her behind . . .

She choked back a hoarse cry as her spine popped and elongated, her skin splitting from the force of her protruding vertebrae. *Stop it,* she told herself. Demanded herself. He had overcome the temptation. He had not deserted her. They zigzagged through the pass *together.* Fled their deaths *together.*

Sameen yanked so hard on the reins that Namali slammed into his back. The stifling walls had fallen away. As she peered over his shoulder, her stomach dropped with a whispered, "No."

A massive serpent uncoiled above them, up and up and up, tall enough to block out the sun. Its long, tapered head was a thing of nightmares. Orange slits for eyes. Black scales hard as diamonds, shimmering with the strength of a million suns. Two white fangs jutted from its open mouth, the tips beaded with a clear substance, what she assumed to be venom. In horrified fascination, she watched a bead drip onto the sand and burn a hole clean through.

"Don't," Sameen muttered from the side of his mouth, "move."

He certainly did not have to tell her twice. She was stone. Rock beneath the earth.

The serpent's neck exploded forward like a glittering black whip. They swerved to avoid the fangs driving toward them with the purest, deadliest aim, a whiff of rotted air billowing against their backs as its jaws snapped together behind them and a fleck of saliva singed a hole through Namali's robe. Her jaw locked tight. Screaming was useless, for they were alone, and even if they weren't, no one would risk their life for a demon girl.

She did not have time to process how close she had come to an agonized, flesh-eating death. Its mouth gouged into the hills and valleys, its eyes like two licks of fire doomed to set them aflame. The creature tunneled beneath the sand, gone for one heaving breath, before exploding to their immediate left, the luster of its scales capturing the light so it ruptured into white fire. Namali flung up a hand. She may have screamed but couldn't be sure. Then the sand came to life beneath them, rolling into one monstrous, frothing wave, and suddenly she was flying through the air, her tether having snapped with frightening ease. She clawed at the space around her, seeking something solid to grab—a rock, a tree—but there was nothing, and her feet flipped over her head, sent her vision into a spin, before the ground punched into her back.

The serpent slithered toward her.

Get up get up get up—

Teeth chattering, she scrambled to her feet. Thoughts flitted through her head, things she should have said and done. And at the heart of everything was Baba, who was her world and didn't even know it. Regret was a clinging emotion. It grew as you grew. She should have said goodbye to him. She should have told him she loved him, even the parts she did not understand. Why was it that death broke down walls in ways life never could? Now he would truly be alone. No wife, no daughter, no family.

The beast halted within striking range. It coiled its body, as thick as five camels standing abreast, beneath it, those dark, oily scales reflecting Namali's terror in their rigid surfaces: round eyes, pupils fully dilated, sweat coursing down her pallid cheeks. A ghost. She was looking at a ghost.

But then the beast jerked back with a blood-curdling shriek. Namali clapped her hands over her ears and squinted through her blurred vision to watch Sameen yank his dagger from the serpent's vulnerable underbelly, stabbing it over and over as bubbling black ooze dripped down his arm.

"Run!" he cried.

The serpent shot forward in a blur, chasing Sameen down, but Namali was right behind it, her own dagger clenched in one white-knuckled fist. Her mind was empty. She only knew the pounding of her feet and the hungry rush of her blood. She had to save Sameen, save them both. She would not run. She would not turn her back on her friend.

Launching herself at its back, Namali wrapped her legs around its curved body and sank the blade to the hilt between two rigid scales with a savage snarl, parting the flesh like water. She yanked down, down, tearing into muscle, sinew. The scent of blood plowed into her, and she was plunged into that black, black night, alone with the weeping man. The sand hawk's screech as she butchered the camel, the air foul with the stink of its innards. Two lives cut short by her hand.

Namali dug her claws into the shallow space between the armored hide as the serpent flailed in an attempt to fling her off its back. The first incision was the blow that broke her open, let free the churning masses, the *need*. The dim guided her hand. She yanked the blade free, stabbed it a second time, the suction of metal parting flesh pleasing to her overstimulated ears. On the back of this ancient beast, she was a god, this blade a sword, the violence a show of her power and might. A half-mad laugh tumbled free.

With a shriek, the serpent snapped to the side, dislodging Namali in the process. And, like a god, she fell.

"Over here!"

Its head whipped around. Sameen waved his arms, drawing the serpent's attention as Namali lunged forward with a helpless *no*, diving to grab hold of its tail. The smooth scales slipped through her outstretched palms, and she tumbled to her knees and let loose a scream as though the world, her world, had imploded, for against the sweeping field of blue, a great cloud of sand plumed, and when the wind swept away its remnants, Sameen was gone.

Shakily, Namali stood and peered around. No, not gone . . . hiding. If she looked at the place where he had stood long enough, he would appear. His face would rise behind the dune, bright as the sun. He would show her that lovely smile, that beautiful foot, and how very much alive he was. They would continue on their journey—together.

But the land was still. Nothing stirred. Not even the slightest breeze.

Sand was sinking around her, pulling her into a deep, dark place. "Sameen?" One step forward before she stopped. She searched the area more frantically, certain she had overlooked him in her haste. He had been right there. *Right there.*

But he wasn't there now.

As the seconds passed, as Namali watched the Saraj and waited for him to appear as she knew he would, because he was *always* there, her chest caved inward. It hurt to breathe. It hurt to consider a world without Sameen, for now something had become absolutely clear.

She loved him.

And then she could not breathe at all, because now she knew the terrible mistake she had made. Not for loving him. Never that. For loving him and never telling him what she felt in her heart. And now it was simply too late.

"Sameen?" she called again. "Sameen!"

She waited for his answer. She waited in vain. But Namali realized the silence was answer enough, for those who are dead cannot speak to the living.

Namali stumbled, fingers pressed to her mouth to stifle a sobbing wheeze. She was drifting. "Don't . . ." *Go.*

Sameen was gone. He was well and truly gone—just like that.

Every part of her felt raw. How she wanted to close her eyes and let the darkness fully in. The void scraped against the walls of her mind with its sucking force, eroding the barriers stone by stone, and it took every ounce of strength to keep her trembling legs from collapsing. She didn't want to fight, but she must. She didn't want to continue on this journey alone, but she must. She had survived thirty days of hell, and to give up now? It was not an option. She needed to go on.

Namali was so overcome with shock she did not realize the serpent had returned until its snout crashed into the place she had stood seconds before. The present danger awakened the part of her having gone numb, jolting her limbs into motion. She slogged through deep, soft sand, up a mountainous dune. Heavy, labored breaths clotted her chest as if she breathed through a screen of damp wool. She needed a plan, and she needed one fast.

Namali reached the top when its massive shape shifted in the corner of her eye, and she dove to the side, rolling and tumbling down, head snapping back from the momentum while sand clung to her sweaty body. She hit bottom. Forced her aching body into motion, to stand and fight, to not give in. If she stopped moving, she would die.

The serpent struck, again and again, its rank breath scratching at her exposed neck. Her legs throbbed. Her throat burned with the need for water. Every second pushed her nearer to an end she wasn't ready for. The demon was so far away, an immense distance. She'd never reach it in time. The beast would kill her first.

And yet a memory was taking shape. Faded, yet familiar. She held it in her mind's eye, brushed the fine dust from its surface. Soon the image grew clear: a blanket spread out beneath a violet sky, and a camel, and a cup of steaming tea, and an old man who had claimed people possessed both light and darkness inside them. And she was just desperate enough to listen.

Taking a breath, Namali concentrated on the thread pulsing low in her belly. Over the days and weeks this bond had strengthened, twining tighter and tighter around her core until she could not separate herself. She was both Namali and the daeva, a demon and a girl. Brushing her fingers along the thread, it warmed beneath her touch. With a bit more coaxing, she could make it purr, make it sing.

Do not forget me, she whispered to it, *my brother, my kin. Do not leave me behind.*

The demon turned around and came back.

"Namali!"

The world slowed, and stopped, and started again. A shred of hope warmed her chest. Warmed, and bloomed. She whirled around, palm to heart. All was forgotten but the lingering of his voice.

There.

As Namali charged forward, half-sobbing in relief, she knew his was a face that would never leave her. She would know it blind. His soft, tender mouth, always so quick to smile. The creasing at the corners of his eyes, like the fanning of a river delta. His nose, which did not fit his face until he let slip free a laugh. She would know it in distance, in memory. She would know it in death.

Namali slammed into him. They tumbled to the ground, a tangle of limbs, and she sobbed, blubbering against his chest, "You were dead. I watched you die. H-how? I can't believe it . .

." She gasped before another wave of sobs hit, breaking her open again.

"Shh, it's all right. Everything's all right." He wrapped his arms around her and squeezed. "I was buried, that's all." He hauled them to their feet and caught the demon's reins. "You climb on first."

Once she mounted and extended her clawed hand, Sameen leaped up and settled behind her. Then they were racing away, over and around the dunes while the serpent roared its rage and dove in and out of the sand, trying to catch up.

"I'm sorry, Namali. For everything. I shouldn't have left. I should have stayed. I should have talked to you." His forehead pressed against the space between her shoulder blades. "It's not an excuse though. If I could take back what I did, I would."

Her veil whipped wildly about her face. She had half a mind to tear it free. "It's all right. You did what you believed was right."

"No, it's not," he said, his arms like iron bars around her waist. "It was cowardly."

She could not concentrate on both this conversation and leading them to safety. "Sameen, now's not the time—"

"I need you to do something for me."

She flinched from another wild shriek. "What?"

"Whatever happens to me, I don't want you to stop. I want you to keep going."

They veered left to avoid an explosion of sand. She couldn't pick apart her emotions amidst the chaos. What he asked her was absurd. She couldn't leave him behind. To leave him was to leave her heart, and without her heart, she'd be lost. "Are you suggesting I abandon you?" she hissed, digging her heels harder into the daeva's sides. *Faster, faster.* The gall he had, to think she would give him up so easily. "I won't do it. How could you even think—"

"Please."

The word stripped her of thought, for the emotion rippling underneath suggested something she had not heard since before her mother's passing. What she heard was an impossibility.

"Don't stop," he said. "Don't endanger your life for mine."

Clenching her teeth, Namali blinked back tears threatening to rise again. Long nights of indecision had broken her down in the worst way, laying bare her basest needs. She thought she had wanted his surrender. But she had been wrong. "What are you saying, that your life isn't worth saving?" The serpent screeched again, the sound fainter now. A glance back showed it had stopped chasing them. "I'm not going to let you die. *Do you hear me?*"

Lowly, he said, "I don't care about what happens to me."

"But I do." Too much. Far too much. She wiped the wetness from her cheeks. "I don't want to talk about this anymore."

"Namali—"

"I said I don't want to talk—"

"It's the merchant!"

She swore and urged the beast faster, gentling her grip on the reins to allow the demon the swiftest path across the red-gold fields. He appeared out of the corner of her eye, his men trailing him, his yirasaf a scab that would not heal. The distance between them closed. With the weight of an extra person on its back, the daeva would unlikely outrun the fastest horses wealth could buy. It wasn't enough. They needed distance, speed.

The land rose on a sharp incline. Namali tightened her legs around the daeva, whose shadowy form streaked upward. They were close. She could feel it. A voice, deep and dark and persuasive, reminded her of the task at hand.

It must have looked like this, in the beginning. In the void of beginningless time, when all was smudged and empty and aimless, and all was unknown beneath the sea of eternity, there at some point came a shift, a yielding that gave way to the undark. An arrival put into measure all that had passed, a seemingly perpetual journey having reached its culmination, and as Namali topped the rise, the barren land spread out before them save a white speck shimmering in the heat, she knew the Lost City was the undark, a pinnacle she had finally reached.

"Namali, look."

There, against the backdrop of the Lost City, the sun drew her eye like the glint of a pale coin, its fiery edge overshadowed by a sliver of darkest night.

The final solar eclipse had begun.

CHAPTER 27

THE DAEVA THUNDERED toward the Lost City with the might of a sand hawk intent on decimation, Namali and Sameen clinging to its back. The outer wall wrapped around the city's pallor, keeping the Demon King out while his heart lay hidden within. A heart that lay unbeating until it joined with its master once more and released him from his underground cage forever.

A whip-like *crack* lashed the air, followed by a scream. Namali kept her eyes straight ahead, ignoring the poor fool's demise. If the fall hadn't broken his neck, someone would end him by other means.

"Where's the merchant?" she asked, ducking her head. Sand particles sliced into her exposed skin.

Sameen's chest pressed more firmly against her back as he shifted for a better look. "Behind us. A hundred yards. You have three more men on your left."

"Seven hells. Go!"

Incredibly, their speed increased. The wind pummeled them, growing more vicious the closer they came, but they pushed through the mighty wall. The Saraj could howl all it wanted. It would make no difference. The wish burned brightly in her mind, an ever-present star, guiding her to an incomprehensible treasure. Nothing could keep them from the prize.

"Turn left!"

Startled, she steered the demon without thought, realizing too late it was the wrong direction. Sameen struggled against her back, fighting a man she was blind to. She did not have time to recover before someone gathered a fistful of fabric between her shoulder blades and yanked, and she screamed, clawing at the reins, but could not grab the rope with her bandaged hand. Betrayed by her own body.

The fall drove the air from her lungs. She scrambled to her feet to face a middle-aged man wielding a scimitar, his face thin and cruel, with lines like rivers carving through deep rock. Namali unsheathed her dagger, eyeing his weapon as he circled her low to the ground. Her heartbeats tumbled one over the other. She could run or she could fight, but right now she hadn't the ability to choose, for his black eyes ensnared her, reminding her of what lay ahead: the end. She had learned long ago how to read someone's eyes, and his told her she would die today.

The man lunged. A rush of air stirred her hair as the blade whipped past. Teeth gritted, she stabbed at his shoulder. Missed. At his counterattack she danced aside and struck again, driving the blade with a steady hand the way Sameen had taught her, cool and in control, but the man knocked it aside as easily as a leaf.

They circled one another, the other competitors forgotten. Her chest heaved. The man feinted right, swung the heavy weapon toward her skull. She ducked, slipped, but managed to keep her footing as he struck with a combination of middle and high blows, counting on his offense to give him the advantage, yet it left him poorly guarded, the fool, and she snaked under his arm to bury the blade in his chest.

A death rattle burst from his lips, fueling the fire in her dark heart. One vicious twist, and Namali yanked the dagger free.

There was little time for victory. Another man charged her, a curved blade in each hand. He quickly overcame her, barreling through any defense she might have had. Arms, legs, stomach—she bled at the touch of his blades, burned from the fire of salt in her wounds. Namali gasped, slashing wildly as his swords kissed her chest with razor lips. This lower block, this dodge—nothing else mattered but his blade against her own, indication that she was still, miraculously, alive.

The man's leer caught the light. He drove her back, down a steep dune so he gained the high ground. She couldn't move fast enough. Blood pooled in her legs, weighing them down, and then she was falling, and as she twisted to catch herself on her uninjured hand, the dagger flew out of her grip. It was lost. *She* was lost.

The man was upon her with a hungry grin. His black eyes swallowed the light, swallowed *her*. Namali clawed at the sand for her weapon, then gave up and chucked some into the competitor's face, the distraction allowing her the time to locate her precious dagger, slide it between his ribs, and end him.

A silent figure intruded into her line of vision.

The elegant robe was little more than tatters. His hair hung in limp, oily locks, his yirasaf strangely absent, most likely having been torn away from the wind. She shoved the body off her and stood, shaking in the scalding heat.

"All right, Namali, you've proved your point," the merchant said. "Now it's time to come home."

Her traitor legs trembled, threatening to buckle, but she straightened with every last bit of strength. He would see no weakness from her. Never again. "How do you keep finding me?" It should not have been this easy to locate a single person in a million square miles of sand.

His gaze flicked to the metal bracelet clasped around her wrist, and something cold and heavy settled in her belly. It appeared as a regular piece of jewelry, unless of course it had a twin used to keep track of the other. The merchant must have had it all this time, traveling in the direction where the gemstone burned brightest. The direction that would lead him to her.

Namali didn't hesitate. She ripped the burning metal from her shadowy wrist and dropped it in the sand. The burden, the chain, was gone. Let the desert lay claim to it. "I'm not going back with you."

His brow furrowed slightly. "I know things are . . . *tense* between us. I shouldn't have treated you so poorly. I should never have hurt you." His attention fell to her bandaged hand. "I'm truly sorry for what I did."

The moment he had placed his selfish needs above her safety and well-being was the moment he had revealed his true self. She nearly spat at his feet. The apology was little more than hot air. His actions, however, would linger, each time she grasped at something, a girl with nine fingers instead of ten. She owed him nothing.

"I do not forgive you," she said, and it felt free.

His next words tumbled out. "Maybe not now, but if you let

me prove to you how good of a husband I can be, it might change your mind."

"Are you even listening to me? Have you *ever* listened to me?" She didn't know whether to cry or claw his eyes out. "With the way you treat others, it's a wonder anyone can be around you for more than a few minutes. Is that honestly what you want? A wife who hates you?"

"Bijala didn't hate me."

"I'm not Bijala," she growled, lips peeled back.

"Please . . ." Palms up, the merchant stepped forward.

And Namali picked up the sword lying near her feet.

He stopped. The skin around his mouth pinched, adding to his overall haggard appearance. "You can't run from me forever."

He was right. She couldn't run forever. But standing here, facing him at last, she realized she'd stopped running from him a long time ago. Instead, she had been running *to* something. A life she loved, a life she *lived*.

For the longest time, strength had eluded her. Strength was for her mother and father, the old man living down the street, Sameen and his brother, Mirza, children without a roof over their heads, struggling in a world with so much less than she. There were times when she had wished for it, fervently, clinging to the possibility that she deserved it, too. Yet each time, without fail, she snuffed it out. *Not me,* she thought. *Never me.* As if she hadn't the right to such a privilege.

And now Namali wondered why she had ever thought such a thing. Strength was not a privilege. It was not gold or jewels to be hoarded, owned by only those who could afford it. It was built brick by brick, in the steel of her spine, the power in her arms, the steadiness of her voice, culminating to a surety in the most chaotic of times. Something that had carried her thousands of miles across heat and sand, pushing her onward even in the hopeless shadow-dark. Something that had led her here, to the Lost City, in the last hours, on the last day, of the Demon Race.

With a white-knuckled grip, she hefted the heavy blade, ignoring the dull ache worming up her arms, and pointed it at his chest. "Don't come any closer." The rush of power made her lightheaded.

The merchant studied her with a dull-eyed gaze. "You think you have it in you to kill me?"

She had killed strangers with a dagger through the heart and back. What was one more?

Before she could answer, he snatched at her arm, probably hoping to catch her unaware, but she had anticipated the attack. Namali swung, the weight throwing her off-balance. Her muscles screamed. The skin around her wounds tugged, and it was like being sliced open all over again. The merchant flew forward, skirting the blow, catching her around the waist.

They slammed into the sand, Namali snarling and thrashing and carried upon a wave of vehemence. She kneed him in the groin. Cursing, he rolled to the side, allowing her to scramble to her feet and level the blade at his throat. Her arms trembled from the urge to ram it through. It would be so, so easy.

"Let me make something clear," she hissed. "You do not have the power here—I do. You do not have control—I do. Now listen, and listen closely. I am a human being, and I deserve resp—"

An arm wrapped around her neck, cutting off her air. She dropped the weapon to curl her unwounded hand around the band of muscle. The pressure increased to bruising. Her head swam as he choked the life from her, a life she was only beginning to live.

Somehow, she managed to press her mouth against his arm, and she tore into the man's salty flesh with her canines, the warm tang of blood flooding her mouth. The man howled and wrenched away.

"Behind you!" Sameen cried.

She rolled away as the merchant grabbed for her while Sameen struggled against the fat man, their blades hilt to hilt. Enemies and demons alike blazed past, heading for the shimmering gold wall, the entrance gates, thick clouds of dust trailing them. Many had already disappeared into the city.

A grunt, a spurt of blood, and the enemy collapsed. Sameen panted, poised in a crouch, his sword, which she assumed he had taken from one of the bodies littering the ground, pointed at the merchant. Sweat poured down his face. "Namali, go to the city."

It took a moment for the words to puncture through the haze of bloodlust. Surely she'd heard wrong. "Sameen—"

"Just go." His attention flicked to her, then back to the merchant, his eyes holding unwavering resolve. The eyes of a warrior. The eyes of a friend.

The merchant glanced between them, face pinched. "Think about what you're doing, Namali," he said, voice raw. "I can make you happy, give you everything you've ever wanted. This poor boy cannot."

As Namali took her first step toward the merchant, picking up the sword she had dropped, it felt like coming awake after an eternity of sleep. She was not weak. She would not be cowed. The time had come to make a stand. Today. Now.

A choked sound emerged from Sameen's mouth when she reached his side. "What are you doing?" The hand holding his sword trembled.

"What does it look like I'm doing?"

"Go. I'll handle this."

"We stay together." They had guarded one another in the beginning and would do so until the end. There was no one she would rather be with when the darkness came. "Besides," she added, pressing down on his wrist so he lowered his weapon, eyes never leaving the merchant, "This fight is mine."

Sameen grinded his teeth together, clearly unhappy with this change in events. Indecision rooted him. "Are you sure?"

If she had not already fallen for him these past weeks, she would have done so in this moment, here on the brink of great change. He would not deny her this fight, but he would support her efforts, and carry her, should she ask. Namali never asked, had never needed to. He spoke the language of her heart.

"I'm sure."

He retreated with a quiet, "Remember to keep your knees bent," before standing guard at her back.

The merchant said, in genuine sadness, "I wish it didn't have to come to this."

And Namali replied, "I wish a lot of things." Then she swung her blade toward the merchant's unprotected side with all the strength she possessed.

A clash rang in the air, carrying over the land, the song of Lomorian steel.

The force of his block ripped through her shoulder joints. He retaliated in a series of high and low strikes, his blade a dangerous line of silver, never satisfied, never still. His wealth belied his expert swordsmanship, a certain poise she lacked. Indeed, he did not appear worried in the slightest. Namali thrust the thought aside. Maybe she wasn't an expert, but she had come far. Invisible, but no longer. She had two hands and a will carved of black stone.

It quickly grew clear, however, that he did not take this fight seriously and did not intend to harm her. He slapped her ribs with the flat of his blade, the sting hot and sudden. Then again to her other side, no better than a scolding toward a disobedient child.

Blood flushed from her neck to the tips of her ears. Was that what this was? A lesson to be taught? Even with a sword in her hand and murder in her eyes, he would never view her as anything more than an unfortunate inconvenience. She owed it to herself. To be feared was to be respected.

Instead of avoiding his next blow, she stepped *into* it. As he pulled back in surprise to readjust his stance, Namali rammed her shoulder into the center of his chest with all her fury, all her fiery might, watching in satisfaction as he tipped backward, dragged down by gravity's heavy hand. She smiled. Let him discover what came of those who did not learn.

He hit the ground on his back. It pleased her more than she could say. He was a bug she might squash beneath her heel.

With a heady sense of power, Namali lifted her sword. Stared into his eyes. Dread, horror, denial—all emotions she had felt as he brought the dagger to the base of her smallest finger. And then, pain. She would be glad to return the favor.

"Namali." A warning.

Namali faltered, sword still raised. She had forgotten Sameen was there, keeping watch.

Kill him, kill him, kill him, the sword screamed, and oh, how she wanted to, but at the last second, she twisted her hand and slammed the pommel against his skull instead. He slumped to the ground.

A touch to her shoulder brought her back from the edge. In the distance, the hawk-man yanked two people off their mounts with a sandy tentacle while a towering bull of a man slaughtered three more. "You didn't . . ."

"Later," she cut in, not knowing how long the merchant would remain unconscious. "Let's go."

Grabbing his hand, she pulled him toward the city. Men abandoned their mounts to give chase.

"Faster," Namali panted. The outer wall, a fortification of impossible splendor, touched the very roof of the world. She pushed her legs harder, bulling through the paralyzing burn creeping up her calves and thighs, but the deep, soft sand combined with Sameen's limp prevented them from moving faster than a slow jog.

"Namali—"

The distance between them widened.

"We're almost there." She squeezed his fingers in reassurance, their skin slick.

Sameen stumbled. "I can't—"

"Only a little farther."

"Namali, wait. Wait." He slowed, half-bending at the waist to catch his breath. His chest heaved beneath his grimy robe. "You go ahead. I'll catch up."

The moon cloaked the burning orb of the sun halfway, leaving one side bright, the other black as night. Her heart thumped like the hollow beat of a drum. "What are you doing? They're getting closer." Even as she spoke, two men melted into daevas and tore the hawk-man to shadowy streams.

"I'm slowing you down. My foot—I can't run as fast as you."

She didn't dare look at his foot, though the urge was strong. Instead, she looked to the gates. Burnished gold. And so far away. "That's fine." What else was there to say? If she had the strength she would carry them both, but her heart felt as if it were one beat away from expiring. "We'll . . . we'll go slower then."

His eyes were serious. "We both know only one person can get the wish."

She could always count on Sameen to be realistic, but this wasn't the time. They stood amidst a killing field while blood rained down. "You don't know that. If we reach it at the same time, we'll both get the wish." Namali bit her lip, spared another glance. "Come on." She tugged on his hand.

He didn't budge. "You know that won't work."

Frustration warred with the fear that he was right, that all she had believed possible was lost. "It will." She would make it work, whatever it took. "Somehow . . . somehow it will work. I know it."

"Just because we both want this to happen doesn't mean it will."

She blinked back tears. "I don't *care*. All I care about is you and me making it to the end." How could he not see that?

His mouth, that beautiful mouth, twisted in pain. "You're running out of time."

Panic swelled, and she stepped closer with urgency. "You mean *we're* running out of time."

"No, I mean you."

Then he did something that left her breathless.

He dropped her hand.

The chasm in her chest widened. She had never experienced such emptiness before. Not like this, like being crushed beneath a black void. "Why are you doing this? We can both win. It will work if we try." It had to, because if it didn't, one of them would lose—everything.

Maybe I've already lost.

"After everything you've been through," he said, "you deserve the wish. You deserve to live the life you desire."

"And you don't? You deserve the wish as much as I do." He wasn't selfish like her. He was good. He was light. "You take it. Use it to save your brother."

"And the merchant?"

Thankfully still unconscious. "He knows where I stand on the issue of our marriage."

Face grave, he shook his head and pulled her to the side, out of range of the worst of the fighting. They were still far enough away from the entrance to not pose much of a threat. "He won't stop until he gets what he wants. You take the wish. Use it to be free of the marriage."

What he offered . . . she could no longer bear to look at him.

Namali turned to survey the land. An absolute bloodbath. Worse than those killed were those mortally wounded, forced to suffer hours beneath the beating sun while their bodies bled out. "But your brother will die," she whispered. Choice—it had the potential to free her or tear her apart.

He tunneled his fingers through his shaggy hair, head bent. At some point, probably as they fled the sand serpent, he had lost his yirasaf. "There might be another way," he replied, more to himself. "Another cure."

They both knew there was no such thing.

"I want you to be happy," he said.

Covering her face with her hands, Namali burst into tears. This was wrong. All wrong. How could she be happy with herself by allowing Sameen's brother to die? What would that prove? "I can't let you do this to your brother. I can't."

His callused hands gently removed hers so he could look into her eyes. She felt his openness, how he wanted to share with her this moment, both quiet and separate in the storm. "I love my brother, Namali. I love him from the bottom of my heart."

"Then why?" She didn't understand.

"I've learned that sometimes Mahurzda has a path for you, and it's different from the one you're on."

"But how do you know? How do you know it's meant to be, that it's the right path? It could be the wrong one. It could be a mistake."

His lips trembled. The touch of grief to his mouth was foreign to her. "Faith. Faith that everything will be as it should. If Mirza dies, then that's what the Good Lord meant to happen. At least . . . at least he won't be in pain anymore." His voice cracked, mirroring the fissure down her heart. "At least his soul will finally be able to rest in peace."

"Don't do this, Sameen." She clutched his hand to her chest, against her pounding heart. "Don't make me choose."

His dark lashes swept his cheekbones, settling like the softest of petals. "I'm choosing for you," he whispered, "so you don't have to."

She was crying so hard she couldn't see him clearly. It was not supposed to end this way. She didn't want this pain. Not at all.

"Please—"

Sameen shifted closer, a whisper of space lingering between their bodies. He skimmed his fingers across her veiled cheek, and the pull between them tightened, a sweet, dark ache. "I love you, Namali. I love your courage, and your kindness, and your heart. I didn't enter this race expecting to find love, but I did. I'm only sorry it's taken me this long to tell you."

Starlight burst inside of her, flooding all those dark, hollow pockets with light. For a brief moment, all thoughts of the Demon King fled to make room for the healing touch of his words. He loved her. All of her.

She sobbed, "Why do you have to be so kind?"

His mouth bowed upward. A beautiful smile. It reminded her of the sun, for when it appeared on the horizon it bathed the land in gold, and when it disappeared she waited in vain until it showed its face again.

Namali glanced at the competitors barging through the entrance gates. There was still time, but she couldn't help but hang on to this moment, this man, for as long as possible, because she knew once they parted, nothing would ever be the same again. "I didn't want to feel these things for you. I didn't want it." Mahurzda was cruel. As she had learned, wanting left her unsatisfied. "I never expected . . ." She swallowed and looked down.

"Whatever you have to say," he said, placing a finger underneath her chin to tilt up her head, "don't be afraid."

Namali trembled. The truth lifted inside of her, light as air, but it was too huge, too daunting to face. She wasn't ready.

"I . . . I want you to know I never expected to . . . care for you this much."

Silence. The type that existed in places untouched by light. Silence dark and utterly alone.

When she glanced up, his smile was too brittle, too bright. She was a terrible person for hurting him this way, for answering his truth with lies.

Stepping away, he released her chin and allowed his hands to fall at his sides. "I'll hold them off as best as I can."

"Sameen—"

He looked to the wave of swords and daggers barreling toward them. "Go, or I'll never forgive myself."

There was not enough time in the world to consider whether her decision was right and the consequences if it was not. The eclipse, Sameen, their circumstances—all played a part in shaping the future, and the future could not wait.

So she ran. Ran and did not look back. Ran toward the Lost City as fast as her weighted legs could carry her, wondering how a gift so priceless came with such a heavy burden to bear.

CHAPTER 28

THE AIR INSIDE the Lost City hung still and undisturbed, empty in the way of places long since inhabited. Bone buildings protruded from the murk, glowing like faint apparitions of the past, yet there was no one to witness their stark and silent beauty. An air of abandonment and ruination clotted the once pristine city. Grime caked the jeweled streets and bone surfaces, and the towers clawed at the dark sky. Sparse, defeated, a tumor where a flowering garden once flourished. All this space with no one to fill it. Nothing grew here. The weeds were emeralds, mossy green. The flowers were rubies, amethyst, and diamonds, cracked and dulled. And the trees were not trees at all, but rather spears sculpted of black onyx, hammered into the earth and forgotten.

From the sight of bodies littering the ground, the first competitors to reach the city had already come and gone. Namali stepped around the fallen, unable to avoid the crimson pools. Her sandals splashed through the warm, rusted liquid. A small thrill surged up her spine. This was where she must restore her master's heart, and it would not come easy. The others, too, fought for the privilege of his favoritism. At least some of the work had already been done for her. A single pair of bloody footprints led away from the carnage to end at a corpse, its stomach split open, innards strewn among the broken limbs. The vultures were already feasting.

A cry snapped her attention to the entrance, where demon-men swarmed through the gates. Some wobbled on two legs, others on four, and the crowd was so massive it was difficult to distinguish any one person. Screams and snarls, the flash of slithering, shadowy bodies. Men and beasts alike piled up between the gates, forcing others to climb over the remains, making for easier targets. Blood ran rivers down the street.

Namali bolted down the road, onyx columns whipping past, and veered right. More cracked spires and domes, a lonely bridge having once spanned a rushing river, dilapidated dwellings. Her mind raced, and her heart raced, and her feet thundered against dusty jewels, pushing her through the eerie gray light, and she didn't care where she was going, so long as it was away. The wave of men and beasts was coming. The promise of it burned like a fire at her back.

After passing what appeared to be an abandoned ice house, she reached a fork in the road. The clash of blades rang closer than before. Namali studied one path, which veered toward an empty courtyard, the other vanishing into a rolling fog.

If this fork told her anything, it was this: she knew nothing. She did not know where these trails would lead because she did not know what to look for. She did not know what to look for because no one did. Only young Delir, who was long gone save his story imprinted between the musty pages of a book. Even then, his tale did not reveal the Lost City's secrets. The wish could be buried in a box fifty feet below ground for all she knew, in which case this was futile.

When a soft growl reached her ears, Namali sucked in a shallow breath. The fog encased her legs, a gradual shift she had not noticed. She felt the demons before she saw them—cold, slithering tendrils clinging to her ankles like leaches, sucking out her warmth. They emerged from between two buildings, teeth bared. An entire pack of them, longer of leg, wider of chest. She had not heard them approach. They truly were night incarnate.

Namali backed up slowly, reaching for her dagger as they formed a half-circle around her, the largest of the four flanking the two smaller ones. She had time enough to grip her weapon before they were upon her.

Snarls ripped from their throats as they snapped at her legs and drove her to the ground. Namali kicked out at one, slashed her dagger at the other, but it jumped out of reach and slipped under her guard to strike once more, tearing into her arm until she screamed. Fire rasped its forked tongue deep into the wound, scouring flesh, the anguish intensifying with each passing moment. Three competitors raced by, ignoring her pleas. She blinked as they passed, lashes wet, vision too bright. The sound of her pain chased them through the city.

She kicked again, catching one demon in the muzzle. The other she stabbed in the eye, and the beast's howl shook the buildings. It did not bleed as she bled. Rather, white smoke poured from the gouge. Namali nearly broke free, but then a third rammed into her head, snapping it back so it slammed against stone and stars burst behind her eyelids.

They were everywhere. Sucking away the light. Feeding on her despair. Her body was a raw, lit nerve, her throat hoarse from screaming. She clawed at the ground to pull herself away, but another demon tore into her shoulder. Her sobs grew to shattering wails. Her blood dripped rubies among the jewels.

Help would not come. The dagger lay beyond arm's reach. Bloodied fingers stretched toward it, her teeth gritted, face shiny with perspiration. She kicked half-heartedly at the beast nipping her legs, and its fangs sank into the meat of her thigh. She choked on a cry as her fingers brushed the dagger's metal base, their trembling causing her to accidentally push the weapon a few inches farther. Slippery, slippery blood.

She did not want to die.

Namali dug deep to where her last bit of strength lay. With a violent screech, she lunged for the knife and slashed at her captors with everything she had. This was for Sameen, and her mother, and her father, but most of all, *most of all*, this was for herself.

This was for the girl borne of stories.

This was for the girl shaped by tragedy, her coward's heart.

This was for the girl set free.

And this was for the girl she would become, in time. The girl she had yet to fully meet.

One by one the beasts fell, sliced into ribbons of black smoke struck through with white.

The daevas did not move again.

Namali slumped onto the ground, breathing hard. Sweat and blood dripped from her skin onto the cold hard jewels. It was too much and yet not enough. How could she want to flee and continue on at the same time? What madness had overtaken her?

The ground trembled.

Her head snapped up. Two men sprinted toward her, and Namali lurched to her feet and hobbled away from the path, into the deep, watchful shadows. If she wanted to survive, she must disappear.

She stumbled through the buildings, weaving between cracked, broken columns and magnificent crumbling temples, and left the road far behind. The city cast a ghostly glow, as though the protective outer wall would not let darkness penetrate. She fell into the tangle of passageways and corridors and conquered ruins, into a story long ago foretold. There were secrets here, buried deep within the earth. Slumbering. The umbra whispered its history. A city of mortals and gods, loved by both, claimed by neither. It was as close to a heaven as she would ever experience in this lifetime.

After some time, Namali slowed. Her ears strained for sound. She could have sworn she'd heard her name spoken, a whisper in the hush. Perhaps she had been mistaken.

But the voice came again, saying, *Namali,* and she knew she had not.

Her feet moved. First a walk, and then a run. Down the long, gloomy road stretching beyond like the throat of a monstrous beast. Hunger swept through her body until the bones of her legs fused together, knee caps snapping backward, and she was running in an awkward half-walk, half-lope motion. Soon she would join her kin, become a servant in her true form.

Soon.

A vague shape sprouted from the center of a deserted crossroads, hidden behind the film beginning to claim her eyes. Namali approached the fountain warily, as there was something familiar about its shape. She traced the central sculpture, claw points scraping over gritty stone. A swirling sun. The birth of fire. She snarled. Mahurzda. The Demon King's betrayer, his *brother*. The Good Lord had a choice, on that day, to be merciful, yet had chosen something infinitely more permanent. At least now she had the chance to right his wrong.

Stepping away from the offensive sculpture, she glanced around. Four roads diverged from this point, heading north, east, south, and west. It seemed the city was laid out on a grid. One of these paths led to her heart's desire. The others led nowhere. South seemed like a good choice, though so did west . . .

North.

Namali raced down the road heading north, allowing her sandals to slip free, as they would not be needed much longer. The buildings towered overhead, crowding close. Whispers slid through the empty spaces, soft murmurings of lives that had long since become dust. The path cut through one of the courtyards, the desiccated pools, before veering into one of the elegant temples. She tore down a corridor, through darkness and vast, empty chambers. The columns were pale, spindly ghosts. The few mirrors clinging to the walls and ceilings caught glimpses of her reflection, but Namali didn't slow, didn't tear her gaze away from the bottomless space beyond, for if she looked, if she met those eyes in the mirror, she would wonder how she had ever denied herself this one true thing: to accept the skin she lived in.

Eventually, she reached a second fountain half-buried beneath rubble. Broken, along with everything else. A statue depicted Mahurzda with two enormous wolves flanking him. His gilded eyes followed her as she circled it once on four legs and again on two, then a third time to make certain, her muzzle alternating between sniffing the air and ground for clues. An image, a word, something to show her the right path. Time was the enemy, creeping up while her back was turned. She scoured every inch, even going so far as to dig around the fountain base, but it was bare of inscriptions. Nothing to indicate which direction the wish lay.

She paced back and forth, and as she did, her robe burst into black fire and left behind a shadow cloak. Her spine bowed forward, forcing her completely onto four legs. The moon began to part from the sun, and still she searched, as she'd been doing her entire life, but for what? She didn't know what she should be looking for. She was lost. In her head, in her heart, and now in this city where nothing grew.

The whispers were stronger now. Wisps of sound coaxed and cooed with sweet promises, things that *could* be, if she only let them in. The buildings fell into disrepair the farther she ran, their roofs collapsed and fissures creeping up their crumbling walls. Her breath rushed out, harsh and wild in her ears, and she would run forever if it meant reaching the end, gaining the prize, putting a halt to this madness.

When the jeweled road became a dirt path, her pulse soared in anticipation, but upon reaching the stretch of outer wall, Namali skidded to a halt in confusion. Was this some sort of trick? A maze of roads leading nowhere?

Dread sank into her. This couldn't be it. There had to be more. More roads, more fountains, more *something*. She didn't come all this way, cross the entire Saraj, only to find there was nothing here.

But the wall was answer enough.

There was nowhere else to go.

Had she misinterpreted the information? Overlooked a key detail? It didn't make sense. If the Demon King required the wish to return to power, then why make it impossible to find? Unless . . . was the wish hidden with his heart, and she must seek both?

Her ears twitched from a faint scrape behind her—a treading foot, reluctant to draw attention to itself. Fangs flashing, she whirled toward a shadowy figure. Fear leaked from his pores, thick and sweet, and her nostrils flared in response.

"Namali?"

That voice. Familiar, and not in a good way. She circled the man who reeked of cloves and sweat and longing, her body rippling at the edges as she moved. "Who are you?" she cried, and the sound splintered through her. It was the braying of hounds on a hunt. The deep and mournful wail of grief.

She thought he would recoil at the sight of her form, closer to that of a demon than a girl, but he did not. "Hazil Abdu, your . . . husband."

She stopped circling him. Her throat cinched with the memories she would rather forget. "You lie."

He wiped the sweat from his brow, hand trembling. "I do not. We are betrothed."

It seemed like a lifetime ago that she had sat in a room with this man. The conversation had been a blur. But she remembered his yirasaf: red. She remembered the feeling of a cow being led to slaughter. "You are mistaken."

"We belong together."

She bared her teeth, darkly pleased when he flinched. "I belong to no one."

"You—" His throat worked. He looked so confused, as if he

no longer knew the reason for his being here. The Saraj did not discriminate from whom it took, and how much. "You would not give me another chance to prove myself?"

"Never."

He studied her for a long moment, long enough for Namali to shift in unease. "Then perhaps there's a way I can convince you otherwise."

He unsheathed his scimitar.

The void in Namali's heart expanded, stretching so far and wide no light could escape. She laughed a bitter laugh. "What will you do? Kill me?" In many ways, she was already dead. After all, what remained after death but darkness?

His fingers twitched around the hilt and lay still. "Maybe," he said. "Or I can get the wish myself and force you to stay with me. If you don't belong to me, you don't belong to anyone, least of all that peasant boy of yours."

A growl rumbled in her chest. She'd nearly forgotten Sameen. "What did you do to him?"

He shrugged, and his eyes hardened. "The poor boy could hardly fight with a twisted leg. If you don't care for your own life, then what of the boy's? How far would you go to stop me from slitting his throat?" He mimicked the motion with his sword.

The merchant had crossed an uncrossable line, one which separated those Namali loved from those she did not, her heart from her mind, her most hidden secrets from the rest of the world. She could not stand by and allow this human to hurt the people she cared for. She could not let this man hold power over her any longer. He would take and take until she was empty. He was a hot flame needing to be snuffed out.

Her feet were moving, though her mind was still. There was no thought as she lunged, claws extended. As she slammed into the merchant with the force of a stone wall and brought him down. She would not ask. She would demand. She would fling her voice to all corners of the world.

"Let's make something clear," she hissed, shoving her muzzle into his pale face. "Sameen is twice the man you'll ever be. He treats me with kindness and respect. You treat me like dirt." And what did she do to those who mistreated her? What did the Demon King order his servants to do?

Punish them.

Namali increased the pressure so her claws punctured into muscle and he screamed and thrashed from the pain. *Good,* she thought. *Good.* Let him scream. Let him understand.

"Please," he begged, his voice a high whine. "Please."

"Was it worth it? Was it worth everything you've done? Was it worth intimidating me into marrying you? Was it worth chasing me across the Saraj to prove your power over me?" She snarled the words. "Well?"

The merchant's grief-stricken eyes rolled upward. She wondered if he believed in a heaven, and if he could glimpse it through the dark huddling around them. "I don't—I don't know. Please!" He tried to shove her off as fat tears rolled down his cheeks, soaking into his beard. "I beg of you, Bijala."

"My name is not Bijala."

He blinked in genuine puzzlement, hands slack. "How—"

"What would your wife think of you?" She spat the words like venom. She was a monster, yes, but so was he, so was he. "What would she say to the man you've become?"

The merchant flinched. "Don't speak about my wife that way. You know nothing."

Before the Demon Race, she had lived her life behind a curtain of innocence, but now . . . now she knew too much. "I know you're a lonely man. I know you loved your wife deeply, and she was taken from you too soon."

"Stop it."

She would not. He would hear her, and she would not need to speak above the barest whisper. "No matter how much you wish for me to be your wife, it will never come to pass." Her laugh was rough, strained. "I used to be afraid of men like you. I used to be afraid of becoming trapped in living a life that was not mine to control. Tell me, how does it feel to be powerless? How does it feel knowing your word is worth nothing? Less than nothing?"

Something in the merchant's expression shifted. A slow glide, like smoke shifting under glass. "You're hurting me," he said hoarsely.

"*I'm* hurting *you?*" She leaned her face closer so the shadows from her body flowed down his neck and shoulders. He shivered from the shock of cold. "What about all the ways in which you've hurt *me?*" Her claws sank deeper, yet it wasn't enough. An eye for an eye, her people said, but if she went one step further and ended his miserable life, it might make up for the pain he'd caused her. Let the Saraj bury him beneath a sandy grave and beat his bones to dust. "Why do this to yourself? To me?"

"Please—"

"Answer the question," she snarled. Time was slipping.

Covering his face with his hands, he sobbed, loud and long and unable to breathe, "I loved her. I loved her so much. And now she's gone."

His sobs punched low into her gut. His grief was so thick she could nearly taste it. She choked on the air as if it were a knot of rope. "What does that have to do with anything?" Her voice lost some of its rage.

"I just wanted some way to be with her, to be happy again."

Namali closed her eyes, grasping for the threads of her control. No. *No.* He shouldn't have the right to mourn, not after what he'd done to her, the scars he'd inflicted. He had stolen away her comfort and security. He had injected fear into her heart until it festered and spread. It wasn't fair that he should live to hurt others for the sake of his selfishness. Where was the justice, the order? She should kill him for both their sakes.

Namali shook from reining in that black wave, the urge to fill his eyes, nose, and throat with eternal night. The bottomless hunger swelled, and the need punctured through, curled in. How she wanted to. It would be a sweet release for him, a gift. One long exhale into nothingness.

But when she looked into his eyes, she froze.

These were eyes she knew, somehow. Large, dark, vulnerable. Broken and lost and full of questions. Brown and turbulent, snapping with anger, swimming with tears, shining with joy, dancing with amusement. She'd seen them before. She'd seen them in mirrors and in water's smooth reflection. She'd looked through them for seventeen long years.

These were *her* eyes.

Except how could that be? This was a man who had spent the last thirty days breathing down her neck. His warped, twisted soul, desperate for a shred of what he once had. Black intentions, and an even blacker heart.

As Namali stared down at the merchant, however, she knew that to be untrue. When she looked at him, *truly* looked at him, she saw all of him. The black *and* the gray. The ugly *and* the misunderstood. He was not one thing, but many. All these parts of him, all these parts of her. Different path, same direction. She had forgotten, had lost what made her human and complicated and flawed. Human life was not favored as the gods were. It was messy and confusing and often without purpose. What the gods were gifted, they had to carve out with every breath.

Removing her claws, Namali stood. The amount of power she had by merely looking down at him astounded her. "We are done, Mr. Abdu. We are done."

With a sob, the merchant curled around himself, wallowing deeper in his grief while the air shifted beyond his huddled form, twisting in a counter-clockwise motion. Eventually, a door solidified—large, arched, and shimmering as if born from sunlight.

Heart pounding, Namali approached and curled her claws around the bone handle.

Need seared through every pore and cell, almost bringing her to her knees. At long last. The wish lay beyond this door, thrumming with the power to change everything. Her master would be so proud of his servant. So proud.

Without looking back, Namali stepped through the doorway and shut out the city behind her.

CHAPTER 29

NAMALI PADDED INTO the oval-shaped room on all fours, her paws sinking into plush, heavily tasseled rugs of violet and green. Curved walls soared into a vaulted ceiling like the hollow innards of an empty bowl. There was light here, faint, casting the room in a mist-like glow. She did not know where it came from. The room was windowless, lampless, candleless. But not, she noticed, mirrorless. This must be hell then. A gaping, echoing hell. Why else would mirrors line every inch of wall, each a facet of some mutinous insect eye, unless it was to remind her of how she had turned?

Warily, she approached an ornate chair situated on a dais in the center of the room, memorizing the layout with one sweep of her eyes. The air was cloying, though not unpleasantly so, and it wavered as if she pushed through a viscous substance. The sensation prickled.

"Hello?" Her voice bounced off the cavernous walls, the distance softening its edges until the sound melted into air.

"Hello, Namali."

She whirled around, but saw only the emptiness of a too-large room. "Who are you?"

"You mean you don't recognize me? Of all people, I was sure you would."

"Well, I don't." She didn't, right? She was certain she had never heard this voice before. "Now answer the question."

"I am your eyes," said the voice. "I am your ears. I am the ground beneath your feet." The voice paused. "I am in your heart, too."

Lies.

"I can assure you, I have no reason to lie."

Prowling the room, Namali investigated the floor and walls in hopes of finding this disembodiment, this man who hid himself from her. "How did you know what I was thinking?" If he knew her thoughts, he knew her hunger for the wish, and if he knew that, he must know she'd use it for sinister purposes. And by knowing all of this, she had no secrets, no power, no leverage.

"I am ancient, Namali. I know many things."

Her hackles rose. Then he must know of the girl she had been, poor fool, and the beast that had set her free. "Everything?"

The gruff voice chuckled. "Well, maybe not everything. But most things I know. Yes, most things."

She leaped onto the chair, perforating the silk cushion with her claws. If the wish was in this room, then the man—voice, whatever it was—must know its location. "Are you going to show yourself?"

The silence deepened, and the light in the room dimmed. "Now why would I need to show myself when you already know who I am?"

"I thought I made it clear I don't know who you are, so I'll ask you again. *Who are you?*" Her roar shook the ceiling rafters, pieces of stone showering onto the carpet. Her skin felt too tight. The turmoil pitched and rolled, pitched and rolled. She shredded the pillow in satisfaction, the air swarming with gossamer feathers.

The voice rumbled with laughter. It was thunder in the distance, an earthquake beneath her feet, a great oiled drum. "How the Saraj changes people."

A shudder ripped down her spine as the light in the room bled further into twilight. She leaped from the chair and stalked from wall to wall. Felt a throb, a wave of power from the Demon King's calling. Her master, betrayed, seeking revenge.

The voice continued. "You ask me who I am, but I think the more important question is, '*Who* are *you?*'" The voice darkened. "Why don't you look into the mirror and find out."

Namali turned. Her eyes, cruel and fathomless, two deep punctures in her skull, met those in the mirror and slid over the twisted four-legged creature with revulsion. The flowing dark fur absorbing any and all light; the misshapen form, her head a bulbous growth, legs tapering to twigs; a scrap of tail; the ribs protruding beneath paper-thin skin. The sight chipped at her, piece by piece by piece. It was not gentle. She became a shower of stone, broken by failure, hardened by life. The loss she felt at her own abandonment, the guilt of not having done enough to prevent this atrocity. The impossibility that she had once been a girl at all.

She looked away from the beast's hideousness, trembling. Her stomach roiled. There was nowhere to hide, no need to pretend anymore. Now the world knew what she was.

Whirling, Namali paced the room, returning to the task at hand. She did not need another distraction. "Whoever you are, I know you have the wish." Her hiss seethed between her fangs. "I'm not leaving until you give me what's mine."

"Is this who you are?" the voice wondered. "Is this all there is?"

Is this all there is?

Grief exploded in her chest and drove her in circles around the room. She had been someone else once, a shy and fearful girl, painfully inexperienced in the way of life. What had happened? How did one descend so quickly into insanity? Was she too weak then, too soft? Or had she been so determined to escape her life she had tossed herself aside without reservation?

She was like the blade of one who has oversharpened it, the metal brittle as consequence of seeking a finer, more deadly point. Unbalanced, unstable, unsustainable. But she could be kind *and* assertive, generous *and* firm, loving *and* seen. She wished she could tell past-Namali there was no need to strangle what she had believed to be weaknesses just to prove a point. That person was gone though, torn apart by darkness. She would never know of that girl again.

Springing forward, she slammed into a mirror, scrabbling at the reflective surface with her claws. The glass cracked and shattered, rained onto the carpet. It sliced into her pads, sliced into *her*, and though blood flowed like shadows, there was no pain. What she felt was beyond pain, an acute human experience. It lived and died inside of her. An animal. A disease. Without shape, without name. Yet it touched her so deeply in ways she could not explain, only *feel*. It was all of her, and it was a wound, tight and throbbing, and she thought maybe there was a way to go back, to ease this terrible load, this suffering that was herself.

"Remember who you are. Remember."

A second mirror cracked and shattered, followed by a third. She could not. It was now, not then. *Too late, too late.* Darker than a moonless night. Savage and chaotic and entirely feral. She had left Benahr with hope in her heart, and instead of keeping to the light, she had forged a path of ruination and death. One by one the mirrors cracked, the sound like a snapping branch in the quiet. She would destroy them all, destroy herself. They deserved to be broken. All of them. And she deserved to be broken, too.

The last mirror fell to pieces, leaving gaping walls and shards littering the floor. Namali stopped, panting heavily. Something was shifting inside her chest, tightening, building in pressure until it grew to a fierce ache that stole her breath. These were emotions she had known, once. If she were still human, she would claw at her hair and claw at her eyes and scream until the screams led to tears and her knees gave out and she collapsed onto the piles of jagged glass. The voice said to remember, but how could she remember when she only thought to destroy? It consumed her. All the wonderful things she had known—love, hope, forgiveness—gone. All gone.

The darkness rose up as one mammoth wave. Crashed over her. Namali fought its strength, but it was not enough. It pulled her into deep fathoms, tugged her down to where the sun couldn't penetrate, where all was what it had been before the dawn. This deep, so far away from everything, it would be easy to succumb. No pain, no confusion, just absence. Like dying, only . . . less.

How did one turn from the dark? How did one change course

after drifting for so long? At times, the dark comforted her, because she did not need to hide from its penetrative gaze. Here, she could be cruel, and angry, and heartless, and selfish, and spiteful, and vindictive. All the things light did not shine favorably on. Here, she could be true.

And so she would live her life. If she could not turn from the dark, she would become it. Live in death. Mourn in death.

Serve in death.

She was tired. She was so tired she might very well sleep for an eternity if she closed her eyes. This was what the Demon King wanted, right? And did she not want this, too, in some ways?

But what about all the things she loved, the people she'd leave behind? They were important, too. What about Baba?

What about Sameen?

To love was to be brave, for it was both the storm ravaging your existence and the shelter in which you sought. The path she'd trodden before meeting him had been painfully empty. When she thought about it, truly thought about it, she realized she had carried that gaping emptiness with her for years. But life could be full of so many wonderful things, if only she let in the light.

Warmth spread down her neck, driving away the searing cold. For a moment, she imagined it to be the brush of Sameen's fingers running through her shadowy fur, skimming across her veil.

No, that wasn't right. She was a daeva, and daevas wore no veils. But if that were true, how did she know the warmth of her mother's laughter, the bow of a boy's beautiful mouth, the beauty of forgiveness, grace?

How did she know her name?

Namali.

The edges of her vision burned bright. The song of it poured into her, a stream of pure, liquid light. A song she knew.

Namali. That was her name.

She remembered now. She remembered the light in her heart.

Mouth agape in a silent scream, Namali tore free of the bonds, shedding the clinging shadow, the crippling doubt, until only the girl remained.

Her legs liquified. She slid to the ground, shaking so hard her teeth clacked together. The dim had vanished, and it was so very bright, like being born. The world was new in that way. She touched her teeth—normal. And her hands . . . her hands were smooth and free of shadow.

It was done.

The dam broke, and a river poured from her eyes, down her cheeks and down her chin and onto her hands, dripping like a steady rain onto the glass-covered ground. She couldn't stop. Her heart was a cup filled to brimming, raining relief down her face until all the crushing blackness that had built in her chest these past thirty days vanished.

Thank you, she thought. And again: *thank you.* Namali did not know to whom she spoke. Herself. The universe. Whatever faith had led her, blind, from the shadows. For she was human. Beautifully, painfully human, and she would never take it for granted again.

Behind her, a man cleared his throat tentatively. "Better?"

Her attention slid to the jewel-encrusted chair, where a familiar old man sat, his beard pooling into his lap.

Being careful not to cut her hands on the glass, Namali pushed to her feet. She met the man's steady gaze, wiped tears from her cheeks. "Mahurzda," she said, and it was truth. The all-powerful Lord of Light, who looked as if he might cave from one strong gust of wind.

The Good Lord dipped his chin. "You have come far, Namali Hafshar. Farther than I believed you would."

She curled her fingers into her grimy, tattered robe, recalling every horrific memory she'd experienced these past thirty days. She did not disagree.

He gestured her nearer with a bony hand. "Come closer, child."

"You're a fraud."

His hand fell into his lap. Twitched, then lay still.

"People worship you," she said, stepping forward. "*I* worship you." The Good Lord, who walked the path of darkness alongside her. It was personal. Faith was personal. And now it felt coated in filth as if having been dragged through the mud. "They think you're the answer, that you can do no wrong." Her voice held an undercurrent of steel, and she did not know if it was for their behalf or hers. "You killed your own brother."

She did not think it possible, but he seemed to age a thousand years before her eyes. "Technically, the divine cannot die."

"That's not what I meant," she snapped, and he knew it.

Mahurzda scrubbed his shriveled hands, like brittle bird bones, over his face, the fatigue of a man haunted, doomed to never find peace. "Do you think I don't regret my decision? I have had an eternity of guilt and shame, and I still wish I had chosen differently."

"Then why did you do it?"

His expression grew distant as he studied a point beyond her shoulder. "He stole my daughter from me, my only child. I feared her lost. I feared I had failed her."

At his words, Namali curled her arms around herself, and thought of Baba.

"My brother never knew of family. It was in part my fault. I did not stand up to our father when my brother was sent away. I accept the blame. So when he took Barandi, I feared she would become like him. Spiteful. Empty." His beard swung like a ratty pendulum. "You know fear well, Namali. I'm sure you can understand why I did what I did."

She looked around the room, at the mirror shards littering the floor. So sharp and unforgivingly cruel. "Yes," she said, more to herself. "I do."

"I did what I felt was right at the time, even though now I see it was wrong."

"Do you blame him?"

"How could I?" A pained curve of his mouth. "I turned my back on him, so he turned his back on me. He was carved from the life our father sentenced him to. I cannot blame him for that."

"So then what about the race?"

"I would have given anything for the Great Pack to be restored, for light to return to the world the way it once was. But I needed someone with a selfless heart to accomplish that, for mine was too filled with want."

That gave her pause. It was strange. Why did she suddenly feel as though she peered through a door that had formerly been closed? She had believed the Demon Race a strategized move, yet wondered how the Demon King would have the power to grant someone a wish in his eternal prison. There had always been a missing piece.

"*You* created the race, didn't you."

He inclined his ancient head. "Of a sort. The daevas already sought the Lost City every thousand years, on the day the mortal and immortal realms opened to one another. It was simply a matter of turning the process into a race and offering a reward to people who were willing to risk their lives. The wish would prove if someone possessed a heart free of greed. If they used the wish for something other than benefiting themselves, then the Great Pack would be freed. If they didn't, I would have to wait until the next solar eclipse in hopes that someone new would come along and change things."

"Except the Demon King took advantage of the race, too."

The Good Lord leaned back, frowning. The chair practically swallowed him. "Unfortunately. Had you wished for his soul to be restored, I would have had no choice but to do so. It was a necessary risk."

Then thank Mahurzda she had been strong enough, true enough. "Can I ask you something?"

"Of course."

"Whatever happened to Delir? In the stories, it's written that he reached the Lost City, but it never goes into detail about what happened afterward."

"Delir." He shook his head at the memory. It reminded her a bit of her father, the way fondness could look so akin to sorrow. "Such a spirit that boy had."

She was afraid to hear what he had to say.

He sighed. "It's true he reached the Lost City. But the young man's heart wasn't pure. Why do you think the race still exists?"

Namali ran her tongue along the bottom of her teeth. Her mouth and jaw had yet to feel natural despite the shift back. She continued to anticipate the sting of sharp points sinking into her lower lip. Maybe there would come a day when she did not flinch, but today was not that day. "Did Delir, I mean, was he . . ." She gestured, unable to say it.

"Saved?"

Her arms dropped, and she nodded.

"No," said Mahurzda. "He was not."

"I don't understand," she whispered. "Why was his heart not pure? He reached the end, didn't he?" Her voice pitched, the words strangled. She had hoped differently. "Say I used the wish to cure Sameen's brother. Won't that prove I have a selfless heart?"

Mahurzda smiled in sympathy. "Unfortunately, no. The very act of you wishing for Mirza's improved health, even though it may benefit him, remains an act of selfishness because your happiness directly correlates with the outcome of that wish."

"But you're Mahurzda. Can't you just order people to free the Great Pack?"

"Ah." He lifted one wrinkled finger. "That is both the beauty and downfall of a mortal life. It is not for me to decide how you live."

"So then how is the Great Pack supposed to be freed?"

Mahurzda stared at her for a long moment. "I think," he said, with deliberate articulation, "we should discuss what you intend to wish for."

She wiped her sweaty palms on her robe, at a loss. Either he did not have the answer, or he chose not to reveal it. So what now? He offered her the world, but such a gift required great responsibility. She did not know if she was ready for it. She could wish for freedom as she had originally intended, or she could wish for something else, something to prove her selflessness. But where did the balance between what *she* wanted and what the world expected of her come into play? If she had learned anything on this journey, it was this: she was not less, and so she would not act in ways to make it so. She deserved her best life.

Namali rubbed her tired eyes. It was hard. Harder than she would have believed for a girl willing to do almost anything to shed the skin of her old life. "Can I ask you something else?"

"Certainly."

With a quiet sigh, she let her hands fall to her sides. Her body throbbed. "What would you wish for?"

Like a child offered a sweet, his face came alight. "Me?"

She nodded, and wondered if Mahurzda had ever been asked such a thing. Never, probably. He was, after all, a god.

Tapping his chin, he considered her question. "I suppose . . . I suppose I would wish for a friend. It gets rather lonely up there, especially with the Great Pack gone."

This mattered to him. It mattered that she'd asked. Even when someone had everything in the world, it still wasn't enough. The wants of gods and men were infinite.

"I don't know if this is allowed," she said, finally reaching a decision, "but I'd like more time to consider my wish. I don't want to rush into anything."

He gave a slow, solemn nod. "I think that can be arranged."

Rising from his chair, Mahurzda reached into his beard and

removed a clear, perfectly spherical jewel, a rainbow shimmering at its core. With the wish nestled in his palm, he descended the dais and offered it to her. "When you decide to use it," he said, voice low and serious, "touch it to your lips, say what it is your heart desires, and your wish will be granted."

"Many thanks," she whispered, sliding the wish into the pouch hidden in her robe. With a final bow, she headed for the entrance.

He smiled, childlike once more. "You are most welcome, Namali Hafshar."

CHAPTER 30

NAMALI REACHED THE entrance gates within minutes, halting at the edge of a violent red sea. Seven hells. The wave of fallen men swept far and wide, their bodies stinking beneath the blistering sun. The daevas were gone, sucked back into the earth, but a few horses loitered near their dead owners. The deaths were too many to count. The stench of rust plowed into her gut, and flies swarmed thickly around the carcasses, crowding into their orifices. The dead air shimmered with heat.

She stepped forward, lightheaded. Scanned the ground for a blue yirasaf before remembering Sameen had lost it. She couldn't distinguish the men in death, crumpled and broken as they were. "Sameen?"

"Namali." A rasp.

She whirled, raced toward a huddle of shadow slumped against the city's outer wall. At her approach, Sameen struggled into a sitting position, then grimaced and drooped back down. His hand, coated in blood, pressed against the oozing wound in his side. "I'm here," she whispered, touching his ashen cheek. His features were human again, like hers.

A cough wracked his weakened body. "I was afraid you had left without me."

It was clearly a joke, but she replied, strained, squeezing his fingers so hard they bulged white at the tips, "I wouldn't. I would never."

"I'm glad, You know how much I wanted to . . . see the world with you."

Her hand clapped over her mouth to muffle a sob. He was slipping away. To a place she could not reach.

His eyes clouded in pain and fluttered closed.

"*Sameen.*"

He opened them, and her skin flushed hotly with mounting, clawing, frenzied panic. He needed medical attention. The red dampness pooling beneath him spread. "You're going to be fine. Look, I have the wish," she said, fumbling for the pouch hidden in the folds of her robe. The rest didn't matter. They were things, objects. He was beloved. He could not be replaced. "I'll use it to heal you."

He laid a palm on her arm, stopping her movements. His eyelids drooped over his glassy-eyed stare. "I won't have you sacrifice your freedom to save me. If it's my time to go, then that's Mahurzda's plan for me."

"You're not thinking straight."

"For the first time, I think I am."

She gritted her teeth, blinking back tears. "Stop trying to be a hero."

His body sagged deeper into the sand. "I'm no hero, Namali. Just a boy in love."

Impossible, that her heart could break even further. Her lips trembled, and she pressed them tighter to hold in the sob climbing up her throat. She refused to lose him, refused to even consider the possibility. "Don't . . ." *Die*. "Just stay awake, all right?" She looked around. Vultures descended on the dead, pecking at their sightless eyes. The landscape was void of human life.

Except for one man who stumbled through the entrance gates, collapsing on the sand among the dead.

"Keep putting pressure on the wound," she told Sameen, before running to where the merchant lay, coated in blood and grime. He was as filthy as she, and hanging on for life like the rest of them.

"Mr. Abdu."

The merchant, curled on his side, tilted back his head. "What do you want?"

"I want you to help my friend."

"If you think—"

Her dagger snaked up to kiss his throat, halting his words. They were meaningless anyway. "You're going to help him, or I'll shove this blade down your throat." She would not, although he didn't need to know that. "Now tell me where the nearest town is."

He didn't so much as flinch. "Zeminir is fifty miles east," he said tonelessly, with a glare bordering on loathing, "but the most advanced healers live in Ahkbur." A pause. "He has a few days, maybe."

Her grip on the hilt slackened. The distance to Ahkbur might kill Sameen. Then again, it might also save his life. "Do you have any healing supplies?"

"Sandroot. It will help clot his blood."

It would have to do. "Help me carry Sameen to a horse and I'll let you go."

Surprisingly, the merchant stood without argument. The Saraj had broken him. He had been Hazil Abdu, wealthiest merchant in Malahad, a king. Now he was nothing.

After feeding Sameen the sandroot, the merchant helped Namali heave the younger man onto the saddle and fasten a rope around his waist to prevent him from falling off. Namali mounted behind Sameen's unconscious form and curled one arm around him protectively while the merchant held the horse steady. She gripped the reins. For a man who had shown her such cruelty, the merchant was perhaps the last person who deserved her gratitude. But the sun would rise and set each day, and life would go on whether she wanted it to or not. "Many thanks, Mr. Abdu."

He stared at her, face blank.

"Mr. Abdu?"

He didn't respond. Heading to the wall, he settled against it and closed his eyes. Shut his gaze from the girl who had destroyed him with something as small as her voice.

Not wasting any time, she dug her heels into the horse's sides and left the Lost City, the merchant, and the dead behind in a cloud of dust.

She rode through the baking afternoon and the cool, dark night. Flat, rocky ground replaced the great mounds of sand while Sameen's skin grew pale and cold. She tried her best to rub warmth back into his limbs, but after almost losing her balance, she settled for wrapping an extra blanket around his prone form. The strike of hooves against the earth was the drum to which they fled.

Namali stopped less than two hours each day to sleep, water the horse, and reapply the sandroot. Then they were off, racing through sand and sun. She pushed their mount hard, much harder than she normally would have, to the point where sweat lathered its flanks and saliva flung from its panting mouth, but she would never forgive herself if Sameen died. He slept fitfully, his breath wheezing through half-parted lips. Clutching him tighter, she imagined her strength flowing through him, filling him the way his love for her filled her heart to brimming. "Hold on," she said. "Please hold on."

On the fourth day, as the first spark of gold alighted in the east, Ahkbur rose from out of the dust. Namali kicked the horse into a sprint the last few miles, not bothering to slow down once inside the town. She dismounted before they came to a stop and barged into the healing tent.

"I need a healer," she gasped, her voice carrying to all corners of the room. "My friend is wounded."

A stout woman with thick gray hair paused in the middle of chopping herbs and hurried forward. If Namali's disheveled appearance disturbed her, she said not a word. "Show him to me."

After untying Sameen, they hauled him into the tent and laid him on a folded rug in the corner.

"Water!" the woman barked, and two healing apprentices rushed to obey.

Namali's attention flitted between Sameen and the healer, who pressed two fingers against the side of his neck to check for a pulse. "Is there anything I can do?" One of the apprentices cut away his bloody robe. *Hurry,* she wanted to scream. *Save him.* His skin was so pale. "I can pay you—"

The woman held up a hand. "Pay me when he is well. Now let me be. I have work to do."

Namali looked at Sameen's sweaty, ashen face, not knowing

if it would be for the last time. After sending a brief prayer to Mahurzda, Namali slipped from the tent, leaving her heart behind with him. She sat near the entrance, knees up, arms resting on her knees, hands hanging loosely. Should he wake, she would not be far. She stared at the ground, dazed.

The wish burned a hole into her pocket, useless. She should have used the wish on Sameen. Technically, she still could. It was her choice, after all. But it was his choice, too, in deciding his fate, and she would not take that from him. So she waited. The sun rose higher, and the ground burned hotter, and still she did not move. Crowds flocked to the marketplace, shouts and laughter and screams dissolving into a roar of noise. Namali hardly noticed when her stomach growled. Her eyes remained unfocused. They saw nothing.

Hours passed, but the healer did not emerge from the tent. No one did. Late afternoon brought the brush of cooler air, the smell of burning wood. The voices inside the canvas walls had died down long ago. If Sameen had taken a turn for the worst, surely the healer would have informed her. Then again, maybe not.

A twinge in her neck forced Namali to raise her head. Her attention fell on the vendor across the street lounging beside his tent stall, and she froze.

Could it be?

Quickly, she went to search her horse's supply pack. When she found what she was looking for, Namali approached the vendor, her shadow sliding across his withered face.

The man glanced up. "I'm closed at the moment."

She smiled at the irony. So he didn't remember her. "I'm not interested in a sale." Yes, she was thinner, her skin darker, but it was not her appearance that distinguished her from the naïve girl who had sold her father's kerespa over a month ago. Rather, it was the way she held herself: back straight, chin up, gaze direct. "I'm here for my kerespa."

He stilled, recognition dawning. "That's not possible."

"I believe it is," she said, holding up the rope for him to see. Technically it was the merchant's rope, but the man did not need to know that. "Your rope."

"Yes, well, about that." He cleared his throat and pushed to his feet. "I, um, sold him."

"You *what?*"

"I didn't think you would actually survive the race."

"Who did you sell him to?"

He tapped his fingers together, gave a nervous, breathy laugh. "A very rich man from out of town."

Namali stared at him long and hard. It wasn't that she didn't trust this man . . .

Actually, she *definitely* didn't trust this man.

"What was his name?" she asked.

"You know, I can't recall. It started with an A, I believe. Amir something-or-other."

"You're lying. Where is my kerespa?"

"Excuse me, Grandmother?"

Namali turned to a scraggly boy dressed in a dark brown robe, pupils large in his sooty face.

"I saw him tie the beast up over there." He pointed to their right, behind a pen of goats.

The man sputtered his disbelief as she dropped the rope on the ground and followed the boy to where Khorshan dozed, passing him a ruby as thanks. Her old friend huddled in what little shade the tree provided, his shadow splashed across the cracked, sizzling rock like a blot of spilled ink. Namali's throat swelled with emotion. Here was a piece of home, something she had thought lost. She examined his sleek form, checking for lost weight, an injury, any noticeable difference. By the luster of his scales, he had been well taken care of in her absence.

Namali stepped toward him, her lips sliding into a smile as natural as breathing. At her soft whistle, Khorshan's head lifted, and he watched her with those piercing green eyes. His tongue flicked out, catching her scent.

The effort of standing still was too great. She thought once he recognized her scent he would come toward her, ears perked, speaking the language only they knew. In her heart, she held this tremulous hope close. He would come to her. He would.

Except he didn't move. He stood there, head cocked in confusion as the wind whipped around them, and Namali remembered passing off his reins, how Khorshan shifted in unease, the approach of change.

Namali's heart cracked clean in two.

She pressed her fingers against her mouth. *Fool,* she thought, and very nearly crumbled. Of course he would forget her. She'd abandoned him. Had traded him for a piece of *rope,* for Mahurzda's sake. She was no friend to him. And even if—

Khorshan stepped forward. One small step.

She didn't dare breathe.

And then, as if tearing down the wall between them, Khorshan was moving toward her, and she toward him, until they came together, his snout nuzzling her shoulder, her arms wrapped tight around his sun-warmed neck, clinging as tears leaked down her face. And it felt so good, to embrace and be embraced.

He was here. With her. Khorshan, her friend.

"I missed you, boy," she whispered against his neck. "I missed you so much."

"Excuse me."

Slowly, Namali drew away. The healer was staring at her with her arms crossed.

"Your friend insists on seeing you," the woman sniffed.

The world went slow and luscious and wonderfully warm. Her heart was filled with beating wings.

Sameen.

After Namali tied Khorshan to a post closer to the healing tent, she entered the enclosed space. Sameen, propped against a small mountain of pillows with a bloody bandage wrapped around his abdomen, grinned at the sight of her. She had never known a smile to hold such love.

She knelt by his side, smiling shyly behind her veil. "You look better." His skin, no longer pale. His eyes clear and bright.

"I feel better," he said, taking her hand. "And I have you to thank for saving me."

Ironically enough, Sameen had saved her, and she hadn't known until this moment.

I guess we both needed a little saving.

"I have something for you," she said.

He quirked an eyebrow. "A gift?"

"Something like that."

Reaching into her pocket, Namali drew out a bracelet woven from black thread, the one she had worked on in her free time during the race. "I used to make these with my mother a long time ago," she said, holding it up for him to see. The memory was soft, having lost some of its hardness along the way. "I know it's not much," she added more uncertainly, "but I wanted you to have it."

Everything about Sameen softened, his mouth most of all. She loved seeing him this way. "It's lovely, Namali."

She gestured to his hands. "May I?"

He held out his right arm, and she tied the bracelet around his wrist. It was the perfect fit.

That done, he fiddled with her fingers. "Did you get your wish?"

"You mean you don't remember what happened when the race ended?" What she had proposed doing to save him?

He shook his head in puzzlement.

"I did," she murmured, and left it at that.

Silence settled between them. It was the drop of a stone down a deep well, the wait for its echoing splash. If it were up to her, she would happily wait until nightfall, for she knew what he would ask. She knew he would not wait.

"Well?" he pressed. "What did you wish for?"

With reluctance, Namali withdrew the small pouch from her robe, tipped it upside down, and caught the wish in her hand, her skin growing warm from where it touched. A rainbow of color shimmered against the tent walls. "I didn't use the wish."

The skin around Sameen's mouth tightened. "Why not?"

Because I love you.

But the words would not come. "I'm not going to wish for anything," she said, offering him the glimmering jewel, "because I'm giving the wish to you."

He made no move to touch it. Stubborn, so stubborn. She

wished he would. It would make things so much easier. "I won't take it, Namali. It's yours. You won it fairly."

Her chest pinched. This was backward. Both had fought for the wish in the beginning, but now neither wanted the responsibility of the other's unhappiness. "If it's mine, then I'm allowed to do what I want with it," she argued, thrusting it against his chest. "And I choose to give it to you."

"*No.*"

Namali flinched. When she tried pulling her hand away, he tightened his hold and said, "Nothing you say will convince me to take the wish from you. I made my choice. I made it a long time ago."

"But what will you do?" she whispered. "What about your brother?"

It was some time before Sameen spoke. "What I've always done: keep looking toward the future. As for Mirza . . ." He stared at the ceiling for a long moment, and kept staring as he said, "I'm going to return home to be with my family, and I'm going to make my brother as happy and comfortable as possible for the remainder of his life." He swallowed, struggling to keep his face a carefully composed mask. "Sometimes that's the only thing you can do for someone—just be there."

"About Mr. Abdu. It doesn't have to—"

"Stop." He rested a palm on her knee. His fingers trembled. "You can and you will. I'll never forgive myself knowing I had sentenced you to a life with that man."

She shook her head, slowly at first, then faster. "I can't do it. I can't."

He tugged on her hand. "Can I show you something?"

She released a shuddering breath. It didn't help much. "All right."

Bare-chested, Sameen led her from the tent and across town. Namali hurried after him, blushing as curious onlookers watched from their homes. No doubt the healer would reprimand him for moving about so soon after his injury, but the woman had made herself scarce. Outside Ahkbur's wall, Sameen stopped and stood behind her, gripping her shoulders. "Tell me what you see."

She squinted through the searing light. The rolling dunes were high and mighty. The sky was a clear, perfect blue. The wind rippled over the sand, churning it like water. And there, too far away to see clearly, lay the rest of the world.

It was waiting for her.

"I see the Saraj," she said. "I see the sand and sky." Both endless. "I see my home."

He sounded his agreement, the vibration faint against her back. "I see those things, too. But I also see something else."

"What?"

"Opportunity."

Beneath the surety of Sameen's guiding hand, her eyes changed. The world was somehow both a friend she had known for a long time and someone she had only just met. "I see it."

Hands tightening on her shoulders, Sameen turned her to face him. "So what are you going to do?"

Her heart quivered from the depth of emotion in his eyes. "I'm . . . I'm going to take the wish and hold it as tightly as I can. And I'm going to take the freedom that comes with it and run."

She saw how her words broke him. Felt how they broke her, too. "I want you to find happiness in your life," Sameen said, "because you deserve more than I can give you." He ducked his head. "You deserve so much more than me."

"That's not true." How could he think, after everything they'd been through, all the words and memories they'd shared, that he was not enough? That she would choose someone else?

She had already found the person worthy enough to love. He was right here, steady and unshakeable, everything she could ever want. "I wish we had met under different circumstances," she croaked. Maybe if she used the wish to change things . . .

Sameen caught on to her thoughts. "No," he said. "Don't wish for that. You know I want to be with you."

She closed her eyes. Bowed her head. "I know." And she did. In the deepest, most secret part of her heart, she knew. How lucky she was to know. And how tormented. "But I also know I need to take this journey alone. Right now your family needs you," she whispered. "You have to help your mother take care of your brothers, and I need to try and repair the relationship with my father."

He gripped her hands hard, pulled her close. "If we were to stay together, regardless of whether or not the merchant was in the picture, I would hold you back. I have no money, no means to provide for you." His mouth drooped. "I don't want you to regret not having seen the world just to be with me."

Mouth trembling, she laid a palm against his cheek. He was right. If she wanted to see what was out there, to grow and learn who exactly Namali was, she would have to leave Malahad. She would have to leave Sameen behind. "I didn't think it would hurt this much," she whispered as her heart swelled and cracked.

He placed a hand over hers. Smiled, or at least tried to. "Just do me a favor."

"Anything."

"Don't forget me when you go out and do great things."

She made a sound halfway between a laugh and a sob. And he knew exactly what to say to wear her down. "How could I forget you, Sameen? You're the only one who has ever seen me for who I am."

He brushed away the tears clinging to her eyelashes. "I believe in fate, Namali. I believe we were supposed to meet, just as you were meant to get the wish." His voice was low and private, just for her. "But this is not the end of our story. We'll meet again, in a year, or three, or five, and when we do, under different circumstances, I think . . . I think we may have a chance."

She clung to his words with all the strength in her heart. Yes. This was not the end. Only a brief separation, a bridge for two halves to meet. "I'll come back for you," she said. "I promise."

His face softened. "I believe you."

Namali tore her gaze away, each heaving breath bringing her closer to falling apart. It hurt to look at him, knowing it was for the last time in a long time. The day would end soon. She wasn't ready for it.

Sameen tucked a stray hair behind her ear. "Wherever your journey takes you, just know I'll be thinking of you. You will be here, in my heart, and I will be in yours, and that will be enough for now."

She was crying, so hard she could barely breathe. His words touched the most secret part of her, tore down those walls she had so carefully and painstakingly built.

She could not keep the words inside any longer.

"I love you, Sameen." And it hurt. It hurt so badly.

His face crumpled, and now Sameen was crying, too. "I love you too, Namali." He touched his forehead to hers. "You are the whole of my heart."

Was it worth it, to love and be loved, knowing this was all there would ever be? If he gave her so much of himself, perhaps there was something she could give him in return.

"You see me," she said. "You see me, and I see you, and . . . I want to show you something."

She began to pull up the edge of her veil.

He stilled her hand, his face grave. "You don't have to do that."

"I know." But she wanted to show him this small gesture, give him a piece of herself that no one else had.

"Wait—"

"Sameen," she murmured. "I know what I'm doing."

After a moment, Sameen let go and allowed her to remove the fabric. The hot desert wind kissed her cheeks, and she closed her eyes from his gaze. Now he truly saw her. The real Namali. Not a phantom image he'd created in his mind. He saw her huge nose; her wide mouth with its thin, almost nonexistent, upper lip; the blotchy purple birthmark covering one side of her lower face. She tried not to cringe. He probably expected a great beauty.

When I wore the veil it was almost like I was one.

Warm, callused fingertips skimmed her cheek, and she inhaled at the gentle touch. When his fingers wandered upward to graze her ear, she began to tremble. "I know I'm probably not what you expected."

"Namali."

"I've always hated my nose."

"Namali, please look at me." Not an order, but a request.

Biting her lip, she opened her eyes, watching Sameen through a shield of unshed tears.

His smile warmed her like a second sun. "Beautiful," he said.

CHAPTER 31

THE NEXT MORNING, under a still-night sky, Namali and Sameen said their goodbyes. Namali mounted Khorshan, leaving the merchant's horse in Sameen's care, and set off southwest toward Benahr. She didn't look back.

The journey was leisurely, never more than a walk or light trot. Any urge to race and feel the wind tugging its fingers through her hair had died. She was tired in her heart, tired in her bones. She knew too much of pain and not enough of happiness, and it had sucked her dry.

The wish weighed down its pouch, awaiting her decision. The thought of wishing herself free of the arranged marriage had faded, little more than embers, and another idea was beginning to take shape. Now that she no longer viewed the world behind bars, now that she knew of the strength in her heart, perhaps she could use the wish for something . . . more.

The moons swept across the velvet backdrop, two swaths of light amidst the dark. Night melted into day, and day melted into night, and time slowly unraveled. Namali stopped to rest, to eat and think and dream and *breathe*. Simple things, but the Demon

Race had taught her there was nothing simple about the taste of water, or filling her lungs with air, or even a moment of quiet. Each was its own freedom, a piece of time standing still long enough for her to experience it.

On the third night, a few hours before sunrise, Benahr grew from a tiny dot in the distance to the humble town from which she was born. Dismounting Khorshan, Namali led him inside the wall, his claws clicking against the hard brown brick. Benahr was smaller than she remembered, and quiet. Goats and camels huddled together in their pens for warmth. Moonlight slanted across the mud-brick dwellings with their darkened windows and tired structures. Places she had known all her life. Places utterly unfamiliar now.

Eventually, she reached the paddock where Baba housed their camels. Upon counting them, her heart sank. Two less animals than when she had left. Her father must have had to sell some in order to make ends meet.

After unsaddling Khorshan and locking him in the corral, Namali climbed the crumbling staircase leading to the front door. She pressed a palm against the smooth wood, her pulse beating like thunder in her ears. A part of her wanted nothing more than to back away and disappear into the Saraj once more, but it was a very small part. She could do this, say what she needed to say. It was her future, her life. The time for running was past.

She took a deep breath before removing her sandals, pushing open the door, and stepping inside her dark, quiet home. It smelled the same as when she had left, like cardamom and turmeric and wanting, and it was a smell she had outgrown.

Closing the door, she started for her bedroom, then stopped. Would it look the same, or had dust gathered in the corners, on the bookshelves, the windowsill? Her worst fear was having been forgotten.

A light winked at the edge of her vision, and she turned. Baba, holding a fat tallow candle in one hand, stared at her as if she were a ghost. His bare feet peeked out from beneath a sleeping robe six inches too short. His hair had turned almost completely gray.

"Namali?"

A whisper in the dark.

Her throat tightened. She wanted to run to her father, to throw her arms around him and tell him how much she had missed him and beg for him to love her, but she didn't say anything, and she didn't move. Where did they stand, after all this time? She was afraid. She was so afraid she couldn't convince her muscles to move.

Setting the candle on the ground, he took a tentative step forward. Then another, his feet silent on the cool mud floor. Mere feet separated them, but it felt like miles and miles of desert, a place where nothing had grown for a long time. And he was trying to cross it.

Her father stopped two feet away, his face hidden in shadow. "I thought . . ." He swallowed. "I thought you were dead."

Namali bit the inside of her cheek. Surprisingly, and as if by some miracle, she wasn't. "Well . . . I'm not."

Lifting a trembling hand, Baba touched the edge of her face. His skin hung from his frame in bags, and deep wrinkles fanned from his unsmiling mouth and eyes. "So you entered the Demon Race."

Namali nodded, her throat too swollen with emotion to speak. With the truth so solid between them she saw no reason to lie.

If they wanted to rebuild and move forward, they needed to be honest with one another. She was willing to do whatever it took.

But was he?

"Mr. Abdu sent a message. He told me what happened." Her father shook his head. "I thought . . ." He ran his fingers through his hair, dropped them at his sides. "Why did you do it, Namali? Why did you leave?"

"I'm sorry, Baba. I told you I didn't want to marry Mr. Abdu, but you didn't listen. I entered the race because it was the only way I could think of to change things. Can you understand that?"

He sighed. "Maybe. I don't know."

"I did bring Khorshan back."

He didn't give any indication he had heard her.

She tried again. "Did you miss me?"

His eyebrows snapped together. "You're my daughter. Of course I missed you. I prayed every day for your safe return. But—" He shook his head again. "I have to figure out how to speak with Mr. Abdu."

A sinking sensation spread through her gut. In so few words, he had managed to snatch away her tenuous control over the situation. "Why?"

"I don't want there to be any animosity toward us."

"Animosity?"

"He told me what you did to him."

Heat crawled up her neck and flared in her cheeks. He was taking the merchant's side. A stranger's word over his daughter's. The worst part was she had expected this, and it stung. It always would. When would her father open his eyes? When would he open his heart to her again? "Yes, but what about all the things he did to *me?*" She shoved her bandaged hand in his face. "Did he tell you this? Did he tell you he cut off my finger?"

Startled, he blinked at her bandaged hand. "Are you all right?"

"Fine," she mumbled. Her hand would heal. There were other, more important, wounds to address.

He turned so the candlelight deepened the hollows of his face, sharpened the angles to severe points. "Namali, there's still time to fix this."

She bowed her head against the dark pressing upon her, the familiar helplessness pulling her into its heavy folds. Nothing had changed. "Baba—"

He was more adamant now, pacing back and forth. "I can invite him over, you can apologize, and—"

"Stop it," she hissed. *"Just stop talking."*

He stiffened. "What has gotten into you?"

Be brave, Namali. No one will be brave for you.

"Even after all this time," she said, "you're still not listening to me."

He stepped forward, his expression stony. "I am listening to you—" Each word bitten off, spewed forth. "—but I don't know what you're trying to say."

Pent-up emotion beat against the walls of her skin. Trapped, with nowhere to go. It should never have reached this point. "Then let me be absolutely clear," she said. "I will *never* marry Mr. Abdu. Ever. *Do you understand that?* Can you understand how your daughter would feel, given to a man without warning? Can you imagine her fear? Can you imagine her belief that she wasn't important, that she didn't matter, that family meant nothing?"

Baba looked away, a flinch for each scouring truth. It sounded as if he had stopped breathing. "What are you trying to say?"

A sharp twinge in her chest, as swift and sudden as a knife driving through. This wound was old. It was old and largely ignored, and it would not bend to her will no matter how hard she tried. Did she have to spell out something so obvious? He truly did not know how she felt. The pain was nothing she had ever experienced, a splintering ache, too great to hold inside.

It destroyed her.

Namali covered her face with her hands as the tears came fast and hard, and it was too much to bear, this pain. Her legs could barely hold her weight. "All I want is for you to love me," she cried, and at last came undone. "That's all I've ever wanted." He had denied her the one thing she had ever asked of him, and it had broken her heart.

"You . . . you think I don't love you?" Hitched breath.

She curled her arms around her stomach, trying to quiet the sobs. Tears clouded her image of him, and she wondered if this was how it would always be, questioning if the blurry form she saw was real or if she only wished it were. "I don't know," she whispered. "I just don't know." And that was the saddest part of all.

He appeared to gather himself, saying, "I've shown you plenty of times how important you are to me."

"When? Every time I try to talk to you, you turn me away."

"That's not true," he said, but his voice quavered.

"When was the last time you looked me in the eye? When was the last time you asked me how I was without the mention of chores?" Her knees started to shake, and she sobbed harder, so hard her temples throbbed. It hurt, but more importantly, it was a relief. "When was the last time you held me?" She couldn't remember a time it had been so long. This man, her own father, a stranger.

Her baba stumbled back as if from a blow. "You don't mean that."

Namali swallowed. "I do," she said, and she had never spoken truer words. "I really do."

He stood there, unmoving, for an immeasurable moment while the candle flickered, nearly gutted out. A single light in the heavy, hopeless dark. She saw how it cast its warmth on her father's face, exposing the tightness of his jaw, the slight tremor of his lips, pressed together to hide his weakness. And she saw, too, the moment it happened. A wall toppling down, stone by stone, as his mask crumpled. Just . . . fell apart.

"Have I failed you?" he cried, hiding his face with his hands. "Have I been such a terrible father I've driven you away?"

Namali was speechless. Her father, crying. Tears on his sunken cheeks, like rain falling onto a parched and dying land. It was his pain, yet her pain, too. Years and years of it, enough to fill an ocean of sand.

The truth was, she didn't know who to blame. They had both treated each other unfairly, toeing a line neither wanted to cross. They had both made assumptions, mistakes.

But they were here now, on even ground. And maybe they could begin to move forward.

Steeling herself, Namali wrapped her arms around her father for the first time in three years while his body shook with ugly sobs. She squeezed harder. This man had done so much for her. He was not perfect—no one was—but he tried. Together, they broke themselves down and began anew. He wept into her shoulder, and she wept into his.

And it was enough.

"You know I love you," she whispered, "right?"

He clutched the back of her robe fiercely, unwilling to let go. "I love you too, Namali." The words shot straight through her chest, filling a piece of herself she had thought empty. "I'm sorry I haven't shown you. I'm so sorry."

Namali closed her eyes, tears receding, allowing the moment to absorb into her skin. Home was not a place or a dwelling, a roof over her head or walls surrounding her. It was her father's voice and being held close. The comfort someone's love brought like the warmth from a fire in the hearth.

"I'm sorry too, Baba."

"Can you ever forgive me for what I've done?"

"I forgive you. Of course I forgive you. The race taught me many things, especially forgiveness." Chest tight, she drew away. "It also made me realize I need to go away for a while."

Her father lowered his gaze.

"Not forever," she reassured, squeezing his hand. "I just . . . need to find myself."

Two tears trickled into his beard. "How long will you be gone?"

"I don't know." The world was a door she had only just opened. Exploration, discovery—these things took time. She did not want to rush, for there was so much to see. "But I don't want you to worry about me."

Some of his sternness returned. "Of course I'm going to worry about you. I'm your father."

"I can see you're not happy, Baba, and haven't been in a long time." She linked her fingers together and went on. "You know Mama would have wanted you to be happy. She would have wanted you to move on."

"I know," he replied, and it was with the voice of a man too broken to recognize his own unhappiness. "Do you know where you'll go?"

She wanted to make one stop in particular. Other than that, she would travel until she reached the edge of the Saraj, and continue even beyond to places she had heard of but never seen. "I'm going to head toward Shun. I've heard they have mountains there. And rivers. I'd like to see them." She waited until her father looked up. "Do I have your blessing?"

"Yes, Namali." He kissed first one cheek, and then the other. Slowly, so as to remember the feel of his daughter's skin. "Go with my love. And take Khorshan with you," he added. "You'll need him more than I do."

"Many thanks, Baba."

His dark eyes, so much like her own, shimmered with pride. "I love you, Namali. I will always, always love you."

Namali looked away, took a breath, and met his gaze.

This was the beginning of something beautiful.

"You know," she said, "I wasn't planning on leaving for a few days at least. Maybe . . . maybe I could tell you about some of my adventures from the race." She smiled tentatively. "If you're interested."

Baba reached across the space between them and gripped her hand. "I'd like that, Namali." His smile soothed her wounded heart. "I'd like that very much."

EPILOGUE

COLORFUL STRIPS OF muslin and wool livened the doorway of the crumbling mud house at the end of the street, bright pops of color against the black sky. All was quiet. The people of Yanasir slept, safe in their homes, for it was early still, too early for the sun to rise. Beside the front door, someone had planted a flower in a cracked clay pot. Miraculously, it was growing.

Namali stepped onto the sagging front stoop, her heart racing impossibly fast. Sweat dampened her palms, and her hands curled into the folds of her robe. She didn't know if this was the right thing to do, and she probably never would. She only knew she was here, driven by a need to see change.

Her arranged marriage was no more. The last she'd heard of Hazil Abdu he'd packed up and moved to a town on Malahad's eastern border. Plenty of women for him to search for a bride there. Plenty of women who were not her. Still, she wished him well, wished him peace in his life.

With unhurried movements, Namali reached into her robe and pulled out the wish, the moonlight reflecting off its lustrous surface. So much bloodshed for a thing so small. It was strange, but the more she examined it, the more she believed the wish to look like a regular old rock, easily overlooked. She ran a finger along its curve, pondering. Maybe it was because some of the magic had gone out of it.

Or maybe it was because she didn't need it anymore.

Namali dropped the wish into its pouch, along with a note she had written, and placed it by the front door. She knocked hard— once, twice—then dashed away to crouch behind a nearby home where Khorshan awaited her.

After a minute, the door opened. Sameen, rumpled and bare-chested from sleep, peered around the deserted street. At the sight of his face, her stomach quivered. *This is not the end of our story,* he had told her. It promised a future, one they would both share. Not yet, but someday, if the stars aligned. First, she must explore. First, she must push herself, love herself. So for now she would hold those words close, keeping them safe until the day they met again.

Sameen looked down, and that smiling mouth she had grown to love wilted as he picked up the pouch.

"I'm sorry," Namali whispered. It was not enough, would never *be* enough unless they were together, but for now this was all she could offer. It was all she could give.

Face grave, Sameen untied the pouch and removed the message. He stared at it for a few seconds before unfolding it. Then he began to read.

Dear Sameen,

I can't thank you enough for everything you've done for me. After much thought, I decided to leave home and travel for a while, so I'm heading east, toward Shun. I don't know how long I'll be gone, but I don't want you to worry. I have Khorshan with me, and my strength. It's more than I could have ever hoped for.

I know you thought I deserved the wish more, but I've decided I no longer have the need for it, as Mr. Abdu and I are no longer betrothed. Please take it. Use it to save your brother. Touch your lips against the wish, say what it is you want aloud, and it will be granted.

I love you.

—Namali

Sameen's lips began to quiver, and he upended the cloth so the wish dropped into his palm. His gaze darted left and right, lingering in the shadows like a lost boy searching for his mother. He stumbled onto the road. He turned in a circle, dazed. "Namali?" A hoarse whisper.

He received no answer but the wind.

"Namali?" Then louder: "Namali!"

Squeezing her eyes shut, Namali clapped her palms over her ears, breathless. The knife of his voice pierced her chest. It twisted and drove deeper, slicing through any defense she might have. Limping up and down the street, Sameen sought her in the dark, clinging to the hope that he would spot her face, the glow of her eyes. When minutes passed, filled with quiet, he slowed to a halt. He stood in the middle of the road, head tilted back, hands limp at his sides, his eyes full of stars. Finally, he fell to his knees and wept, understanding he now held a miracle in his palm. An impossible reality.

After a long time, Sameen went inside and shut the door behind him. Namali stared at the place where he had been, anticipating his return, and when he did not, she brushed herself off and rose to her feet. It was time to leave.

As she mounted Khorshan and turned east, movement shifted on the horizon. Shadows twisted and unfurled, flowing from the ground like ink. They rode the wind, up and up and up, shedding their darkness like a second skin. What remained caught her breath: the Great Pack, shining bright as stars, free from servitude. Their howls crested, an upwelling of liquid gold that set the air to ringing. *We are here,* they told the world. *We are alive.*

Namali watched them climb to infinity, and when they disappeared, she kicked Khorshan into a gallop across the stark, silent land. Though the moons hid their faces from her, she was not afraid.

The night was dark, but her heart knew the way.

ONE YEAR LATER

IT WAS DAWN. Night had lifted its gray veil, a streak of pale lavender blooming along the horizon, overshadowing the faintest hint of gold. Spring. How lovely. The Saraj did not flower from the earth, but rather from the sky. Pinks and yellows and sometimes greens, the tender shoots of new buds. Namali wondered how she had never noticed this before.

A warm breeze tugged on the edge of her veil as she and Khorshan traversed the last of the colossal dunes, a shy tug of recognition, of *welcome home* after a twelve-month absence. Gentler than she remembered. The whistle of wind over earth carried, lifted, a voice, a song. The land, it seemed, could be joyous, too.

When the sand finally hardened to the baked clay of Yanasir, Namali slipped from Khorshan's back with a grateful sigh and looked behind them. The trail of footprints leading east had already vanished, brushed clean with each sweep of the breeze. Still, it took shape in her mind's eye, a messy, winding path of exploration.

As Yanasir was a small town, it did not take long to reach the end of the street where Sameen lived, all jittery nerves and sweaty palms, a commingling of anticipation and fear. After many weeks dreaming of this moment, it did not feel entirely real. Another dream, then? If so, it was lovely.

She walked the narrow dirt road and remembered. This was where he had cried out for her. Where she had kept her silence. Maybe it had been cruel to let him think her gone, but deep down, she always knew she would return.

Stopping in the scant shade of a wilted bush, she observed Sameen and a young boy playing a game of marbles in the dirt outside their home, shoulder to shoulder, heads bent close. Their voices crested and died, the words lost to her. It didn't matter. When she looked at them, she saw togetherness. Safety. It was physically painful to stand here watching them, watching *him*, separate and unnoticed. But she didn't want to disturb them. And, truthfully, she did not know if she was welcome.

Sameen nudged the younger boy playfully. The boy nudged back. A few moments of wrestling ensued, and Sameen was tackled by who Namali now believed to be Mirza. Their laughter carried, high-pitched and low-pitched. Brothers. Free.

They slumped together, hair and limbs askew, chuckles dwindling to shallow pants. They returned to playing marbles, though Mirza's focus was obviously elsewhere. Namali, who thought herself well-hidden, noticed Mirza watching her with curiosity. As the boy pointed in her direction, drawing Sameen's attention to where she stood, she caught her breath. She had missed much about Malahad, but not a day had gone by where she did not think of this sight before her: a line of white teeth against a browned face, with eyes softened by love.

When his gaze locked onto hers, it was as if no time had passed and they stood in the congested arteries of Ahkbur, seeing one another for the first time. Then, she had not known how drastically their lives would change, the battles they would face, the strife. But they had fought together. Laughed together.

Loved together.

Slowly, Sameen rose to his feet, his expression slack with shock. "Namali?" The marbles rolled to a stop in the dirt, forgotten.

Her stomach fluttered from the timbre of his voice. Deeper than she remembered. His body, too, had changed in the twelve months she was away. This taller, broader, older Sameen. The blue yirasaf, however, remained the same, burning like the purest jewel.

When he did not immediately approach, Namali hesitated in stepping forward. It was entirely possible Sameen's life had shifted in ways she was no longer a part of. The thought was a hot knife driving into her. If that were so, what then? It was well within his right. She had not asked him to put his life on hold while she ventured into the unknown. It was neither practical nor fair. At least, she told herself as much.

But then her focus settled on the threaded bracelet tied around his wrist, and she inhaled sharply. Her heart gave one hard thump. "You're still wearing it."

His initial bewilderment softened into something distinctly more intimate. He did not question what she spoke of. He just knew. "Did you think I wouldn't?"

Thick emotion lodged in her throat. "No," she whispered. The thought had never crossed her mind.

Leaving Khorshan to doze in the shade, Namali approached him with an unwavering gaze, forcing herself to walk slowly, to revel in the delicious simmer of anticipation. With each step, the pressure behind her eyes built, and soon they were full, brimming, and she could not see him clearly behind the stinging blur. She had journeyed far and was near-dead with exhaustion. But it was over now.

They met as one, two streams merging after having drifted thousands of miles apart. As if in a dream, Sameen lifted his hands and cupped her face in his rough palms, the gentleness of his touch unleashing a flood of tears from within her.

This was home. Here, with him.

He touched his forehead to hers. Exhaled as he fought for composure. "You . . . you came back."

She gave a watery giggle and wiped her nose. It was nice to know that, even when she smelled like death, he didn't seem to mind. "I promised, didn't I?"

His shoulders shook in low laughter, his eyes shining with overwhelming affection. The joy of his smile pierced her heart straight through. "You did. You most certainly did." Tugging her close, he wrapped his arms around her, and Namali returned the embrace, letting herself feel—everything. On her travels, she had experienced the highest highs and the lowest lows. Euphoria. Destitution. Turmoil. Confusion. Determination. Her trials had torn her down and built her up: stronger, fiercer, wiser. She intended to continue on this path for as long as she had breath in her lungs.

"Eh-hem."

A rush of heat scalded her cheeks, and Namali jerked away from her friend's embrace, having forgotten they were not alone.

"And who is this?" she wondered, turning to the boy who peered at her curiously from behind Sameen's legs.

Sameen cut the boy a glare, his expression an endearing combination of frustration and adoration. "My brother, Mirza." He clapped a hand on the boy's slender shoulder. "Mirza, this is Namali. She's the girl I told you about. The one I traveled with during the race."

With a shy smile, the boy ducked his head and tugged his brother's sleeve. Sameen crouched down so Mirza could whisper in his ear, rather loudly, "She's pretty."

Sameen smiled crookedly. It made her heart do funny things.

"Will she stay for dinner?" Mirza wondered.

"Oh." Namali looked to Sameen in uncertainty, not sure if it was exactly proper. Benahr was near enough to reach by nightfall, if needed. "I don't know . . ."

"Please do." The intensity of his gaze made her blush. *Stay.* "I insist."

"Your mother won't mind?"

"Are you kidding? After everything you did for my family?"

"I know, but—"

"Mirza, please tell Ma we have a guest tonight."

Well. *That* was settled.

Once Mirza disappeared into the house, Sameen turned to her. "So . . ." He released a slow exhale through his nose. "I have to ask. Is this return permanent or temporary or . . ." He glanced away, his attention returning with a snap, as if afraid she would disappear when he looked elsewhere.

Namali shifted a few inches closer. The rise and fall of Mirza's voice sparked through the nearby open window, breathless with excitement at her visitation. "I do plan on staying awhile." She smiled as she spoke, because there was much she had missed.

Though she may drift in the wind, she would always return to her roots. "At least until Asraba is over."

Next month marked the beginning of the three-day holiday, and she looked forward to celebrating the way she and Baba used to, bringing back some of the joy they had lost. They had written one another during her travels. *I miss you,* and *be careful,* and *when are you coming home?* But a written letter was not the same.

"And after?"

After . . .

Across the sloped back of the Spine, the air smelled sweetly of jasmine. In the lowlands, where the rivers converged, the water ran clear. The earth was green. The branches bowed, heavy with red blossoms. She remembered, during her first month in Shun, when a fisherman offered her fresh trout in return for helping him carry supplies to the local market. The old man's laughter as she shrieked upon realizing the fish were not, in fact, dead.

"There's a Shunese festival that takes place in mid-autumn. It's . . . unlike anything you've ever seen. There's dancing, traditional ceremonies, fresh sea food. And the people there are so *kind.*" The pale touch of his gaze drew her attention, and the love she felt for him, for this wonderful, compassionate, understanding man, spilled over in a flood of light. "I want to experience it with you."

To watch surprise and pleasure overtake him—it was a gift. And if she could spend even a fraction of her life doing just that, well, there would never be a day when she would not feel full.

"I know you're needed here," Namali rushed on, "but we won't be gone for more than a few weeks. I have some money saved. And there's a friend I know in the capital. We wouldn't need to pay for lodging . . ."

Reaching out, Sameen snagged her hand, lacing their fingers together, and asked, with mischief in his smile and promise in his eyes, "When do we leave?"

ACKNOWLEDGEMENTS

IT'S A SURREAL feeling to be standing on the other side of my first published novel. This story is over three years in the making, and while writing is, for the most part, a very solitary activity, I could not have reached this point alone.

To Jennifer: you may never read this, but if you do, thank you for taking a chance on this story, and for all the work you put into making it the best it could be. Here's a cup of Luke's coffee, on me.

To Cassandra: your insight and critique helped shape Namali and Sameen into stronger, more well-rounded characters, since apparently I forgot that little thing called a character arc! Thank you for being such a wonderful editor.

To Beth: there is no doubt that you have gone above and beyond as a critique partner. Thank you for your wonderful feedback and support. I always value our conversations!

To Melanie: your perspective has been invaluable for the early drafts of this story. Thank you.

To Maia, Kris, and Jennifer: I truly appreciate the early

constructive criticism. Overall, your comments helped strengthen the manuscript ten-fold.

And lastly, to my family: thank you for believing in me. To my parents: thank you for instilling my deep love of reading, and thus my love of writing. Thank you for listening to me say, for years, "This is The One!" Ha. I guess this *was* The One.

To anyone who reads this: it's an honor, truly.

About the Author

ALEXANDRIA WARWICK is the #1 fan of Avatar: The Last Airbender. *The Demon Race* is her first novel.

•••

alexandriawarwick.com
@alexandriawarwick